TEMPTED

ELISABETH NAUGHTON

sourcebooks
casablanca

For Tonia Wubbena and Rita Van Hee…
my go-to first readers and biggest fans.
Thank you for your honesty, support, and mostly
your never-ending love of the written word.
This one's all yours.

Ah, but the man—cursed be he,
Cursed beyond recover,
Who openeth, shattering, seal by seal,
A friend's clean heart, then turns his heel,
Deaf unto love: never in me
Friend shall he know nor lover.

—Euripides, *Medea*

Chapter 1

TEMPTATION HUNG LIKE A THICK MIST IN THE CLUB, calling to the desperation seated deep inside him.

Demetrius swallowed back the shot of whiskey and slammed his glass on the table. Heavy bass pulsed around him, lights flickered over bare skin, strips of leather and dangling chains, and bodies ground against each other in time to the thumping music.

He couldn't remember where he was—LA, Houston, Atlanta?—but he didn't give a rat's ass. One human city was just like the next, and sleazy clubs like this that fed the deviants on the fringes of society were easy to find. Yeah, he was in the mood for pain tonight, and right now he didn't care if it was he or the brunette in the skimpy dominatrix getup across the dance floor who got to dole it out.

She shot him an I'd-hit-that look and smiled when he nodded her over. As she turned away from the two shirtless losers in dog collars she'd been talking to and headed his way, lights rippled over her cleavage, her long legs, her dark brown shoulder-length hair. A scar marred her upper lip and her makeup was way too heavy for his taste, but that was okay. He wasn't beautiful either. So long as she *wasn't* petite and pale and perfect, that was all he cared about.

She stopped at his booth in the shadows, gave him the once-over. He knew what she saw—a big-ass, tattooed, scarred, and menacing biker dude dressed all in black. And obviously, from the gleam in her eye, she approved. But it was what she couldn't see that should have scared her shitless.

She braced both hands on the table, leaned forward so her breasts all but spilled out of her leather bustier. Three small triangles were tattooed just above her left breast. The Greek symbol delta repeated.

His gaze flicked up to her eyes, outlined in thick black. Her fake lashes curled almost all the way to her eyebrows. No, he was sure she wasn't Argolean, didn't possess any link to the ancient Greek heroes who'd been the first to settle his realm thousands of years ago. As an Argonaut, born of the guardian class, his sense of perception was strong. She was definitely a mere human.

That little bit of conscience dogging him pushed in, twisted through his gut.

"I'd ask you how it's hanging, stud, but"—she drew in a breath that seemed to give her pleasure—"I have a feeling I already know the answer: Well. Very, very well, by the looks of you."

Bind me, *hurt me*, and *fuck me* were written all over her heavily made-up face. And when she sent him that come-and-get-me look, what was left of his conscience slid to the wayside, just that fast.

He flipped cash onto the table and pushed to stand, refusing to think of the reason he was here, in this human club, desperate for the all-too-familiar pain that would make him forget. "Where to?"

"There's a dungeon room below."

"Good enough."

Excitement flared in her eyes as she turned, giving

him a nice view of her ass in the barely-there leather bodysuit. Not perfect, but it would do for tonight. "Follow me."

He made it four steps before he caught movement to his left. And two faces that shouldn't ever be in a place like this popped into his line of sight.

"Whoa." Gryphon, Demetrius's guardian brother in battle, stopped feet away, eyes wide as he took in the interior of the club. He pointed to his right. "Is that woman naked in that cage?"

"No way." Phineus moved into the light so he could get a better view of the cage hanging from the ceiling above the dance floor. "She can't be—holy crap, she is!"

Demetrius clenched his jaw. He didn't have time for this shit tonight. He was off duty, damn it. It was the first night in months he wasn't on patrol with the Argonauts, searching for the daemons Atalanta had unleashed from the Underworld because of her twisted need to control and annihilate. And the last thing he wanted to do was stand here with these two yahoos, ogling something he didn't want. He glanced toward the far side of the room. His dominatrix stood in ice-pick heels on steps to a hallway that disappeared around a corner. Her what-the-hell's-the-hold-up? look said he was running out of time.

"Dude," Gryphon said with a wide grin, eyes locked on the woman in the cage, now rubbing against the bars, "you've been holding out on us. This is where you go when you leave our asses behind in Argolea? I am *so* following you from now on out!"

Demetrius shot the blond Argonaut a withering glare, then looked back toward his dominatrix. She was already moving back into the crowd, searching for someone else.

No. His muscles coiled. He'd been sitting here for the last hour, scoping out the scene, and she was the only one who fit his requirements. She was the only one who in some way didn't remind him of—

"...Isadora's vanished. Like into thin air."

Demetrius whipped around at the sound of Phineus's voice and focused in on the dark-haired guardian. "What did you just say?"

"For shit's sake," Gryphon yelled over the pulsating music. "Didn't you hear a damn word we said?"

Demetrius glanced between the two Argonauts, who'd given up gawking and were now focused solely on him. Humans had taken notice of their conversation, but drawing attention was suddenly the least of his worries. As if his brain had just come back online, he realized Gryphon and Phineus should be in the royal temple. Right this minute. Witnessing the princess's binding ceremony. Not here in this seedy club with him.

"What do you mean, vanished?"

"Gone," Phineus said, snapping his fingers for effect. "Into thin air. No one knows where she went and Theron wants your ass back in Argolea, like now, to help find her. If the Council finds out she's missing..."

Demetrius's chest went cold as Phineus's words faded in his head. He thought of the Council of Elders, of their desire to see Isadora ousted as soon as her elderly father, the king, passed and she assumed the crown of their realm. It was no secret they didn't want her to rule. Then his mind shot to Atalanta and what the goddess would give to get her hands on Isadora. As a descendent of the Horae, the three goddesses of balance and justice, Isadora had powers yet untapped.

Then again…

Wouldn't it just be like the princess to run off again? Except now…this wasn't about her anymore. This was about all of them. Didn't she realize she was screwed—that they were all screwed—if Atalanta got her claws on her?

Plan for tonight forgotten, he pushed by his fellow guardians and stalked to the door as his mood grew blacker and that dark mist he lived with every day of his damn life roiled and boiled inside him. Bodies parted as he passed, but he didn't need to look to see the fear in the eyes around him. Normally he'd enjoy scaring the shit out of a group of humans, but right now all that mattered was getting outside so he could open the portal and flash back to Argolea, then find that bloody princess before she screwed up everything for good. And when he did? Oh, when he found her—after he laid down the law—he was going to haul her skinny butt back to the castle and make sure she was exactly where she should be.

Bound. Forever. To any Argonaut who wasn't him.

"Demetrius! Dammit." Gryphon sighed at his back before he reached the exit. "What in Hades crawled up his ass and died?"

"I don't know," Phineus said. "I've been wondering that for over a hundred years. You ever figure it out, you let me know."

~~~

She felt as if she weighed a thousand pounds.

Isadora tried to get up but couldn't. Her arms and legs were heavy, her mind nothing but a thick, murky fog.

She shifted her head, groaned when pain stabbed her skull. Faintly, she thought she smelled basil burning. And…clove.

Peeling back her eyelids, she looked through hazy vision that seemed to come and go. She was in some sort of dark room. The air was cold, and light flickered over the walls as if from a candle.

Her father often used candles to light corridors in the ancient castle of Tiyrns, but something in her gut said this wasn't any room in the royal castle that was her home. At least not one she'd ever been in.

Apprehension churned in her stomach. To her left, a soft voice murmured, "Are you sure this is safe?"

Isadora recognized the voice. She blinked several times and peered up at a woman dressed all in black. A hood shielded her face, and she stood with both hands extended and hovering above Isadora's abdomen.

"Perfectly. She won't be harmed. Much."

"I don't know," the first voice whispered.

The hooded figure reached for something behind her. When her hand returned, it glistened with moisture. She touched Isadora's forehead, the spot between her breasts, and then, lightly, she traced lines over Isadora's bare belly.

Gooseflesh prickled Isadora's skin. Her mind was like a worn gear caught in a wheel, trying to catch, over and over, yet slipping each and every time.

"Demeter," the female chanted, "goddess of fertility. Come to us so that she may bear thy fruit."

Bear fruit? Isadora went cold all over as her mind stopped its frantic search for answers and she focused in on the female above her. Tiny tendrils of fear slithered down her spine.

"She's awake," the familiar voice said. Though pain raked her skull, Isadora shifted, looked that direction. She knew that voice. Strained to make the connection she was sure was on the tip of her mind. Then froze when she realized who it was.

Saphira. Her handmaiden. Her trusted confidante. The one female who knew her better than any other.

Saphira didn't meet her gaze, but thoughts, memories, images swirled in Isadora's hazy mind as she stared at the female she considered a friend: Sitting at her vanity on the day of her binding ceremony to Zander, peering into the mirror, seeing the first glimpse of the future she'd had in several weeks. Realizing she was trapped, that if she didn't get away, there was no way the vision she'd just witnessed wouldn't come true. And Saphira. Coming to her rescue. Kneeling at her feet. Bringing Isadora tea and claiming she had a way out of the entire mess.

Isadora struggled again, glanced up when she discovered her arms were tied to some kind of bar. Frantic, she tried to lift her head again and this time succeeded, only to peer down the length of her body and learn she was bare but for a sheet low across her hips. Red lines marred her skin, fanned outward from her belly button. Lines that looked like they were drawn in blood.

Oh, gods…

A scream bubbled up Isadora's throat, but the sound came out muffled and ragged. Belatedly she realized a gag was stuffed in her mouth, tied behind her head. Terror clawed its way up her chest.

"She'll hurt herself," Saphira said as Isadora thrashed again.

"No, she won't."

Isadora's eyes shot to the woman in the black cloak, and anger welled inside her as the female lowered her hood.

Isadora had met her before, she was sure of it. Spiky red hair, sharp green eyes. Isadora squinted, tried to see through the haze, but still couldn't make the connection she knew was right there.

"Yes," the female breathed, leaning closer, her gaze coming to rest on Isadora's face. "We have met, Princess. Patience. It will come to you if you let it."

"Isis," Saphira warned.

Like a light bulb flicking on, the face and the name converged. This female was a witch. She and her consorts manned the secret portals in the Aegis Mountains Isadora had used to cross into the human realm unseen. And the lines on Isadora's stomach…Her eyes shot down her body again. Now she recognized the shape. The lines of blood were drawn into the shape of a pentagram.

No. No. Gods, no…

Isadora arched her back, tried to kick and claw herself free, fought with everything she had in her. But the bonds holding her were too tight, the slab of granite beneath her body unforgiving and cold as ice.

"Shh, *paidi*," Isis said, rubbing a hand over Isadora's forehead. "We wouldn't want you to expend all your energy just yet. You're going to need it for what lies ahead."

Isis moved away, came back with a small black dagger. Isadora's eyes grew wide all over again as she looked up at the double-edged blade, at the twin curves of silver metal that made up the guard—one up, one down—at the gleaming black handle, at the ball at the end that formed the shape of the pentagram. When she recognized the sun symbols of Medea running up and down that handle, her vision blurred.

An *athamé*. The ceremonial dagger used by Medean witches to direct energy when invoking a spell. Holy *skata*.

Saphira moved around the table, sprinkling something on the floor. The scent of roses drifted to Isadora's nose. Isis passed the dagger through the smoke of burning herbs, then through the flame of a black candle. From her pocket she produced a handful of brown granules— dirt?—and sprinkled them over the dagger and Isadora's belly. Finally, Isis dipped her hand in a bowl and flicked liquid over the blade and Isadora.

Fear rendered Isadora immobile; the bonds held her tight. All she could do was watch as Isis held the dagger over her belly and chanted, "Child of earth, of wind, of fire and sea. Into our lives, we welcome thee. As I will it, so mote it be."

A fertility spell. They were casting a fertility spell?

"Are you sure this will work?" Saphira asked.

"Have faith," Isis replied.

"I do. It's just…" Saphira wrung her hands. "Is this the only way? I mean…" Her voice lowered. She refused to look Isadora in the eye. "The dark one…he'll hurt her."

"Atalanta knows what she's doing."

Atalanta? Dread welled in the bottom of Isadora's chest.

"You know she is our chance for freedom," Isis said before Saphira could answer. "If our powers are to grow and we are to be free of this prison as we so desire, we cannot afford to let this deal with Atalanta slip by."

Deal with Atalanta. None of that sounded good to Isadora. She struggled against her bonds again.

Saphira grimaced, nodded.

A wicked smile spread across Isis's face. "Trust me, Saphira. She will enjoy what is to come. Before this is over we will all get what we want."

"But, Isis…" Saphira's voice dropped to a whisper. "You know she's of the royal family. That she's untouched. That she is a—"

Isis held up a hand. Saphira closed her mouth. She didn't argue again even when Isadora screamed, *"Fight for me!"* from beneath the gag.

Isis set the dagger on the table behind her and returned with a flaming black candle, which she held over Isadora's stomach. Isadora's eyes jumped from Saphira to the witch now swirling the candle over her abdomen. "The circle is cast and we are now between worlds. Beyond the bounds of time, where night and day, birth and death, joy and sorrow meet as one. It is in this place we invoke the tantric powers of Hecate."

No, no, no…

Isis set the fat black candle on the center of Isadora's belly, right over the pentagram outlined in blood. Then she held her hands over Isadora and the candle and chanted, "Mother, goddess, we call on thee. Set this female's inhibitions free. Let her have dreams of lust and desire. To ready the way for our rebirth through fire. As I will thee, so mote it be."

Unbridled lust? Passion? Oh holy hell…*no*. Panic and a sense of urgency welled in Isadora as she wrestled against the bonds. Isis lifted the candle, titled it sideways. Isadora's eyes grew wide and she struggled harder. A single drop of melted wax rolled over the side of the fat candle to drip down toward her bare flesh.

Her back arched off the table when the wax made contact. A scream tore from her lungs as the tender skin between her breasts sizzled and burned. Tears flooded her eyes, and her vision blurred. And though she fought it, she felt as if something were crawling into her skin, settling deep in her bones, dragging her down into a murky abyss.

She couldn't see the black magick taking hold, but she could feel it. Slowly, her limbs grew heavy again. That fog descended. Her muscles relaxed one by one, even though her soul screamed for freedom.

"That's it," Isis said from what seemed like a great distance. "Good, *paidi*. Let the magick work. Let it flow through your body. See? We're going to make this good for you. In a while, Princess, there will be nothing to fear. Only mindless pleasure."

A hand ran over her forehead. One that was warm and gentle. And though Isadora struggled to stay conscious, darkness edged in. A single tear slipped from the corner of her eye and rolled down her temple.

"Sleep now," Isis said softly. "And rest. Your future has taken a new path, *paidi*. Your new queen is waiting. And through your desire, we will be reborn."

Chapter 2

CASEY KNEW WHEN SOMETHING WASN'T RIGHT. THIS was one of those times.

"Are you sure you questioned all the castle guards?" Theron asked.

Zander rubbed a hand across his jaw, studied the map on the desk in front of them—the desk that sat in the middle of what used to be the king's office, but now served as HQ for Argonaut business. "All of them. No one's come or gone in the last hour. Theron, the place was locked down for the binding ceremony. There's no way she could have gotten out without someone seeing something."

Theron sighed, ran a hand over his shoulder-length dark hair as he studied the map more closely. They were both dressed in the traditional Argonaut fighting gear they wore when they battled daemons in the human realm, and were roughly the same height and size—over six and a half feet tall and built like tanks. And with their heads together like that, they could have passed for brothers. If, that is, one ignored the fact that Theron, their leader, was dark and Zander looked like a larger version of David Beckham.

Casey watched, tormented by Theron's frustration. Her husband was a worrier. It was part of his job. Part of who he was. Every minute his guardians were out on patrol, his concern for their safety consumed him. But this was different. This wasn't simply worry over Isadora's disappearance just before her scheduled binding. This was fear. That something had happened to her. That she was in trouble. That if something truly had gone wrong, Isadora wasn't the only one who would be affected.

His eyes lifted, almost as if he sensed Casey's thoughts, and held on hers. Midnight eyes. Ones she never tired of looking at. Ones that said, *You are mine and I won't let anything happen to you*. "Acacia? What is it?"

Casey sighed. She wasn't helping his anxiety. But then, how could she? She and Isadora weren't just half sisters, they were linked through prophecy. Though they'd yet to test the boundaries, they couldn't be separated too far or too long before the illness that had racked them both once before returned. And while Casey didn't feel sick—yet—she sensed this entire situation was not at all what they thought.

She took a step toward the desk. "Theron, she didn't just run off."

"And what makes you so sure of that?"

All three glanced toward the open doorway where Demetrius stood, scowling into the room. Behind him, Gryphon rolled his eyes and Phineus looked like he wanted to be anywhere but here.

Casey set her jaw as Demetrius stalked into the room with the others at his back. He was the biggest of the Argonauts, at nearly six feet eight inches and three hundred pounds, with short dark hair and a case of mean-cuss Casey hadn't encountered before. He didn't like anyone, didn't care about monarchy business, and his contempt for Isadora was widely known.

"Because she's not stupid, Demetrius," Casey said, "contrary to what you may think."

"You don't want to know what I think, human."

Casey crossed her arms. She wasn't entirely human. She was Misos—half human, half Argolean. And his prejudices were wearing on her already-frayed nerves, especially since all Argoleans—including him—were descendants of the great Greek heroes who had established this realm in the first place. "You seem to forget that some small part of you is human too."

"Don't bet on it."

He was trying to intimidate her. But it wouldn't work. "You don't scare me."

His gaze narrowed. "I should."

"Demetrius," Theron cut in, "enough."

At the sound of footfalls out in the hall, they all looked to the door again. Callia, Zander's mate, hesitated in the opening, her auburn hair tousled around her shoulders, her eyes wild.

Zander instantly read the alarm in her eyes and moved toward her. "*Thea*, what?

"I…" Callia curled into Zander's touch. Showed no resistance when he slipped his arm around her and pulled her close. And their connection was touching to watch, especially when Casey remembered that only hours ago they'd both been resigned to the fact the king was going to hold Zander to his agreement to marry Isadora. Thank God Casey's father had come to his senses. Anyone within a mile could tell these two were meant for each other. Callia tipped her face up to Zander's. "I felt something. A—"

"A tingle," Casey finished from across the room.

When Callia and Zander both looked her way, she added, "I felt it too."

Theron glanced from one female to the other. Then to Zander. He could sense anytime Callia was hurt or in danger, but that didn't extend to her sisters and their connection as the modern-day Horae.

"I didn't feel anything," Zander said. "I'm linked to her"—he nodded at Callia—"not the other two."

Theron's growing frustration was evident in his eyes as he rubbed his forehead. "No, that'd be too much to ask, now, wouldn't it?"

Voices kicked up in the room, speculation about where Isadora had gone and how they were going to find her. Theron ran a hand down his face as he listened to varying theories, rested his palms on his hips, and looked like he had a headache the size of Mount Rushmore.

The marking on Casey's lower back, the one that looked like an omega with wings and was identical to what Callia had on her neck and Isadora had on her leg, started to pulse. She caught her half sister's gaze across the room and knew Callia's marking was pulsing as well.

She put herself between Theron and Demetrius. "Stop it, right now. She didn't run off."

Demetrius glared down at her. "I ask again, human, what makes you so sure?"

"Knock off the 'human' shit, Demetrius," Theron warned.

Warmth spread through Casey's chest at Theron's protectiveness, but on this she didn't need his help. She hadn't lied. She, unlike Isadora, wasn't scared of Demetrius. "Because there's no point to it."

"She's done this before," Demetrius pointed out. "When the king betrothed her to Theron, she—"

"She came to find me. Yeah, I know. But this is different. She wouldn't run now because there's no point. She can't hide in Argolea—"

"She can in the human realm," Demetrius cut in.

"—and she wouldn't be dumb enough to go to the human realm alone."

"And why not?" Demetrius sneered. "She seems to like it there. In fact, she likes causing trouble in general, getting us all stirred up so we have to drop whatever we're doing and go look for her."

Casey could barely believe what she was hearing. "Do you honestly think that's what she's after? Attention?"

"I think that's *exactly* what she wants."

Casey's temper flared. "For your information, Demetrius, she wouldn't go to the human realm now unless someone forced her."

"And why is that?"

"Because she knows Atalanta is hunting the Horae. And she wouldn't risk jeopardizing our world for her own satisfaction."

"I'm not so convinced."

That did it. Casey took a step toward him. "Well, maybe this will convince you. She also wouldn't go there because if something were to happen to her there, what waits for her is a thousand times worse than marrying someone she doesn't love."

"*Meli*," Theron warned behind her.

She ignored her husband, shook off his hand trying to pull her back. His Argonauts needed to know what they were facing. This wasn't another of Isadora's attempts to sway the king's decision where she was concerned. Something bad had happened to her. Casey could feel it. And she was going out of her mind with worry.

"She traded her soul to Hades," Casey said, glancing from one Argonaut to the next. "She did it to save me when she thought our father's attempt to complete the prophecy of the Chosen was going to kill me. And Hades is holding her to that bargain, even though he— the sick bastard—knew we would both survive." When Demetrius only stared at her, she added, "Do you get what I'm telling you? Living, with even one of you, is a thousand times more enticing than spending eternity with Hades. Besides, she's way too loyal to do anything that would put me or anyone else in jeopardy. Someone forced her to leave. She would not have run this time."

"Casey's right," Callia said. "Even though she didn't want to be bound to Zander, she wouldn't have run."

Silence fell over the room. And Casey knew what each Argonaut was thinking. There was no proof. Only her gut feeling against Isadora's track record. But in her heart, Casey knew she was right.

Theron ran a hand over his brow. "*Meli*, the castle's been under extra security all day for the ceremony. And no one's seen a thing. She couldn't have—"

His words broke off when footsteps pounded outside the door. Casey glanced over to see Cerek and Titus move into the room. Titus's dark brown waves had slipped free from the leather strap he usually kept tied at the nape of his neck. Cerek's short dark hair flew every direction, as if he'd just walked through a wind tunnel. Both Argonauts' faces were flushed as if they'd been running.

"Saphira's missing," Titus said as he crossed the royal seal in the middle of the floor.

"Who in Hades is Saphira?" Theron asked.

"Her maidservant," Cerek said.

"How do you know?" Callia asked. "And when?"

Titus shook his head. "Not sure. No one can find her either, but we found this under the ottoman in Isadora's room." He held out his hand. In his big palm he cradled a silver bracelet with sun-symbol markings over one shiny side. "Saphira was the last one alone with the princess."

"Holy *skata*," Theron mumbled.

"What?" Casey asked, stepping close to get a better look. "What is it?"

"That's the symbol of Helios." Callia moved forward.

Casey's mind skipped back over her mythology. "The sun god. He was a Titan, wasn't he?"

"Yeah." Theron clenched his teeth. "And Medea's great-grandfather." He looked at his guardians. "The handmaiden's a witch? How did no one know that?"

Casey was still having trouble following it all. She took the bracelet from Titus, studied the stamped silver as voices picked up in the room. "Wait," she said. "Wait!"

When eight sets of eyes glanced her way, she asked, "What would a witch want with Isadora?"

"I don't know." Theron shook his head. "But I intend to find out. Titus, Cerek, find where the witch lives."

"On it," Cerek said as they both headed back for the door.

"Phin and Z, scour the princess's rooms again, talk to every guard. If the witch cast a spell to get them out of the damn castle, someone knows something. Find it."

Phineus nodded. Zander kissed Callia and whispered

something Casey couldn't hear, then Phineus and Zander took off for the door.

"D, Gryphon," Theron said, "I want you to check the portal, make sure no one's crossed—"

"Oh, gods, the portal," Callia cut in.

The blood drained from Casey's face when she made the connection too.

Theron glanced between the two. "What now?"

Casey turned to her husband. "The secret portals. I told you that's how Callia, Isadora, and I crossed into the human realm when you and the guardians were at the Misos colony. We couldn't use the main portal because the Executive Guard was monitoring it and they never would have let us through."

"I remember. What—?"

She placed her hand on his forearm, right over the Argonaut markings, ancient Greek text that ran up and down his arms and signified him as the warrior descendant of one of the seven greatest heroes in all of ancient Greece. "Theron, the secret portals are manned by witches. Orpheus took us there. They recognized Isadora the day we crossed. I didn't think anything of it then, but now—"

"Orpheus," Demetrius growled at Casey's back.

Casey whipped around and did a double take at the malice in Demetrius's eyes. Demetrius stalked to the door without a word, his long black coat flapping in his wake.

"Gryphon," Theron said quickly. "Your brother—"

"I'm on it." Gryphon jogged for the door. "I may want to kick Orpheus's ass now and then, but even I wouldn't sic D on him."

When the room fell silent, Casey turned toward her husband. She knew he was doing everything he could, but the heavy weight on her heart and that tingling near her lower back told her something was very wrong. "Theron," she whispered.

"Shh, *meli*." He pulled her close. "We'll find her."

Casey leaned into his touch and glanced at Callia. Across the room her half sister crossed her arms and chewed on her thumbnail. And in her eyes Casey saw the dread she felt reflected right back at her.

The black mist rolled through Demetrius as he flashed to the sidewalk on Corinth Avenue in the Draco region of Tiyrns, the slum that was home to the lowest life-forms in all the city. Dusk had just settled in, and the streetlights above glowed orange in the fading light. He took in the trash in the gutters, the run-down buildings, the bars on the windows, and the swaying signs from businesses that had long ago called it quits in this part of Argolea.

He knew this area well. Knew the pub across the street, with its blaring music and raucous laughter. Knew several who inhabited the seedy establishment even better, because they came here for the same things he did. But there was no way Isadora could have known about this place. And just the thought of her walking these streets to find Orpheus sent that black mist boiling.

He spotted Helios, Orpheus's "shop," halfway down the street, and headed in that direction. Oh, the irony that Orpheus's shop bore the same marking those damn witches glorified.

"Hold up, D," Gryphon called. "Shit, wait for me, would ya?"

Demetrius ignored the guardian and didn't stop until he was outside the shop's door. The sign said "Closed" but he turned the handle and found it unlocked. Stepping inside, he glanced around the dimly lit interior with its tables and shelves overflowing with trinkets. Human shit. Things Orpheus had no doubt pilfered from the human realm and brought to Argolea to hawk.

Gryphon moved past Demetrius and picked up a snow globe on a nearby table. A soft chuckle came from his throat as he turned the globe in his hand and little white flakes floated through the clear liquid inside. "Man, the Council's gonna love him when Uncle Lucian finally retires." His eyes shifted to Demetrius. "Can you see good ol' Orpheus on the Council of Elders, advising the king or Isadora or whoever in Hades is running this place by then?"

No, Demetrius couldn't see Orpheus as any kind of advisor to anyone. It was a sick twist of fate that he and Gryphon were the only living heirs to Lord Lucian, the leader of the Council of Elders. Since Gryphon already served with the Argonauts, that left Orpheus as the only eligible *ándras* to replace Lucian on the Council when he finally retired. But Orpheus was no lord. He was only out for himself. He obviously had no qualms about opening the portal, about letting Argoleans roam back and forth between their world and the human realm. Didn't give a shit about the dangers that lurked there or the daemons that couldn't wait to infiltrate Argolea and destroy their home. And he obviously didn't give a flying fuck about the monarchy, if he was the one who had led Isadora to those witches.

His jaw clenched. Before he could tear into Gryphon about his lazy-ass scheming brother, he spotted a door along the back wall and headed in that direction.

"D," Gryphon called. "Dammit."

The doorway led to a dimly lit hall that ran through the length of the building. From the far end, voices echoed.

"Come on," a male voice said. Orpheus's voice. "Ignore what you heard and refocus. Act like you're enjoying yourself. Attitude is half the battle."

"I am," a female replied. "Stop bitching at me."

"I would if you'd just open yourself to this. We don't have all night."

That darkness brewed deeper in Demetrius's gut, like a mist rising up to envelop him. He moved around the corner and into the room.

A female with long blond hair stood at a rectangular table, a bowl of what looked like water in front of her. For a moment Demetrius thought it was Isadora, but then he remembered that the last time he'd seen the princess, her hair had been short. And Isadora was thinner than this female, more wiry, and definitely prettier.

The female's hands hovered over the surface of the liquid and her eyes slid closed as she chanted softly to herself. Behind her and to the right, Orpheus stood with his feet apart and his arms folded over his chest, a scowl on his face as he watched.

He was as tall as the Argonauts and, because he was Gryphon's brother and hailed from Perseus's line, just as muscular. But he wasn't as well trained, and even though he was a scrapper, Demetrius knew he could take him in a hand-to-hand.

As the water in the glass bowl swirled, the female

chanted, stepped back, and lifted her hands outward. The water rose up, swirling higher until it was at least four feet tall, a mini cyclone twisting above the bowl.

"Yes, that's it," Orpheus said, dropping his hands. Sandy brown hair fell across his forehead. "Keep concentrating. You're doing it. You are fucking doing it. What do you see?"

The muscles around the female's eyes contracted. "Faces."

Demetrius stepped fully into the room. The female's eyes popped open and shot in his direction.

"Dammit, Aellô," Orpheus said quickly. "Focus!"

With the female's concentration broken, the cyclone stopped spinning and gravity grabbed hold of the water, drawing it down to slap against the table and floor and spray over her and Orpheus.

The female yelped. Demetrius went right after Orpheus. He grabbed hold of Orpheus's shirtfront and slammed him against the wall. "Where is the princess?"

"*Skata*," Gryphon muttered. "Demetrius, let him go."

A sinister smile spread across Orpheus's face. "Don't tell me you boys lost her again. I guess the rumors are true. None of you are man enough to satisfy her after all."

Demetrius pulled forward, then slammed Orpheus back against the wall again, but before Orpheus's body made contact he disappeared. Poofed right out of Demetrius's hands.

Demetrius's eyes widened. He looked at his now-empty hands and whipped around to find Orpheus standing behind him, a murderous expression on his face.

"Don't fuck with me, Guardian. Aellô, we're done here. Gather your stuff and head home."

The female cast each of them a nervous look but quickly picked up her cloak and bag from the floor, stepped over the puddle of water, and hightailed it for the door.

"Now," Orpheus said, crossing his arms over his chest as he glanced from his brother to Demetrius and back again, "to what do I owe this…surprise?"

Demetrius took a step forward, but Gryphon's forearm against his chest stopped him.

"The princess is missing, Orpheus," Gryphon said.

"And that concerns me how?"

"Because you took her to the portal."

"I don't know what you're talking ab—"

Demetrius pushed past Gryphon's arm. "Dark magick hovers all around this place. That female you had in here was a witch."

Orpheus's gray eyes settled on Demetrius, and for a second they flashed green. Green? That wasn't right. "Be careful, Guardian."

"Orpheus, listen," Gryphon said, moving by Demetrius with a glare. "Isadora went missing from the castle just before her binding ceremony to Zander. No one can find her. She doesn't even know the king called off the proceedings."

At those words Demetrius finally pulled his gaze from Orpheus and shifted it to Gryphon. "The king did *what*?"

Gryphon frowned Demetrius's way, but refocused on his brother. "We found a bracelet in her room. One with the Helios marking. This store. Those witches." He gestured to the door Aellô had just left through. "Casey told us the portal you took her, Callia, and Isadora to was manned by witches."

Orpheus's gaze shifted from Gryphon to Demetrius and back again. "The king called off Isadora's binding?"

"Yeah." Gryphon's brow wrinkled. "Wait. You were supposed to be at the ceremony. You should know this already."

"I decided not to go. Why did the king call it off?"

"Because it's clear Zander and Callia are meant to be together."

Orpheus's eyes narrowed. "Who did he give her to this time?"

"No one."

"No one?" The words shot out of Demetrius's mouth before he could stop them. Gryphon glared his way again with a *what the hell is wrong with you?* look that tightened Demetrius's stomach and told him what the guardian said was true.

The king really hadn't betrothed her to anyone else? Fuck. *Fuck!*

"Translation, little brother," Orpheus said with disdain, flicking a curious look between the two. "The king didn't have a chance to force her on yet another Argonaut she doesn't want because she ran off before he could."

"Ran off or was kidnapped."

The brothers stared at each other, and in the tension crackling it was clear that they both knew something Demetrius didn't. The darkness inside him tingled with awareness.

"Will you help us?" Gryphon asked.

Orpheus's eyebrows lifted. "You're asking, not ordering?"

"Yeah. This time I am."

Orpheus nodded at Demetrius. "And what about that one?"

"He wants to find her as much as the rest of us do."

"I wouldn't be so sure of that. Something tells me he has other, contradictory motives where your princess is concerned."

Demetrius had sensed Orpheus and the princess had some kind of connection in the past. Knew it now by the way Orpheus glared at him. What was she to him? And what was he to her?

The dark mist churned and boiled inside Demetrius as he imagined the two of them alone together. This was her choice? This piece-of-shit, rat-bastard, scheming *nothing*?

Orpheus's eyes slid back to Gryphon. "I'll take you to the portal where I took the girls. But if she already went through—"

"We know," Gryphon said. "There's no telling where she could be by now."

Orpheus grabbed a cloak from a nearby closet, led them outside, gave them a location in the Aegis Mountains, and disappeared in a flash of light. With no other choice, Demetrius followed. He cleared his mind and imagined the location, then he was flying, flashing from the sidewalk on Corinth Avenue to a wooded area at the base of Mount Parnithia.

Orpheus was already there waiting when Demetrius opened his eyes. Seconds later, Gryphon arrived. They followed Orpheus up a hill toward a small tent city made up of colorful fabrics. Flags flew in the wind, streamers of greens, reds, golds. A large pavilion with three flags marked with sun symbols took up the center area. As

Demetrius glanced around, he counted twenty, thirty, maybe fifty witches in this gathering alone.

Fifty witches. The darkness inside condensed even as disgust roiled through him.

Faces turned their way as they moved into the camp. Voices died down and movement stopped. At his side, Demetrius saw Gryphon ease his hand toward the blade he kept strapped to his thigh. Even he didn't completely trust his brother. Not when he'd led them into the center of a witch's brew.

Orpheus spoke in Medean to a young female standing near the pavilion's door. Her eyes grew wide. She nodded and disappeared inside. Seconds later she came back with an older female, this one with long, straight, snow-white hair, a youthful face, and piercing blue eyes. The witch looked only about thirty, but Demetrius sensed she was much, much older.

The witch's eyes narrowed, passed from one to the next, and swept back to Orpheus. "These are not the Horae."

"No."

"They have no need for our services." She started back into the pavilion, but Orpheus caught her by the arm.

"We're looking for one I brought through here days ago. The blond. You remember her?"

She studied him closely. "The princess?"

"Yes. Did she pass here in the last day?"

"None crossed the portal as of late."

"What about the other portals?" Demetrius asked in a low voice.

The witch's gaze snapped his way and held.

Knowledge passed over her eyes. Tension gathered in the air around them and anxiety pricked the edge of Demetrius's control.

She knows. The words reverberated in his head. There was a reason he steered clear of witches. They were too perceptive. And they recognized their kind with ease.

"All requests come through me," the witch finally said. "If the other portals had been crossed, I would know."

When she looked back at Orpheus, Demetrius let out the breath he'd been holding. But his relief was short-lived when she added, "Why do you come to me?"

Orpheus held up the bracelet Gryphon had brought with them. "This was found in her room."

The witch muttered in Medean, but the words were too quiet for Demetrius to make out. Her gaze darted up. "Come." She gestured with her hand. "Come inside."

Her urgency set off a tingling in Demetrius's skin. He followed Orpheus and Gryphon as they ducked beneath the tent flap. The inside of the pavilion was set up as a gathering area, with a circle formed in the center, chairs and rugs scattered around the perimeter. A few females looked up from their conversation on the far side of the circle and went silent.

Magick hung in the air, as did the scents of incense, herbs, and oils. A primitive part of Demetrius reacted to the scents, but he pushed it down as he focused on the witch again. She stopped near the circle, turned, and wrung her hands together. "That bracelet belongs to an apprentice of mine. I made it myself. But I fear she may have given it to her sister."

"Does this sister have a name?" Orpheus asked.

"The sister…" The witch paused. "She's just a young

girl. She works at the castle during the day. Her name is Saphira."

Foreboding slid down Demetrius's spine.

"The princess's handmaiden is called Saphira," Gryphon said.

"I know." The witch swallowed, ran a hand over her brow. "Oh, dear. I think we may have a problem."

"What kind of problem?" Demetrius ground out. "What would your witch want with the princess?"

The witch looked back to Orpheus. "Isis has gone missing as well. I thought perhaps she'd gone into Tiyrns to see her sister, but now I fear that's not the case."

"Who in Hades is Isis?" Gryphon asked.

"The witch who took Isadora across the portal days ago." Orpheus focused on the witch. "Where did they take her, Delia?"

Unease passed over Delia's face. "It's the eve of the full moon, and the feast of Hecate draws close. This time of year the dark powers will do anything to break free of their bonds. I cast a binding spell on the Horae when you were here with them so others wouldn't see what they were, but if Isis recognized them—"

"Shit," Orpheus muttered.

Demetrius didn't like the direction of the conversation, and that tingle in his skin was now a roaring vibration.

"What?" Gryphon asked. "Man, I am having so much trouble following this conversation."

"The witch has taken her to Apophis," Orpheus said from between clenched teeth.

"The warlock?" Gryphon's eyes grew wide.

"Yeah, dammit." Orpheus looked back at his brother.

"There's good and evil in this world, little brother, even among witches." He turned back to the witch. "What do you know about their plans, Delia?"

Delia wrung her hands together. "The word we're hearing is that Apophis has banded forces with Atalanta."

Demetrius stiffened and the blackness inside jerked.

"Son of a bitch," Orpheus muttered. "They're going to hand her over in exchange for freedom from their prison. Is that what you're telling me?"

"Yes," Delia said with a pained expression.

"How?" Gryphon asked. "And what prison?"

Delia looked his way. "Apophis was once an *ándras* like any other male in our region. But two thousand years ago he discovered a way to harness the black arts and used them to fuel his immortality. As his strength in this realm grew, the covens knew the horror he would unleash if he was free to roam Argolea. They united their powers to confine him to Mount Parnithia. Trapped there, he constructed Thrace Castle around him, but he's been recruiting those from our race to his side for years, and he's never stopped searching for a way out."

Demetrius clenched his jaw. That was all they needed. A fucking warlock with godlike powers, set free in their realm to wreak havoc. And now he was working with Atalanta? Holy Hades.

Orpheus looked back at Delia. "Did you know Isis had joined Apophis's horde?"

"No, I didn't. But looking back…" She wrung her hands again. "She was acting strangely after you and the Horae went through the portal."

"Shit," Orpheus muttered. "How long do we have?"

"Not long. The feast of Hecate is all but upon us. At the full moon's crest, Apophis and his band of witches will be able to open their own portal and send the princess across undetected. Once she's there, Atalanta can then open the portal for the rest of them, if she so chooses."

"We need directions to Thrace Castle," Gryphon said.

"It's protected by black magick. You'll not get close."

"We'll get in," Demetrius growled. "How many man the gates?"

Delia finally looked his way again. "At least fifty. But take heed, Guardian. Those in service to Apophis are not only of our kind. They've traded what's left of their humanity to him in exchange for enhanced powers. And he uses that humanity to strengthen his immortality. Though his followers may look like common witches, they are not."

She glanced over her shoulder. A witch near the far wall came running. "Selene will take you as far as the outer wall. Her powers can mask you that far, but no farther. From there, it'll be up to you. We can't go in with you. Apophis will sense us. But I don't have to tell you, if he and his minions are set free in the human realm…"

Then Atalanta won't be the only immortal being roaming the world with a major-ass case of pissed-off.

"Understood." Orpheus looked toward Gryphon again. "You might want to use that fancy medallion of yours and call your guardians. Three against fifty isn't gonna cut it."

Gryphon reached for the Argos medallion that hung around his neck and worked like a GPS between the Argonauts. And as he did, Demetrius pictured Isadora behind the dark castle walls with that *thing*, doing who the hell knew what right this very minute. His stomach clenched. The female couldn't stay out of trouble for five fucking minutes. And just like every other time she'd gotten herself in a bind, the Argonauts were being sent in to save her. He was sick to death of playing royal baby-sitter. At what point was he going to be free of her for good?

Never.

As that blackness simmered and churned inside of him, Demetrius made himself a promise. If she wasn't dead yet, he just might kill her himself.

Chapter 3

SOMEWHERE CLOSE, ISADORA HEARD THE CRASH OF waves, felt the gentle push and pull of the water. The sounds were relaxing, the tide freeing. And the tingle in her skin was as intoxicating as the strongest wine in all of Argolea.

Something brushed her calf. Sparks of electricity zinged along her nerve endings. She drew in a breath, relaxed as the touch crept up her leg, over her hip to her abdomen. Warmth gathered there, teased her, pushed up to the undersides of her breasts. A thick heaviness pulled on her body, called to her from a place outside herself. Unfulfilled need puckered her nipples. Her blood warmed, beat in her veins, slid lower inch by inch, until she had to press her thighs together to keep from moaning.

You like that, don't you, Princess?

Excitement leaped in her chest. The voice was male, deep, and sinfully sultry. A hint of darkness hovered along the sexy edges, calling to someplace deep inside her. Her mind struggled to make the connection she knew was on the tip of her memory, but awareness eluded her.

She rolled to her back. Arched. Needed…something more, though she wasn't sure what. More of his touch. More of those strokes that were making the blood pound in her ears. More of him.

He chuckled low, near her ear. Hot breath fanned the

sensitive skin of her neck, sent delicious shivers up and down her spine. *Tell me, Princess. Are you wet?*

This time she did moan. Because his barely there caress, those erotic words, and that wicked voice all condensed until a fire ignited in the center of her core.

Hands pushed between her legs, spread her thighs. Flames licked at her center even before she felt the first contact.

Open your eyes, little one. Look up at me. It's time.

Her body blazed with white-hot desire and scorching flames filled with need. Slowly, she peeled her eyelids open and stared up at the blurry image above. Short dark hair framed a rugged face, onyx eyes, and a strong square jaw, with the slightest dent right in the middle of his chin.

Demetrius.

Alarm rang through her head like a bell being tolled, and yet still her body arched toward his, toward his lustful gaze and that decadent promise of ecstasy hovering in his dark eyes. But it was wrong. He was cruel. And she *had never* wanted and *should never* want him like this.

Her mind protested as she tried to move. A groan tore from her chest. She rolled onto her side, sucked air, and tried to break his wicked pull even as her body continued to hum with unfulfilled cravings.

Hands grasped her hips, and she cried out as they easily rolled her back. Warmth gathered in her center all over again. She didn't want this. She didn't want him. Why wasn't her body listening?

"Wake up, *paidi*, it's time."

This time the voice wasn't male and deep and sinfully

erotic. This time it was female and clipped. And the hands hovering against her skin were small and cold.

Isadora blinked, shook her head, tried to see through the fog still hanging around her like a shroud. The room came into view. It was circular, made of stone. A chill spread down her spine when the temperature registered. An old iron chandelier hung from the high ceiling, shining light over the stone floor, over her. Over Isis standing at her side, smiling a sinister grin.

Isis. The witch. The scene from earlier raced through Isadora's mind. She darted a quick look to her left, then her right. This room was not the same one she'd been in before. It looked like a bedroom chamber with high arching windows, a four-poster bed, a chest of drawers, and a large, cold, unused fireplace on the far wall filled with dead embers.

"It's time, *paidi*," Isis repeated. "We must ready you for your journey."

"Wait—"

Hands gripped Isadora's arms. She resisted, but they pulled her easily from the bed. The sheet fell to the stone floor, revealing her naked body. Desire still thrummed through Isadora's body, combined with the chill air to tighten her breasts. Embarrassment washed over her, but the two witches with death grips on her arms barely seemed to notice. They dragged her across the room, lifted her as if she weighed nothing, and dropped her into a steaming bath set near the blackened fireplace.

She wanted to escape, needed to run, but the water was warm, the scent of roses soothing. Her body immediately relaxed and the hands pressing down on her shoulders kept her immobile.

Isis sprinkled some sort of oils into the water. She chanted in Medean, then sent Isadora a smug grin. "Atalanta wants you in peak condition when you cross the portal."

Atalanta. Those alarm bells rang louder. Isadora didn't have a clue what the hell Atalanta had planned for her, but whatever it was it couldn't be good. Atalanta had been pissed at the Argoleans for millennia—ever since she'd been denied the rank of Argonaut herself. Until recently, she'd been living in the Underworld, gathering an army of daemons in her never-ending quest to destroy those who'd shunned her. And now that the Argonauts had stolen from her the one thing she needed in her quest for ultimate control, she was even more pissed than ever before.

Isadora's mind churned and sputtered as the witches cleaned her. She blocked what they were doing and focused on what she knew. She was in some kind of castle. The stone walls and floors, the chill, the darkness, all were things she recognized. And this witch had just settled one of her fears—at least she was still in her own realm.

Panic edged its way into her chest, but she pushed it aside. Focused again. She couldn't flash through walls, but if she could get clear of this castle, if she could just find her way outside, she could flash home. But first she had to summon enough strength to get the hell out of here.

The witches pulled their hands from the tub, motioned for Isadora to stand. She did, her mind plotting and planning as they dried her with towels. From a hook on the wall, one of the witches reached for a garment, turned back, and held it up against Isadora's naked flesh.

"Yes, yes," the other witch said with excitement. "Perfect, yes. Let's get her into this. Quickly. Quickly."

The first witch removed the thin black garment from the hanger and lifted it over Isadora's head. Her arms slid through the long sleeves with apprehension; the hem fell at her bare feet. She looked down with horror as she realized the garment was sheer nearly everywhere, showcasing her skin, her left hip, her belly button, the swell of her breasts. The only places protected by diagonal strips of velvet were her nipples, the juncture of her thighs, and—she glanced over her back—thankfully, her ass.

Dear gods. This wasn't a gown. It was a negligee. One that didn't hide nearly enough and showed more than anyone had ever seen.

She couldn't come up with one logical reason Atalanta would want her dressed like this. That panic clawed its way up her chest, wrapped itself around her throat until she wanted to scream. She glanced up and around, searched for the exit. Behind her, Isis chuckled.

"Relax, *paidi*. The spell is working. You will enjoy this."

She had no idea what "this" was, but earlier she'd been dreaming about Demetrius. And though nothing about him could be good, anything that had to do with Atalanta was a thousand times worse.

"Bring her," Isis said, starting for the door.

The witches wrapped their fingers around Isadora's arms, and something inside Isadora screamed that if she went with them it would be the end for her.

"No. Stop." She braced her bare feet on the stones, pulled back. "You can't."

"We haven't much time," the one to her left said.

"No. Please." Isadora struggled as they pulled her out into the cold dank corridor and dragged her along. "Please!"

But her cries went unanswered. And the arms pulling her were too strong. Tears rolled down her cheeks when she realized she was trapped. For so many years she'd thought her father's will and his intent to bind her to one of his Argonauts—even Demetrius—would be the worst thing she could imagine in this lifetime. Now she knew the truth. Nothing compared to the horror that waited for her somewhere in this castle.

———

Frigid air blew past Demetrius's face as he stood with the rest of the guardians hidden in the dark forest to the southeast of Thrace Castle. A thick fog enveloped the stronghold built into the side of the towering mountain. Aside from the great wall that ran around the base of the fortress, the only sections of the castle that could be seen were the cold gray spires above the clouds, illuminated by the moon, nearly at its crest above.

Anticipation thrummed in Demetrius's blood. Beside him, Theron ran through the layout of the castle one more time with the witch Selene, who'd guided them this far.

"Yes," Selene said. "Once you get past the outer wall, you'll have to be careful. The witches on guard will be scanning for anything out of the ordinary. If you can get through the inner wall, the princess will most likely be held in one of the four towers."

Four towers. Demetrius glanced at the witch, shivering

in her puffy black coat, then to the spires he could see rising above the shadows and mist. Eeny, meeny, miny, fucking moe. Just their luck Isadora wouldn't be in any of them. And just their luck this castle was built for defense. Sheer rock wall on one side, drop to bone-jarring glacial water on the other. There was only one way in and out and that was through the main gate. Which was, no doubt, guarded by at least twenty witches.

"Apophis's minions have the power to alter perception," Selene went on. "So be careful. What you see may not be what's actually real."

Lovely. They were so screwed it wasn't even funny.

Theron looked up from his map, swept a glance over each of his guardians. "Zander and I will distract the guards while the rest of you go in. Orpheus has agreed to help us out on this one. Demetrius, Gryphon, and Orpheus take the west side, Phin, Cerek, and Titus, the east. We need to make this short and sweet, boys. Once you find the princess, set off your medallion and the rest of us will clear the road so you can get her out. This is a rescue mission only, not an attack. Are we clear on that?"

Heads nodded in unison.

"And if any of you run into that warlock Apophis—"

"Bend over and kiss your ass good-bye," Titus muttered.

Theron's irritated gaze shot in Titus's direction as he rolled up the map. "I was gonna say, get your ass out of there as fast as you can. You won't last two minutes against the kind of power he wields." He looked at the rest of the group, handed Selene the map. "The only advantage we have is that his powers can't cross the castle walls. Don't go until you hear our diversion. After that you're all clear. Any questions?"

Energy vibrated around the group. Eyes darted from face to face. No one said a word.

Theron nodded once. He looked toward Zander standing to his left, dressed in the same fighting gear they all wore. "You ready to go tease some witches?"

A wide smile broke across Zander's face. "You betcha. Just don't tell Callia. Wouldn't want her getting jealous or anything."

Across the group, Titus huffed.

"Get moving, lover boy." Theron swept a glance back toward the others. "The rest of you, don't get dead."

As Theron and Zander headed off toward the main castle gate, Selene held out her hands to the rest of them and muttered in Medean. Demetrius knew she was casting the last of her invisibility spell so they could reach the castle walls unseen, but a part of him prickled just the same. He avoided magick at all costs, any kind. And this was just one more thing he had to hold against Isadora. When he found the little vixen…

"D," Gryphon said, "let's go."

Looking up, Demetrius realized the others had already left. He followed Orpheus and Gryphon as they made their way to the west side of the castle. The darkness of the forest opened up to brilliance as they reached the edge of the trees, the light of the near-full moon illuminating the area as if it were daylight. This close, Thrace Castle towered above, the stark peak of Mount Parnithia a black shadow, hovering. Gruesome gargoyles glared down from perches along the outer wall. Off in the distance, torches flickered near the castle's main gates.

"Well, boys," Orpheus said, shrugging into his black cloak. "This is where I leave you."

Surprise registered, but not shock. Demetrius never expected Orpheus to play by the rules. Some instinct deep inside said not to trust the scoundrel alone with Isadora for even a second, though. Demetrius grasped the *ándras* by the arm before he could get a step away. "Hold up. Just what is your claim to the princess?"

"Careful, Guardian."

The flare of green in Orpheus's eyes was unsettling. Almost as unsettling as why Demetrius even cared what Isadora was to this guy. "If you intend to harm her—"

"No, hurting females would be your specialty, not mine."

"Orpheus," Gryphon warned.

Orpheus ignored his brother, narrowed his gaze on Demetrius. "What is she to you, *Guardian*?"

The darkness vibrated in Demetrius's chest, pushed against his ribs, screamed to be let free. "A burden."

"Well, that's where we differ, Argonaut. To me she's an opportunity. She and I have an arrangement. And she owes me something I intend to collect. Now if that's it for the inquisition"—he glanced down to where Demetrius held him by the arm, waited until he let go—"then I'll see you both inside." He lifted the cloak around his head and disappeared.

Demetrius darted a look at Gryphon, who only rolled his eyes. "Invisibility cloak. Don't ask where he got it. Trust me, you don't want to know."

Demetrius looked back to where Orpheus had stood only moments before.

"He can also poof through walls, in case you didn't

know. Which means he's probably already inside. Where in Hades is that signal?"

As if on cue, an explosion rocked the front gate and shook the ground. Screams and shouts erupted; a fireball ignited near the moat. Demetrius caught Gryphon's eye. Gryphon nodded and flashed. Demetrius followed. When he opened his eyes he was on the top of the outer wall walk. He turned just in time to see three witches running his way, blades drawn, mouths open in blood-curdling screams.

Holy Hades. He tensed, had just enough time to draw his parazonium—the ancient Greek dagger they each carried—from the scabbard at his back and swing out and around in a defensive move before the first witch reached him. But his blade made no contact, swept through nothing but air. Jolted by the lack of matter, he shifted his attention to the middle witch, who screeched and swung up and over with her sword, bringing it down dangerously close to Demetrius's shoulder. He shifted out and around, heard Gryphon call his name from farther down the wall walk, and kicked out, knocking the witch off balance. She hit the stones at his feet, jumped up, and swiveled in the air like a kung fu fighter.

Blade met sword. The witch was small but strong, and Demetrius felt the dark magick clinging to her as she fought against him. The third witch disappeared and reappeared at the edge of his vision, an exact replica of the one he was fighting. As he swung again and again and advanced, he realized she was casting illusions, trying to confuse him.

. *Fucking witches...*

He pushed her closer to the gun battery. She growled,

shifted the sword in her hands. Venom shone in her eyes. Her back hit the stone wall with a thwack. Knowing she was cornered, she stared at him, and a slow smile spread across her twisted face. "Come to me. Join me. You know you can't resist for long."

"I don't think so." He swung up and over, catching her arm with the flat of his blade, knocking the sword from her grasp. It clattered against the hard ground.

Her eyes flew wide, and her irises turned neon yellow…which was just freakin' *wrong*. She shifted forward, raised her arms, and pointed her fingers at his chest. "Mother goddess of the—"

"I'm not wild about that one either." He placed the heel of his boot against her chest and pushed just hard enough to get her attention. Her back hit the wall again. "Surrender."

He spent his life killing. Daemons weren't a problem, and if a random human got in the way of his goal, it was an acceptable loss as far as he was concerned. But he had a mental hang-up when it came to fighting a female, even a witch. He didn't want to gut her, but he also knew the depth of her powers and he wasn't about to let her cast a spell over him.

"I'd rather die first." The witch lifted her hands again.

Before she could hex him, he pushed with the sole of his boot. A cracking resounded just before the stones gave way and her body tipped over the edge of the wall. He reached out to grab her, but she slipped out of his grip. Her scream echoed up as she dropped into the clouds below.

"Demetrius!"

Damn it. At the sound of his name, Demetrius tore

to the other side of the wall walk and looked across the ward to the inner wall, where Gryphon had flashed and was now fighting a handful of witches. Only these didn't look like illusions. They looked real and pissed and abundant.

"*Skata.*" Demetrius closed his eyes and flashed to the next wall, behind the horde of witches. He kicked out at one, knocked her off balance. She leaped to her feet, twisted around, and hissed. When she charged with her sword high, he arced out and slashed through her abdomen. Lights flickered around her like a halo as blood spurted from the wound. But it wasn't red, it was neon yellow, and when a drop hit the skin of his hand, it sizzled and burned.

Holy motherfucking...

Her shriek yanked his attention. In a daze he watched her beauty stutter and fade, leaving behind a wrinkled, gnarled, and warped being with razor-sharp teeth and snakes shooting out all over her head.

No way. Delia hadn't lied when she said these things weren't Medean anymore. They were like Furies, without the fucking wings. Any apprehension he had at mowing them down evaporated. He used his blade to take down one, then another. Each time he struck, that acid spurted from their wounds, charred any bits of his flesh left exposed.

They were relentless, coming again and again. By the time he reached Gryphon's side, he was bloody and bruised, his hands charred and aching, and he was breathing heavily, a trail of dead witches behind him on the wall walk.

Gryphon didn't look much better. "I never thought

I'd say this, but I think I prefer fighting daemons. These witches are fucking brutal. At least the damn daemons go down easy."

Demetrius wasn't about to compare the two. His gaze shot to the courtyard below. "We have to get inside that keep before they bar the doors."

They each flashed to one side of the gatehouse entrance, where two witches were working to roll the massive wood doors closed. Demetrius nodded once at Gryphon, then jumped up to the steps and went after the first witch. She was agile and turned on him like a wraith. Her scream echoed through the chill air, but he struck out and around with his blade and caught her in the chest. Her face contorted and morphed into her ugly image, her neon yellow eyes flying wide just before she fell at his feet.

Demetrius looked up in time to see the blade in the other witch's hand catch Gryphon at the chest. Gryphon roared as metal sliced into flesh, went down to one knee. The second witch screeched and lifted her sword for the kill blow.

Demetrius charged with his shoulder and plowed into her abdomen before she could make contact. The witch sailed through the open door and smacked into a pillar on the far side of the hall. Her eyes went glassy; her head lolled on her shoulders. As her glamour faded, the snakes that made up her hair hissed and twisted around her face. She slumped to a heap against the floor.

Demetrius righted himself, reached for Gryphon.

"I'm fine," Gryphon grumbled, pushing up to stand. "Shit, that burns." He shook off Demetrius's help. "I said I'm fine."

Outside, shouts resounded and footsteps drew closer. The cackles and screams were clear indications that what was coming their way wasn't Argolean.

"*Skata*." Gryphon pointed toward a circular staircase with his blade. "There. Go!"

They made it halfway up the stairs before they were overrun by five more witches rushing down from the second level.

They swung, battled, chopped, and kicked. For every witch that went down, another seemed to come out of the woodwork and join the fight.

"Holy Hera," Gryphon shouted over the battle. "They're reproducing like rabbits!"

Just about the time Demetrius thought they were losing ground, Orpheus appeared on the landing above, his own sword raised as he drove the remaining witches down. Metal clanked against metal. Shouts resounded. Cries and screams of effort and agony echoed in the vast stone space.

"I leave you boys to do one simple thing." Orpheus sliced through one witch's leg. When she howled, he kicked her in the stomach. She tumbled down the staircase to land on a pile of dead and mutilated bodies.

Demetrius wiped a hand across his sweaty brow and peered down at the ruin below. "No way there's only fifty witches in this freakin' castle."

"The witches are the least of our problems right now, boys." Orpheus's eyes flared in that strange way of his. "I found her."

Orpheus turned and skipped steps to get to the top. Blades drawn, Demetrius and Gryphon followed. When they reached the third floor, Orpheus held up a hand, stopping them. Down the long arched corridor, an open doorway at the end glowed with a surreal blue light. Dark magick hovered all around, and a vile evilness coated every inch of space.

Demetrius stared at the blue light, transfixed by the glow, his chest rising and falling as he worked to regulate his breathing. That darkness inside him leaped with excitement.

He swallowed hard, gripped his blade. At his side, Gryphon did the same.

"This is where we separate the men from the boys." Orpheus's eyes flicked to his brother. "You wanna run home?"

Gryphon shot him a glare. "And let you have all the fun? I think not."

Orpheus smirked, looked to Demetrius. "How about you, cowboy? Did you ever wonder what Pandora let out of her box?"

Demetrius tensed. There was no way Orpheus could know who and what Demetrius really was, but the intense expression, coupled with the look in the *ándras*'s eyes when he tipped his head toward the door, gave Demetrius a strange hitch in his gut, as if Orpheus knew way more than he should.

Orpheus took one step toward Demetrius. "Some things are better left unseen. You know what I'm talking about, don't you, *Guardian*?"

Knowledge and secrets lingered in Orpheus's words, drifted in his empty eyes. The black mist pounded at Demetrius from every side. The two parts of him he kept locked off from the world, the blackness inside and his so-called *gift*, strained to be set free. To finally be used.

Temptation was closer than it had ever been. All he had to do was lift his hands, give in to the power...

An ear-shattering scream rent the air. Demetrius looked past Orpheus toward the blue glow. And his chest grew impossibly tight. He knew that voice.

Instinct pushed him forward without a second thought. "Isadora."

Chapter 4

ISADORA THOUGHT HADES WAS THE MOST TERRIFYING immortal being she'd ever faced. She'd been wrong.

Shakes racked her body as she stood in the center of the great hall. Behind her, lightning flashed outside, illuminating the space through three high arching windows. Far below, the crash of waves against rock drifted up in a roar that churned and rolled in time with her fear. But what held Isadora's attention wasn't the lights or sounds or even what the witches were muttering. It was the glowing blue being floating across the ground toward her.

Floating.

Holy *skata*, it was *floating*.

Her heart pounded like a gong against her ribs. Terror gripped every inch of her soul and urged her to flee, but she couldn't move. Even if the witches hadn't been holding her, she'd have been frozen in this space. Because evil hummed and vibrated in front of her—the kind that was on a par with Atalanta and Hades and wasn't supposed to exist in her realm—and she was powerless to do anything but stare and quake.

"You," the glowing thing said in a raspy voice that sounded as if it rang out from the dead. "You are…more than I expected."

Isadora had no idea what he meant. Her gaze was fixed on the silver hair that fell from a part in the middle of his skull and hung to his hips. A gray moustache seemed to rise from two clumps under his nostrils to frame his twisted mouth. Not a single hair swayed; the only thing affected by his movement was the long black robe he wore, which hovered inches above the weathered stone floor.

He stopped mere feet from her. The sallow wrinkles on his face pulsed with energy as he breathed deeply. And as his pupils dilated until there was no white around his irises, just one giant gaping black hole, Isadora knew this thing—whatever it was—had come to steal what was left of her freedom.

"My name is Apophis, wee one. Do you know who I am?"

Terror rendered Isadora speechless. Apophis. The mythological warlock. It couldn't be. She'd heard stories of him as a child, but she'd never thought he was real. And now he was standing before her? No way.

"Atalanta was wise to hide your true power from me," he said in that eerie voice when she didn't answer. "She was also naïve to think I would not find out."

"My lord?" the witch to Isadora's left asked.

His glowing gaze stayed locked on Isadora. "With this one at my side, Isis, I will be more powerful than Atalanta. I will rise to the level of the Titans."

The Titans...*shit*. They were the gods who had spawned the Olympians. Isadora's anxiety skyrocketed.

Isis stiffened. "But, my lord, she is nothing more than a weak child."

"Not a child. And not weak." His lips twisted into an evil smile. "She is one of the Horae, Isis. Do you know what that means? Atalanta tricked us into thinking she only wanted the princess because she was royal, but this changes everything." Excitement flared in his eyes. An excitement Isadora knew was going to equal bad things for her. "She has the power to look not only into the past and future, but the present as well."

Isis gasped. And Isadora's brow wrinkled as the warlock's words set in. No, that wasn't right. Her sister Casey had the gift of hindsight, and Isadora herself had the gift of foresight, but both of their powers were unpredictable. And they'd only recently discovered that Callia, their other sister, was the so-called balance between them, but they didn't yet know what that meant.

"I thought the Horae needed each other to harness those powers," Isis said.

"For themselves, yes," Apophis answered, "but with the power of the dark arts I can harness the strength in this one alone. Imagine what I will be able to do once she and I are joined. I will be able to see everything. Past, present, future. Even what the gods have planned."

The impact of what he was implying rushed through Isadora like a wave, shutting down all other thought. If he was right, then it meant together she and her sisters had the power to look into the present, to visualize what was happening elsewhere, to tap into the future and see what others had planned, even Atalanta. And it also meant, with the strength of the Argonauts behind them, together they could ensure no one man, creature, or deity disrupted the balance of the world.

Something inside her chest solidified, as if years of wandering finally made sense. Isadora's father, the king, had once told her she would play an important role in the world—if, that is, she stopped being so darn timid.

Could it be this was her role? Not simply to rule over their realm as queen as she'd thought he meant, but to aid the Argonauts as they carried out Zeus's ancient decree that the Eternal Guardians protect not only Argolea, but the human realm as well?

She was so lost in her thoughts she didn't realize Apophis had moved close until she felt the chill from his hand hovering over her chest. Startled, she looked up to see one bony, gnarled hand with razor-sharp black fingernail-like claws inches from her skin.

"Yes," he muttered. "Yes, she will do nicely. Not only is she Horae, but she is untouched." He lowered his hand. "We will not be sending her to Atalanta as planned. We will keep her. Her virtue will fuel my powers, and once the union of our bodies and souls is complete, I will have the strength to open the portal on my own whenever I choose. Then Atalanta will bow to me, not the other way around." He turned to Isis. "Prepare her for the ritual."

Union of bodies and souls? Ritual?

Hold on…wait a minute…

Isis scurried off. One witch secured Isadora's left arm to a horizontal bar that hung from the ceiling as Apophis moved across the room to reach for something from the wall. Another witch chanted in Medean at Isadora's side. And Isadora knew right then, if Apophis so much as touched her, the world—both Argolea and the human realm—would be forever altered. Survival instincts welled inside her, triggered her anger and what little training Orpheus had given her to this point. She wasn't going to sit back and do nothing. She wasn't going to let this thing have her.

She dug down deep for her courage. And when Isis moved around the warlock and reached for her other arm to secure it as well, Isadora struck.

She grabbed the *athamé*, the black dagger hooked in Isis's belt. Her fingers closed around the handle. She pulled back and swung. The blade caught Isis's upper arm. The witch howled, stumbled back. Her eyes flew wide and glowed—oh, *skata*—yellow. Fear leaped in Isadora's chest as Isis hissed and advanced with fury coating her features. Panicked, Isadora swung out blindly again, this time catching the witch across the jugular.

Bright yellow blood sprayed across the room, splashed over Isadora and the ground. She screamed when it connected with the skin on her forearms, sizzled, and popped. Across the room, Apophis screeched and jumped back, as if the blood had burned him too. Isis's eyes went bug wide; her hands flew to her neck. As her body slumped to the floor, her face twisted and transformed. The youthfulness and beauty faded before Isadora's eyes, leaving behind gnarled and wrinkled skin, canary yellow eyes, sharp pointed teeth, and hair that was no longer short and stylish but made up of hundreds of small snake heads, striking and hissing.

Horror pounded against Isadora's chest. The burns on her arms forgotten, she shifted toward the other two witches. They both hissed and jumped back. Their eyes turned the same neon yellow as Isis's as they began to chant again.

Isadora swallowed hard and gripped the dagger tighter. She tried to move back but her left arm was still secured above her.

Across the room, Apophis yelled, "*Quai!*"

She'd almost forgotten about him. Isadora twisted in his direction, then wished she hadn't. The warlock was no longer the size of a regular man. He'd sprouted to nearly seven feet, the blue glow now a blinding glare.

"You are mine, *paidi*." He held out his hand, curled his fingers forward. "And you shall not enjoy a moment of what is to be." As if he were grabbing hold of something in the air, he yanked. Isadora's body jerked forward as if her spine were being pulled right out of her body.

Blinding pain tore through her stomach, her hips. The dagger flew from her hand, smacked against the wall, and clattered to the stone floor. Her knees gave out. A sharp stab rocketed through her shoulder as her body slumped and her weight shifted to her wrist, shackled above.

Apophis advanced, menace blazing in his soulless eyes. "For the glory of Hecate I claim you here and now."

Isadora lifted her head. Stars fired off in her line of sight and her shoulder felt as if it were being yanked from the socket, but all of it was overridden by the knowledge that he wasn't going to end her suffering. He was going to torture her. And then…then she didn't want to even think about what he would do.

Apophis's vile voice echoed in her head as he drew closer. Shouts and screams ricocheted off the rock walls around her. Tears burned her eyes. She wanted nothing more than to curl into herself, but the blood-curdling roar from the doorway tore her eyes open.

A figure bolted through the opening, blade held high, malice coating his features. A body and face

Isadora knew well. She blinked twice, barely believing the sight.

Demetrius. Only this wasn't the almost-lover she'd envisioned in her dream. This was death and destruction intent on annihilation, pulled straight out of a nightmare.

His blade blurred silver as it sliced through air and slashed into Apophis's robe at the arm. The warlock screeched, the sound a spine-chilling howl that vibrated through the stone-cold floor and into Isadora's bones.

Two more males stepped into the room behind him. Orpheus joined the attack on Apophis, while Gryphon set his sights on her. Apophis lifted his arms out and shot electricity from his fingertips. A bolt hit Orpheus in the shoulder, sent him sailing backward, slamming him into the doorway. Demetrius dove to the side, narrowly missing a shot to the chest.

The witches at Isadora's side screeched, and Isadora whipped around as they rushed Gryphon, who had made it past Apophis and was racing her way.

"No!" Isadora's adrenaline surged. The pain dulled. She reached up with her free arm, grabbed the bar with both hands, and pulled herself up. When the witches got close enough, she swung her legs up and kicked out as hard as she could.

Bare feet met flesh and bone. The closest witch fell into the other with a howl. They both slammed into Apophis, sending him careening off balance. He hit the ground, twisted, and surged to his feet. Demetrius charged again. Apophis flicked out his arm and backhanded Demetrius in the face. A flash of blue erupted where they made contact and sent Demetrius staggering. The two witches scrambled to their feet. Orpheus swung out and caught the first across the chest with his blade before she could strike out at Isadora again, then plowed into the second, shooting her across the floor and into the wall.

Gryphon reached Isadora. "Hold on." He worked the bind on her hand above. "Can you walk?"

Isadora's energy lagged, but her will to live had never been stronger. And she'd never been as grateful to see the Argonauts—Demetrius included—as she was right now. "Y-yes. Hurry."

Across the room, Apophis roared. His arms darted out and an electrical bolt shot from his fingertips. Demetrius swung out with his blade, nailed Apophis in the back, but it was too late. The current was already flying, sailing at light speed in their direction.

The beam struck Gryphon square in the back. Energy jolted through him. His eyes flew wide and his whole body jerked and seized. He dropped to the ground like a board.

A scream tore from Isadora's chest. Demetrius swung at Apophis again. Orpheus attacked. The remaining witch pushed up from the floor and turned her fury on Isadora with a shriek.

Isadora scrambled back as far as the bar still holding her arm would allow. She glanced down and found Gryphon's blade at her feet.

The training sessions with Orpheus condensed in her mind. Instinct ruled. She focused on the parazonium and envisioned it in her hand, breathed deep to center herself. Energy gathered near her Horae marking on her thigh. Power surged up into her body and shot down her free arm. Gryphon's blade rocketed into her hand. Her fingers closed around the grip with deadly intent, and she swung as hard as she could. The blade stabbed deep into the witch's chest.

The witch gasped. As she staggered backward, the blade pulled from her chest cavity, creating a sucking sound that echoed across the chamber. Yellow goo spurted from the wound, droplets searing Isadora's cheek. She recoiled at the burst of blinding pain. The witch dropped to her knees, then slumped to the floor.

Across the room, Orpheus struck the warlock's leg with his sword. Apophis screamed and went down to one knee, whipping Isadora's way. Crimson blood oozed from numerous cuts and scrapes across his body. Unlike his witches, he was still mostly human. And he bled. Bright red. Just like her.

Sweat poured down his face. That perfectly ordered gray hair was now a knotted mess around his grotesque features. His eyes took in the dead witches, darted back to where Demetrius and Orpheus prepared for the kill blow.

"You haven't seen the last of me." With one final glare Isadora's way, he poofed into nothingness.

"That's right, motherfucker," Orpheus muttered. "Run back to your hole and hide like the pussy you really are."

Demetrius crossed the room in three strides and reached for Isadora's bound arm. He didn't speak as he worked and Isadora was too juiced to care.

Orpheus finally caught sight of Gryphon out cold on the floor and rushed to his brother's side. "Gryph! Shit." He dropped his blade, rolled Gryphon onto his back. Burn marks marred both the front and back of the guardian's clothing. "Dammit, Gryphon. Wake up, you moron."

Isadora's hand jerked free and she fell into Demetrius. He caught her around the waist. Faintly she was aware of the blood and sweat coating his clothing, but his arms were strong and warm and crushing as they closed around her. And she didn't give a rip that he smelled like witch goo. He was solid. He was real. Right now he was everything she needed.

He was also gone way too soon. He set her back, made sure she was steady on her feet before he let go, but then he was gone, sliding his blade into its scabbard and kneeling on Gryphon's other side as he and Orpheus worked to wake the unconscious Argonaut.

She was still too stunned to feel anything as she turned to watch them work. But the scream that resounded from the doorway drew her immediate attention.

Saphira, Isadora's handmaiden, charged with her sword out like a spear. Only this wasn't Saphira as Isadora had ever known her. This female's eyes were a frightening neon yellow, her face a horror of menace and rage, and the murder gleaming on her face was a clear indication that what was left of her humanity was long gone.

"Fuck," Demetrius muttered when he caught sight of the rabid witch. "Orpheus!"

Orpheus twisted, grappled for his sword. Demetrius's hand darted to his back for his blade.

Isadora didn't think, she reacted. She lifted Gryphon's parazonium, still in her hand, and hurled it end over end. The tip of the blade impaled the witch dead center in the chest. Her eyes flew wide, she stumbled, and her mouth dropped open in shock. The sword fell from her hand as she grappled to pull the weapon free. But there was no time for even a scream to slip from her throat. Her glamour flickered and died as she collapsed forward on the cold floor and the blade pierced flesh and bone to protrude from her back.

Isadora's hands cupped her cheeks. As she stared at Saphira's lifeless body, she couldn't help but think of the thousands of times she'd looked at that face and trusted she was her friend. The energy that only moments before had propelled Isadora forward rushed out of her on a wave. She took a step back just as her knees went out from under her.

"I've got you."

Strong arms closed around her. Still reeling, she looked up to find Demetrius holding her tight against him once again.

Demetrius?

Yeah. Demetrius.

She focused on his face to keep the panic at bay. On the bloody and bruised skin streaked with dirt. On the faint lines fanning out from the corners of his eyes, that hard mouth, the slight dimple in his chin. On the strong cheekbones and his intense gaze, which seemed to be looking all the way through her, right into her soul. This was the same Argonaut she'd seen in her dream. The same one she'd cowered from so many times she couldn't count. Only this time something felt…different.

He pushed her hands away from her face, focused on her burn, and muttered, "Bitches." Gently he blew on the tender skin and his breath, cooling against the sting of the burn, heated other places inside her she definitely shouldn't be aware of right now.

Her body reacted, shifted deeper into his arms. Even though some small place in her mind screamed, *What the hell do you think you're doing?*

"Sonofabitch," Orpheus said from across the room. "Um, guys. We've got a problem. A big-ass problem."

Somehow Isadora tore her gaze from Demetrius and looked toward Orpheus, who was standing at the doorway, peering down the long hall.

"What now?" Demetrius asked.

"Wave number two," Orpheus said. He crossed the floor in quick strides, reached for his sword from the floor. "Only this time they're not fucking around."

"*Skata.*"

Isadora tensed in Demetrius's arms. "What does that mean?"

"It means we need to haul ass out of here." Demetrius looked down at her. "Can you walk?"

"No, but I can run."

"Good girl." Demetrius let go of her, dropped to Gryphon's side, and slapped the guardian on the face. "No more dicking around, Gryphon. Wake up."

Gryphon grunted and stirred.

Orpheus checked the door again, swore. "We don't have time to run." Then to Demetrius, "You'll have to take them through the portal."

Demetrius's gaze shot to Orpheus's as he pushed Gryphon up to sitting. "She can't go to the human realm."

"It's either that or die, smart guy. Gryphon's not strong enough to flash out of here and you're not leaving him behind, so make a choice. We've got seconds here.

I can hold them off until you get through the portal, but that's it."

Fear leaped in Isadora's chest. She twisted to Orpheus. "You're coming with us."

He flicked her a look as he pulled on his black cloak, stained with blood and gore. "Would love to, Isa, but someone's got to be the man around here."

"Wait. You don't have to do this."

"Careful, Isa. I'll start to think you really do care."

"Orpheus—"

He turned to her before she could touch him and the humor left his features, stopping her feet. His eyes flickered green before returning to their normal gray color. Isadora stiffened when she saw the daemon in him shimmer forward and retreat.

"I can hold my own," he said. "You know that."

She did know that. She was the only one who knew his secret. Not even Gryphon knew that his brother was part daemon. He was right. He could take down just about anything that came at him, but he wasn't invincible. And somewhere in the back of her mind she realized she'd foreseen this moment long ago. "Orpheus—"

"Go, Isa," he said, softer. "You managed to save me; now do it for my brother. Get Gryphon home. I can hold them off long enough for all of you to get through. This time I need *your* help."

She swallowed hard. Out in the hall, footsteps pounded and mixed with screams and shouts and cries of war.

Isadora took a step back. And another.

"Go!" Orpheus shouted. His eyes flashed again before jerking from her toward the doorway, which was suddenly filled with a horde of witches, all seething and hissing and bearing weapons like nothing Isadora had seen before.

Fear surged. Isadora turned and ran as Orpheus dropped down for attack.

Demetrius brought his hands together in front of him. "Run!"

The portal fractured and opened, illuminating the room in a burst of light so bright it blinded Isadora. She dropped her hand to block the glare, dug her bare feet into the slippery floor, and pushed off as hard as she could. Weapons clashed behind her. Screams and shouts resounded. Terror plagued her as she thought of Orpheus left here alone. But when she reached Demetrius and Gryphon, she didn't hesitate. She sprinted through the opening toward salvation. And prayed somehow it would find them all.

———

"D?"

Behind Demetrius the portal popped and sizzled in a band of brilliant light that shimmered over the dark clearing. With one arm wrapped around Gryphon's waist, the other holding the guardian's arm at his shoulder to support his weight, dread welled in the bottom of Demetrius's chest. "Yeah?"

"Tell me I'm hallucinating," Gryphon muttered.

Dozens of glowing green eyes peered their way.

"Neither of us is that lucky."

"Mother…" Gryphon winced in pain. "The portal didn't improve our situation."

No shit. As the daemons in the field turned and headed

their way, exit strategies raced through Demetrius's mind. A descendant of Perseus, the great hero who'd defeated Medusa, Gryphon had the power of paralysis, but he rarely used it. Not only was his power unpredictable, but using it drained him of strength and left him blind until the weakness passed. The Argonauts didn't like him to call up his power unless they were in dire straits, and though that's exactly what this was, in his current state there was no way Gryphon could freeze-frame their enemies without possibly killing himself in the process. That left battling their way out of this mess, which didn't look all that promising from where Demetrius was standing.

No, Gryphon was wrong. Demetrius would take fifty witches over a pack of daemons any day.

Moonlight cascaded over their seven-foot-tall bodies, over their catlike faces, doglike ears, and horns that looked like something off a rabid goat. He glanced sideways to where Isadora was standing still as death, staring out at what now faced them.

His adrenaline surged. No way he could open the portal again and send her and Gryphon back to Argolea. Not with those daemons so close. If even one got through...

They didn't have time. He unhooked Gryphon's arm from around his shoulder. Pushed the guardian toward Isadora. Gryphon stumbled, but Isadora was right there to catch him. "Get back. Both of you."

"Demet—" Isadora started.

He unstrapped the knife at his thigh and pushed the handle into Isadora's small hands. It wasn't much of a weapon against hell's monsters, but it was better than nothing, and hopefully it'd give them a chance. A slight chance.

Sonofabitch. He'd thought they were fucked before? This topped that by a mile.

The black mist swirled and deepened, condensed in his chest. He whipped the parazonium from its scabbard and turned to face the coming doom. The daemons were now in a full-out charge, headed right for them. "Run, already!"

There was no time to look and see if Gryphon and Isadora had listened. The first daemon flew through the air, blade swinging, claws thrashing. Demetrius's parazonium made contact with the daemon's sword, the vibration of the hit ricocheting down his arm. Five, maybe six, he could handle on his own. But not the forty or so that were out here. And wasn't it just his dumbass luck that he hadn't paid attention to where he was opening the portal in the human realm, had simply opened it to the last place he'd come from. Which had been days ago, at the half-breed colony, when he'd been here with the other Argonauts helping to fend off a daemon attack.

A scream rang out. He stabbed the daemon in the chest and pulled his blade from the unholy's body as he whirled around. Gryphon and Isadora were thirty feet from him, flanked by two massive daemons. In a daze he watched one daemon swipe out with razor-sharp claws, saw Gryphon go down. Isadora stepped closer to Gryphon's body, wielded the knife like a pro, and though he was momentarily shocked by her courage and skill, he knew that wouldn't keep the beasts back for long. The three daemons making a beeline for her didn't look like they cared about her bravado or the puny weapon she held in her hand.

Demetrius's chest pounded, his throat closed. He'd never reach her in time. His mind tumbled with options, but when the daemon smacked the knife out of her hand and her body spun from the blow, he didn't even think.

The magick that was as much a part of him as his eyes and hair and teeth, but which he denied at every turn, gathered in his hands. A chant rose in his mind, circled, and swirled until the words poured from his tongue without encouragement.

"Earth, wind, water, fire, grant to me your growing power." He felt the force push through his hands, zing out his fingertips. Imagined his arm shooting across the distance and his hand wrapping around the daemon's throat. Sensations rippled through him. The instant he felt contact, he clamped down and yanked.

The daemon lost its footing. Jerked back ten feet before it slammed into the ground. Isadora scrambled to her feet. The daemon jumped up with murder in its green eyes as it searched for whoever had grabbed him.

He homed in on Demetrius and charged. Demetrius had just enough time to brace himself. He darted a look toward Isadora and the remaining daemons closing in tight. The daemon launched just as Demetrius swung out. His parazonium caught the beast across the chest, tore into its thick flesh. Demetrius swiveled out from under its weight.

"Isadora! Run!"

Blood spurted over him as the daemon hit the ground and rolled. From the corner of his eye Demetrius saw Isadora sprinting toward the trees. But the monster was up again, charging, blocking his view of her, teeth bared, fangs unsheathed, eyes a blinding glow in its grotesque head.

Isadora screamed again. A loud crack resounded through the chill night air seconds before the daemon slammed into Demetrius, knocking him to the ground. His head hit hard, stars fired off behind his eyes, but panic over what he couldn't see happening only yards away had him swinging out again and again with his blade.

He couldn't make headway. Didn't have enough time to focus and draw on his magick. The creature knocked the blade from his hand. Metal pinged against rock as his parazonium clanked across the ground. The beast reared back, blood-coated claws seconds from annihilation.

"Stop!"

The daemon above hesitated. His gruesome head swiveled toward Gryphon and Isadora and the daemon who'd shouted the order.

Demetrius looked too. Ten or more daemons had gathered around Isadora, blocking his view. The daemon kneeling on the ground nodded toward the beast that still had Demetrius pinned. "Bring him."

The daemon curled its claws into Demetrius's shirt and yanked. "Get up, asswipe."

Demetrius staggered, caught his balance, stumbled again as he was dragged across the ground. The daemon threw him to the dirt near the others.

Pain seared every inch of his body, but he pushed up on his hands, searched through the sea of tree-trunk legs and arms for Isadora. Sweat and blood rolled into his eyes, but he barely cared.

Isadora's face was bruised, her arms limp, her head

tipped to the side. Blood trickled down her temple. More dried blood caked her short blond hair and matted the side of her head. One foot was twisted at an odd angle, and her chest neither rose nor fell.

No. Oh, skata, no…

The daemon who'd summoned him stepped in Demetrius's line of sight, blocking his view. He wrapped his meaty hands in the front of Demetrius's shirt and jerked him to his feet. Demetrius didn't fight back, didn't try to defend himself. All he saw was the image of Isadora lying dead on the ground.

The daemon's glowing eyes roamed Demetrius's face, and that black mist brewed in Demetrius's chest with every passing second. Two hundred and eighteen years of life had come down to this. To making one monumentally fucked-up mistake that had just toasted all three of them and sent Isadora straight into Hades's clutches for good. "Just kill me, you fucking prick."

The daemon's lips curled back in a grisly smile to reveal stained, pointed teeth. "And risk the wrath of Atalanta? I don't think so."

The daemon set Demetrius on his feet, but instead of the blinding pain from claws or teeth or blade, what came was a pat on his back as if they were old friends. The daemon turned to face the others. "What we have there, my comrades, is of royal blood. And lucky for all of you I realized this before you killed her."

Demetrius's gaze snapped to Isadora. She wasn't dead? Hope erupted in his chest.

"Atalanta has been waiting for her," the daemon went on. "What a lucky twist of fate that we are the ones who will bring her to our queen." He turned and looked Demetrius's way. "And she will be most pleased you are the one who brought her to us."

That hope fizzled and died. Trepidation coursed through Demetrius as the leader's chest swelled with pride. More daemons gathered to see what was happening. Murmurs and throaty whispers rose up in the night to circle the field like a malicious, pulsing halo of evil.

The leader of the pack held his arms out wide. "Warriors, pay homage to this Argonaut who will change the tides of our war. For Atalanta's son has succeeded in his duties. Your brother has finally brought us our prize."

Chapter 5

ORPHEUS FELT LIKE HE'D BEEN RUN OVER BY A semitruck. The skin on his hands and forearms was fried from all the acidic witch blood. His shoulder hurt like a bitch where he'd taken a blast of Apophis's energy. And he had enough nicks and cuts from claws and swords everywhere else to last him into the next millennium.

Man, the Argonauts owed him big-time. As he flashed to Delia's tent city in the low hills of the Aegis Mountains, he corrected himself. *Isadora* fucking owed him.

And this time he planned to hold firm to his word and make sure she paid up.

Delia rushed out of the pavilion just as he lowered the invisibility cloak's hood. She grasped his forearm, her fingers digging in deep to his already-seared skin.

He winced as pain shot into his arm and tried to pull away. But the witch had a death grip and her wide-eyed expression put him on instant alert. One look around and he realized the Argonauts weren't here, where'd they'd planned to reconnoiter after rescuing Isadora.

"Where are they?" he asked.

"They left."

Left? Why, those ungrateful motherfu—

"They sensed one of their own open the portal."

"I know. The big one opened it to get the princess away from Apophis."

Delia shook her head, white hair flaring out all around her shoulders. And his last thread of patience snapped. He'd nearly gotten fried, had risked his own neck so Demetrius could get Gryphon and Isadora the hell out of there, and then they'd gone and ditched his ass so they could—

"It didn't reopen."

"What did you say?"

"I said the portal didn't reopen. They didn't come back through. Not here, not in Tiyrns."

His brow wrinkled. "How can you—"

"Because I sense anytime the portal opens, anywhere in Argolea. How do you think I'm able to monitor our mobile portals?" Her hand tightened on his arm. "I sensed it open to the human realm, but not back again. Orpheus, I don't have to tell you, as one of the Horae, it's not safe for the princess to be in the human realm."

No, it wasn't safe for Isadora to be in the human realm, but that wasn't what set off a tremor of unease deep in Orpheus's gut. Thinking about Gryphon unable to stand on his own when Demetrius had taken him through was foremost in Orpheus's mind.

He didn't bother to answer Delia, simply closed his eyes and pictured the castle in Tiyrns, then flashed to the grand foyer.

The guards at the front door caught sight of him and hollered, surprised he'd flashed inside walls. Turning, he looked up the massive staircase to where Theron and a few of the other Argonauts were coming down.

Footsteps pounded across the marble floor. Theron waved a hand from above. "He's with us."

The leader of the Argonauts stopped at ground level,

motioned Cerek over to take care of the flustered guards. Then he turned his attention on Orpheus. "Glad you made it back."

Yeah, right. "What happened?"

"I was hoping you could tell us."

"We were overrun. Demetrius took the princess and Gryphon through the portal to get away. I stayed back to give them a chance."

"How in Hades did you get out?"

Orpheus didn't like the accusation. The guardian might command this ragtag group of warriors, but he didn't hold a damn thing over Orpheus. "I have my ways."

Theron studied Orpheus for a long beat, and in his eyes there was skepticism and distrust, the kind Orpheus was used to seeing. But not when he'd *volunteered* to help. And definitely not when he'd nearly gotten zapped to smithereens as a result. This is what he got for being a fucking Good Samaritan.

He set his jaw, was just about to lay into Theron, when the guardian said, "They never made it back. What did they say to you before they left?"

Nothing that would help the Argonauts find them, that was sure. They could be anywhere. Except…"Gryphon was injured."

"Where? How?"

"That piece of shit warlock hit him with some kind of energy. He could barely stand on his own. If they didn't come back right away—"

"*Skata.*" Theron looked over his shoulder. "Zander, get Callia. We're going to need her."

As the blond guardian headed back up the stairs, Orpheus's irritation with this whole fucked-up situation reached its limit. "Can't you just track them with those fancy medallions you all wear?"

"The medallions work like a beacon, one way, and only if they're pressed. Someone has to activate them for—"

Boots clomped on the floor above, and all heads turned to see what the ruckus was about. Seconds later Titus rounded the newel post and skipped stairs to reach them at the bottom. He was out of breath when he said, "I got it. Just came in." He waved some kind of hand-held gizmo. "Gryphon's medal went off."

"What about Demetrius's?" Theron asked.

Titus shook his head. "Hasn't been triggered. Theron, man. They're at the half-breed colony."

"*Skata,*" Theron muttered again.

It didn't take a rocket scientist to figure out that was the worst possible place to open the portal. The colony had recently been overrun by daemons, and the Misos— half human, half Argolean—were in the process of setting up new digs somewhere in Montana. If Demetrius had opened the portal there, odds were good they'd run into a shit storm of daemons, still running patrols and searching the area for stragglers. And with Gryphon injured, their chances of getting out alive diminished radically.

"Get Nick on the horn," Theron said to Titus. "He's still in Oregon rounding up his people and getting them moved over."

"Got it," Titus said, skipping back up the steps.

Zander was just coming back down the massive stair-case with Callia at his side. "T," he said as Titus rushed by. "What's up?"

"Nothing good," Titus muttered, then disappeared around the corner.

One hand gripping Zander's tightly, the other holding her healer's bag, Callia couldn't hide the worry shrouding her face. She stopped at the base of the stairs, looked from Orpheus to Theron and back again. "Zander said Gryphon was hurt. How bad?"

Theron shook his head then focused in on Zander. "T tracked them to the colony."

"Shit," Zander muttered. "What the hell are they doing there?"

"Your guess is as good as mine. We'll need to go in carefully, pick a location well enough away so the bastards can't sense us."

"I'm coming too," Callia cut in.

"No," Theron said. When she flicked him an irritated look, Theron gentled his tone. "No, Callia. It's too dangerous. Until we know what the scene is like, you stay here. But I want you ready at the Gatehouse. If it's safe and we need you, Z will come back for you. If not…we'll figure out a way to get Gryphon back to you ASAP."

That didn't seem to appease Callia, but she nodded, then turned to Zander. The two exchanged quiet words while the other Argonauts muttered among themselves. And watching, Orpheus had the distinct impression he was systematically being shut out.

His jaw clenched. "I'm going with you."

"No," Theron said without looking his way. "We can handle this on our own."

Fuck that.

The muscles in Orpheus's eyes constricted, and though he fought it, he couldn't stop what was about to happen. Callia glanced his way and gasped. Several of the Argonauts turned to look. But before his eyes shifted to complete glowing green, he closed them tight and flashed out of the castle and straight to the portal.

Screw the Argonauts.

In this case he was lucky the Council had replaced the Argonauts with the Executive Guard. It took him microseconds to hit the Gatehouse, pull up the hood of his invisibility cloak, and sail right past the morons and through the portal.

The Council thought they knew best, that they didn't need the Argonauts to protect their realm, that the Executive Guard could do it just as well by standing guard. They didn't have a clue what kinds of evil lurked on the other side of the portal. But Orpheus did. He knew because he lived it every damn day.

Since he'd been at the half-breed colony only days before, he knew the coordinates in the remote Oregon wilderness, and it was easy to open the portal just beyond the cave's entrance. A flash of light erupted as he stepped through, then sizzled and popped into nothingness.

He lowered the hood of his cloak, stood where he was, his eyes and ears adjusting to the sights and sounds around him. The Douglas firs were eerily quiet, the light from the full moon illuminating the thin layer of fresh snow on the forest floor with a surreal gray light. A whisper of frigid air ran down his spine, prickling the hair on his back, and the scents of earth and pine and decay filled his nose. That and blood. Lots of blood.

The daemon in him pushed forward, but he fought it back, thankful this one time his heightened senses would draw him to what he was looking for. He moved through the forest without a sound, like the dark shadow he knew he was, and reached the edge of the clearing moments later. It was just as he'd remembered days ago—wide, snow-covered, and bloody. Except this time it was empty.

The storm the last two days had covered the battle from before, when the daemons had overrun the colony, so he knew this blood was fresh. As he moved over the meadow, he studied the footsteps in the soft powder, stopped to examine the blood sprays and other fluids he found staining the ground. He knelt down, ran his bare fingers over one wide patch of red, and brought the blood to his nose to sniff.

"Not exactly a winter postcard, now is it?"

Nick. Orpheus recognized the voice of the half-breed leader. Though Nick Blades and the Argonauts didn't exactly get along, Nick and Theron had formed some sort of alliance in the war against the daemons and aided each other whenever necessary.

Orpheus looked up at Nick's shaved head and scarred face. A highly trained warrior, he was dressed in boots, thick black pants, a heavy black military-type sweater, and his signature fingerless gloves. It was easy to see this Misos was built like the Argonauts and was just as deadly. But unlike the Argonauts, Orpheus considered Nick an ally. Usually. Today he was too juiced to think of anything other than finding his brother.

He sensed the portal open and close in the woods behind him, so he knew the Argonauts weren't far behind. As he went back to checking the ground, a pair of boots stopped just at the edge of his vision.

"Daemon?" Theron asked.

Orpheus rubbed the blood off on his pants, rose, and looked around the barren meadow. "No. Argolean."

"My men killed four daemons in the woods on the way over here," Nick informed Theron, "but we haven't seen anything else."

"*Skata*. Fan out," Theron announced to the rest of the guardians. "Z, you and Phin keep an eye out for the bastards. I don't want any surprises while we check the scene."

No one said a word as they worked. A handful of Nick's men joined the search. Minutes later, Cerek's voice rang out near the tree line. "Over here!"

Orpheus followed Theron and the others to where Cerek stood holding a knife of some kind. Theron reached for it with gloved hands.

"It's Demetrius's," Cerek said, pointing to the letter *D* carved into the handle.

"Yeah." Theron turned it over, looked up and around the battlefield again. "There should be bodies. If they got hit by daemons when they came through the portal, D and Gryphon should be here. Even if the motherfuckers recognized Isadora."

"We're in the right spot," Titus announced, studying the screen in his hand. He tapped it with his finger. "Gryphon's medallion is going off right"—he turned to the left and faced the trees—"here."

Orpheus glanced up and around while the Argonauts and Nick discussed what could and couldn't have happened. He saw nothing but snow and trees, a few shrubs here and there, rocks, and an old-growth, moss-covered log that looked like it had dropped twenty years ago and was now home to rodents and snakes.

Come on, Gryph. Where the hell are you?

He scanned the tree line again, taking in every boulder, every tree trunk someone could hide behind, every—

His gaze swung back to the old-growth log. And his heart picked up speed as he headed that way. Someone call his name but he didn't turn. His senses kicked in the closer he got to the log and he smelled blood again. This time fresh. And very, very Argolean.

He bounded to the top of the log, at least six feet off the ground, and looked down. Dread welled in his stomach at what lay on the other side. "Shit."

He dropped to his knees beside his brother. Gryphon lay with his torso tilted at an odd angle, perched against the log. Blood oozed from various cuts over his face and arms and legs and seeped through what was once his white shirt.

"Dammit, Gryph." When the guardian shivered, Orpheus whipped off his cloak and tucked it up around his brother's shoulders.

"You…" Gryphon's teeth knocked together. "Don't look so…happy to…see me."

"I'm never happy to see you, dumbass." But there was no heat in Orpheus's words, and as he worked his gut churned with urgency.

Damn it, he needed Callia, like *now*. Orpheus wasn't a healer, but even he knew Gryphon had taken a blade to the ribs and had already lost too much blood. Yeah, he was an Argonaut and as such healed faster than most, but there was no telling what Apophis's energy had done to him.

Footsteps and voices echoed as the others came around the log. "We're gonna get you home, brother," Orpheus whispered.

Theron dropped down on Orpheus's right. "Hey, Gryph," he said softly. "How you doin', buddy?"

"Never better," Gryphon breathed as another shudder racked his body. He looked up at the others, his voice no more than a whisper. "You guys make a helluva lot of noise. Thought you were never gonna…find me."

Worry ran across Theron's face. He glanced at Orpheus, who nodded at Gryphon's side, where blood was already seeping through the black cloak. "Ribs. We need to get him back now."

Gently, Theron lifted the cloak, swore, then replaced it. "Orpheus is right, Gryphon. We need to get you home. We'll do it gently, but we need to hustle. There's no telling how many daemons are out in these woods. We—"

Gryphon shook his head, stopping Theron's hands from shifting under to lift him. "No. None. They're gone."

"How do you—"

"They left…" Gryphon shivered again. "With D."

"What do you mean 'left with D'?" Theron asked. "You mean the daemons captured Demetrius? Him and the princess?"

Gryphon shook his head again. "No. Not captured." He grimaced, bent forward at the waist as if he was in excruciating pain, then eased back. Sweat marred his brow as he said, "Demetrius opened the portal here on purpose. I heard him. They thought I was down, but I heard the head…daemon congratulate him on finally bringing them a prize."

Oh shit. Orpheus had been wrong. Demetrius's biggest secret wasn't that he could harness magick.

At Theron's perplexed expression, Gryphon shivered

once more and added, "Theron, man. Demetrius…He's Atalanta's son. The motherfucker double-crossed us."

———∿∿∿———

"I'm sure you're anxious to see Atalanta." The archdaemon—Phrice, Demetrius was sure he'd heard him called—cranked the key in the engine of the old rusted-out cargo truck.

The daemon on Demetrius's right snorted. "I guarantee she's eager to see you."

Yeah, Demetrius just bet Atalanta was anxious to see him. Anxious to see him, gut him, then stick his head on a stake for all the Argonauts to see.

He kept his mouth shut as the rig bounced over the frozen ground. In the hours since he and Isadora had been wrenched from the half-breed colony, they'd ridden on a small plane, landed somewhere in northern British Columbia, and were now driving across the barren tundra to hell-if-he-knew-where. As daemons were bound by the same limitations as Argoleans, they couldn't flash from one place to another on earth, which meant hauling back a hostage or two took a long-ass time.

The only plus in the entire situation was that Isadora was still unconscious. Until he knew where they were headed, Demetrius had to play it cool, not show any outward sign he was frantically plotting a way to get Isadora far enough away from these monsters to open the portal and get them both out of this nightmare.

They drove for twenty minutes, and as the truck drew close to an enormous lodge-style wilderness retreat, that black mist inside grew stronger.

The truck pulled around the side of the structure, then headed for an outbuilding roughly two hundred yards away. Phrice shoved the truck into park and popped the door. "Get out."

The hair on Demetrius's neck tingled as he slid out of the cab and dropped to the ground. There was very little snow here, but the ground was frozen solid and brown as death. At the back of the vehicle, the cargo door slid up, and seconds later a daemon walked around the side with an unconscious Isadora tossed carelessly over his shoulder.

"This way." Phrice motioned for Demetrius to follow.

"He said move, maggot."

Demetrius stumbled, turned to glare at the daemon who'd shoved him. The beast smiled a stained and challenging grin.

Two massive doors to the warehouse at his front were pushed open. Phrice led them into the building, then through another door that disappeared down a rectangular staircase and into an underground passage.

Orange lights spaced every fifteen feet in the ceiling illuminated the corridor. The scents of earth and mold and sweat stained the air. The only sounds were the heavy clomp of boots against the concrete floor and the rapid breaths of both beasts and man.

Demetrius's anxiety amped up as they neared the far side, two hundred yards from where they'd started. A black door carved with strange symbols beckoned. All around it, a pulsing halo of dark smoke hovered, the stench of brimstone sharp. Inside his chest, the darkness shifted to the forefront, as if inexplicably drawn toward what lay beyond the door.

His pulse picked up speed as he stared at the door. Behind him, the daemons chuckled.

"What are you waiting for, maggot?" the one directly at his back asked. "Don't you want to see Mommy dearest?"

This time Demetrius was ready for the shove. And he didn't fight back the pulse of darkness that clawed its way up his chest. Before the daemon could knock him off his feet, Demetrius whipped around and caught the monster by the throat. They were roughly the same height, close to the same size. The daemon grappled to pry Demetrius's hand loose, but the blackness had claimed him, and words left Demetrius's lips without even a thought as he called up the Medean powers he normally kept locked down.

The daemon's arms dropped to his sides. The spell paralyzed his limbs but didn't take away pain. Demetrius squeezed tighter and cut off the beast's windpipe. Phrice chuckled and muttered, "Oh yeah, this is definitely Atalanta's offspring." Then louder, "I told you not to mess with him, Zepar."

The blackness coiled and wrapped itself around Demetrius like a python squeezing out its victim's last breath. The daemon's eyes flickered; death beckoned. Demetrius reached for the sword at Zepar's waist and drew it halfway out of its scabbard before Phrice yelled, "Enough!"

The two daemons behind Zepar plowed into Demetrius, one from each side, breaking the spell and ripping Zepar from his grasp. Demetrius went down hard. His head cracked against cold, unforgiving concrete.

"Get him up," Phrice barked.

The daemons growled and hauled Demetrius to his

feet. As they dragged him toward the door, the inky darkness inside radiated outward from his chest, sending tentacles through his limbs and up into his brain, as if taking control the way it had longed for years to do. The pain in his skull subsided as the door came into focus.

"Watch this," Phrice muttered. "I've seen her do it a time or two. But only one from her line can work this charm."

Phrice lifted Demetrius's hand and placed it on a carved symbol in the center of the door. The surface burned his flesh, a loud hiss echoed through the corridor, and steam erupted all around the edge of his skin. His eyes grew wide as he watched his hand sink into the door as if it were liquid, and though blinding pain rushed up his limb, he didn't cry out. Whatever was on the other side of that door—inside it—fed the darkness in the depths of his soul and called to it on a level like nothing before.

Give in. Come to me.

Power erupted in Demetrius's chest, in his limbs, fueling him with strength and energy. The darkness surrounded him, invaded him, drew him forward. The door popped open with a hiss, and his hand broke free.

Phrice nudged him forward. Demetrius took a step. Though his night vision was sharp, the air felt heavy and thick, and he couldn't see more than a foot in front of his face. His other senses clicked into gear, but he picked up nothing. No sounds, no scents, nothing but a sublime, vast emptiness in every direction.

The daemons pulled him to a stop. A faint whiff met his nostrils. A sweet scent, like cotton candy, one he was sure he'd smelled before.

"None shall disturb me in my chamber of solitude. The penalty is death."

"Forgive me, my queen," Phrice said, his voice wavering, "but what opens the door is a gift. Something…of great value."

Silence ensued, then faintly, voices whispered. Moments later the entire room burst into flame, hundreds of candles of differing sizes and shapes set in a circle around them flaring to life.

The illumination burned Demetrius's retinas. He blinked to clear the spots from his vision. When he finally adjusted to the glare, Atalanta was sitting on a blackened throne in front of him. Piercing onyx eyes held his as if they were the only two in the room. And that darkness, now a part of him he couldn't deny, leaped with excitement in his chest.

Give in. Come to me.

She pushed out of her chair and moved forward, the hem of her long red robe whisking across the ground. Phrice stepped back out of her way. The daemons on Demetrius's right and left dug their fingers into the meat of his arms to hold him still, but they needn't have. The blackness held him in place with a pulsing exhilaration.

Atalanta's gaze ran over his face, taking stock of his features one by one. Finally her focus ran back to his eyes, and one corner of her bloodred lips curved in a wicked smile. "*Yios.*"

The vileness inside him purred like a stroked kitten. And though something in the back of his mind whispered *Be careful*, the thrill of power pulsed all along his nerve endings, so intoxicating, it was a high like he'd never experienced.

She lifted her hand and ran icy fingers along his jaw. A chill slid down his skin, into his bones, and condensed along his soul. "It's been a long time, *yios*. I was beginning to think you'd forgotten all about your *matéras*."

His *matéras*. She was, wasn't she? His. Why had he tried to forget her?

A strangled sound echoed behind him before he could answer. His gaze flicked that way, and he caught sight of the pale blond female over Phrice's shoulder.

Atalanta peered around him. "What is this?"

"A gift," Phrice answered. "The Argonaut brought her to us."

Argonaut. The word swirled in Demetrius's head, meant something he couldn't quite pin down. That darkness roared in his chest, rebelling against the thought. He watched with detached interest as the daemon holding the female shifted her around so she lay cradled in his meaty arms. Blood and dirt stained her measly clothing, gathered where his claws dug into her tender skin. Pain raced across her features but she didn't cry out, didn't even move. She looked as if she was in some sort of daze, not focusing on any one thing as her gaze darted around the room. But when Atalanta moved toward her, her chocolate eyes grew even wider and a gasp tore from her throat.

Argonaut.

Princess.

Isadora.

Home.

Warmth unfurled inside Demetrius's chest as links, dots, connections clinked back into place and battled the chill and darkness from the brink of consumption. In a rush he remembered who he was, what he was, and just what was at stake here.

His heart picked up speed. Sweat broke out on his skin. Evil black power still teased the edge of his control, but he ground his teeth against the temptation, knowing if he turned himself over to it Isadora would be lost forever.

Stay focused on her. Don't take your eyes off her. Don't forget why you're here…

Atalanta's long-fingered hand hovered over Isadora's forehead, then dropped to her hair. "I've been waiting for you." She looked up at Phrice. "Where did you find her?"

"In the field outside the half-breed colony."

"How many witches accompanied her?"

"None. She was with two Argonauts. One we killed. The other…" He gestured to Demetrius. "His magick alerted us to his lineage. We thought he might be of value."

"None," she repeated, looking back at Isadora. "So Apophis betrayed us. And yet my *yios* brought her to us regardless."

The daemon didn't answer. Long seconds passed in eerie silence. Finally, Atalanta's lips curled and she looked back at Demetrius. "Release him." To the daemon holding Isadora she added, "Bring her." She turned, waved her hand. The candles parted, opening the circle.

Panic rushed through Demetrius's chest as he was pushed out of the illuminated circle into another cavern of black nothingness. Another candle flared ahead, this one set on a high pillar, raining layers of multicolored light down to form a spotlight on the concrete floor.

Atalanta stepped into the illumination and gestured to a long metal table at her right, also within the circle of light. The daemon dumped Isadora on the cold silvery surface and moved back into shadow. Isadora winced in pain as she eased herself to a sitting position. Her hand shook as she tried to shift on the unforgiving table, but she didn't make a sound.

A morbid smile curled Atalanta's mouth. "I sense your fear, Princess. Tell me, child. Do you know what it is like to lose something of great value?"

Demetrius's gaze scanned the circle, his mind flipping through exit strategies as Atalanta spoke. But the blackness inside jerked when he spotted the drain set into the concrete floor beneath the metal table.

Atalanta leaned down so she was eye to eye with Isadora. "You and yours took something that belonged to me. Did you think there would be no repercussions?"

Atalanta reached behind her into the darkness and came back with a small twelve-inch dagger. Isadora's eyes widened as the goddess grasped her arm in one swift move and held the shiny blade against her small wrist.

"No," Isadora whispered.

Every muscle in Demetrius's body tensed. Around him he sensed the daemons watching and waiting in the shadows, their excitement fueling the blackness inside him all over again.

"The hand is a marvelous thing. A gift, wouldn't you say, Princess? Something of great value? One can exist without it, but the pain of loss is immense. They say those who lose a limb can still feel the blood pulsing in their missing veins long after the wound has healed." She leaned closer and her voice dropped to a malicious whisper. "This is a good trade, don't you think, *Princess*? Your hand for what you stole from me?"

What was stolen from her. Atalanta was talking about the boy. Max. Callia and Zander's son, who'd been taken from them as a baby and raised by Atalanta herself. She needed Max because he was the son of a Hora, and with that link she could wield the Orb of Krónos, the magical medallion that would give her the power to control the human realm. Once she had that power…she could unleash her revenge on the world.

The Argonauts had rescued Max not more than a week ago, and Atalanta was obviously still pissed she'd been vanquished.

"No, please." Isadora struggled, but Atalanta held her too tight.

The tip of the dagger pierced Isadora's pale skin and she cried out. Atalanta's hand tightened on the grip of the dagger, the tip of the blade digging in deeper.

Skata. Think…

"Please," Isadora cried as blood ran down her inner arm.

"If you cut off her hand," Demetrius said, fighting to keep his voice steady, "she'll be of little use to us."

They both jerked in his direction. The blade stilled against Isadora's wrist.

"Perhaps you would prefer I took her foot?" Atalanta asked.

He didn't answer. Isadora trembled as she peered into the darkness.

"Come into the light, *yios*."

Demetrius hesitated, then took a slow step forward. The instant he passed into illumination, Isadora gasped.

He steeled himself against the look of utter betrayal that crossed her face, but it was the hardening of her eyes that cut through him, the confirmation he was the evil she'd always believed him to be.

"Her foot, then?" Atalanta asked again.

He pictured Isadora's pale, petite feet. The trimmed toenails that she'd painted a fiery red. And tried not to imagine all that perfection mutilated and destroyed.

He shrugged. "I don't care. But you go hacking her up and she's bound to dislike you. And we all know a happy hostage is a useful hostage."

Atalanta's eyes held his. He knew she was debating just whose side he was on. She wasn't stupid. And there was no love lost or loyalty between them. The blackness rumbled again but he worked like hell to tamp it down.

Slowly, she lowered the blade. Isadora let out a relieved breath. Atalanta set the dagger on the table at Isadora's side, but she didn't release the princess's wrist. With her eyes still locked on Demetrius, she drew the index finger of her free hand across Isadora's wrist, gathering a droplet of blood, and brought it to her mouth.

Isadora's horrified gaze darted from Atalanta to Demetrius and back again.

A feral smile crossed the goddess's face. "The witches succeeded in one part of our bargain."

Bargain? The witches had been working with Atalanta? Demetrius's mind spun with the ramifications of that, but he pushed it aside, focusing instead on figuring a way out of this hellhole.

Atalanta let go of Isadora's arm and passed a hand

over the princess's face. "We're done with you for now, Princess."

Before Demetrius could react, Isadora's eyes flickered and her body slumped to the table.

Demetrius tensed all over again, but instinct told him Atalanta wouldn't seriously harm the princess. Not yet anyway. She needed her too much.

"Now," Atalanta said, looking back at him. "The princess's presence is not a surprise. But yours is. A pleasant one. I am very happy I won't have to track you down as I'd planned."

As she'd planned. Demetrius had no clue what the hell was happening, but the pinch in his chest said to be careful.

Atalanta stepped forward and ran her ice-cold finger down his cheek. "You see, *yios*, I've put up with your defiance long enough. And now it's time to prove your worth. The Horae will never willingly cooperate, so I ordered Apophis's witches to cast a fertility spell over our fair princess. And you, my son, will be the one to ensure I reap the rewards."

Demetrius's chest tightened. He thought back to the way those witches had Isadora strung up when he and Orpheus had charged the room. To the way the warlock had been eyeing her. To the see-through negligee she was still wearing.

Atalanta tipped her head and stepped closer, until the sickeningly sweet scent of her was all he could smell. "I thought I would have to persuade you, to draw you to my side first. But now I see that won't be a problem. Hera has finally done something right."

The blood drained from his face as her plan finally

registered. She was going to use him to get the link to the Horae she needed.

"Oh, don't look so upset, *yios*." She patted his cheek. "You're going to enjoy this." Her humor faded and she looked down at Isadora, completely out on the table beside them. "The only question is where? Where to send you? I'd originally thought I'd simply keep both of you locked up here until the darkness consumed you, but now I think you'll be better off alone. It will definitely be faster this way. We'll have to bind your powers so you can't open the portal, of course, but you both need time. And a place where you'll have no choice but to keep her close…"

Sickness drifted up from Demetrius's gut, sickness and a foreboding that rang in his chest and echoed in his head.

"Of course," Atalanta said, her excited voice cutting through his thoughts as she whipped back to him. "Of course, *yios*. There's only one place that will work. One place where you wouldn't let this pretty thing out of your sight. I have no doubt you'll keep her alive, though it may become a challenge. But at least all those ingrained heroics of yours will finally be of use to me."

He tensed as she reached out and ran her cold, vile hand over his jaw again. "You, my son, are finally going to live up to your destiny. You are going to give me the ultimate gift. An heir. A legitimate heir, with links to both the Horae and the throne of Argolea. And thanks to Hera, you'll do so whether you want to or not."

Hera. Atalanta was talking about the soul mate curse. Hera's spiteful gift to Heracles and all the Argonauts—one soul mate. Only it wasn't the blessing it should be. It was the cruelest curse imaginable. The one female in the world who was the worst possible match for that Argonaut.

He was Atalanta's son. The spawn of true evil and the enemy to those of his world. He'd suspected Isadora was his curse, had spent two hundred years avoiding her so Atalanta could never use him for her own gain. And now, thanks to one wrong decision, everything he'd done up until this point to protect Isadora, to protect their world, was for shit.

"Sleep now, *yios*, you'll need your rest." Atalanta passed her hand in front of his face. His vision dimmed from the outside in, even though he fought it.

As the image of Isadora asleep on the table faded and the world drifted to black, he knew there was no escaping what was to come. His only hope was that somehow—in some way he'd find the strength he needed to resist the only female he'd ever truly wanted.

Chapter 6

DEMETRIUS SHIELDED THE GLARE OF THE SUN WITH HIS hand and looked out across the barren beach. Water lapped gently at the golden sand and a light wind rustled the trees at his back. Sweat slid down his spine as he took in the miles of sand, the cliffs to his left and right that turned to sheltered forests beyond, and the water… so much damn water.

Atalanta had dumped them on an island. Of this he was sure. Where, he didn't know. The trees, the temperature, the sand though…it was all vaguely familiar. Like a postcard straight out of the Mediterranean. A tingle low in his belly told him there was only one island in the area she would send them to where he'd be forced to keep Isadora close, but he refused to believe his suspicions. For all of Atalanta's scheming, the bitch needed Isadora to live. She wouldn't be so careless as to leave them alone in hell.

He looked down where Isadora was still out cold on the sand. He'd awakened next to her minutes before and, after checking to make sure she was still breathing, had spent the last five minutes taking stock of their surroundings. Knowing there was no imminent threat, he decided he needed to get Isadora out of the sun; to check her leg, which he feared had been broken in that daemon fight; and to figure out what the hell they were going to do next.

He crouched, lifted her into his arms. Her head lolled like a rag doll's, but her breaths were steady and deep. He ignored the silky smooth feel of her skin against his, focused on the way his boots sank into the deep sand, making it hard to move. After carefully laying Isadora in the shade of a palm tree, he dropped down and unlaced his boots, then tossed them behind him.

Sweat beaded his forehead. His toes sank into warm sand as he found a downed branch, checked its strength. Bringing it back to where Isadora lay, he snapped the ends until it was roughly the length of her shin. Then he sank onto his knees next to her and took a deep breath.

Years of disuse left his powers rusty. He didn't even know if he could conjure a healing spell, let alone if it would work, but he had to do something. Wiping his sweaty hands on his thighs, he glanced once at Isadora's face and hoped like hell she didn't wake up in the middle of this.

His eyes slid closed. He held his hands out in front of him, chanting words he'd shunned long ago. As power gathered in his fingers, heat and light radiated outward. Slowly, he lowered his hands to her broken leg.

She jumped but didn't wake. He ran through the chant over and over, smoothing his hand over the broken bone, knitting it back together with a magick he'd long denied. Minutes later, tired and spent from the effort, he sank back onto his heels and wiped the sweat from his brow.

She lay in the same position she'd been in before— her head tipped to the side, her blond hair wild around her face. One hand lay in the sand; the other rested on her stomach as her chest rose and fell with her breaths. He had no idea if the spell had worked. He'd know only when she woke and tried to stand. Brushing his hand across her brow, he leaned down to her. "Wake up, *kardia*. Open those eyes for me."

She didn't move.

Worry pushed in, but he focused on her breathing, on the fact she didn't have a fever, and tried again. "Wake up, *kardia*. Open your eyes so I know you're there. Please open your eyes."

Still nothing.

Disappointment filled his chest, but he refused to let it affect him. She was alive. For now that was all that mattered. Maybe it was a good thing she was out for the time being. At least she wasn't in pain, and sleep would hopefully give her body the chance it needed to heal.

He decided to splint her leg just in case. He tugged off his shirt, dropped it on the ground. Casting another look over the barely-there nightgown those witches had dressed her in, he told himself to stop being a pansy and get on with it already.

He grasped the hem of the gown near her knees and gently pulled it up, careful not to look at what was being revealed. Shifting one arm underneath her back, he lifted her so he could drag the gown over her head. Then he reached for his shirt and slid her arms in one sleeve, then the other, and laid her back down as he tugged the two halves of the shirt closed at her front and started in on the buttons.

Damn these buttons. Why in Hades did there have to be so many? His hands grew slick as he fumbled to cover her as quickly as possible. Catching one button, he moved to the next, this one between her breasts. A flash of skin caught his attention. He tried to look away but couldn't. Her skin was shades lighter than his, smooth where his was scarred, soft where his was rough. The button slipped from his large fingers. He grappled with it again, his knuckles grazing the swell of her breast as he moved.

Heat ignited through his torso, spread to his belly and into his groin. His gaze slid lower, to the strip of skin visible on her belly, lower to the juncture of her thighs…

He jumped to his feet, swiped his forearm across his brow, and turned away. *Sonofabitch*. This was exactly what Atalanta wanted. This was why she'd sent them here to this remote island. Well, she wasn't going to get her way. He was getting away from Isadora before he did something he knew he'd regret later.

After tearing her gown into strips of cloth, he braced the wood against her shin and tied it in place, careful not to touch her more than was necessary. Then he set off into the trees in search of supplies to build a shelter and hopefully to cool himself the hell down.

Isadora was still asleep when he came back nearly an hour later and set to work. The sun beat against his bare skin as he lashed boards together with vines and covered the structure in foliage. When he was satisfied with the result, he carefully picked Isadora up and placed her inside, made sure she was covered again, then turned to look out over the water and the glowing sunset.

Okay, so, injuries looked after, shelter built…Now they needed food. He was good so long as he had a goal. It was the downtime alone with her that he was seriously dreading. He reached for one of the limbs he'd brought back with him, stripped off the foliage, and looked around for a rock to use to sharpen the end into a point so he could go fishing. That's when he heard the howl.

He froze, lifted his head, turned to look back into the trees growing darker by the second as dusk crept in.

No, not a howl, he realized, dread racing down his spine. That was a scream. But not the kind that came from man or animal. This scream was made by a beast, and the roars that erupted around it were the sort that lived in nightmares.

His fingers tightened around the limb in his hand. He looked to Isadora, still asleep in the shelter. And knew—damn it—he'd been right. They really were in hell, and the first part of Atalanta's plan was coming true. He couldn't leave Isadora now, not even for a second. And that meant if he wasn't careful, Atalanta just might get exactly what she wanted.

~~~

Isadora was floating again. The gentle push and pull echoed in her mind, tugged at her consciousness, dragged her from the depths of something murky and dark.

Images drifted through the haze, ones that made no sense and couldn't be real. A seven-foot glowing blue man with floor-length hair. Yellow acid hitting her in the face. A field of daemons and a woman with soulless black eyes wearing a long bloodred robe. And then there was *him*.

Her blood warmed and a tingle ran along her skin as the image morphed and shifted. This male most definitely wasn't blue. He was tall, muscular, powerful. With short jet-black hair and hands that seemed to span the width of her rib cage. She couldn't make out his

face, but his voice was familiar when it whispered in her
ear. And when his arms came around her, his body was
hotter than anything she'd ever felt.

She shifted, tried to reach for him because his touch
felt so wickedly good she wanted it all over again.
Anywhere. Everywhere. Only as she held out her hand,
the image swirled and dissolved, leaving behind only the
swish and sway of the wind.

No, not wind. Water.

Isadora listened closer. A strange sense of foreboding washed through her, pushing out all that heat
from before.

She rolled to her stomach, groaned because every
muscle in her body ached, then drew in a mouthful
of sand. Pushing up on her hands, she coughed as she
dragged her eyes open.

Blinding light burned her retinas. She dropped back
onto her butt and winced as pain shot up her spine and
down her legs. Holding up her hand to block the glare,
she forced her eyes open again.

Her surroundings slowly came into view. She was
sitting on a beach. The sound she'd heard was indeed
water, but nothing seemed familiar.

Her mind spun and tendrils of panic wedged their
way into her chest. Where was she? And how in Hades
had she gotten here?

A figure moved to her right, and she looked that way
only to be blinded all over again by the setting sun. She
winced and squinted at the shadow coming toward her.

The mystery face was shrouded in shadow, dark hair
wreathed in a halo of light from the sun behind. But
even from this distance she could tell he was male. Male

and massive and very impressive, especially wearing next to nothing as he was.

Tingles rushed over her as he drew closer. A smattering of dark hair covered his olive skin and impressive chest, catching the light as he moved. Her eyes drifted lower to chiseled six—no, eight—pack abs, to black pants that rode low on lean hips and were rolled up at the calves, to strong, perfect bare feet throwing sand as he moved with the grace of an Olympian.

For a fleeting moment she had the feeling she was in the presence of a god. She held her breath as he stopped feet from her, and though she tipped her head back and squinted to see more clearly, his face was still cast in shadows.

He dropped a rope on the sand at her side, one she now realized had been hooked over his shoulder as he'd dragged something behind him. Sunlight glinted off his muscular arms and chest, accented the droplets of sweat gathering on his tanned skin, which she could now see was marred with thin white scars.

"You're finally awake," he said in a clipped and familiar voice as he rested his hands on his hips. "About damn time."

Wait. Gods didn't have scars, did they? They were immortal. They couldn't be hurt, not like humans and Argoleans. She tipped her head the other way, tried to get a good look at him. Still couldn't.

"It'll be nightfall before long. Unless you want to get caught out here in the dark, Princess, I suggest you get your ass up and try putting some weight on that leg."

He began pulling seven- and eight-foot sections of

wood from the rope he'd looped around the bundle. Tree trunks, she realized, none more than five inches wide, stripped of their limbs so they formed long poles. Her mind tumbled again. What on earth were the trees for? And who the hell *was* he?

The setting sun flashed over muscles in his arms and back that flexed and rippled beneath his skin as he worked. Three long red gashes, equally spaced, cut across the middle of his back. Another ran down the outside of his left bicep, this one redder and deeper, the puckered ridge indicating the injury had happened more recently than the others.

She tried to make sense of what was happening and who he was. As if he felt her eyes on him, he turned and glared at her.

And in the split second his face shifted from shadow to sunlight, Isadora gasped.

The voice finally registered. She scrambled back on her hands and feet, stopping only when her back hit something solid.

Demetrius's glower darkened but he didn't say anything, just clenched his jaw and went back to loosening the rope around the bundle of logs. But Isadora's heart rate shot into the triple digits. The last thing she remembered was sitting in her suite at the castle, staring into her mirror as she prepared herself for the binding ceremony with Zander, and seeing a vision of her and Demetrius locked in an erotic scene.

Her hand shot to her mouth and her eyes clamped shut. She couldn't even think the words, let alone remember the image—the first glimpse of the future she'd had in over a month. She forced her eyes open and looked across the sand to where Demetrius was now laying out the logs two feet apart.

Holy Hera, what was going on?

He turned before she could collect herself and marched in her direction. She tensed as he drew close and tried to scoot back more, but the wall—no, it wasn't a wall, it was some kind of lean-to shelter built out of more logs and twigs and foliage—stopped her.

His mouth was set in a hard line, his jaw covered in a thin layer of stubble, his dark eyes flat and resigned as he leaned close. For a second she thought he was going to touch her and her body stiffened, the heady scent of sweet male sweat and something else she couldn't quite place drifting in the air to make her light-headed. But instead of grabbing her, he reached past and picked up something at her back, then turned and walked away without a word.

Curious, she shifted forward and that's when she realized he'd grabbed a rope from the mini-shelter at her back. Only it wasn't like any other rope she'd seen before. This one was green and consisted of a number of differing vines woven together like a braid.

She watched as he strapped boards together. He worked in silence, his muscles flexing and relaxing as he moved, his skin shining with a thin layer of sweat. Head still spinning, Isadora sat silent, unsure what to say or do. Glancing around, she took a wider look at where they were.

Behind her, green mountains rose. To the right and left the white sand beach stretched into infinity, bordered with forest and dense brush and the occasional palm tree here and there. The air was temperate, the push and pull of the water familiar. In front of her lay a pile of black ashen logs, as if from a recent fire, and off to her right, just out of her reach, a collection of spears of differing lengths, all made of wood, the tips chiseled to dangerous points.

Trepidation washed over her. There was no other sound besides the gentle lap of water and ropes thwacking wood where Demetrius worked. There were no other people anywhere close, no signs of life either. She knew they weren't in Argolea—at least nowhere she'd ever been—but nothing else made sense. And though she didn't mean to, her eyes kept straying back to Demetrius as he worked. At the play of muscle and bone beneath his tanned skin. At what he was doing with his big, powerful hands.

Warmth gathered low in her belly. A warmth she didn't want and didn't understand. What was going on? Why was he here? And where the heck was *here*, anyway?

As the sun dropped toward the water, she finally realized he was building a ladder.

A loud shriek sounded in the trees at Isadora's back, followed by a howl that seemed to shake the ground. She jerked, every hair on her body standing on end. Instinct had her scrambling out of the lean-to on her hands and knees and looking back into the trees. "Wh-what was that?"

"*Skata*," Demetrius muttered. Rope thwacked board faster. "That, Your Pampered Highness, was either a Calydonian boar or a harpy. Take your fucking pick."

Wide-eyed, she turned to look at Demetrius. His jaw was locked tight and his hands now moved with lightning speed over the boards. "A *what* or a *what*?"

"Not a what, Princess. A when." He dropped the end

of the ladder in the sand and stepped close to pick up a handful of spears. "And if you don't get your ass moving, you're gonna meet one or both up close and personal."

The trees rattled and swayed as the shrieks and roars grew louder. Fear had Isadora struggling to her feet. She took a step back just as her left leg went out from under her.

Pain shot up from her shin and she cried out. Before she hit the sand, Demetrius's arm wrapped around her waist and tugged her tight to his side.

"Fucking lovely," he muttered. He shoved a spear into her hand. "Take this."

She had little time to do anything else. He hooked the other weapons under his free arm, picked up the end of the ladder, and then he ran. Clamped tight to his side, Isadora could do nothing but put her good foot down in time with his to keep her balance and hold on tight to his shoulder with her free arm.

Her leg throbbed and every step sent pain ricocheting throughout her body. She had no idea where they were going, but the roars and screams behind ratcheted up her adrenaline. A loud crashing sound echoed and Demetrius slowed, whipped them both around. A gigantic boar sailed through the air as if launched from the trees and landed hard against the lean-to Isadora had just been sitting in.

The lean-to split apart into dozens of pieces. The boar grunted, squealed, rolled to its side, and righted itself. It whipped around and looked back into the trees. Then it opened its mouth and bared enormous fangs and razor-sharp teeth.

No way. It couldn't be real. Before her brain could

click into gear, a flutter of tree limbs drew her attention. She glanced back to the forest only to see a winged monster that looked like something straight out of a nightmare emerge and hover above the boar.

"*Fuck*," Demetrius muttered.

"Wh-what is *that*?"

The sickeningly gray-colored *thing* that looked like a twisted cross between a woman and a bird shrieked, the sound so loud Isadora felt the sharp stab of pain in her eardrum. She slammed her free hand over her ear and cried out. The creature swung its gaze their way and narrowed bloodred eyes.

"*Skata*." Demetrius let go of Isadora and shoved the end of the ladder into her free hand. "Run. Run hard." Then he dropped the bundle of spears from under his arm and picked up one in each hand.

Terror leaped in Isadora's throat. She had no idea how any of this could be real, but she wasn't about to stand here and get into a debate with Demetrius. Balanced on her good leg, she turned to look behind her. Then had a moment of *Oh, shit*.

They'd run far enough down the beach that she could see around the next set of rocks. Fifty yards away the beach came to a dramatic end, a sheer cliff rising straight up at least four stories.

A hissing sound echoed at Isadora's back. She turned just in time to see the winged creature open its mouth to reveal three rows of razor-sharp teeth dripping with blood. An ear-shattering shriek erupted from its throat and then, with a great flutter of wings, it charged.

Horror enveloped Isadora, held her tight where she

stood. Her legs trembled as the monster flew through the air.

"Run!" Demetrius yelled just as it reached him. He swung out with the spear.

Screams and grunts mixed with the clash of Demetrius's spear against flesh and bone. The beast's claws arced out and caught Demetrius across the abdomen. He swiveled. Blood spurted from his wounds. He reached back and hurled the spear hard.

The spear caught the monster by the wing, tearing a large hole that gushed bloody fluid. The monster screamed and dropped to the ground.

Across the sand, the boar roared and dashed forward, as if it had suddenly realized it was about to miss out on all the fun.

Demetrius hooked another spear with his bare foot and kicked it up in the air. "Fucking *run!*"

His voice cut through the terror-filled haze. Isadora stumbled backward, caught herself on her good leg before she went down.

The boar charged. The winged creature screamed again, righted itself. Its eyes seemed to grow even redder.

Oh, shit. *Oh shit oh shit oh shit…*

The pain in her leg only a dim thought, Isadora tore off across the sand as fast as her weak leg would let her. Her heart pounded hard as she dragged the ladder with one hand, which now made a sick sort of sense, and held the spear in the other.

Like she'd even know what to do with a spear. Like she stood a frickin' chance if those things got by Demetrius. She'd only just learned how to use a blade—thanks to Orpheus's help—and only when she thought methodically about how and where to strike. But a spear? A *spear*?

Oh, gods.

A fresh wave of panic consumed her when she reached the base of the cliff. Up close it was much higher than she'd thought. The ladder wouldn't even come close to reaching the top. Fear closed her lungs, made it hard to breathe. Her heart pounded hard in her ears, drowning out the sounds of clashes and grunts and screams and roars behind her, where Demetrius still battled the two monsters.

She swallowed hard and pulled the ladder up so she could maneuver it against the cliff. It rose at least fifteen feet, not to the small lip that jutted out a good distance up but—yes!—close enough. Maybe if she could get high enough, she could pull herself the rest of the way up.

Her eyes flicked from the tree-trunk poles to the green woven-vine rope. Would it hold her weight? He'd lashed it together quickly. Would it splinter as soon as she was high enough to fall and break her neck?

A roar shook the ground. Isadora grasped the rung above her head and climbed.

The muscles in her arms quivered and ached as she tried to use her strength to pull herself up instead of putting weight on her bad leg. Fear stabbed into her chest like a hot, sharp knife. When she was three-quarters of the way up, breathing heavily from exertion and trying not to look down, the ladder shook.

Both hands clamped on to the rung in front of her. A scream tore from her mouth. Below she heard Demetrius yell, "Climb faster!"

A high-pitched shriek sounded from somewhere

close. She didn't look, knew she couldn't. Instead she grabbed the rungs faster and climbed higher.

When she made it to the top of the ladder she reached for the closest rock sticking out of the cliff. She perched her bare foot on the uppermost rung, grabbed on, and hauled herself up. Her free hand reached the four-foot ledge. Her fingers dug into rock and dirt, and pain shot through her joints and muscles as she pulled with all her strength.

The creature screamed again at the base of the ladder.

"Go!" Demetrius yelled below her.

Her arms ached in protest, but somehow she managed to pull herself up and over the ledge. She fell onto her back, sucked air into her burning lungs. Demetrius appeared at the ledge before she'd taken three good breaths.

He didn't even look winded as he hauled himself onto the ledge and jerked the ladder up with him. He placed it against the cliff again, reached for her hand, and yanked her to her feet. "This isn't a pit stop, Princess. Move!"

Sweat covered every inch of Isadora's skin. She was so tired she could barely move, but when that *thing* below screamed again, she realized he was right. This was no place to rest. He might have injured the beast, but that didn't mean it couldn't fly anymore, or—oh, gods—climb. She grabbed the ladder when he pushed her toward it, hooked the foot of her bad leg on the first rung, and pushed herself up.

Blinding pain shot from her leg to her skull, and she screamed out as she felt something crack. Her vision swirled and she nearly let go of the ladder, but the horrific cry of the thing below reminded her that if she gave up, she was going to be lunch. Gritting her teeth, she paused, drew in deep breaths. Then with Demetrius's urging she kept climbing, letting her arms and good leg do as much of the work as they could.

She tried not to think about how high they were, about how unstable the ledge their ladder was perched on could be, about how close Demetrius was, right below her feet, or how much weight rested precariously on the rungs of this makeshift ladder. The next ledge was below the end of the ladder so she didn't have to struggle so hard to make it to the top. She fell off the ladder onto her side on the hard rocky surface and just tried to breathe. Demetrius stepped off after her, pulled the ladder up again, and grabbed her by the arm, hauling her with him and pushing her toward the ladder again for the last climb.

"I can't." Her determination wavered. She leaned into him. The pain in her leg was so great she couldn't put even an ounce of weight on it. Exhausted, she tried to push him away so she could sink back to the ground, but he was like a solid stone presence, preventing her from doing anything but what he wanted.

He picked her up at the waist, shifted her around, and placed her hands on the rungs in front of them. "You can do it. C'mon. We're almost there."

Tears burned the backs of her eyes. Gripping the rungs, she tried to pull herself up with the sheer weight of her arms, but her good leg slipped, and a scream tore out of her when she realized she was going down. Strong arms caught her and she felt Demetrius move in right behind her and place his hands over hers on the crossbeams. "Just a little farther, *kardia*."

It took every ounce of strength she had to keep going.

That and Demetrius pushing her up from behind. When they finally reached the top of the cliff, she collapsed onto the ground on her back and sucked in as much air as she could to stop the world from the crazy spin cycle it seemed to be on.

He yanked the ladder up from the last ledge, tossed it to the ground at her side. Wind whipped his dark hair back from his face as he held out his hands in front of him, closed his eyes, and chanted in a language that was oddly familiar.

Pain momentarily forgotten, Isadora watched, unable to tear her gaze away. With the waves crashing far below, the wind picking up speed to lift the hair away from his face, and blood and dirt staining his weathered skin, he looked like a god. Like Poseidon calling forth the seas, or Zeus preparing to unleash his wrath on the world. But when the language he was speaking finally registered, she knew the male in front of her was no god at all.

Run!

Instinct kicked in, drowned out the fear she'd felt earlier. She scooted back on her hands, winced when pain lanced up her leg and prevented her from moving.

The winged monster shrieked in anger. From his waistband Demetrius drew a three-foot spear, opened his eyes, and peered over the ledge to the beach below.

He hurled the spear down toward the beach. An agonizing cry echoed up to where Isadora lay watching in horror, and then all sound ceased but for the gentle whistle of wind through the trees and the crash of waves against rock at the base of the cliff.

No, not a god, she realized as she stared at him. This

male was something else. Something dark and menacing, and if she wasn't careful, a thousand times worse than the monsters they'd faced earlier.

He turned his gaze on her. His dark eyes were as focused as she'd ever seen them when he stalked in her direction. She tensed, closed her hand over a rock at her side to defend herself if need be. He picked up the end of the ladder and snapped the bottom rung off, leaving sharp ragged points of wood on one side, then dropped to his knees at her side.

Isadora's whole body went rigid, unsure what he was going to do next. There was nowhere for her to go, no way to get away from him. When he reached for her bad leg, she flinched. "What are you doing?"

"I think you re-broke your leg. Hold still." He immobilized her with ease, as if she were nothing but a child, then began unwrapping something from the bottom of her leg.

Isadora looked down and realized the shin of her left leg was wrapped in a sheer black gauze-type fabric. "What? When did I—"

"In the clearing with the daemons," he answered without looking up at her. "I didn't see it happen." He removed the last bit of wrap and cringed. "Dammit." He reached for the wood he'd broken off the makeshift ladder, picked at the ends so the jagged edge wasn't quite so sharp. "Hold still. I'm not very good at this. It'll probably hurt."

Hurt? What was he going to—?

He set the wood near his knee, then placed both hands over her shin. Before she could ask what he was doing, he closed his eyes and chanted in that unsettling language again. Excruciating pain swirled and condensed in that one spot, stole her breath, and darkened her vision. Isadora cried out, tried to push his hands away, but the torture was too much and she dropped back against the rock in agony.

The pain seemed to go on and on. Just when she was sure he was killing her, the edges softened and inch by inch the roar in her head and leg turned to a dull throb. When the worst was over, she gasped for air and tore her eyes open to stare up at a swirling gray sky.

His hands shifted; the chanting stopped. She tried to focus on one single cloud to ground herself, couldn't seem to make it work. His hands moved again as he braced the wood against her leg and rewrapped it with the same gauzy black fabric as before.

"You shouldn't walk on this for at least a day." His voice was thick as he worked. "I knit the bones back together, but it still needs to heal."

Knit the bones?

Isadora blinked several times. Found one cloud she could focus on. As she worked on simply breathing, her mind wandered. Who the hell was this guy? Not a healer, that was for sure. She'd heard that chanting before. Recognized the language.

Medean. He'd been speaking Medean. Her stomach rolled with understanding, but the one thing circling loudest in her brain was the fact he'd just tried to heal her, not harm her.

Him. Demetrius. The one guardian who hated her more than any other and made no bones about the fact he thought she wasn't qualified to burn toast, let alone rule Argolea. He'd never been nice to her, not once in

all the years he'd served with the Argonauts, and yet…
he'd not only just healed her broken leg with—she swallowed hard—magick, he'd saved her from two monsters straight out of a nightmare when he could have sacrificed her and gotten away with ease.

Questions hit her from all sides. Questions she needed answers to *right now*. Gritting her teeth, she pushed up to her elbows and looked down her body to where he still knelt, wrapping her injured leg.

She opened her mouth, then noticed the oversized white dress she was wearing wasn't a dress at all but a male's long-sleeved shirt. And the hem had ridden up so high on her thighs it was clear she wasn't wearing anything beneath.

Warmth rushed through her body all over again. A heat that came out of nowhere seared her center with an intensity that stole her breath. Tingles she didn't want or understand ignited in the skin beneath his hands and traveled up her leg, seemed to gather in that spot just barely covered by the edge of the oversized shirt. She tried to push her legs together, but his hands held her immobile.

He must have felt her tense because his fingers stopped moving on her lower leg. Her pulse ratcheted up as his eyes traveled up the length of her bare leg and zeroed in on the hem of her shirt.

"Fuck," he whispered.

Yeah, that's what she was suddenly thinking about too. With him. Here. Now. Any way he wanted. Which, considering her history and his history and the fact they couldn't even stand each other, was utterly and mind-bendingly *insane*.

Chapter 7

DEMETRIUS PUSHED UP FROM THE GROUND AND TURNED so fast he stumbled and nearly fell on his ass.

Graceful, dickhead. And really fucking heroic. If you wanted to stare at her body, you should have left that sheer black nightgown on her instead of giving her your shirt.

Pinching the bridge of his nose, he tried to wipe away the image of Isadora's near-naked lower half from his mind. Which was as productive as trying to open the friggin' portal right this minute, because all he could see were her sleek bare legs, those creamy inner thighs, that little treasure that was hidden just under the hem of his shirt…

His face grew hot and his pulse beat so hard he could hear the blood pounding in his veins. Damn it, he didn't want her. He didn't like her. She wasn't even his type.

He thought back to that girl at the club. The dominatrix with the delta tattoo and fuck-me boots. Now *she* was his type. She was the kind of female he was attracted to. The only kind he deserved.

Isadora cleared her throat. Scowling, he glanced sideways and saw she'd crossed her good leg over her bad and pulled his shirt down over both legs as far as she could, then wrapped her arms around herself in a don't-even-look-at-me move he'd have to be a moron to miss.

Okay, just fucking refocus.

He stalked across the ground, picked up what was left of his weapons. He was going to need to make more. The invisibility spell he'd cast on the edge of the cliff wouldn't last long, and with the sun setting they needed to find shelter. Two days on this island had already taught him the really nasty stuff came out at night.

"I didn't realize you were a…" Isadora swallowed. "A witch."

"I'm not."

"Yeah, right." Louder, she added, "You're from Jason's line. It shouldn't surprise me, since he shacked up with a sorceress. Do the other Argonauts know?"

"I don't give a flying rat's ass what they know."

"That would be a no," she muttered.

Her disgust hit him square in the chest, and before he could stop it that blackness circled, latched on, and squeezed. "I also don't care what you *think* you know. But don't lump me in with your little witch friends. I'm not the one who turned you over to a warlock." *I'm the one who fucking saved you, dammit.* He reached for another broken spear from the ground.

"Oh my gods," Isadora whispered. "Apophis's witches. You were there."

Her shocked voice brought his head up, and too late he realized *bingo*. Thanks to him, her brain had just snapped back into gear. She'd been out the whole time they'd been here, while he'd been getting his ass kicked trying to find a way off this damn island and at the same time making sure nothing snacked on her when he wasn't looking. And though it would have been nice if she'd been awake instead of deadweight during all that, her consciousness now ignited a whole other set of problems. Namely, what did she really remember, and how the hell was he going to explain any of this?

Way to go, dumbass.

"I...I didn't think anyone was going to find me."

He definitely didn't need to hear the quiver in her voice. And he sure as hell didn't want to think about what that twisted warlock had done to her in the hours she'd been in his castle. Demetrius had already played every scenario around in his head a dozen times, then promised himself that when he got off this freakin' island he'd go back and kick some warlock ass just to settle the score.

"How did you find me?"

Her soft words cut through his thoughts, and a little voice in the back of his head cautioned *Ignore her.* But instead of listening, he heard himself say, "Your handmaiden."

"Saphira." Her eyes slid closed. "She came to me in my chamber. I was...upset." Her cheeks turned the softest shade of pink before she added, "She gave me tea, only it wasn't tea. It was something else. And then... then I was out."

"Nice handmaiden." If the witch weren't already dead, he'd add her to his takedown list. "Too bad the king didn't call off your binding ceremony to Zander earlier."

And whoa, why the hell did he even care? And since when had he turned into Mr. Noble? He gave his head a swift shake and glanced toward the thick forest to the west in an attempt to clear his gray matter.

"My father did *what*?"

The shock in her voice nixed his thoughts and brought his head around before he could stop it. "You didn't know?"

"No. He…" Her surprised chocolate eyes skipped over the ground. "He decided to let Callia and Zander be together?"

Demetrius shrugged, though inside that darkness brewed deeper. If the king hadn't reneged on the original arranged binding between Theron and Isadora weeks ago, neither of them would be here now. "Don't know. Wasn't there. Really don't care." He pointed toward the west. "I think our best bet is through those trees."

"Wait. What was…?" She swallowed. "That thing looked like a Fury."

Thank the flippin' gods she'd changed the subject. He gathered the last of what was left of his weapons. "Furies have snakes in their hair. Like Apophis's witches." *And trust me, Princess, they're a thousand times worse.* "That was a harpy."

He moved to pick her up, but she blocked him with her forearm. "What happened to my leg? The last thing I remember is stepping through the portal from Apophis's castle into a field full of daemons. How did we get here? And"—her eyes widened—"what happened to Gryphon? He came through with us."

Demetrius fought to keep his shoulders relaxed as he straightened. Here came the questions. He should have picked up his damn pace. "I don't know."

"What do you mean, you don't know?"

"I mean, *Your Highness*," he snapped, at the end of his patience with her and this place and all of it, "I don't know what happened to Gryphon. When I opened the portal to get us the hell out of there, something crisscrossed and we wound up here."

"Crisscrossed? That's your best explanation?"

"That's the only one I've got." *And the only one you're gonna get*.

"So where is Gryphon?"

"I don't know."

She stared at him, and then slowly her eyes narrowed to thin slits. A demeaning look he was used to seeing on her pale face. "What you really mean is you don't care."

His head snapped back as if she'd hit him. She obviously couldn't consider the possibility he was as worried about Gryphon as she was. But then why would she? She thought he was a son of a bitch, which wasn't far off the mark. And considering what had been running through his head a few minutes ago, if he wanted to find a way to get her off this island before Atalanta's little scheme clicked into gear, it was better all around if she went on thinking he was nothing more than a righteous prick.

But it still cut. Just as it always did when she refused to look him in the eye or turned the other way when she saw him in the castle. Even if that was the only way it could be.

"Yeah," he muttered as he rested his hands on his hips and glared down at her. "You're right, *Princess*. I don't fucking care."

Her mouth snapped shut. She crossed her arms over her middle and looked down at her legs. If she was at all still hurting or upset, she didn't show it. The tight line of her shoulders was a clear sign she was well and truly pissed. Which was exactly what he wanted, wasn't it?

"Where the hell are we?" she asked without looking up.

Oh yeah, her adrenaline swing was in full gear. She'd morphed from scared shitless to ticked in the span of a few seconds, thanks to him.

Well, good. He handled pissed a whole lot better than freaked-out and vulnerable any day of the week.

He shifted his legs wider, crossed his arms over his chest. "Why don't you tell me? Since you're the expert on everything. Where the hell do you think we are?"

"Harpies and rabid boars—"

"Calydonian boars. There's a big difference"

"Whatever. They don't really exist."

"Tell that to the two dead monsters down on that beach."

Her eyes met his. Eyes, he noticed, that weren't quite as enraged as he'd originally thought. Lurking behind the tough-girl shield was true fear.

Which, *skata*, he did *not* need to see.

"The Argonauts extinguished the lines," she protested. "Thousands of years ago, that was the first thing Zeus commanded them to do. To sweep the world, gather the monsters wreaking havoc on humans, and destroy them. It's in all the history books. They did that. They—"

"Your history books were obviously wrong. If you ever left that palace you call a bedroom suite, you'd know that." Refusing to be moved by her shocked expression, he added, "Look around you. The Argonauts didn't kill anything. They gathered and they dumped. Right here in the middle of the Ionian Sea. And lucky us, we followed."

"Ionian Sea?" Shock flicked over her features. "Pandora isn't a real island. It can't be. It—"

"Looks pretty damn real to me." He glanced up, noted the sun had now completely dropped behind the water and that dusk was creeping in fast. They were about out of time. The fresh kills down below were like blinking beacons to the nasties. They needed to get the hell out of here before the really ugly shit woke up and went hunting.

Far off in the forest below, a bloodthirsty howl echoed. Isadora's head snapped in that direction and her eyes grew even wider until a halo of white surrounded her golden brown irises.

"Sounds pretty fucking real too. Let's save the bickering for later, shall we? We need to make tracks."

"Wait," she said when he bent toward her. "Open the portal and take us home."

He clenched his jaw. "I can't."

"Why not?"

"Because whatever crisscrossed to get us here screwed with my ability to open the portal."

She pressed a hand against his chest when he lifted her into his arms. A hand that was warm and soft and ignited a tingle in his skin he liked and hated all at the same time. "Demetrius…"

Bloody hell. He did *not* like the way she said his name. Didn't like the sudden soft lilt to her voice or the way the sounds rolled off her tongue. And it didn't make him think of hearing her say his name just like that when she was naked, beneath him, her head kicked back on a pillow—

"Pandora can't be real. It can't be."

"Why the hell not?" He pushed the image out of his mind and looked down at her this-can't-be-happening expression. It was all he could do to keep his face neutral as that tingle spread lower and his mind flashed back to the revealing black nightie she'd been wearing when he'd first found her. To the way her skin had peeked out from beneath the sheer black fabric. To the sway of her hips, the roundness of her breasts, the soft indent of her belly button…

"Because," she whispered, "if the creatures are real, if Pandora is real, it means the myth is real. And according to the myth, there's no way off the island. No one who's been here has ever lived to tell about it."

Like he didn't know that? Reality snapped back firmly in his face. *Welcome to my hell, Princess.* Dying on this island wasn't his greatest fear. It was being stuck here alone with her that scared the shit out of him.

He headed for the trees. "Then we're gonna have to figure out a way to prove the myth wrong now, aren't we?"

"Yes, but—"

A scream joined the howl far below. Her hand gripped his shoulder. She pulled her body close to his on reflex. His skin warmed in response and before he could stop it, a whole host of electrifying tingles erupted beneath her fingers where she held him, beneath her breast pressed tight to his bare chest, then rushed straight down his torso right into his cock.

Which he *so* didn't need, now or ever.

He ground his teeth to the point of pain. And shoved a whole lot of I-don't-give-a-shit into his voice when he said, "I liked you a lot better when you were unconscious."

───※───

Orpheus stared across the room toward Gryphon, out cold in the center of the bed. A series of monitors beeped and hummed above his head. Wires and tubes ran into the Argonaut's hands, resting on the thin blanket covering his body. His chest rose and fell as if he was deep in sleep and his face looked as it always had. Only nothing was the same.

Three days. Gryphon had been unconscious for three days and nothing Callia had done or was doing was reviving him. The daemon inside Orpheus vibrated with the need to grab Callia and shake her until she healed his brother. The Argolean in him kept his feet rooted firmly in place against the wall of this room on the fifth floor of the castle. As he crossed his arms over his chest, he willed Gryphon to sit up and start bitching at him as he'd done thousands of times over the years.

Callia moved over to the bed, studied a monitor near Gryphon's head, reached down, and felt for his pulse. She jotted numbers on a clipboard, then stepped back to enter them in her little high-tech computer with its virtual screen, near the windows.

Footsteps brought Orpheus's head around. Zander stepped into the doorway and cast Orpheus a tight smile. "Hey, man."

Orpheus went back to watching the bed.

"Zander." Surprise and relief lit Callia's face as she put the clipboard down and moved to embrace the blond Argonaut.

Zander nodded toward the bed. "How is he?"

"Fine," she said easily. Way too easily.

"When was the last time you took a break, *thea*?"

"I…" Callia's eyes strayed to Orpheus. "I don't need a break. I'm fine."

"You're not fine," Zander said. "You're about ready to fall over from lack of sleep. Even you have limits."

He unlooped the stethoscope from around her neck and set it on the table to his right. "No arguing."

"But—"

"O?" Zander asked. "There's an empty room across the hall. She needs an hour or two of rest. If something changes, you'll come and get her, right?"

Orpheus didn't look at either of them, kept his gaze firmly on the bed. He wanted them both gone if they were going to stand here and bicker. "Go."

"Come on." Zander pulled her toward the door.

Callia paused at the threshold. "Orpheus…"

The concern in her voice was too much. He set his jaw. "I'll call you if anything changes."

"Okay," she said softly. But his peripheral vision picked up the uneasiness in her eyes, the compassion rushing over her features. And that space in his chest that was already tight as a drum stretched even tighter.

They disappeared out into the hall. Footsteps sounded on the wide marble floor, then the snap of a door. A rasp of cloth met Orpheus's ears, followed by the press and slide of two mouths joined in a heated kiss.

His overly sensitive hearing picked up every nip and suck and lick, even through closed doors and soundproof walls. Normally he'd get a sick kick out of listening to what they were up to in that other room, but right now all he could think about was the fact that if something didn't change soon Gryphon was never going to have that. Not that rush of want or the carnal fire of desire. Not with his soul mate. Not with any female. Not ever again. All because of him.

Theirs was a relationship anchored in animosity. Mostly on Orpheus's part. And yet in all the years

Orpheus had dissed his brother or undermined what the Argonauts were doing, Gryphon hadn't given up on him. The guardian had a serious case of heroics, and on more than one occasion Orpheus had told his younger brother he wasn't worth saving. But Gryphon had never believed him.

"Oh, Zander," Callia whispered across the hall. "Nothing's working. He's not getting better."

"It's only been three days, *thea*. The knife wound he took was pretty deep."

"You don't understand. The wound in his side has completely healed. That's not what I'm talking about. It's what the warlock did to him."

"You said the burns on his skin are already gone. I thought—"

"They are," she cut in. "But I ran some extra tests this morning. Zander"—her voice lowered—"the burn has condensed *inside* his chest. And it's growing."

Silence met Orpheus's ears. Callia's words swirled in his brain and his brow lowered with curiosity.

"What are you saying?"

"I don't know," she said softly. "It's like the burn or energy or whatever is consuming him from the inside out."

"Consuming him?" Zander asked. "How is that even possible? You said his body was healing. He's looking stronger every day."

"I know." Orpheus pictured Callia pressing her fingers against her forehead as she tried to figure out what she was missing. He'd seen her do it several times over the last few days, and even though he wanted to drop-kick her into action, he knew she was doing all she could. "I've tried everything. I even had Max take a break from sitting with my father to come down and help me direct a healing energy, hoping that would make a difference, but it hasn't. Whatever the warlock hit him with was so strong…"

Max was Callia and Zander's son, and his power of transference was an aid to Callia as she drew on her healing powers. But the fact she'd needed Max's help with Gryphon wasn't what set off a tremor of unease in Orpheus's chest. It was the way her voice trailed off and the words she held back that put him on alert.

"So what does that mean, Callia?"

"It means," she whispered, "there's nothing else I can do for him. It's not his body being destroyed. It's his soul. And my powers aren't strong enough to heal the soul. Nothing is. Even if I could figure out how to stop the damage, if he were to awaken right now, he wouldn't be the same, Zander. His soul is dying one piece at a time."

A lump formed in Orpheus's throat and his eyes shot to his brother's face. No, that couldn't be.

But even as he thought the words, he knew they were a lie. He'd taken a shot of Apophis's energy during that fight too. The blast had knocked him off his feet, sent him spinning into the wall. But he'd been able to shake it off and get back up. Gryphon hadn't.

There was only one difference between them. As brothers, they shared the same father, the same lineage, the same link to the ancient hero Perseus, the same blood that made them both bigger, stronger, tougher than most. And yet Orpheus had walked away from Apophis's attack without a single scratch.

Because he was part daemon. Because what was vile in them lived in him. Because he had no soul to destroy.

The tightness in his chest that had been holding him together snapped like a rubber band. And a green glow illuminated the room as his eyes shifted from gray to the calling card of the daemons.

"Have you told Theron yet?" Zander asked in a gruff voice.

"No. I…I don't know what to tell him."

Silence fell, and then Zander said, "Come here, *thea*." Cloth rasped again. "We'll figure something out. There's still time."

Not much, Orpheus realized. Not much at all.

A heavy weight pressed down around him. He was responsible for this. He'd taken Isa to the witches. Even though he wasn't directly responsible for her abduction, he'd been the one to tempt that witch with exactly what she wanted. And then he'd taken it one step further and led Gryphon to his death by thinking he could play hero for a few hours and rescue the princess himself. In the end all he'd done was fuck things up worse than he ever had before.

Out of nowhere he thought of the Orb of Krónos. Even with the four chambers empty of the classic elements—earth, wind, fire, and water—the Orb held a power like nothing else. It had kept Max safe when he'd escaped Atalanta and her daemons. Maybe it could put a stop to whatever was killing Gryphon.

He rushed out the door and down the stairs, a renewed sense of urgency pushing him. There were servants coming and going who could alert Callia if Gryphon's conditioned changed before he got back. He didn't care that retrieving the Orb from its hiding place would put his carefully constructed plans into chaos. Didn't care that he was about to give up everything he'd ever wanted. All that mattered was Gryphon.

Which was fucking ironic, wasn't it? He'd never given a shit about anyone else in his whole life. He hadn't thought a soulless being could develop a conscience.

As he hit the foyer of the castle and stopped on the gleaming marble floor, he closed his eyes and imagined his shop on Corinth Avenue. And ignored the voice in the back of his head warning that an Argonaut without a soul was a very dangerous thing.

Chapter 8

I LIKED YOU A LOT BETTER WHEN YOU WERE UNCONSCIOUS.

The fear gripping Isadora morphed into resentment with each step Demetrius took through the trees. Yeah, well, she liked him a lot better when she was unconscious too.

Rather than drumming up snippy comebacks that would get her nowhere, she thought back to what had happened when she'd been with the witches. She had flashes of chanting. Of a dagger. Of someone dipping her into a pool. The discombobulated images didn't make sense, but she was sure they'd done something to her in that cold, dank castle. Something that explained the roller coaster reactions she was having to Demetrius today. Attracted to him? Tingly? Achy with need? Those were not logical or appropriate physical responses for her to have to any Argonaut, especially to the most callous of the bunch. And especially not now when her life was in danger and she was stuck here with him for what looked like an indefinite amount of time.

Howling echoed in the trees to both her right and left. She tensed but didn't grab on to Demetrius. She wasn't about to give him the satisfaction, not again. And freaking out wouldn't get her off this island any faster.

The thick cypress trees opened up to a rocky ledge that fell away nearly two hundred yards to a canyon below. Isadora's eyes scanned the dark mountains on the far side, the river that wound through the small valley, the splashes of color against a deep green canvas. Then her gaze swung to the ruins on the hillside to her right.

The fading light made it hard to see, but Demetrius spotted the crumbling stone structure at the same time and shifted in that direction without a word. Rocks and grasses covered the steep hillside. Acacia and wild fig trees littered the landscape leading up to the edifice. The scents of sage and thyme, rosemary and oregano greeted her senses as they drew close.

At first Isadora thought the ruins were some sort of temple, but as it came more fully into sight she realized it was a garrison. What little she knew of Pandora filtered through her mind. No one lived on Pandora. No one could survive the monsters.

Wind whistled past her ears, sent a shiver down her spine. The quickly fading light cast shadows over the stones and battered steps. More cypress trees, palms, and eucalyptus shared the top of the hillside with the ruins, flanking the man-made with the natural.

Demetrius eased her down to sit on the broken steps and handed her a short spear. "Take this while I go have a look around."

She accepted the weapon without a word. The tip was still sharp but she doubted she'd be able to do any damage with it, especially considering she couldn't walk. Something was better than nothing, though.

Massive columns ran along the front of the structure. Demetrius disappeared inside. Somewhere across the valley a howl erupted, drifting on the air like an ominous warning.

Another shiver ran down her spine, this one not from the temperature but from everything lurking out there in the shadows. How in the name of all the gods had Demetrius opened the portal here? Not for the first time since she'd awakened did she have the feeling he wasn't telling her the entire truth.

Long minutes passed during which Isadora tried to piece together the fractured memories swirling in her mind. Growing more aggravated by the minute, she tapped her fingers together while she waited, the only sounds now the whistle of the wind through the trees. Just when she was sure Demetrius had ditched her, he appeared from around the far side of the building and stalked across the rocky ground toward her.

Her heart tripped at the sight of him, a reaction that made her draw in a startled breath. As he moved, her eyes shifted to his bare chest, to the slight dusting of dark hair there, to the muscles and sinew flexing beneath his tanned skin. The wounds on his belly had already scabbed over. His black Argonaut fighting pants were bloody and ripped at the knee and he'd lost his shoes at some point, his bare feet making him look more like a mortal man and less like the warrior she knew he was. But it was his face that kept drawing her back. His hard dark eyes, his jaw covered in two days' worth of stubble, his mouth set in a grim line.

It wasn't excitement over seeing him that stirred something inside her. It was relief at knowing she wasn't alone. It had to be.

Her gaze focused on his full lips as he moved closer and out of nowhere she heard his husky voice in her head. Only it wasn't the condescending, angry voice he usually used with her. This one was deep and gravelly and filled with emotion.

Wake up, kardia. Open your eyes so I know you're there. Please open your eyes.

Kardia. My heart. Why would he ever call her that? Her pulse stuttered, caught, and picked up speed.

He stopped at the base of the steps and raked a hand through his disheveled hair as he glanced around the ruins. "The place looks empty. It's got to be an old outpost. Pre-Archaic period, I'm guessing. Most of the roof's gone but the walls are sound, and there are a few rooms off the main hall with enough shelter for the night."

She had trouble comprehending his words. Was still busy trying to make sense of that voice she'd heard in her head. Was it a memory? Was it a vision of the future? Had he been talking to her?

Demetrius's dark eyes slid her way. "What's wrong with you?"

His harsh voice cut through the fog and she blinked even as her heart continued to race beneath her breast. "I…"

He frowned and stooped down to pick her up again. "Since you're no help to me, you might as well just get out of my way."

She didn't argue, had no idea *what* was going on or why. As he carried her into the main hall, which was flanked by two rows of columns, chipped and broken but still standing, she mentally focused on her surroundings instead of his strong arm beneath her legs or the bare skin of his chest pressing into her side or the heat radiating from every inch of his body.

Her eyes skipped over shadows and light. The ceiling was missing but the walls rose around them like a security barrier, and the first twinkle of lights from the night sky shone above. Halfway down the hall he ducked under an archway and stepped into an octagonal room.

Windows devoid of glass looked down over the open valley. A slight breeze blew through the large room with its pointed dome ceiling missing pieces here and there. Pottery shards and rusted metal littered the floor. Demetrius set her down on a bare section of stone against the wall that faced the wide open windows along the eastern side, then kicked debris out of her way.

"I'll be back," he announced.

Her heart pounded hard in her chest as he looked down at her. She didn't nod when he spoke, was too busy trying to figure what was wrong with her. Scowling, he shook his head and disappeared beneath the archway once more.

Alone, she drew deep breaths to settle her racing pulse, but it did little good because her mind wouldn't slow. *Kardia*. She was almost sure he'd called her that when they'd been climbing that cliff face too.

A soft echo drifted in through the windows. Happy for the distraction—any distraction—Isadora pushed herself across the floor and eased up to look over the low ledge to the ground beyond.

The rocky outcrop on this side of the fortress dropped off steeply to the sea below, churning against rocks and sand. Soft moonlight cast eerie shadows over the uneven ground and shimmered off the water. As far as strongholds went, this was a perfect location. Nothing could surprise you, nothing could attack you without warning, and no one would even know you were here unless you lit a fire or sent up smoke signals. That settled her anxiety, at least for the moment.

Her gaze ran back over the ground, then stopped and held when Demetrius stepped into view. Moonlight highlighted the dips and ridges of his powerful back. Mesmerized, she watched as he looked out to the water and pulled in a deep breath. Just as he had on the bluff, he held his hands in front of him and closed his eyes. His voice drifted on the wind, no more than a hum, a murmur, a silent curse. He turned a slow circle, his lips moving with muffled words, and when he'd made a complete rotation he knelt down and lifted a handful of soil, which he then proceeded to sprinkle as he rose and walked around the ruins, disappearing from sight.

Unnerved, Isadora eased back down to the cold floor. Again the sense that Demetrius was not who and what she'd always pegged him to be ran through her mind.

Wrapping her arms around herself, she scooted into the corner of the room so she could lean her head against the wall. She was so tired. And weak. And not just because of her bad leg. Something else had happened to her. Something before, during, or after her time with Apophis that she couldn't quite remember but which weighed heavily on her soul. And she was too exhausted and worn out to figure out what that was right now.

Her stomach rumbled, but she ignored it. For just a moment, here in these ruins, she felt safe. Whether or not that was because of Demetrius, she didn't want to know. She just wanted to forget.

She drew in a deep breath. Let it out. Relaxed into the wall as sleep drifted over her. But her mind kept twisting back to what she'd seen. And one image it wouldn't relinquish.

Demetrius.

Darkness closed in, faded to gray, and then grew lighter. Through shadows and mist she saw him standing on that cliff, his hands outstretched, his hair whipping around his lean face. Looking like an Argonaut, a sorcerer, a god, all rolled into one. And she heard his voice. Deep, rich. So damn sexy it set off a tremor deep in the center of her being.

Wake up, kardia. Open your eyes and look at me.

She did. Slowly. Blinked several times. Only she wasn't in an ancient garrison anymore. She was in a dim room illuminated by hundreds of twinkling candles. Massive marble pillars rose around a circular raised platform and a flat altar of granite. Symbols were etched into the side of the altar, into each of the pillars midway up. Symbols she couldn't quite read but faintly recognized.

She saw herself dressed in nothing more than a short black robe that hit mid-thigh, parted in front to reveal the long supple line of her neck, the mounds of her breasts, and the deep valley of her cleavage. Her legs were sleek and bare, her hair a wild mess of gold around her face. She looked like a sex goddess sent to seduce, and lying over a bloodred velvet chair, staring into Demetrius's wicked, searing eyes, it appeared she planned to do just that very soon.

I've waited so long for you.

His lips didn't move, but his words echoed in her mind, and her body answered with a rush of warmth that ignited a wild, uncontrollable desire. Heat gathered in her center as a slow smile slid across her mouth. She rose languidly from the lounge and slinked across the room, up the three marble steps toward the immense stone altar where he stood waiting, wearing nothing more than loose, low-riding black silk pants.

He captured her hand as she drew close, pulled her in for a hot, wet kiss that vibrated all the way to her toes. And just as she felt herself melt, give in, *crave*, he lifted her around the waist, laid her out on the altar, and untied the black sash around her waist.

She shivered as the halves of her robe fell open, revealing the length of her bare body.

Open your eyes, kardia, and look at me.

Slowly, she did. And gasped as his face shifted and morphed into that of the Lord of the Underworld.

A depraved, victorious sneer ran across Hades's face as he drank in every inch of her naked flesh. Horror pressed in and she opened her mouth to scream. But the only sound she heard was his heinous voice closing in to smother her.

Soon you will truly be mine.

———

Demetrius paused outside the open, arched doorway and listened to the slow steady rhythm of Isadora's breathing.

Thank all the gods she was asleep.

Tired himself, he placed a hand against the cool stones and debated the urge to take a peek at her. Then he remembered the fear in her eyes when they'd been attacked on the beach. When she'd broken her leg all over again. When she'd watched him casting the invisibility spell on that bluff so that damn harpy couldn't see them anymore.

Too bad he also remembered the disgust.

Bitterness brewed in his stomach when he thought of the way she'd said *witch*, but he welcomed it. Welcomed the familiar feeling and the distraction it brought as he pushed away from the wall and headed for the passageway he'd found hidden in the northwest corner of the ruins.

With the protection spell in place, he was able to breathe a little easier. Any monsters lurking in the shadows wouldn't be able to get past the circle he'd cast, at least for now. His powers were nothing more than tricks, really. He wasn't strong enough to cast a spell for any serious length of time. Tomorrow night he'd have to cast the damn spell all over again, and there was a good chance it might not even work. And judging by the way his luck was going…

His jaw clenched as he moved down four dusty steps that took him into what he suspected had once been a kitchen or dining hall but was now nothing more than rock and soil and open sky. Stars twinkled overhead and moonlight shimmered down, casting shadows and light over the uneven ground. He moved around a corner and paused near a six-inch gap that ran from floor to what used to be a ceiling at least ten feet high, where two walls intersected in the shape of an *L*.

He might have passed right by this spot earlier if he hadn't felt the chill brush his face. Now he was just plain curious. He ran his fingers over the edge of the gap. The air leaking out was cool, but not frigid. Grasping the edge of the protruding wall, he pulled, and like a door opening, the wall hinged outward.

The space was just wide enough to slide through,

no wider. He paused inside to let his eyes adjust to the darkness. From the moonlight shining at his back, he realized he was looking at another wall of solid stone.

He was just about to turn around and head out the way he'd come when the cool air slid over his bare feet. Kneeling down, he ran his fingers along the bottom edge of the wall and the inch-high gap that stretched the width of a door.

A false wall, he realized. Stepping as far back as he could, he squinted and discovered what faced him wasn't solid stone but an arched doorway. He pressed his palm against the center of the door. Pushed. Nothing happened. Lifting his gaze, he looked over the entire space, and that's when he noticed the ancient text inscribed into the stones surrounding the door. Faint, weathered from time and the elements, but readable.

Only he who hath been chosen shall pass unto this sacred place. Speak ye hero and enter.

A shot of apprehension rippled through him. What could possibly be sacred on this miserable island? His brow wrinkled as he read the words again and realized it was nothing more than a riddle. He'd never been good at riddles. Never really cared. And yet…

He glanced at his forearms, and two words came to mind. The ancient Argolean words for Eternal Guardian. A name he and the other Argonauts were never even called anymore because it had fallen out of use. "*Aionios Kidemonas.*"

A loud scraping sound echoed and the door opened inward all by itself.

"Whoa."

He stepped inside the circular room, which looked like home to nothing more than wide dusty steps that spiraled down into a black abyss. He listened, the only sound the rapid beat of his own heart. Beside him he spotted a metal ring embedded into the stone, roughly shoulder height, with what looked like a wooden torch perched within.

He swiped the cobwebs away, lifted the torch from its holder. Touching the rag wrapped around the end, he brought his fingers to his nose to sniff.

Oil.

Apprehension turned to wariness. His senses went on high alert. Were he and Isadora really alone on this island?

Muttering one of the easy spells he remembered from childhood, he waved the fingers of his free hand over the end of the torch and watched as flames ignited in the cloth to illuminate the downward-spiraling room and cast eerie shadows over the walls. He took a step down, then another, and as he descended he couldn't help but consider the irony. He'd used his powers more in the last two days than he had in the last two hundred years combined.

The steps dropped what had to be thirty feet. The air was cooler down here, mustier. At the base of the steps, he held up the torch to shine over the massive space ahead.

"Holy mother of Zeus," he whispered.

A long hall was flanked on both sides by massive marble pillars that ran up to the ceiling. Between each pillar sat a lone steel trunk. Three on the left, three on the right, and at the very end of the hall another, though this chest was bigger than the first six and was decked out with gold hinges and trimmings and the symbol of Heracles.

He moved toward the wide flat stone table that stood on a raised platform in the center of the room and held the torch waist high so he could read the words carved into the base.

Aionios Kidemonas.

The hair on the back of his neck prickled as he turned a slow circle, glancing from one chest to the next, each monogrammed with a different Greek symbol.

The Hall of Heroes.

No way.

A lump formed in his throat. It couldn't be real. Not here on this island of all places, hidden away from the world.

His eyes flicked over the second chest from the end, then came back and held. He focused in on the ancient symbol of his forefather, Jason.

His heart beat hard as he stopped in front of the trunk. Glancing around, he noticed more steel circles embedded into the pillars, as if to hold luminaries. He slid the torch into the closest, then flexed his fingers and refocused.

There was no lock. No magick words to speak. Grasping the lid of the chest, he lifted. Aged metal groaned as it hinged up and back. He peered inside and froze.

"No fucking way." His hands slid into finely spun golden wool. Slowly he lifted the fleece from its resting place and stared at the mythical object, which looked like nothing more than a ram's skull and horns with a head full of golden curls. The search for the Golden Fleece had been Jason's one major quest. The journey that had propelled him to hero status. The mission in which he'd fallen under Medea's spell. It had set events into motion that now could not be undone, and which had condemned Demetrius and every other of Jason's ancestors.

It didn't look like much to him. He turned it in his hands, noting not a flicker of power anywhere in the damn thing. Just bones and wool and history. Frowning, he set it aside and looked down again, then felt a burst of excitement.

"Now this is what I'm talking about." The parazonium with its black handle and red jewels was the perfect weight in his hand. He swung it right and left, brought it back to center. "If only…" He touched the edge with his free hand and winced. The blade sliced through the tip of his finger as if it had just been sharpened.

He brought the tip of his finger to his lips and sucked until the blood flow slowed and stopped and he felt his skin begin to heal. Wiping his finger on his pants, he looked back in the chest. Then smiled when he spotted a shield with Jason's markings, a steel breastplate with the same, and shoes.

"About time you did one damn thing for me." He set the parazonium and shield on the massive stone tablet and bent over to push his foot into the well-used sandal.

Not a pair of hiking boots, but a thousand times better than bare feet. He'd left his shoes on the beach and had been kicking himself ever since for taking them off in the first place. Looking back in the trunk, he realized there was only one sandal, not two.

"Figures." He tugged the sandal off and tossed it in the chest. Digging deeper, he found a spell book that had to have come from Medea, a bag of rocks he had no clue what to do with, a sheepskin rug, blankets, and a bunch of black candles.

His distaste for witchcraft reared, but with the monsters he'd seen the last two days, he wasn't about to be picky. He'd use whatever the hell he could. Hooking the belt and scabbard over his shoulder so it lay diagonally across his back, he slid the parazonium in its sheath. After replacing the other items back in the box, he stepped to the next trunk, the one with Achilles's symbol branded into the metal, then flipped the lid and smirked as he lifted the Pelican Spear from its resting place.

Achilles's great spear, which had aided the famed hero in defeating Agamemnon's enemies. He bet Zander'd like to get his hand on this. He turned it in the light. Now it was nothing but cold tarnished metal.

From trunk to trunk he moved, taking note of the objects that might just come in handy. When he was done, he gathered what he needed for the night, replaced everything else, closed each trunk, and headed back toward the spiral stairs.

At the top he extinguished the torch, replaced it in its holster. As soon as he stepped through the arched doorway, the door slid closed with a deafening thwack.

Sweet. That was the best fucking security system he'd ever seen.

The ruins were silent as he made his way back to the main hall and the small room off the north side where he'd left Isadora. With any luck she was out like a light. He'd toss a blanket over her, then park himself across the hall where he'd spotted another small room with a view down the hillside, toward the ravine below.

He climbed the four short steps to the main hall. Rubbed a hand down his face. And was twenty yards away when she screamed.

Chapter 9

THE CASTLE WAS A FLURRY OF ACTIVITY BY THE TIME Orpheus made it back. He flashed to the fifth-floor hall outside Gryphon's room and was greeted by a metallic crash from inside that set his nerves on high alert.

"We're losing him!" Callia yelled.

Machines beeped and whirred. Something hard scraped the floor. Orpheus tried to muscle his way past the two guardians blocking the doorway but it was like swimming against an ocean of stone.

"No admittance," someone said in his ear. A hand clamped over each of his arms.

"Shit, Orpheus," Phineus mumbled on his left. "It's not a good idea for you to be here right now."

Screw that. Orpheus tried to wrench his arms free. The meaty hands tightened.

"Theron," Callia said from inside the room, "hold him down. Zander, I need that syringe. *Now.*"

Panic and rage pushed in as Orpheus flashed free of Cerek's hold and reappeared at Callia's side. "What happened?"

Callia spared a quick glance his way before depressing the syringe of clear liquid into Gryphon's IV line. The guardian's eyes were closed but his face was scrunched in serious pain and his body thrashed against the bed and pillow. The only things that kept him from sailing off the bed were Theron's massive hands pressing down on his shoulders, holding his upper body in place.

"Sonofabitch," Zander said at Orpheus's back.

"Not good." Callia tossed the syringe on the table to her right, then pressed her fingers against Gryphon's carotid artery to feel his pulse. Her eyes zeroed in on her watch. "Step back, Orpheus."

"What happened? When I left—"

"Zander?" Callia asked without even looking up.

Another hand closed over Orpheus's upper arm. "Come on, O, give her some space to work."

Orpheus felt his eyes shift before he could control it. He wrenched free of Zander's grasp with his surging strength. "Fuck that! Tell me what happened!"

Voices rose up in unison around him. Gryphon got off a good kick with his right leg and sent a cart full of medical supplies crashing to the ground. In the pandemonium, Orpheus was forgotten as Zander and Cerek moved in to pin Gryphon's legs. The machine on the wall behind Gryphon's head picked up its incessant beeping. Then Gryphon's entire body seized and his back arched off the bed. Another machine off to the right set off a high-pitched alarm.

"He's flatlining!" Callia shifted around and reached for something behind her. A loud hum echoed through the room. She moved back with two large white paddles in her hands, placed one paddle just beneath Gryphon's collar bone and the other on his left side, down by his ribs. "Clear!"

Theron, Zander, and Cerek all let go of Gryphon. A zapping sound echoed. Gryphon's body jerked.

Callia looked at the monitor. "Again. Clear."

As Orpheus watched the seconds tick by with no change in his brother's condition, and Callia started CPR, the tightness in his chest returned. Only this time it was razor thin and brittle. And he knew if he didn't do something now it would fracture and shatter, splitting him forever in two.

He pulled the Orb from his jacket pocket. The disk was cool in the palm of his hand, the chain heavy between his fingers. The symbol of the Titans deeply embedded into the center stared up at him, as did the four empty chambers waiting to be filled. But the Orb didn't need the classic elements to work. It carried a power like no other. And right now it was the only hope Gryphon had left.

Gently, Orpheus laid the Orb over Gryphon's bare abdomen and let go. For a second, nothing happened. And then it began to glow. Pink at first, then brighter, until it was a blinding circle of red.

"Holy shit," someone muttered.

Realizing something was happening, Callia paused and looked over. Her eyes went wide when she caught sight of the Orb. "What the hell are you doing?"

Before she could grasp it, Gryphon shot up like a bolt of lightning, the movement so strong it threw Theron back and down to the ground with a thud. Gryphon's arm arced out to the right, knocking Callia off her feet. She screamed as she crashed into a medical cart behind her.

"*Thea!*" Zander yelled.

Theron pushed to his feet in a flash. The other guardians took a step in. The Orb slid down Gryphon's stomach and dropped into his waiting hand. And then Gryphon opened his eyes.

Movement in the room came to a screeching halt as Gryphon looked from face to face. And as his head slowly swung Orpheus's way, a collective gasp echoed through the room. When his brother was finally staring at him, Orpheus realized what was wrong.

The eyes that bore into his own were the same as they'd always been. Deep set, light blue, the same wide almond shape Orpheus always remembered. But this time they were empty. Vacant. As soulless as if…as if there was no one home.

A monstrous grin inched its way across Gryphon's face and his hand tightened around the glowing Orb. "My master thanks you, *adelfos*."

Brother.

In a poof of smoke, Gryphon disappeared. Leaving behind only rumpled bedding and swinging tubes and wires.

"Motherfucker," Theron muttered on the far side of the bed. "Orpheus, what the bloody fuck did you just do?"

Voices kicked up again as questions swirled. Zander helped Callia to her feet at Orpheus's side. The Argonauts argued around him about where the Orb had come from and what had just happened. But Orpheus barely cared. All he saw was the image of his brother disappearing into nothing.

"Dear gods," he heard Callia whisper at his side. "Orpheus. Your arms."

In a daze, he looked down. The ancient Greek text that marked all the guardians was slowly emerging on his skin. The writing was exactly the same as what had been on Gryphon's arms, noting him as the guardian from Perseus's line.

Voices trailed off. Someone swore. But the words

didn't register for Orpheus. The tightness in his chest cinched until he gasped in a breath and then it cracked and shattered, blinding him with pain. And then all of it trickled out. Until there was nothing left behind but a vast cavern of nothingness. Until the line that was his one connection back to humanity was finally severed.

"Oh, shit," someone muttered.

"Um, guys?" Titus said from back near the door. "O's the least of our worries right now." Heads turned to look. But not Orpheus. He was still staring down at his forearms.

"What now?" Theron asked.

"I caught a glimpse of Gryphon's thoughts—well, um, *his* thoughts—before he poofed out of here. And it wasn't good."

"What do you mean 'his'?" Theron asked, stepping forward.

"'His,' as in the warlock," Titus answered. "Apophis. Spawn of Hecate. Underling of the devil. Whatever the shit you want to call him. This guy's got some serious control issues. He made a deal with Atalanta to get the hell out of Thrace Castle, but he's been planning to double-cross her all along. And that little energy blast Gryphon took? It did exactly what Callia said it would, it killed off his soul. Only Gryphon's soul didn't go to the Isles of the Blessed like it should have. It went straight to the Underworld, leaving behind his body and mind for the warlock to do whatever the hell he wants with it."

Orpheus's eyes shot to Titus, standing in the doorway.

"Fucking A," Phineus muttered.

"That's not the worst of it," Titus said, his gaze

skipping from Phineus to Orpheus and then finally to Theron. "From reading Gryph's—*his*—mind, it's clear Apophis knows Atalanta has the princess. And now that he's got the Orb of Krónos—"

"Oh, dear gods," Callia whispered. "He's going to go after Isadora on his own."

"*Skata*," Theron said, running a hand over his hair.

"You can say that again," Titus muttered. "Sometimes I'd really rather not know this shit." He crossed his arms over his chest. "Hell is coming, boys. And it's coming fast."

Demetrius skidded to a stop just outside the arched doorway that led into the room where he'd left Isadora sleeping. Heart pounding, he dropped the bundle of blankets he'd brought with him and reached for the parazonium at his back, then inched over to glance around the corner.

Across the moonlit space Isadora leaned against the corner of the room. Her eyes were tightly shut, her head flailed from side to side as if she were in pain, but the thwacking he'd heard from the hallway was nothing more than the splint on her lower leg hitting the wall as she moved. There was no one else in the room with her. No Harpies or boars or a hundred other threats he'd imagined on his sprint up here.

He let go of his weapon, stooped to pick up a blanket, and crossed the floor quietly so as not to wake her. It wasn't comfort, he told himself as he dropped to his knees next to her and laid the blanket over her trembling body. It was…survival. If she broke her leg again, she'd be another few days of dead weight. And he needed her healed so they could get their asses off this damn island. An Argonaut could open a portal into their realm wherever he chose, but since Atalanta had bound his ability, that left everything up to Isadora. Regular Argoleans needed holy ground to open a portal. And that meant he needed her in walking shape so they could scout out that holy ground sooner rather than later.

"Stop fidgeting."

She kicked out with her good leg, tossed her head his way. "No. Don't…"

Definitely having a nightmare. Probably about Apophis and his gnarled minions. She flinched before his hand caught the edge of the blanket. "Don't touch me. Don't…"

He didn't want to, but he also didn't want to waste more of his energy on healing spells when he knew he'd possibly need that energy for other, more important spells tomorrow. Gritting his teeth, he leaned over her, hooked his arm around her blanket-covered thigh to pin her bad leg in place so she couldn't swing out and whack it against the stone wall. "Dammit, Isadora. I said hold still."

What his voice didn't impact, his touch did. Her body went still beneath his, and just as he was taking a breath of relief, she shifted into him, rolled her weight onto his, and pushed him back so he was pinned against the wall.

His head hit the stones with a crack and he cringed as pain lit off behind his eyes. But the throb only briefly registered because in the split second he was caught off guard, she slid her leg up along his thigh and shifted her torso over his so her face fit in the hollow between his shoulder and throat. And then the only thing he felt was heat.

He tensed. Braced his hands against the cold stone floor and had a moment of *What the bloody hell do I do now?*

She drew in a deep breath and blew it out slowly, her entire body relaxing into his with the movement. Her hand landed against his bare chest, her bad leg draped over his, trapping him in place. But it was the blood humming in her veins and the beating of her heart right against his that really did him in.

Sweat broke out on his forehead. His heart kicked up to the beat of a marching band. He thought through his options, but every single one involved waking her up and he definitely didn't want to do that. He chanced a look down at her face tucked into his shoulder and caught his breath.

Smooth porcelain skin stretched tight over exceptional bone structure. Light brown eyelashes feathering delicate cheekbones, and a mole next to her sweet, tender mouth.

His heart tattooed a blinding rhythm against his ribs as he stared at her. The thousands of reasons he'd avoided her over the years hit full force. He needed to push her off him, to get up and run far, far away before he did something he'd regret later. He needed—

"Softer than Hades," she mumbled.

Was she awake?

"Not bony," she mumbled. "And warm. Hades... so cold."

A shudder ran through her and she burrowed closer. No, the Isadora he knew would most definitely not huddle this close to him. He shifted his shoulder against the wall at his back.

"Stay," she murmured, tensing. "Don't wanna go back to him. Hate going back to him."

His chest tightened when he realized she'd been dreaming about Hades, not Apophis. Casey's revelation that Isadora had traded her soul to Hades to save Casey's life ran back through his mind. And with it a whole host of images of what *could have been* and *probably was* done to her when she'd been in the perverse god's realm.

Just what had she been thinking? Didn't she realize a deal with Hades was forever? What kind of idiot made that sort of transaction without weighing the consequences? Especially for someone she didn't even know?

Anger creasing his brow, he opened his mouth to ask just that, then stilled when she drew in a long breath and let it out slowly. Even through the thin blanket he felt the tips of her nipples brush his chest. His skin tingled with awareness and blood pooled hard in his groin, bringing every one of his senses to attention. And when she shifted her leg higher so it grazed his inner thigh, electricity coiled tight in each of his nerve endings.

Oh, man. That felt good. Way too fucking good.

Bad idea. Wrong person. Get the hell away before she wakes up.

The only problem was, his body wasn't responding to his brain's commands, and suddenly the only things he could think of were a host of erotic images that involved her, him, and all kinds of sinful positions he'd never let himself imagine before.

Which, if he wasn't careful, would lead him exactly where he couldn't go.

Chapter 10

SHE WAS HOT AND ACHY AND COULDN'T SEEM TO get comfortable.

Isadora groaned, shifted to her stomach, flipped to her back. Heat pulsed along her ribs, spread to her abdomen. The tips of her nipples tightened to painful levels and her breasts grew heavy and stiff.

When the ache spread lower and she couldn't find a position that eased the throb, she pulled her eyes open and stared up at the ceiling that wasn't really a ceiling after all.

Yesterday wasn't a nightmare. Her spirits dropped as her eyes skipped over the weathered stone that made up the walls of the ruins.

She pushed up and swung around to ease her head back against the cool stones. A blanket covered her; another had been pillowed beneath her head. Before she could figure out where they'd come from, the ache returned, stronger than ever.

Something was wrong with her. Perspiration beaded her forehead. Her skin grew hot. She pulled the shirt away from her chest and tried to cool herself down. It didn't work. If anything, she felt worse than before, achier, and ugh...now she couldn't get comfortable at all.

She scooted closer to the windows to let the cool air wash over her. Her gaze strayed down the bluff toward the beach on the north side of the island to where Demetrius appeared to be maneuvering what looked like huge wooden crates around on the sand.

Sunlight glinted off his tanned skin. He was at least two hundred yards away but she could still see the way the wind ruffled his hair, the flex of muscle beneath his skin, the way the light caught his toned abs and that dark dusting of hair on his chest that circled his navel and dropped beneath the waistband of his pants.

Heat exploded in her veins, pulsed everywhere. Groaning, she shifted away from the window and closed her eyes, breathing through the heavy throb now settled between her thighs and gathering in her breasts.

Why did looking at him make the ache stronger? She reached up with both hands to squeeze her breasts, but instead of killing the ache like she'd hoped, a tingling sensation erupted in her nipples and shot shards of plea-sure straight to her core.

She moaned, eased back farther against the stones. Her legs dropped open as waves of pulsing heat gathered between her thighs. She saw Demetrius as he'd been on the beach yesterday when she'd awakened—hot, sweaty, dark, and dangerous. She saw the flare of heat in his eyes when he'd healed her shin and his gaze had traveled over her naked thigh. She felt the warmth of his body against hers as he'd carried her to the ruins. In her hip. In her ribs. In the side of her breast pressed tightly against his muscular chest.

Oh, gods. She squeezed her breast with one hand, dropped the other to her thigh. Her fingers ran over her Horae marking, then higher, pushing the long shirt she wore out of her way. The pressure between her legs was almost too much to bear, and every time she pictured Demetrius it grew by explosive levels.

She couldn't take it anymore. She needed relief. She needed something to ease the pain. She popped the top two buttons on her shirt, reached inside to squeeze her breast tighter, and passed the fingers of her other hand over the curls between her legs.

Pleasure arced at the first touch. She sucked in a breath, moved her hand lower. As her heart rate picked up speed, she pressed against her wet, sensitive folds and saw Demetrius's face in her mind. His dark eyes, his square jaw, the tiny dent in his chin. She imagined him kneeling in front of her, pictured his hands touching her naked flesh, cradling her tender breast. Felt his hot breath on her skin, and moaned all over again.

She drew her knees closer, tipped her head back, circled until she found the source of her ache. With her other hand she flicked and tweaked her nipple. Each stroke eased and amplified the throb all at the same time. Her skin grew hotter, her body tighter.

And then she heard his voice. Just like in her dream. One word.

Kardia.

Pleasure radiated outward from her very center, ignited a rush of tingles that spread all along her nerve endings and exploded in a blinding glare behind her eyes. Every muscle in her body tightened, tearing a groan from her chest that left her limp and gasping for air.

She slumped back against the wall, sweaty, breathless, but still craving something she didn't understand. Her cheeks grew warm all over again when she imagined

Demetrius standing outside the ruins, watching her touch herself as she'd just done.

Why him? Why now? And dear gods, what was she going to do about it?

———ᴧᴧᴧ———

Holy fuuuuuuck.

No, don't think about fucking. Whatever you do, do not *think about fucking.*

Demetrius whipped away from the arched stone doorway where he'd spent the last minute frozen in place and hoped like hell he moved out as soundlessly as he'd moved in.

No way he'd just witnessed what he thought he had. No way he'd just seen Isadora pleasure herself in the middle of the ruins in broad daylight.

Heat and liquid fire erupted in flames that licked at every part of him. Stopping on the wide front steps, he dropped the bundle of supplies he'd brought up from the beach, stepped over the scattered mess, and headed around the building as fast as he could move.

His dick was a rod of steel, his balls tight as a drum, and he couldn't see shit where he was going, because the only thing *he* could see right now was Isadora on the floor in that room, her knees open, one hand squeezing her breast, the other moving beneath the hem of her— shit, *his*—shirt.

He stopped at the edge of the bluff, blew out a long breath, rubbed a hand down his face. Good gods, if she'd done that last night when he'd been sitting with her…

Okay, yeah, so think of something else. Daemons. Right. That was good. Think about slicing and dicing the motherfuckers. Not sexy. Not hot. Not the most erotic thing he'd ever *fucking* witnessed.

Shit. This wasn't working. Thinking about daemons made him picture Isadora in that field outside the half-breed colony, standing up to the monsters with that puny knife in her hand. Wearing that slinky black negligee thing that showed off the swell of her breasts, the curve of her hips, the soft indent of her belly button, and her toned abs that led lower to the tiny treasure between...

"Holy fuck." He grabbed two handfuls of his hair and pulled until his scalp burned.

Beach. Supplies. He needed to get back down to the crates and dunk himself in the ocean about fifteen times so he could cool his ass off.

Before he could change his mind he stalked back to the ruins and stomped as hard as he could so she'd hear him. He picked up the supplies, moved inside, and dumped them on the ground in her room without looking at her.

"Demetrius," she said in a surprised voice. Cloth rustled. "When did you get here? I thought...I thought you were on the beach."

Yeah, no shit. I should have stayed on that fucking beach.

"About time you woke up."

Cloth rustled again, as if she was moving around, then a thwack resounded and she let out a yelp.

He glanced up to see her lips compressed in pain, her hand braced against her lower leg. One look down at the splint and he swore under his breath.

"Graceful as ever, I see." He crossed the floor and dropped to one knee by her feet.

Focus, breathe, stay in control. He could be professional about this. He'd just forget what the hell he'd seen earlier.

"That's probably healed by now." His fingers made quick work of the ties on her splint. From the corner of his eye he noticed the Horae marking on her inner thigh and his blood warmed all over again. *Skata.* "Do you mind covering yourself?"

Her cheeks turned pink. She pulled the blanket over her lap. Was she thinking about what she'd done moments before? He gave his head a swift shake— *Focus, dammit*—and went back to untying the last knot.

Several moments passed before she asked, "What time is it?"

"After noon."

"Why didn't you wake me?"

"You obviously needed sleep." Though in retrospect, maybe he should have woken her. Holy Hades, did she wake up horny every morning? If so, he was fucked. And not in the way he wanted right now. He removed the splint and pressed his fingers along her shin, probably harder than he needed. "Does that hurt?"

"Um, no. It feels…good."

He let that go, told himself not to overthink the word *good*. He felt all around her lower leg and when he didn't sense anything out of the ordinary, he shrugged. "I guess we'll see when you stand. You need to get up anyway. Daylight only lasts so long."

Happy to get away from her, he pushed to his feet. Instinct had him holding out his hand before he thought better of it.

She slid her fingers into his palm. The same fingers

that had just touched and squeezed her naked breast. Electricity zinged up his arm and heated his skin all over again.

He let go quickly. "Try walking around."

She reached out to the wall and tentatively took a step with her bad leg. Slowly she made her way down the length of the wall.

"How is it?"

She turned at the corner and made her way back. "Okay. Whatever spell you cast seems to have worked. For now."

"Well, I am a half witch, *Princess*. Maybe you'll luck out and it'll break all over again."

A hurt look rushed across her face. She glanced to the side, crossed her arms under her breasts. "What's all that?"

He wasn't going to feel guilty. "Supplies."

"From where?"

"Crates that washed up on the beach from some sort of shipwreck."

He moved for the blankets and tossed a small box her way. She caught it with two hands. "The most I could find was junk food and some toiletries. But it's better than nothing."

She looked down at the box, turned it, and read the word *Crest* on the side. "Toothpaste? You found toothpaste?" She ripped the box open and rubbed the minty paste all over her teeth, then moaned as if she'd just eaten the most decadent dessert or experienced the most pleasurable orgasm.

The image of her head kicked back in pleasure rushed into his mind. And just that fast his cock jumped to alert.

Damn. Time to refocus. Again.

He turned away and pointed off toward the trees. "There's a stream through there. We're going to need water. I brought up some plastic buckets I found."

"What about those creatures?"

He grabbed the buckets and headed out toward the front of the ruins. "We're safe in the daylight. The creatures on this island are nocturnal."

She struggled to keep up, but he didn't slow his pace. The more distance he put between them right now the better.

"What do you mean, nocturnal?" she asked at his back. "That harpy came out into the sun. So did that boar."

"I didn't say they were vampires who couldn't go out in the sun. I said they're nocturnal. They rest during the day, hunt at night. I need to run back down to the beach and gather the rest of what we'll need."

She trailed along behind. "I'll go with you."

No way. He needed to be alone right now. "I'll take you to the river, help you fill the buckets. You should be able to carry them back on your own. While you do that I'll go to the beach and get the rest of the supplies."

She didn't argue, which was the first thing she'd done all morning that didn't amp him up. But after five minutes of her slowly picking her way around rocks and limbs and anything that might send her off balance, he realized that at this rate it was going to take them an hour to reach the stream.

"Oh, for crying out loud." He turned back and swooped her up in his arms. Then regretted it, because white-hot heat erupted everywhere their bodies touched. He ground his teeth together.

"Are you okay?" she asked.

"Fucking fantastic."

"You don't look fantastic."

His face burned. It was all he could do to keep his eyes off her and on the path in front of them. "I'll be better when I'm back on the beach." *And away from you. And your body. And oh, shit, stop thinking about her hot little body.*

She was silent a moment, then asked, "Um…so how do you know those crates are from a shipwreck?"

Finally, a topic not related to sex. "Know much about Pandora?"

"Obviously not. Before yesterday I thought it was mostly myth."

"Pandora exists in the human realm, but no one's ever been able to find it."

"That's a little convenient, don't you think?"

A sexy crease wrinkled her forehead and he took a deep breath to avoid looking at her full-on. "Imagine what an unsuspecting human would think if they landed here by accident."

"I see your point."

"The first guardians trapped the monsters here and then sealed off the island."

"With what? And by whom?"

He frowned. "Are you always full of a thousand questions?"

"Always. As the future leader of our realm, I find it interesting no one's bothered mentioning any of this to me. Aside from a few brief history lessons in school, this is news."

"Your father probably didn't think it was a big deal.

Like I said, no one's ever been able to find it. The area around Pandora messes with electronic readings of any ships and planes that venture into the area."

"You mean like the Bermuda Triangle?"

"You know about the oddities in the Caribbean?"

"Who doesn't? Another myth."

"Most civilizations are rooted in myth. Ours as well. And many that disappeared from the map are also entrenched in myth."

"Wait. You mean like Atlantis? Are you saying Atlantis is somewhere in the Bermuda Triangle? That *that's* the reason for the strange shipwrecks and disappearing planes in the region?"

He shrugged. "I don't have proof. But yeah, that's what most of us think."

"'Most of us.' As in the Argonauts?"

He didn't answer, but he also didn't miss the shocked expression on her face. As she pondered the ramifications of that, he kept his mouth shut and kept walking.

Finally they reached the stream. He set her down and moved off to crouch by the edge and splash as much cold water on his face and arms and chest as he could. Not the same as dunking himself in the ocean, but it was better than nothing.

"Are you sure you're okay?" she asked.

"I told you I was fucking fantastic. Stop asking the same damn questions over again."

"You must like that word. *Fucking*. You use it a lot."

The sound of her dainty lips uttering that one graphic word reignited the erotic image from earlier in his mind, then triggered an all-new one: her naked on all fours in front of him. His body pressed in tight behind her, thrusting deep while she mouthed the word *fucking* again and again.

Blood pounded straight into his cock. He grew hard in an instant. The only thing that kept him from losing it was the fact he was angled away from her and couldn't see her face.

Focus, breathe, stay in control.

He dropped the buckets by the edge of the water and rose as fast as he could. He had to get out of here. He couldn't stay. And he definitely couldn't give in and show her just how much he really did like that word.

"Don't linger," Demetrius said again as he looked anywhere but where Isadora wanted him to look.

"I won't." What was wrong with him? He was avoiding eye contact like he was the one who had something to be embarrassed about, not her.

Thank the gods he hadn't seen what she'd done in the ruins. Heat rushed to her cheeks all over again. If he'd been just a few minutes earlier…

"Fill the buckets and head right back. Got it?"

"Yes."

He looked as if he wanted to say something more. Birds chirped high in the canopy of trees, and the small river, roughly six feet across, gurgled and swirled over rocks and downed tree limbs. It was darker in here, but the trees were spaced far enough apart so plenty of sunlight filtered through the canopy. There was no hint of danger, no sound out of the ordinary. Scowling, he pulled a small dagger from his waistband and handed it to her. Their fingers grazed and heat trickled over her

skin, but he didn't seem to notice. He didn't even look at
her. "Just in case. Go straight back, do you understand?"

"Yes, I've got it. I'm not an invalid, Demetrius."

He harrumphed as if he didn't agree. Then he flicked
her an irritated look before heading off through the trees.

She was never going to understand him. Wasn't sure
she even wanted to. And yet these hot, wicked fantasies kept running through her head, all centered on him.
Isadora watched until he disappeared. Feeling a strange
sense of loss at his departure, she sighed, then turned to
glance around the streambed.

Across the brook, grass and plants edged the river
and turned to trees, which thickened until she could see
nothing beyond. Reminding herself not to dawdle, she
eased down, set the dagger on the moss beside her, and
filled the first bucket.

The water was cold and fresh. She ran her hand over
the smooth surface, lifted the bucket, and took a deep
drink. Droplets slid down her chin to land on her chest,
cooling her overheated skin. After filling the remaining
buckets, she set them to the side and eased her feet into
the creek.

Heaven. Her eyes slid closed. She took deep breaths as
every muscle in her body relaxed. She'd told Demetrius
she wouldn't linger, but the water felt too good on her
feet to ignore. Two minutes. That's all she'd take.

She waded out into the middle of the stream, then
held her breath and dropped down to dunk her whole
body. She came up gasping, the shock invigorating.
Brushing the water out of her eyes, she stood up, feeling a thousand times better than she had minutes before.
She was just about to turn and head back to gather her

things when she spotted movement to her right, toward the dark trees.

Slowly, she shifted in that direction. And came face to face with a shadowy wraith with red eyes, massive claws, and razor-sharp teeth.

"Oh, *skata*."

Too late she realized the birds had gone silent. Even the wind seemed to have died down as if it too were afraid to move. Isadora's pulse shot into the stratosphere as she glanced to where the dagger Demetrius had given her—just in case—lay on the moss, feet away.

The creature opened its fanged mouth and screamed. She had an instant to make a decision.

She sprinted for the dagger. Water splashed up around her. Something sharp stabbed the back of her neck. Her hand flew to the spot as she cried out in pain. But before she even reached the far side of the mossy shore, her vision blurred and her legs buckled beneath her.

And then she was falling backward. Going down. This time with no one to save her.

Chapter 11

CASEY BIT HER LIP AS SHE WAITED OUTSIDE HER father's suite. She'd promised Theron she would try to take a nap before dinner, but seriously, that was just an asinine request. Who could sleep at a time like this?

The door to the king's rooms opened and her half sister stepped out. Callia closed the door quietly at her back, drew a deep breath, and rubbed her forehead.

"I know that feeling," Casey said.

Callia's head came up. "How long have you been out here? You should have come in. He—"

"He's not the one I've been waiting to see."

"Probably best. I had to give him a sedative. He's not handling the news about Isadora well." Callia glanced back toward the door. "This is pushing him closer to the end."

A space in Casey's chest pinched at the thought of her long-lost father, the king, dying so soon after she'd found him. It wasn't right. It wasn't fair. But it was life. And if there was one lesson she'd learned over the years, it was that you made the best of what was thrown your way. Even when you didn't like the pitch.

The door opened and Callia stepped back as Althea, the king's personal attendant, moved out with a scowl on her face. "I can hear you both plain as day. Shoo. He needs his rest. Take your naysayer attitudes somewhere else."

Casey, familiar with Althea's bossiness, rolled her eyes. The frown on Callia's lips shifted to a smirk.

"I'm thirsty," Callia said to her sister. "Grab a drink with me? You look like you need one more than I do."

"I'm fine," Casey said. "You don't need to worry about me."

"I'm a healer. It's my job to worry."

"Actually," Casey said hesitantly, drawing Callia up short, "Theron asked for you."

"Is there any—"

"No. No news. This·is more about Demetrius." At Callia's perplexed expression, Casey motioned toward the hall. "Come on. I'll explain on the way."

The two fell into step down the massive corridor. The king was rooted in tradition and it showed in every inch of the castle. Massive Grecian columns lined the hallway, rising at least thirty feet to the soaring ceiling. Candles in sconces lit the way. Rich-colored throw rugs and plush furnishings lined the rooms they passed. Casey explained what little update she knew as they moved, but as they reached the end of the corridor and headed down the grand stairs to the king's study several floors below, she noticed the tightness in Callia's shoulders.

She stopped her sister with a hand on her arm before they reached the bottom step. "No one blames you about Gryphon. You know that, right? You did everything you could."

Callia turned to look at Casey. They were roughly the same height and weight, with the same violet eyes and some of the same mannerisms. Though they didn't share the same mother, the similarities between them were obvious now. "Did I?"

"Yes, you did," Casey said with conviction. "I was there. I saw him. No one blames you. Not Theron, not the other Argonauts. No one."

"Orpheus blames me."

Casey frowned. "Orpheus is—"

"Orpheus is right." Callia held up her hand, studied it as she turned it in the low light. "I can't help thinking if he'd had another healer…" Her gaze shifted from her hand to Casey. "It's fading. I can feel it. Something's wrong with me. When I was treating Gryphon, I needed Max to use his powers of transference for things I should be able to do myself. Every day that passes…I feel like I'm losing a part of myself."

"How?"

Callia huffed. "I don't know. I don't know anything right now. Except that I feel a change. Zander feels it too, only he won't talk about it. I can tell by the way he looks at me though. And I'm tired, Casey. All the time. More every day. Just like I know you are."

Casey's chest pinched at Callia's words. Yes, she was more tired today than she'd been yesterday, but she was trying not to read too much into that. But this… this news that Callia felt it too…She hadn't considered the ramifications of Isadora's absence. As the Chosen, she and Isadora were linked together. Hades had warned them not to separate too far or too long. But Callia…she wasn't technically part of the Chosen prophecy.

She was, however, one of the king's three daughters, and as they'd all recently learned, she was connected to both Casey and Isadora through the Horae, the ancient Greek goddesses of balance, and a paternal link all the way back to Themis, the Titan who'd spawned the

Horae. If Casey was feeling the ill effects of Isadora's separation, it made sense now that Callia, as the balance to the Chosen, would feel it too.

And then there was Zander. The only immortal Argonaut. Only he wasn't quite so immortal after all, was he? The guardians had all assumed he couldn't be killed because he hadn't found his Achilles heel like every other male from his line had. But after 829 years, they now knew he had one vulnerability: Callia. Whatever physical effects she suffered, he suffered as well, and when her life ended, his would too.

Casey's stomach churned and a whole host of new worries lit off in her brain. This now went beyond simply Casey and Isadora. If Isadora wasn't found…not one, not two, but four would die. And the kingdom…

She had to tell Theron.

"Something has to be done," Callia said, her worried voice cutting through Casey's thoughts. "I'm not afraid to die, but I can't—I won't—let anyone turn out my son." Until Isadora produced an heir, Max was next in line for the throne. "Do you honestly believe the Council would let a ten-year-old rule?"

No, Casey didn't believe for a second Lucian, the Council leader, would live up to that agreement. It didn't matter that Callia's son Max was of royal blood, that his father was an Argonaut. To the Council he would forever be the illegitimate grandson of the king. And in their eyes, tarnished. Casey now understood what Theron so adamantly protected every day of his life—not just the order of the Argonauts, but their entire kingdom, their world. The Council did not grasp the depth of Atalanta's vengeance or her hatred. If rule were left up to them, Atalanta would already have Argolea in ruins.

"I can't sit back and do nothing much longer," Callia whispered.

"Hopefully you won't have to." Casey tugged Callia the rest of the way to the king's study and pushed the door open.

Heads turned as they entered. Theron looked up from some map he was studying on the desk and smiled Casey's way, but it was a tight, strained motion that spoke of his stress. Zander crossed to tug Callia close. Max sat in Theron's chair, listening to the guardians, and his face brightened when he saw his mother step into the room. Cerek and Phineus stood by Theron's desk with their massive arms crossed over their chests.

"Where is Titus?" Casey asked her husband.

"He went to see the witches, to try to locate Orpheus."

Casey glanced at her sister, then back at Theron. "Why do I get the feeling that's not a good thing?"

"Because O's gonna seriously fuck things up instead of make them better if someone doesn't stop him," Phineus mumbled.

Theron shot the Argonaut a scathing look, then turned back to Casey and forcibly relaxed his features. "I'm still not sure this is a good idea."

She frowned, because they'd already been through this. Several times. And they'd already agreed this was the best option they had. "We have to know one way or the other, right?"

"Know what?" Callia asked.

Theron looked her way. "Whether Demetrius is

truly guilty of treason like Gryphon said before…*skata*, before he poofed out of here."

"And how do you plan to figure that out?" Callia asked.

"Casey's gift is hindsight, *thea*."

Callia turned to look up at Zander. "So you're telling me she's going to look back to see if he planned to kidnap Isadora?"

"Not his plans," Casey corrected. "I can't see his thoughts. But by touching him—or, well, something of his—I can get a glimpse of his past. I can tell us all if what Gryphon said is true. If Atalanta really is his mother. If she is—"

"Then every one of his badass moods and questionable actions over the years makes a sick sort of sense," Cerek muttered.

Callia's gaze swept over the room and then her eyes settled on Max, sitting in Theron's chair behind the desk, his legs swinging in the air. And as if she'd finally clued in to what was going on, they jumped right to Casey. "You're not strong enough to do this on your own."

"I'm fine—"

"You're not fine, *meli*." Theron looked to Callia. "I won't risk her, even to know this about one of our own. I need to know if it's safe for her to do this. She grows weaker every day Isadora is gone. I don't want to put extra stress on her."

Callia's eyes settled on Casey again and Casey frowned, both hating and loving Theron's protective nature. "I'm fine, Callia. Max is only here as a precaution. In case I need a little extra oomph to look. Trust me, if I was really ill I wouldn't even consider it."

Callia stepped close, held out both hands in front

of her sister but didn't touch her. Her eyes fell closed and she seemed to be concentrating, but on what Casey didn't know. Casey felt a warm tug deep in her chest, then nothing but a smattering of tingles.

Seconds later Callia opened her eyes, then looked back at Theron. "She's telling you the truth. She's strong enough. But it's a good idea to have Max here just in case."

Max swung his legs back and forth, glanced from face to face. His power of transference was the most valuable any of the Argonauts possessed, but he was still only ten, and if Casey's suspicions were correct, what she was going to see in Demetrius's past wouldn't be appropriate for a child.

"I'll tell you if I need Max's help." Casey turned to her husband. "Feel better now?"

The crease in his brow said no, but it was the worry in his dark eyes that softened her. She stepped to him, ran her hand over his jaw. "Stop worrying, okay? Everything's going to be fine."

"Everything will be fine when Isadora is home and I know you're safe," he whispered. "Until then, you'll just have to deal with me."

~~~

Demetrius made it halfway down the steep hillside toward the beach on the northern side of the island before he heard the horrific scream from the trees behind him.

He jerked that way. Not human, not Argolean, definitely monster. But the sound had come from the direction of the stream.

Isadora.

Shit. *Shit!*

He'd *just* left her. She couldn't have gotten into trouble already. Did the female have a target strapped to her forehead?

He scrambled back up the steep hill, his heart pounding hard against his ribs as he moved. Sweat slicked his skin as he raced along the path. When he reached the riverbank minutes later, he found nothing but empty plastic buckets lying on their sides and the dagger he'd given her resting near the edge of the stream.

"*Skata.*"

Worry jumped to panic. "Isadora!"

An ear-piercing scream brought his head around. He reached for the blade at his back and took off at a dead run.

He skidded to a stop where the stream spilled into a small lake. A thick, soupy fog hung all around the water, making it hard to see what lay beyond the western shore, but there was no missing what floated in the middle. Or what hovered above, waiting to strike.

Isadora lay on her back in the center of the water, her eyes closed, her hands fanned out to the side. She looked peaceful, like she was asleep, but above her three shadowy wraiths lingered. Waiting. Licking their chops like vultures ready to devour.

His heart shot into his throat.

"Hey!" He jumped up and down to get their attention, waved his sword in the air. Isadora didn't so much as move, but the heads of all three monsters came up and their crimson eyes zeroed in on him with deadly focus.

Oh, shit. Not wraiths at all. These were the Keres. Daughters of Nyx, sisters of the Fates, female death spirits who drank the blood of their prey. They couldn't kill, not by force. And from what little he knew of them, they waited until death was already drawing close to strike a target.

His eyes darted to Isadora. But she looked the same as when he'd left her at the stream. Asleep, maybe, but she wasn't close to death. She was—

The water around her rippled, and near her bare leg a scaled tentacle broke the surface only to disappear again.

Oh…fuuuuuck!

He charged into the water without a second thought, screaming Isadora's name until he dove beneath the surface. His muscles burned as he swam with everything he had in him. When something brushed his leg, he swam harder. Even under the water he could hear the Keres above shrieking.

He gasped as he broke the surface near Isadora. His hand closed over her arm, but she still didn't move. Not even when he wrapped an arm around her waist and dragged her toward the shore. "Wake up, dammit!"

She was dead weight in the water. It took twice as long to reach the shore, and every time something grazed his limbs he was sure it was some kind of serpent about to eat them. His feet finally hit the silty soil; he stumbled, righted himself, turned and slipped his arms under Isadora's to haul her out of the water. The cotton of her shirt tore.

The Keres screamed their frustration as Demetrius dragged her back onto the shore. As he cleared the edge, a bubbling sound echoed. He looked back to see the water in the center of the lake churning and fizzing. The Keres shrieked and disappeared into the fog.

Dread filled Demetrius's chest as he supported Isadora and watched the water recede as if being sucked in by a giant vortex. Rocks and reeds and tree trunks came into view, but what held his undivided attention was the mighty beast with six heads emerging from the column of water in the center of the lake.

"Holy fucking shit." He looked down at Isadora, out cold in his arms, then back to the creature that was a cross between a serpent and six different dragons. No way he could outrun it. Not with her unconscious. His adrenaline surged. Options raced through his mind. He still had the sword in his hand.

He laid Isadora out on the grass behind a giant shrub and drew her legs in so she was completely hidden from view. Then he swallowed hard and held his hands over her, muttering in Medean, casting the mother of all protection spells and drawing deep from whatever power was left in him.

He was a crappy witch. He'd never developed his craft. He hadn't wanted to, hadn't cared. Now, though…now he wished he'd embraced his heritage at least a little.

With the measly spell cast, there was nothing else he could do but distract and divert. And hope like hell she woke up and got the hell out of there before the monster found her.

He took one last look at her lying on the grass, out cold and soaking wet. And for the first time in his life he wished he hadn't been such an asshole to her. That he'd felt what it was like to have her arms wrapped around his body. That he'd tasted those sweet lips. That he'd just once gotten lost in her softness.

Wishing is for shit.

Yeah, he knew that better than anyone, didn't he? The only bright spot in this whole nightmare was that Atalanta wasn't going to get what she so desperately wanted.

He stepped back onto the lakeshore, stayed in the shadows, and sprinted around the far side of the water, well away from Isadora's hiding spot. Pulse pounding, he slowed to a stop and gripped the sword in both hands. "Hey!"

The water column arced in all directions, splattering across Demetrius and the ground. The beast swung around. Two heads on the monster blew fire six feet out.

"Is that the best you can do?" Demetrius yelled. "Why don't you come over here and try that?"

The middle head roared, then the creature dove underwater and raced toward shore.

Demetrius braced his feet on the soft soil and reared back with the blade, ready to strike. The beast shot from the water like a bullet, flew over his head, and landed on all four feet with a crack that shook the ground. Demetrius whipped around. One head shot forward, the hideous mouth opened. Before it could roast him, Demetrius swung the sword.

The blade sliced through the thick neck. The head fell to the ground with a thwack. The other heads screamed and pulled back. But instead of slowing the monster, the wound seemed to give it strength. Two heads instantly grew from the one severed. And then there were seven.

"Fuck me." This wasn't any monster, this was a Hydra. His mind raced over what he new of the legendary beast. Each time one head was lost, two grew back in its place. Only one head was mortal. Decapitating that one was the only way to kill the creature.

Of course, you had to figure out which one that was. And you had to get close enough to cut it off. And you had to avoid being torched by all the other heads in the meantime.

Oh, man…he was so screwed.

He glanced back to the brush where Isadora lay hidden. Then his gaze shot to the fog.

He waved his sword in the air. "Try again, shithead!" He took off running.

The Hydra heads roared, but the monster took the bait and gave chase. The fog thickened. Demetrius couldn't see more than ten feet in front of him, but he kept running, wanting to draw the beast as far away as possible. Up ahead he heard a loud crashing sound, and not knowing what the hell he was running toward, he veered off into a thicket of trees.

The crashing grew louder. A lion's roar sounded. Demetrius looked back just in time to see flames erupt from the fog in the direction he'd been headed. Holy *skata*, there was something else out here. The Hydra bellowed in response, but instead of following Demetrius into the trees, it charged the newcomer.

Snapping and screams pierced the eerie fog. The two monsters collided with a crack that sounded like a two-ton bomb detonating. They rolled across the ground, taking down trees and stumps and anything in their way.

Demetrius scrambled back out of the way. Only when the second monster jerked to its massive feet and Demetrius got a good look at its size did he realize it was a Chimera, an enormous lion-headed creature with the body of a goat and the tail of a dragon. The Hydra righted itself. The seven heads roared a challenge in unison. The Chimera didn't seem to give a rip. It braced itself, opened its mighty mouth, and vomited a steady stream of fire that seemed to have no end.

Okay, he was not sticking around to see who won this fucked up, no-way-in-hell-this-should-be-real battle. Demetrius sprinted back to Isadora. He was pretty sure his heart was in his throat by the time he skidded to his knees at her side. One quick check confirmed she was still unconscious, but breathing. Another loud roar kicked him into overdrive. He scooped Isadora into his arms. And then he ran.

Chapter 12

ISADORA CAME AWAKE WITH A START. SHE SAT UP, blinked several times, and had a moment of *What the hell?*

The corner she was lying in was dark, but across what looked like a massive room, torches burned bright on marble pillars spaced ten feet apart to form a long hall. In the center, a raised platform held a stone table. Just like from her dream. Or nightmare.

Her gaze darted back to the dark corner around her, and trepidation rushed in when she realized she was naked beneath a thin cotton blanket. She tugged the blanket up to cover her breasts, shifted to the side, and discovered she wasn't on a hard cold floor but some kind of fur rug or hide.

She lurched to her feet. Wrapping the blanket around herself, she made it into the light of the torches before she saw the trunks set between each of the pillars and faltered.

One, two…seven trunks. Each made of antique steel, wool, and leather with a different symbol carved in gold on the front. But it was the one at the end of the room, perpendicular to all the others, that drew her attention. The one that was twice as big as the rest and bore the symbol of Heracles on the front.

Wide-eyed, her gaze jumped from the end chest to each of the others, stopping on the one to her right.

Ιάσων.

In Ancient Greek, Jason's name began with an iota, the ninth letter of the Greek alphabet. And he was Demetrius's forefather.

Curiosity pushed her forward and she took a hesitant step toward the trunk. The wood was cool to the touch. Metal groaned on aged hinges as the top moved up and back.

Weapons, candles, books, a bag filled with…what felt like marbles. She lifted a worn sandal so she could examine it in the light.

"There's only one."

She gasped in a breath, whipped toward the voice. Her heart jumped into her throat as a shadow moved on the edge of the light, then picked up speed when Demetrius stepped down stone steps and moved out of the darkness.

"Oh my gods," Isadora whispered. "You scared me." She pressed a hand against her chest, relieved it was him. Disturbed at the same time, because seeing him set off tiny tremors of awareness all over her body.

"There's only one," he said again. "He lost the other."

She had no idea what he was talking about. Her attention was focused solely on the languid way he moved down the steps, the play of torchlight falling across his broad bare shoulders that cast shadows over his muscular chest.

"The sandal," he said, nodding to what was still clutched to her chest. "Jason lost it in the river Anauros helping an old woman cross the water." He frowned, stuffed his hands into the front pockets of his torn pants. "Only it wasn't just a woman. It was Hera in disguise."

The disgust in his voice when he said the goddess's name was more than evident, but it was the way he was watching her with those intense midnight eyes that sent Isadora's pulse skipping in her veins.

Something was different about him. Long gone was the contempt he'd always sported when he gazed at her. Nowhere in his eyes now did she see animosity or disgust over who and what she was. In fact, standing in the flickering light, she saw only curiosity and concern and a hint of what could only be described as…heat.

Her pulse raced, and a low steady ache settled in her stomach, drifted lower. She clutched the soft blanket tighter to her chest. "I…What is this place?"

He moved up the steps of the raised platform, set a bundle of cloth on the stone table, then stepped down again until he was level with her, where he took the sandal from her hand. His fingers brushed hers in the process and heat flared to life across her skin. "What do you think it is?"

She watched as he set the sandal back in the trunk, closed the lid. "I'm not quite sure."

"I think you are."

She looked around the room again. It was indeed a soaring space. She couldn't see the ceiling, but the columns seemed to go on forever. "Where…?"

"In the ruins." When her eyes settled on his once more, he added, "Under the ruins, actually. I found it yesterday."

Yesterday. When she'd been sleeping, dreaming of him. "On Pandora? Why would they build the Hall of Heroes here? Where it would never be found?"

"So it *would* never be found. As far as hiding places go, this is a pretty good one, don't you think?"

Yeah, actually, she did. If you wanted to guarantee that the secrets of the original Argonauts would never be lost, it made perfect sense to hide them somewhere no one could find them.

That epiphany led right into the realization that no one would ever find *them* either. And knowing that bit of info was too much to deal with right now, Isadora changed the subject. "What happened? You left me at the river and I—"

"I was hoping you could tell me."

His intense eyes seemed to bore into hers, as if he couldn't look away. And awareness resurged in the space between them. She was naked beneath the thin blanket. He wore only low-slung frayed black pants that had seen better days. She should be hesitant and self-conscious. But instead she felt…alive.

"I…I don't really remember. I waded out into the stream. I was hot. I remember thinking a few minutes to cool off wouldn't hurt anything."

His gaze roamed the blanket. But it wasn't a casual sweep as he'd done to her thousands of times. No, there was heat in the way his eyes hesitated on her breasts, slid lower to her hips. And for a moment she wondered if he could see through the thin fabric.

Warmth shot straight to her center. For a moment she *wanted* him to see through the thin fabric.

"What did you do?" he asked, bringing his dark eyes back level with hers.

"I…" Words lodged in her throat. A desire she wasn't used to experiencing seared her veins.

"I…I dipped down to cool myself off, and when I came back up—" The image of that wraithlike beast filled her mind and her breath caught. "There was something watching me."

"A Ker. Yeah, I saw it. Actually, I saw three. Did you run?"

She was still wrapping her mind around the fact the *thing* she'd been staring at was a death spirit. And he said there'd been three? She gave her head a swift shake, not wanting to think about that just yet. "Um…yeah. I'd left the dagger on the edge of the water. I turned to get it. The last thing I remember is something sharp hitting my neck." She clutched the blanket together with one hand, rubbed her hand under her hair with the other.

He let out a breath. "That explains things. Their poison works as a sedative. You must have fallen into the stream when you passed out."

"Out? How long has it been?"

He shrugged, hands still deep in his pockets, but his shoulders relaxed. And she had the strange sense this news calmed him, though why she had no clue. "At least eight hours. It's the middle of the night now. You didn't move a single muscle. Not when I found you. Not during or after what happened. It was like you were hypnotized. I thought…" His voice trailed off, and the worry she heard there caught her dead in the chest, the pain so sharp it was as if she'd been pierced by a bullet.

"But now that we know it was just the poison," he said, "that makes sense. It should be mostly worn off by now."

Her world had just tipped on its axis. Her brain buzzed and her head was so light she was sure it would float off at any moment. Nothing made sense, and yet something…something in her soul for the first time in a long time felt…right.

She swallowed hard, tried to get her thoughts back in line with the conversation. "Wh-what do you mean 'during or after what happened'? Where did you find me?"

He hesitated, studied her intently. "Floating in the middle of a lake."

Okay, that didn't sound so bad.

"With three Keres hovering above you and a Hydra in the water beneath you."

The blood drained out of her face. Oh. Um, yeah. *That* didn't sound good. "H-how did you…?"

"Do you really want to know?"

She studied his eyes, thought about the image he painted. Remembered the harpy and boar on that beach the first day she'd awakened here and the nightmares that still lingered from that little scene. Combined with what she remembered of that Ker…her stomach churned. No, she really didn't want to know what he'd done to get her away from those monsters. And she didn't need to relive it if she didn't have to. She shook her head. And then a thought hit.

"You…you rescued me."

His gaze intensified, and warmth reignited all over her skin under that heated stare. "Rescuing you is turning into a full-time job."

It was. Apophis, the daemons in that field, those monsters on the beach, and now this. Four times he'd saved her life recently. Four times he could easily have let her die and never looked back. But he hadn't. He'd been right there to drag her to safety each and every time. And he hadn't asked for a single thing in return.

Her heartbeat kicked up hard in her chest, beat against her ribs with a rhythm that fanned warmth to her breasts and slid lower. She thought back to the snippy comments she'd tossed at him yesterday, to the way she'd treated him most of her life. Emotions pinched her chest, closed her throat, made it hard to breathe.

He nodded toward the table before she could think of a single thing to say. "Those are some clothes I found in the crates on the beach. Thought you might want them. The shirt you were wearing…well, let's just say it didn't make it."

She looked down at the blanket wrapped around her and realized he'd seen her naked. Again. Heat rushed to her cheeks. But for some reason knowing he'd stripped her bare didn't disturb her, it electrified her.

Slowly, because she knew he was watching her, she moved up the steps to the stone table, ran her hand over the pair of denim shorts and the orange tank top folded neatly on top. "These weren't in the bundle you brought up this morning. You went back?"

"We needed water. I had to go back out anyway. Didn't think you'd want to walk around this place naked with me here."

Her gaze shifted back to him. And in that instant she saw every one of her perceptions where he was concerned shatter like glass against the floor. This was not the stone-cold bastard she'd always believed him to be. This was an *ándras*—no, a hero—of honor.

Who would ever have believed she'd think that? Who would ever have thought she'd feel anything for him besides animosity?

Emotions that came out of nowhere and everywhere

all at the same time pushed her feet forward. "You saved me," she whispered. "You could have let me die."

"Why would I do that?"

"Why would you want me to live?" she asked, turning his question back around as she closed the distance between them and moved down two steps.

He didn't step back or look away, but the wrinkle in his forehead said he wasn't sure what she was implying and didn't know how to react. "It's my job to protect you."

"Is that all?"

"Isn't that enough?"

"Probably, but...you risked your life for me. Not once, but four times."

"Yeah."

It wasn't a question, but a statement. As if it were a fact every other day of his life. And in the silence that followed she knew he was thinking the same thing as she. That something was changing right here between them. And if one of them didn't put a stop to it, their relationship would never be the same again.

"You rescued me," she said softly.

His black-as-night gaze roamed her face, but he didn't answer. And he didn't touch her, though deep inside she felt he wanted to. He just didn't know how to bridge the gap.

"Maybe," she said softly, hoping to bridge it herself, just a touch, "maybe one day I can return the favor."

"You can't save me," he whispered.

"Why not?"

"Because some things aren't worth the effort."

Her heart went out to him right then and there. As

firelight flickered over his chiseled features, she saw secrets brewing in his eyes. Secrets that fed something dark in his past that kept him closed off from the world. For years she'd thought he didn't have a soul, but as she stared into his eyes now, she knew she'd been wrong. He hurt, just as she did. And he longed, the same as she. While she'd curled into herself over the years, letting her father and everyone else make her decisions for her, he'd gone the other way, pushing every single person away until they all thought he was nothing but a cold, evil shell.

How wrong she'd been. How utterly hateful and horrid she'd been to him. As they stared at each other, she didn't see him as an Argonaut. Didn't see him as a fighter or even a hero, really. She saw him as a man. With the same humanity the gods both hated and envied. With the same frailties and faults she possessed.

She moved into him fast, burying her cheek against his chest and wrapping one arm around his waist while the other held the blanket closed at her front. He sucked in a surprised breath, but she didn't let go. Against her skin he was alive and warm, and her body jumped to life everywhere they touched.

Gods, this felt good. This contact. With him. Right here and now. How long had it been since she'd touched anyone like this? Since she'd let anyone get close?

"Wh-what are you doing?"

"Something I should have done days ago," she murmured against him, sinking in deeper. "I'm thanking you."

Chapter 13

HEAT PRICKED EVERY INCH OF DEMETRIUS'S SKIN. Against his chest, Isadora was warm and soft and so damn tempting, it was all he could do to keep his hands at his sides and his eyes focused on the wall across the room.

She snuggled closer, and when the tips of her breasts brushed his chest, his heart rate skyrocketed. Shards of electricity shot from his chest to his stomach, then lower. And ah, gods, this was too damn good for words and the one thing he'd wanted to avoid. He sucked in a breath and held it, afraid if he moved she'd slide even closer and he wouldn't be able to hold back.

She stood on the second step, not quite at eye level, but he felt her gaze boring into him when she looked up. "Am I hurting you?"

"No."

"Your teeth are clenched."

Were they? *Skata*. He relaxed his jaw. "I'm fine."

"Are you sure?"

Sweat popped out on his brow. "No."

The corner of her kiss-me mouth curled, just a touch, and he couldn't help it. His gaze shifted from the wall to her face. To her molten-chocolate eyes—as warm as the torchlight behind her, rimmed all in gold—to her small nose, her creamy skin, to the tiny mole on the right side of her succulent lips. Heat flared in his abdomen as his gaze ran over her face, and that part of him that had kept his distance for so long whispered, *Give in, just once.*

Her gaze settled on his mouth. And though indecision brewed in her eyes, the tip of her small tongue snaked out to lick her lips in a way that was so damn sexy he knew she couldn't have planned it. Even before she pushed up on her toes he knew what she was going to do. Just as he knew he should stop her.

He tensed as her mouth met his, tentatively at first. Soft as satin. But his reaction would have been the same if she'd slammed her lips against his and knocked him to the ground. Sparks lit off inside him, around him, everywhere, like fireworks exploding in the sky, blinding and consuming all at the same time. Until she was all he could feel, see, sense, know. Until nothing else mattered but her.

She broke the kiss way too soon. Uncertainty creased her forehead. She took a quick step back up the platform. "I…I'm sorry. I—"

The loss of her heat shifted his body into immediate action. He closed the distance between them, snagged her around the waist, lifted her off the ground, and drew her back against him. And then he lowered his head and kissed her. The way he'd wanted to kiss her for far too long. The way he should never ever kiss her. Especially now.

Her hand landed against his shoulder. She let go of the blanket, pressed tight between them, and moved her other hand to his chest. Electricity hummed where skin met skin, supercharged his blood, pushed the little bit of rational thought to the back of his brain. A sound came out of her as he licked the seam of her lips—a gasp, a groan, a sigh—and then she opened, drawing him deeper into something he wasn't sure he could climb free from.

Her tongue snaked out, hesitantly slid against his. As her fingers inched into the hair at the nape of his neck and she explored his mouth with her own, he had the distinct impression she'd never been kissed before. That she'd definitely never been manhandled. That he was getting the first taste of something sacred. And just the thought turned his pulse to a roar in his ears and sent desire careening through his veins.

He changed the angle of the kiss, delved deeper, wanting more. More of her sweetness, more of her warmth. More of *this*. He walked her backward until she hit the stone table, then brushed the clothes off and lifted to set her on the smooth hard surface.

She didn't let go of him. Not when he eased back and the blanket fell free of her breasts to land at her waist. Not when he pushed his way between her legs. Not when the hard length of his arousal brushed the juncture between her thighs.

A short gasp slipped from her lips as her fingers grazed the stubble on his jaw, then she kissed him back with ardor, picking up confidence with every stroke and lick and nip and sigh. He let her take the lead, told himself this was new for her and he needed to slow things down. But when her hands inched their way down his torso, settled on his hips and tugged him closer, he lost all ability to think.

He cupped the back of her head, pushed her back to lie against the table, then nipped his way across her jaw to her ear, where he drew her lobe into his mouth and bit down just hard enough to feel her shudder beneath him.

His lips found her neck, the soft column of her throat, back up again to that sensitive spot behind her ear. Her hair was silky against his face, her arms around his shoulders warm and encompassing. And the heat between her thighs where he pressed into her was enough to drive him mad.

"Oh…"

The sound of her voice trickled through his conscience, dimmed the roar just enough so he didn't take her right there and then. Realizing he was mauling her and that she might not be enjoying this as much as he was, he pushed up on his hands and gazed down at her.

Torchlight flickered over her features, made her hair look darker, her skin richer. Her lips were swollen from his mouth, her cheeks flushed and rosy. But her eyes… they were the key. He'd always been able to read her emotions through her eyes—fear, anger, despair, those were the things he saw when he looked at her—which was how he'd always known just what to say or do to get under her skin. But her eyes now weren't afraid. They didn't look upset. There was trust there. And behind it, the flare of desire that sent his libido into overdrive and his cock straining for release.

Her fingers drifted to his cheek, so soft and warm against his rough skin, it sent a shiver down his spine. But it was her whispered word that really did him in. "Demetrius."

How had this happened? How had she come to be lying here beneath him, looking up with those lust-filled eyes, whispering *his* name in the dark? Somewhere along the way he'd made one fateful, horrible mistake that was going to ruin everything, but even knowing that, he couldn't seem to pull away.

His gaze shifted to the long slender column of her throat, to the hollow at the base of her neck, to the fine bones of her shoulders and chest. Then lower, to the luminous skin stretched tight over her succulent breasts, just the size and shape to fit into his hand, his mouth, tempting him to take one sinful taste.

It was his fault she was here in this room naked right now. His fault she wasn't home safe in Argolea, where she should be. Every time he thought about what could have happened to her earlier with that Hydra…

"Demetrius," she whispered again.

"Tell me to stop," he managed. The fingers of his left hand skimmed where his eyes had just traveled—over her neck, to her collarbone, lower to trace the line of her sternum between her lush breasts.

She shuddered, drew in a breath as his hand drifted to her nipple, traced the outline of the areola, then gently brushed the tip. But she didn't pull away, didn't show any sign of fear. Curious, he looked back at her face and watched with rapt attention as her eyes slid closed and her back arched off the table. When she moaned in pure pleasure, he lowered his head and breathed against her ear, "Tell me to stop."

"No," she said on a breathy sigh that supercharged his blood. "No, don't stop. I like your hands."

"You shouldn't." His hand crept to her other breast. Her nipple puckered beneath his fingers. "You shouldn't like anything about me."

Her eyes fluttered open to focus on his face. "There's a lot I like about you. You just never let me see it before."

"You're seeing something that's not there. It's called trauma. Once you go home you'll remember why you hate me so much."

Her delicate fingers drifted to his lips, ran over the sensitive flesh until he wanted to sink his teeth into her skin and feast on her. "I don't hate you, Demetrius. I never did. I just didn't understand you."

"You don't now." *You never will*.

"I'm not so sure about that."

His heart stuttered, but he ignored it. He wasn't going to give in, wasn't about to let Atalanta have what she wanted. But a hundred years of denial left him too weak to put a stop to this as he should. And he was dying to know what she tasted like.

He dropped his head and breathed hot against her left nipple. "Tell me to stop."

"No stopping," she whispered again. "I want this. I want you."

Three little words snapped his restraint. He stroked his tongue over her nipple, felt the tremor run through her body, then drew her into his mouth. She moaned in approval, kicked her head back against the hard stone table, and raked her fingers through his hair.

He didn't ease up, moved to the other breast and repeated the action, drawing out her pleasure one suck, one lick at a time. When her back arched and her skin quivered, he let go and trailed a line of hot wet kisses down to her belly button, paused to run his tongue around the small circle, then continued his path downward, pushing the blanket aside as he went. Stopping only when the soft cotton fell away to leave her bare for his eyes only.

Gods, she was more beautiful than he'd imagined.

Pert breasts, small waist, trim hips, fine blond hair that formed a perfect vee drawing his gaze toward her sex. He remembered what he'd watched her do this morning, and unable to stop, he reached for her hand, brought it to his mouth, and sucked her first two fingers until they were coated with his saliva.

Her eyes fluttered open. Confusion marred her brow as she gazed down at him. He pushed her wet fingers back to her nipple and said, "Touch yourself."

Those brown eyes darkened to a rich chocolate. Hesitantly, her fingers grazed her nipple, traced the small circle, slid over and around as her eyes remained locked on his face. As she teased her breasts into stiff peaks, he ran his fingers up her inner thigh, over the winged omega marking on her leg, to her mound and into her downy curls.

She gasped but didn't push his hand away, and her eyes, so intense and focused on his, screamed *Touch me*.

"Just like that," he whispered, watching her face. "Don't stop."

She didn't, and neither did he. His fingers slid into her folds to find her warm and wet and willing. He groaned at the slick feel of her, circled and swirled until he found her clit, then applied just enough pressure to make her moan.

Her eyes, wide and lust-filled and so intently focused, left him light-headed. Achy. Burning with desire. He rested his thumb on her clit, searched lower, and slid one finger deep inside.

Gods, she was so tight. His cock throbbed. Her head dropped back, her eyes drifted shut. She brought her other hand up to massage her neglected breast while he stroked, searching for her sweetest spot. And when she arched her back and groaned long and low, he knew he'd found it.

The buzz between his ears overrode every rational thought. Lowering his head, he made one long, lingering sweep up her cleft, first with the tip of his tongue, then with the flat. Her entire body nearly burst off the table.

He held her down, did it again. And again. Taking her closer to the edge with every lick. She lifted her hips, moaned his name. He answered by stroking deeper with his finger, flicking her swollen nub with his tongue and finally suckling until she came in his mouth.

"Demetrius..." Her whole body trembled with her release and she grew impossibly tight around his finger. But the only thing he could focus on was the roar in his head screaming *Home*.

That one word echoed in his gray matter, settled in the center of his chest, and clamped on with the ferocity of a lion until he couldn't breathe. She reached for him. Desire built all over again, slammed into him at the speed of light, and swept him under.

He dragged her up against his body, closed his mouth over hers, kissed her hard and deep. She answered by moaning into his mouth, twisting her fingers into his hair, and pulling hard.

He needed her now, had to get inside of her. Couldn't think of anything else. But not here, not on this table. There were just enough synapses firing to remind him she was a virgin. At least there were for now.

He wrapped one arm around her waist, used the other to hook her legs around his hips. Her hot, throbbing sex rubbed against his cock, tightening it to painful levels.

He groaned, squeezed her sweet little ass, and snagged the blanket from the table just before he carried her to the sheepskin rug he'd taken from Jason's trunk and covered with blankets in the corner of the room.

She kissed him harder, deeper, like a woman starved. Her nipples rubbing against his bare chest was the most erotic feeling. Her hot sex straining against his fly had him seeing stars. Frantic to get inside her, he laid her out on the blankets, kissed her again and again, and pressed his hips into hers until they were both breathless and sweaty.

"Oh, gods, Demetrius."

The sound of her voice cut through the screaming need. He eased back just enough to stare down at her. At her swollen lips, her cheeks rubbed raw by his whiskers, her straining nipples, her heaving chest, her naked hips pressed against his, and finally her sex poised to take him deep into her body.

Him. Atalanta's son. The enemy.

She stared up at him with soft, trusting eyes. Eyes that didn't see the real him. Eyes that would be horrified if they ever did.

Sickness pushed up the center of his chest. And reality, harsh and way too real, pressed in until he couldn't breathe.

This couldn't happen. This could never happen. He had to get away from her. He never should have touched her. Never should have tasted her. Holy Hades, *what* had he been thinking?

He jerked to his feet, rubbed a hand down his face. Tried to quell the panic roaring in with the force of a jackhammer, but couldn't.

"Wh-where are you going?"

"Out. I gotta go…out."

She pushed up on her elbows. "But I thought—"

His mind spun with excuses. Latched on to one coherent thought. "That's your problem, Princess. You think too much. I changed my mind."

"But—"

He had to twist the knife. It was the only way he was going to break free. It was the only way he was going to guarantee she never let him near her again. And he knew the one way to do it, even if the thought sent bile sliding up his chest.

"Look, I figured you had a little more experience, but apparently I was wrong. I'm really not into the whole virgin thing. More work than it's worth."

Shock ran across her perfect face, followed by disbelief, then abject mortification. Her cheeks turned bright red and she drew the blanket up to her chin with fingers that shook just enough to tell him he'd done exactly what he intended to do. He'd made her feel as shitty as he did.

His chest squeezed so hard it was all he could do not to drop to his knees and tell her he didn't mean it. Instead he turned for the stairs and forced himself not to look back.

He didn't have to. He already knew what was on her face. The image of her pleasure was now branded into his brain along with the horror of what he'd just said to her. And it would stay with him for a long time. As long, probably, as the knowledge that his suspicions over the years had been right. One taste had confirmed it.

Isadora really was his soul mate.

———

Casey stood in the center of Demetrius's flat in the run-down Tenedos region of Tiyrns and turned a slow circle on the stained carpet as she looked from the barren table and chairs to the threadbare couch across the room.

The fact that Demetrius, one of the Argonauts, lived here surprised her. Especially when she contrasted this to the massive wood and glass house she and Theron shared in the forests outside the city. But what shocked her more than anything was the garbage that lined the cobblestone streets outside, the busted-out shop windows, and the abandoned belongings. And mostly, the ragged people she and the others had passed as they'd come here, watching them with wary eyes as if they were the villains in a B movie.

Argolea was a beautiful realm, a place of peace and safety. But the more time Casey spent here, the more she realized it wasn't Utopia. It had its own share of problems, its own class system and prejudices, just like any country. And, now she knew, its own poverty issue.

"I didn't realize Demetrius was such a neat freak," Cerek said from across the room. He ran his index finger over a side table and held it up to show Phineus not a speck of dust.

"Don't touch anything," Theron warned his guardians. He turned to Casey. "*Meli?*"

Casey shook her head. "It's like he never spent time here. I can't pick up enough of him to get any kind of feeling. Are you sure this is his flat?"

Theron rested his hands on his hips and frowned as he glanced around the empty apartment. Across the room,

Callia, Max, and Zander inspected something on the kitchen wall. "This is his listed place of residence."

A heavy bass echoed through the floor and Casey looked down at her feet, sure they were moving in time with the beat. The rowdy pub one floor below was not what she'd expected either. But then what did she really know about Demetrius to begin with?

"Look around," Theron said. "There's got to be something we can use."

They each fanned out, checking the small flat that consisted of only a near-empty living room, a closet-sized adjoining kitchen, one bathroom, and a bedroom that held no bed. There were no pictures on the walls, no clothes in the closet, nothing in the kitchen that said anyone lived here.

Just when Casey was sure they'd hit another dead end, Max's small voice from the bedroom called, "Here! I think I found something here!"

The bedroom wasn't large enough for all of them to fit inside. Casey pushed her way past Cerek and Phineus and stepped into the room, only to realize Max was all the way in the back of the small closet.

"What did you find?" she asked, moving around Zander to peer inside.

"A door," he said in an excited voice. "And there's a ladder in here. It's just like…"

Max didn't finish the sentence, and one glance at Callia's suddenly taut face told Casey it reminded Max of the door and ladder in Atalanta's prison that led to the small loft she'd kept him locked inside.

Max was a resilient kid, but ten years with Atalanta had left its mark, and Callia and Zander were working hard to make sure he felt safe here. Casey reached into the closet and pulled him out of the small space. "I'll go up."

As soon as he was free from the closet, Callia immediately pulled Max against her and mouthed *Thank you* over his head. Casey shot her sister a sad smile and turned to enter the closet, but Theron's hand on her arm stopped her momentum.

"*Meli*, wait."

"It's all right, Theron. Nothing's going to happen to me up there. I'm the only one who can get a feel for who has been there, so it makes sense I should go up. Besides, this is Demetrius we're talking about. He's one of your Argonauts, not the enemy."

"I'm not so sure anymore," he said with a scowl.

She squeezed his arm and stared into his eyes. And as she did, the connection they shared flared hot and bright. He might worry about her, he might order everyone around and frustrate her with his secrets sometimes, but she knew everything he did was done out of honor and duty and love. The last saved especially for her.

"I will be right back," she whispered.

He rested his forehead against hers. "Or I will bring you right back down."

Her heart warmed at his words and she smiled when he let go and nudged her into the closet.

Darkness closed in around her. The small door Max had found was all the way in the back of the claustrophobic space. As she moved to her knees and reached inside the wall to grasp the rungs of the old wooden ladder, she thought, *There's no way Demetrius could fit in here.*

She started to climb, one rung at a time. The only light that flickered into the tunnel came from below, but it wasn't enough to see even an inch in front of her face. A spray of dust from the rung she grasped hit her face and she coughed several times to clear the debris from her lungs.

"Are you okay?" Theron called up from the bottom.

"Fine." Cobwebs tickled her cheeks and she swiped at them with her hand, closed her eyes tight, and kept going. She climbed another five feet in the inky darkness before her hand hit something solid above.

"I've found something," she called down to Theron.

"What?"

His voice was muffled. He sounded like he was a mile away, but she knew she hadn't been climbing that long. Realizing what she was touching was wood, she felt around until she found what she thought was a handle. "I think…I think it's a door."

"Does it open?"

She slid her fingers into the loop handle, pulled, but nothing happened. Gritting her teeth, she pushed. A scraping sound echoed and then popped with a force that jerked her shoulder in the socket. Using what little strength she had, she pushed the door up and over. "I'm through!"

Brilliant light flooded her eyes and she slammed them shut to block the glare.

"What do you see?"

"I…Hold on a minute and I'll tell you."

Bracing her hands on the floor above, Casey climbed the rest of the way out of the hole and dropped back to sit. Her legs hung down into the dark tunnel below as she rubbed at her eyes and blinked several times to let them adjust to the light.

It took several seconds for her vision to clear, but when it did she realized she was in some kind of lookout room on the top of Demetrius's building. Square windows covered every inch of wall space in the octagonal room, rose at least twelve feet to form a dome above. A pile of blankets were gathered in the corner of the room, wrinkled as if someone had slept there. Books littered the floor, ones about weaponry and warfare and others with the Titan symbol stamped into the leather fronts. Clothes were stacked in neat orderly piles along the floor of one whole wall and laid carefully in boxes along another. Fresh weapons that looked just like the ones the Argonauts used were stacked in the corner. To her right she spied a large telescope that peered out over the rooftops of the city of Tiyrns. But what made Casey gasp, what tore the air from her lungs and sent dread pooling in her stomach, were the pictures.

Along every glass wall, taped up like snapshots, were dozens and dozens of pictures of Isadora. Close ups of her face, ones of her dressed in her traditional gowns, talking to the guards, staring out at nothing in the courtyard of the castle, reading a book on the marble steps. Over and over and over, images of her were repeated like a sickening pattern, with her as the constant focus, the obvious obsession of the person who called this room home.

"Oh, my God." Slowly, Casey pushed up to her feet.

"*Meli?*" Theron called.

"I'm okay," she called back, zeroing in on the telescope. "Don't come up here."

Throat thick, she crossed the room, rose on her tiptoes, and looked through the eyepiece. She felt Demetrius's presence in the room as soon as she touched the telescope, but she looked anyway, needing to know…hoping…

The image focused in the telescope and in a rush she realized she was staring into the windows of Isadora's suite of rooms in the castle. Isadora's disappearance, her abduction by those witches…it all suddenly made sense. "Oh, no."

"Holy *skata*," Theron breathed behind her.

Casey lurched around to see the horrified expression on Theron's face as he pulled himself out of the tunnel and stood in the middle of the room. He turned slowly, and as the enormity of what they'd found sank in, the horror quickly faded and was replaced with a murderous look she knew came from the very core of him.

"It doesn't mean—"

"It does. He's been planning this for gods only know how fucking long. And we let him." His hard jaw ticked beneath the smooth skin she loved to run her fingers and lips over. "Touch something, but make it fast. I don't want you exposed to this vileness any more than you have to be. Just tell me if he's Atalanta's son. I don't want you looking any deeper than that."

Her heart dropped, and with it the little bit of hope she'd held out for Demetrius's intentions. And though she couldn't help thinking that in spite of everything else it didn't really matter, she wondered what Theron would say when she told him Demetrius was also part witch. "I already did."

"And?"

She sighed. "And Gryphon was right."

Demetrius cast the crappy protection circle around the ruins with hands that shook more than he wanted them to.

Disgusted with himself, he stopped, drew in a long breath that did shit to ease the sharp pain in his chest, and stared up at the waning moon splashing sparkling white light over him and the uneven ground. The dim roar of waves crashing against the serene shore far below drew his attention and he stepped out of the circle and crossed over to the edge of the cliff that looked down to the beach below.

From so far above, this island seemed like paradise. The sand, the trees, the blue-green mountains. But when you looked closer you realized what kind of hell it really was. And wasn't it ironic that the creatures on this island weren't the real monsters? He was.

As if on cue, something down the hill in the valley behind him shrieked, and a vicious roar rose up as a deafening answer. He turned to look, thought of the Hydra he'd run from earlier. Of that Chimera he'd stumbled across. And wondered if they'd killed each other or if the battle still raged on. Then he wondered if things wouldn't be better all around if he just went down there and joined them.

"I can tell you how things will end," a female voice said from the direction of the cliff.

He whipped that way to find himself staring at an elderly female dressed all in white. She wore sunglasses, which seemed ridiculously absurd at this time of night, and seemed to float inches off the ground.

"The king will die," she said in a strong voice, "the Council will win, the monarchy will be absorbed, and the portals will be opened. And then Atalanta's daemons will spill into Argolea and destroy not only your realm but what's left of the Argonauts. Your mother will then turn her full attention to the human realm and devour as much as she can until she achieves total domination. Do you think the havoc her daemons are wreaking on humans now is bad? It will get worse. It will get much, much worse."

His mother. Just the reminder sent his blood boiling. He clenched his jaw and looked out over the sea, purposely ignoring the female's words.

He knew she was a Fate. Just as he knew he wasn't lucky enough for her to be Atropos, the Fate who cut the thread of life. No, his miserable life kept spinning on and he couldn't stop it. And this Fate was the one who kept drawing it out. "You set the torches. In the Hall of Heroes."

"I did," she said with a smile in her voice. "It's sacred."

He wasn't so sure of that. Nothing on this island was sacred to him. As he'd so obviously demonstrated with Isadora earlier.

He cursed himself again for that little fuck-up and dug his fingers into his palms until pain was all he felt.

She drifted to the ground, and when she landed he noticed her feet were bare and that her toenails were painted a bright neon blue. She moved to sit on a boulder across the ground, but her feet didn't make a single scuffing sound. "I hate these darn sunglasses, but I am not a creature of the earth." She gestured over her head with a wave of her hand. "Moonlight gives me a headache. You know the story of your forefather Jason, do you not?"

At his bored expression, she chuckled. "Oh, I do like you, Demetrius. You have always been one of my favorites."

"Lucky me," he mumbled.

"Atalanta blames Jason most of all for the fate she was dealt."

He flicked her an irritated look. "He let her sail on the Argos when the others didn't want her to. I'd say she's got a burr up her ass if she blames him for anything."

Lachesis sighed. "She does. More than you know. But that's not why she hated him. The truth is she fell in love with Jason on that boat. And he chose another over her."

He clenched his jaw, looked out over the water. "Medea." The witch. Once again, oh, lucky him. "Yeah, that ended well, didn't it? He dicked around with some Corinthian princess, decided to marry her instead of his supposed soul mate, Medea, and to settle the score Medea killed his children. I'd say that ended really well."

"Depends on how you look at it. One survived to bear your line. If history had traveled down another path, you wouldn't be here now."

"And the world would be a better place," he muttered. "Once again Hera's soul mate curse worked like a charm."

He didn't hear her move, didn't see her shift, not until she was hovering over the ground in front of him, her wrinkled face at eye level. He sucked in a breath and held it as she removed the sunglasses. And then he found himself staring into eyes as white as the moon, with only a pinprick of black right in the center.

"There is purpose in every life in this world, whether you decide to see it or not. Yes, Hera hated Heracles with a vehemence that knows no bounds, and because of it she cursed him and all the Argonauts with one soul mate each, the worst possible match who would torment their existence. But a soul mate is not a curse unless you let it be, Demetrius. Jason made his choice. For right or wrong, he chose his destiny. And now you must choose yours. There are no guarantees in this world save one. If you do nothing, Atalanta will win."

He looked past her. "I don't care."

Tingling at his cheek brought his eyes back level with hers. "Oh, I think you do. More than you've let on these long years. You're not weak, Guardian, contrary to what you think. What you fear most may just have the power to save you. But only if you let it."

Save him. Yeah, right. Not likely. But he still needed to save Isadora.

"Where's the holy ground on this island?"

She didn't answer, only smiled, which drew his frown deeper. The tingling dissipated along with her image, which faded into nothingness right before his eyes. Until he was staring out into the dark, all alone once more.

Perfect. Leave it to a Fate to speak in riddles instead of coming out and saying exactly what she means. Choices? What choice did he have? Where Isadora was concerned, he had no choice: he had to get her off this island before that weakness Lachesis thought he didn't have kicked into high gear and he forgot all the reasons he'd vigilantly stayed away from her over the years.

He headed back into the ruins. Tomorrow, no matter what, he was dragging Isadora out to look for holy ground. The portal drew energy from that which was hallowed. He knew there was holy ground on this island somewhere—it had once been inhabited, before the Argonauts gathered and dumped the monsters here—and he was bound and determined to find it. Now more than ever.

He made it as far as the doorway to the Hall of Heroes before he heard Isadora scream. His adrenaline surged and he cursed himself for leaving her—again. He grasped the blade at his back, tore down the steps, and skidded to a stop in the massive room.

She was alone. Just as she'd been the night before. Thrashing in her sleep. No monsters surrounded her. But something was definitely wrong.

Her eyes were tightly shut, the blanket twisted around her waist, her face scrunched in agonizing pain. Her screams brought the hair on the back of his neck to attention. But it was the two words he made out in her cries that burned in his blood.

Hades. No.

He glanced around the hall but didn't see anything out of the ordinary. A dream. She was dreaming again. Crossing the floor, he knelt on the blankets and set his blade on the ground at his side. "Stop, Isadora. Stop before you hurt yourself."

She didn't seem to hear him. If anything, her thrashing grew more violent.

He reached out to hold her still, and just as it had last night, his touch calmed her in ways his words never could. Her body trembled, but she stopped the fierce flailing.

"That's better," he whispered as he ran one hand

down her arm and tugged the blanket back over her bare breasts with the other.

"Don't want to go back to him," she mumbled, tipping her head his way.

A place deep in his chest squeezed tight at the thought of her anywhere near the sadistic god. "You won't have to."

He continued to stroke her arm until her trembling finally eased and she lay still. Drawing a deep breath he eased away, intent on letting her sleep and putting as much distance between himself and her naked body as he could.

She reached out for him, and the shaking picked up all over again. "No, don't leave. He's waiting for you to leave me."

Demetrius's head came up and he looked around the room as a new sort of wariness crept into his mind. Two of the torches had gone out but three others still burned near the heroes' chests. Shadows flickered and fell over this corner of the room, but there were plenty of dark corners to hide in. Enough shadow to mask anything that might lie in wait, mortal or immortal.

Trepidation tickled his spine. He scooted closer to Isadora and didn't protest when she curled into him and rested her head against his bare chest. This time, he didn't even think to. "I'm not going anywhere, *kardia*," he said softly as he looked out into the dark. "At least not yet."

Chapter 14

ISADORA SENSED DEMETRIUS'S PRESENCE EVEN BEFORE she rolled her head to the left and found him lying next to her, sound asleep on his side, his arms crossed over his middle and his head tipped her way.

Confusion hit first, followed by surprise. Why in Hades had he lain down next to her when he'd made it perfectly clear last night that he didn't want to have anything to do with her?

The things he'd said came back full force, as did the mortification when she remembered what she'd done with him. Rolling quietly away, she tugged the blanket around herself and crossed the floor toward the stone table in the middle of the room.

The clothes he'd brought for her were scattered over the floor. Cheeks heating with memories of his mouth, his hands, how she'd all but begged for more, she stooped to pick them up, then dragged them on. The shorts were baggier than she liked, but they were better than nothing. She didn't look at the table as she dressed, and when she was done she straightened, only to have a wave of nausea that came out of nowhere wash over her.

She reached out to steady herself. Breathed deep until it passed. Then wiped a hand over her damp brow.

That was weird. Yeah, she'd been a little stressed since she'd been here, and she wasn't eating like she should be, but she hadn't felt anything like that since...

Dread spiraled through her and she mentally ticked off days. At least seven had passed since she'd last been at the castle in Argolea. Seven days away from her sister. The ramifications of her situation suddenly hit full force. Regardless of what had happened here with Demetrius, she needed to get home before things turned dire for Casey.

Her gaze strayed to Demetrius, still sound asleep, and her temper kicked up. She moved around the table and flipped open the lid of the first trunk, looking for…she didn't know what. Just something that would help her get the hell off this island. Not his type? Screw him. *He* wasn't *her* type. Mean definitely wasn't her type. Why on earth had she ever thought he wasn't the bastard he'd always been back home?

She moved to the next trunk and silently rejoiced when she found a sword. She turned the blade in the low torchlight still burning from last night and figured it would do. It wasn't as big as the one Demetrius carried, but it fit better in her hand. Orpheus had taught her just enough to wield the damn thing, but she wasn't afraid now like she'd been before. She wanted off this damn island so bad she was willing to search for holy ground without him. She could open the portal on her own.

She turned for the steps, then belatedly remembered the spell book she'd seen in Jason's chest.

What you've got there is more powerful than you or your sisters realize.

Orpheus's words from days ago skipped through her mind. She looked down at the winged omega marking on her inner thigh, visible beneath the hem of her short shorts. Orpheus knew all about spells and drawing power, and if her link to the Horae gave her some sort of advantage where that was concerned, she was going to use it. No matter the cost.

She moved to Jason's chest, set the sword down in front of her, and pawed through the contents until she found the book. The cover was dusty and she blew until the grime cleared and the Helios symbol became visible in the aged leather.

"Aren't we curious this morning?"

Isadora's heart lurched into her throat. She dropped the book, grasped the sword, and whipped around with her arm outstretched. The tip of the blade stopped centimeters from Demetrius's bare chest.

His eyes flicked down to the weapon, then lifted to rest on hers. "I see sleep did you well. You obviously remembered all those reasons you hate me."

Her heart pounded hard against her chest. Relief that it was him and not some monster pissed her off more than if she'd found herself face-to-face with a Hydra. "No, I just remembered your legendary cruelty."

"Very good, Princess."

His low mocking tone clawed at her self-respect, heated her cheeks, and made her remember all over again what she'd done last night. With him. In this very room. The difference was, to her it had meant something. To him it was…

She didn't know what it was to him. A game, she guessed. One more way to humiliate her.

He took a step forward, until the tip of the blade pressed into his chest but didn't break the skin. "Do it. Now's your chance."

She wanted to. She was so angry she could barely

see straight. Every one of his cruel words over the years crashed in to remind her of the thousands of times he'd belittled her. And that, coupled with the newfound fear over her sister, made her unsteady. But when he moved closer still and the tip pushed deeper, she tensed. Her eyes shot to his chest and to the tiny droplet of blood that trickled down the blade.

Her stomach rolled. Yes, she was angry, and yes, she hated that he made her feel anything at all, but she didn't want this. She didn't want to hurt him just because he'd hurt her.

"Go ahead, Princess," he whispered. "All you have to do is push."

Her eyes lifted to his and though she saw indifference in his black irises, she also saw something else. Lurking deep, there lingered...regret.

Her heart stuttered, caught, and picked up speed as she stared at him. The night before spiraled through her memory again, only this time she didn't focus on his words. This time she focused on the look of desire in his eyes, the way he'd touched her, the fact he hadn't been able to get enough of her. And she remembered the way he'd told her to tell him to stop, and when she hadn't, how he'd finally let down his guard and taken her places she never knew existed.

He'd wanted her, and it scared the crap out of him. So much he'd reverted to his old ways to convince her he was the enemy. She lowered the sword, even as her heart raced beneath her breast.

"Your father's right," he muttered. "You're no leader."

His words cut to the heart of her, to every one of her insecurities and what she feared most in this world.

But she didn't dwell on them. For whatever reason, he was trying to make her hate him. And his baiting words belied his actions. Those were what she focused on.

She turned the sword and held out the handle to him. "Maybe I'm not. But I know a lie when I hear one."

For just a split second, confusion crossed his features. And then the mask came up again, the one that said *Fuck you* to the world and *Leave me the hell alone*. But that wasn't the real him. The *real* him was the one who'd rescued her more times than she could count, watched over her, and pleasured her so completely last night without taking a single thing for himself in the process.

His fingers wrapped around the handle of the blade, and as he lowered it to the ground, she knew she had a choice. To let him go on believing that lie or prove to him he was wrong.

She moved into him without a second thought. Just as she had last night, except this time she wrapped both arms around his waist and held on tight.

He tensed, and beneath her ear his heart rate kicked up speed.

The reaction warmed her, told her yeah, she was definitely right. He was trying to keep her away from him. Though she didn't understand why, she wasn't about to let him win. Last night *had* meant something to her. And it had obviously meant something to him as well, if it had spurred him into using his old cruel tactics on her again.

"Wh-why are you doing this?"

"Because you won't." She wiped the droplet of blood from his chest, then softly pressed her lips to the wound that was already healing. She wanted him to know she was serious, that this—*he*—mattered. Because something inside her sensed he never really had before.

Seconds passed as they stood frozen together. For a moment she thought he was going to draw away. And then the blade clattered to the floor at her feet and his large, warm hands landed gently on her shoulders and slid down her back.

Yes. *Yes*.

She closed her eyes, burrowed closer, and hung on to the feeling. The same one she'd experienced last night when he'd kissed her and touched her and made her want.

"Why are you so damn stubborn?" he whispered.

"Why are you so hell-bent on pushing me away?"

"Because I'm no good."

His blunt words drew her back, forced her eyes up. The dim light cast a warm glow over his face, made his skin look darker, the week's worth of beard thicker, his eyes blacker. But there was an odd sort of truth in his words. A truth she didn't understand but wanted to know.

What had happened to him? What had he done or seen in his two hundred years that made him honestly believe that he wasn't good enough for her?

"Good is a matter of opinion, Demetrius. And as far as I'm concerned, nothing about you isn't good enough."

"Isadora—"

She didn't want to argue. She knew she wasn't going to change his mind with words. What she wanted was the chance to make him believe.

She eased up on her tiptoes, slid her hand around his neck, and tugged. He was so tall she couldn't reach his mouth on her own, but he took the cue easily. And then his lips were on hers and all the hurt and anger from this morning seemed like a distant memory.

Gods, he tasted good, felt even better. Days ago she'd sat on that beach, watching him strap those boards together, scared to death about the prospect of being stuck here alone with him for any length of time. And now…now a part of her ached at the thought of their time ending before their bond had a chance to solidify.

His hands slid up to frame her face and he tipped her head, kissed her slowly and deeply and so thoroughly she felt it all the way to her toes. And when he eased back to look down at her with those stormy, emotion-filled eyes, she knew she was right.

"This," he said softly, "is a bad idea. You know that, don't you?"

She smiled because this—what was happening between them—was really the least of their problems on this island. "Why are you so convinced doom is lurking around every corner?"

"Because it usually is." A frown turned his lips. "Once you go home, this—I—will just be one giant regret you'll look back on and wish you could change."

And he was trying to prevent that. Suddenly, his words and actions last night and this morning made a whole lot more sense. "I doubt that."

"I don't."

She rubbed her fingers down the back of his hand and leaned into his touch. "Sometimes the most important things in this world are the ones we have to fight for. I don't believe you're not worth fighting for, Demetrius. Even if you do."

"*Kardia*—"

Her heart swelled at the term of endearment he used without even realizing it. And as she pressed her lips into his palm and kissed him gently, she had the strangest sense he'd called her that last night. After she'd fallen asleep. After he'd come back and lain down next to her.

Whatever doubt she'd carried slithered away. He wasn't the stone-cold bastard she'd always believed him to be. He was so much more. Now she just had to make him believe it too.

Easing back, she smiled again, then bent down and picked up the sword he'd dropped. "I'm hungry. And I was thinking after breakfast maybe you could give me a few pointers on my hand-to-hand combat."

One dark eyebrow lifted. "Planning on battling a few monsters today?"

"You never know. Considering my luck, it might not be a bad idea to be prepared just in case."

A sound that was half snort, half laugh came out of him. "Yeah, I've seen your luck. Up close and personal. Several times."

"My gods."

The humor fled from his face. "What?"

"You are gorgeous when you smile."

His eyes darkened. "I think—"

Too deep. Keep things light. When things got deep he reverted to his old ways.

"That's your problem, Demetrius." She reached up to pat his stubbly cheek. "You think too much. Let's go find that breakfast."

Her smile lingered as she headed for the stairs. She knew he was watching her with that perplexed expression, just as she knew he didn't have a clue what to do about her next. He thought he could push her around, treat her as he had before, and she'd react the same as she always had. Like a coward. Like a weakling. Like the shy little princess who didn't have a backbone. Well, things were different now, and he was partly to blame for the change sweeping over her. If the last week had taught her anything, it was that she was in control of her own destiny.

And he'd better watch out, because she had her sights set on him.

—◆◆◆—

He watched her carefully all day. And two things were clear to Demetrius as he followed Isadora on the narrow path down to the beach on the north side of the island. One, she wasn't afraid of him anymore. And two, she was growing weaker by the day.

Both of those realizations set off a tremor of unease deep in his gut. The first, because it meant he'd have to be more vigilant about keeping his distance from her, which, shit, he was obviously doing a bang up job of already, wasn't he? And second, because enough time had passed since her kidnapping that she should be recovered from whatever had happened to her in Thrace Castle and later with Atalanta.

Early afternoon sunlight bathed her in ribbons of gold. Her pale skin had taken on a warm glow from days in the sun, brought a rosiness to her cheeks that hadn't been there before, but she grew tired more easily now, needed to take breaks to catch her breath when they hiked, wasn't eating nearly as much as she should.

Granted, they hadn't had a real meal in days. Fruits

and the measly snack foods he'd gathered from that wreckage weren't cutting it for him either. As if on cue, his stomach rumbled. Which was why they were down here, on this beach this afternoon, with its reef-protected bay. So hopefully they could catch some dinner before heading back to the ruins.

But still…

What if those witches had cast some kind of deterioration spell over her? What if Atalanta had? Either way he needed to get her back to Argolea and to a healer who knew how the hell to help her.

Isadora stepped out of the waist-high grasses and onto the white sand beach, stopped, and took a deep breath.

"What's wrong?" he asked as he stepped around her, careful not to touch her. He'd purposely avoided touching her all day. Because whenever he did…yeah, this morning was a prime example of him losing his ever-loving mind. Whenever he did, he forgot all about his vow to keep his distance and sank right into her.

"Nothing," she said on a sigh. "I'm just enjoying. If you forget about everything asleep in there"—she nodded back toward the trees—"this place is really beautiful."

Not as far as he was concerned. It was like one giant Venus flytrap waiting to snap.

The contented smile on her face tugged at him, warmed his blood, reminded him what those lips felt like against his. To distract himself, he rolled up his pant legs and said, "Just pick a place to relax while I see what I can find."

She chose a rock near the edge of the small bay, sat, and pulled her knees up to her chest while he waded out and climbed onto a series of flat rocks twenty feet away.

Waves crashed against the reef farther out, but the water in the inlet only rose and fell gently, making it easy to see the sandy bottom and the sea life within.

Roughly ten minutes passed before he heard her sigh. "We searched all morning. How sure are you there's actually holy ground on this island?"

"Pretty damn." He zeroed in on a nice-sized fish, lifted his sword, and timed its movements.

"We searched half the island—"

"A third of the island."

"—and didn't find a single temple or even any sign of burial grounds."

The fish swam close and he tensed, ready to strike, but it darted away before he could thrust the blade into the water. He moved to another rock, one that was closer to the reef. "Any temples are going to be built on higher ground farther inland."

"Why wouldn't they be near the ruins?" she asked.

He caught sight of a big juicy fish with a shimmer of color across its side. "Because the ruins are more recent, built by the original seven after they rounded up all the nasties and stuck them on this island. The temples will have been built by early dwellers who inhabited this island before that. And as such they would have constructed their temples on the highest points so they were closer to Olympus. Burial grounds will be near there as well."

"Why didn't we search farther inland today, then?"

"Because we needed to get the lay of the land." And because farther inland was at least a day's hike, probably more. He wasn't about to take Isadora on a jaunt that long, especially not when she was so weak. It screwed with his plans, but a couple of hours out here with her today and he'd realized he had to wait until she was stronger before they ventured that deep into the island.

Which, yeah, created a whole other set of problems he just didn't want to think about yet.

"That's it, buddy," he whispered as the fat fish swam close. "Just a little more." He lifted the sword, ready to strike.

"I get the feeling you're holding out on me."

The sound of her voice right at his back caught him off guard. His sword stabbed into the water. He lost his footing and whipped around to grab her arm and steady himself. But his center of gravity was already shooting backward, and instead of stopping him from going in, she went down with him.

"Demet—!"

Her shriek turned to a muffled rumble as water rushed over his head. He quickly found his footing in the six or so feet of water, pushed his arms around until he found her, and dragged her up with him.

He gasped as he broke the surface, drew air into his lungs, and had a moment of *Oh, shit* when he realized he could have smacked her head against those rocks or ripped her arm out of its socket or—

Her laughter stopped him cold.

She wasn't unconscious. She wasn't injured. She wasn't anything but soaking wet and laughing hysterically in his arms. Her fingers sank into his forearms, his biceps, and then his shoulders as she pulled herself closer and the laughter died on her smiling lips. "That doesn't count as a rescue. Now I think you're just trying to pad your numbers."

Rescue? What—?

Water sluiced over her face, dripped down her forehead from her short blond hair, made her rosy cheeks glisten in the afternoon sunlight. And her eyes absolutely sparkled as she looked up and grinned as if he were the biggest idiot on the planet.

Before he could stop it, a smile wound its way across his lips as well. "I thought you said you were going to start returning the favor. That was a crappy save."

Her fingers felt like heaven sliding around his neck. He didn't think, simply reacted and let his arms twine around her waist and draw her closer to his suddenly aware, suddenly aching body.

"I'm new at this. You have to give me a little time to practice."

He couldn't help it, he laughed. And though the sensation vibrating through his chest felt foreign, it also felt…good. Damn good.

Her smiling eyes flicked from his down to his lips and hovered. And just that fast, heat erupted in his belly and spread lower, lighting up his groin and every nerve ending in his body.

Her soft little tongue darted out, licked her luscious lips tugged at his desire, and tempted him to give in. She shifted closer, until her perky breasts were pressed up tight against his chest and she was all he felt.

"*Kardia*," he whispered in a warning tone.

"I know," she whispered back, still focused on his lips. "It's a bad idea."

"Yeah." Gods, was that his voice? It didn't sound like him at all.

"And it'll be dark soon."

"Yeah, that too."

"Then we'll have to make this quick."

Her lips pressed against his before he could stop her, and that tongue slid inside his mouth without hesitation. He groaned at the taste of her, at the heat searing his body, at the near perfection of her skin pressed up against his, and gave in completely.

He cupped the back of her head, kissed her deeper, let himself go. Just for a minute.

When they both came up for air, desire darkened her eyes and need flushed her cheeks. A need he could sate right here, right now.

Her gaze roamed his features and she reached up to brush a lock of hair away from his forehead. The move was so tender, something in his chest unlocked right there in that water. Something he'd kept guarded and off limits his whole life.

"I think we might have scared all the fish away," she said.

"Maybe."

"Good thing I like fruit." She let go and swam back to the rocks before he could stop her, pulled herself up and out of the water. She shifted to sit on the rocks and wiped her wet hair back from her face. As she did, her nipples hardened in the breeze, pressing against the thin cotton tank to supercharge his blood all over again.

Oh, man. He was in over his head with her. Every minute they spent together drew him that much closer to her. Especially now, when she wasn't the least bit afraid of him. He needed to stop drooling over her body and remember his vow to keep his distance. Needed to remember what was at stake here.

The only problem? He was starting to forget just what that was. And why the hell he couldn't have her in the first place.

Chapter 15

Isadora leaned back against the wall in the great hall of the ruins and stared into the dancing flames of the fire Demetrius had built to cook the fish he'd finally caught. Stars twinkled overhead where the roof should have been, and not for the first time she marveled at the fact there was absolutely no smoke drifting up to the inky sky giving away their location to the monsters in the trees down the hill below. Maybe witchcraft wasn't such a bad thing after all.

"What are you thinking?" he asked from across the fire. He sat on a log he'd hauled in along with the rest of the firewood, tipped forward, his elbows perched on his knees as he stoked the coals.

She drew her legs up to her chest. Her belly was full, her head felt light, and something about the way he kept watching her told her tonight was going to change her life forever. She might not have her sense of foresight anymore, but she was a female. And as such she still had her intuition.

"I was just thinking that your little tricks come in handy now and then."

He smirked—gods, how she loved the way his lips curled with ease now—and went back to stoking the coals. She'd done that. She'd gotten under his skin and brought out that part of him he'd closed off to everyone else. It still amazed her this was the same *ándras* who'd scowled and snarled and berated her back at the castle.

"Not everyone thinks so."

"Do the other guardians know?"

"No. And it's none of their damn business."

She got that. "Then who—?"

"My father wasn't wild about my tricks."

It was the first time she'd ever heard him talk of his family. And though a small part of her realized it was strange he was suddenly being so open with her, she wanted to capitalize on it. "He didn't have the same gift?"

He harrumphed. "No. Akrisios abhorred all things witch related."

"Even though Medea was his ancestor?"

"*Because* Medea was his ancestor."

That struck her as odd. "Why?"

He shrugged, stared into the flames. "Because Hera tricked Jason into falling in love with Medea. She was one of the first soul mate curses. And in the end, when he realized he'd been duped, he left and she ruined him. She killed their children out of spite and revenge. All but one, who'd gotten away."

She'd heard the legend. She knew how awful the end had been for Jason. "But without her your father would never have lived."

"Doesn't matter. He believed Jason's line would have been stronger without her."

"What do you believe?"

He held his hands out, palms down, to stare at the Argonaut markings on his forearms. "I believe I was doubly cursed because of her."

The acidic honesty was unsettling, and as much as

she wanted to know about his lineage, she wanted to know more about his immediate family more. "What did your father do? When he realized you had her gift?"

"He freaked. Forbade me to light candles with a sweep of my hand or cast spells that turned the housekeeper's hair purple." She smirked at the images he painted. "And when I didn't listen, he used a *tria mastigio* on me."

Her brow dropped low. "What's that?"

"It's a short whip about this long." He held out his hands roughly two feet apart. "It's got three leather strips that stretch out from the handle and each one has a barbed end."

Shock rippled through her belly. "He beat you?"

"I had it coming."

"Because you performed measly tricks on the servants?"

He shrugged again. "He told me to stop and I didn't."

Her eyes rushed over his bare chest, a golden glow in the firelight. She'd noticed scars on his chest and back from battles and fighting, but nothing that indicated he'd been beaten. "Where?"

"Someplace no one would ever see."

She contemplated that, glanced at his legs covered by the frayed pants, and imagined all the muscled perfection of him scarred at the hand of someone else. His words were spoken so casually he could have been discussing the weather, but underneath she sensed disgust over what had been done to him. And a bitter hatred for a father who should have loved him and didn't.

"Where was your mother?"

He shrugged again and went back to stoking the

coals. "I don't know. They weren't bound. According to him, she seduced him one night and I was the unwanted result. Then after I was born she dumped me with him, and because I had the Argonaut markings he was duty bound to train me."

Not love him. She heard the sad truth in his words. "You don't have any siblings?"

"One. A brother. But he was raised in the human realm. And we're not exactly close."

"In the human realm? Where?"

He shrugged and eased back. "Closer than you think."

She wanted to ask more, but the hard line of his words told her he wasn't about to open that box of horrors—at least not yet—so she didn't push. Instead she said, "What he did to you was wrong, Demetrius."

"Why? You didn't like my tricks when you first saw them."

"That was before I knew you."

"You still don't know me."

His low voice set off a tingling in her chest.

"I got him back though," he said in a carefree voice. "We were in the human world. It was during my training. One day we were separated from the rest of the Argonauts and a pack of daemons came upon us. Completely outnumbered. He ordered me to cast an invisibility spell around us. I refused. After all, I wasn't supposed to." He stared down into the flames and his tone sobered. "It was the last thing he ever ordered me to do."

Her stomach clenched. She heard the unsaid words: he'd watched his father die. Could he have prevented it? By then he had to have been how old? Thirty? Forty? If it had been her, if she'd been abused that long, she may have done the same.

Even as the questions hit, something else registered. The way he kept flicking his eyes at her, judging her reaction, checking to see if he'd shocked her. As if he *wanted* to shock her. But why? After everything that had happened between them, why would he want to scare her into thinking he was—

And then it made sense. Being cruel hadn't worked. Telling her no hadn't done anything but push her closer to him. He was as attracted to her as she was to him, and it scared him so much he was reverting to his last defense—shocking her into disgust.

She pushed up from the ground and walked around the fire before she could rethink her action. He looked up with a wary expression as she approached.

"The fire's almost out." She held out her hand. "Let's go to bed."

His gaze dropped to her hand and he swallowed hard. "I—"

Oh yeah. He was definitely pulling out all the stops. Well, so was she. For the first time in her life she knew exactly what she wanted and she wasn't afraid to go after it. "No more excuses, Demetrius. Come with me."

Hesitantly, he slid his fingers in hers and let her pull him from his seat. They walked through the secret doorway into the stairwell together. The door sealed behind them. As she led him down the spiral staircase, her heart thumped so hard against her ribs she was sure he had to hear it. But she wasn't afraid. If anything, she felt powerful.

The Hall of Heroes was dark when they reached the bottom step. He waved his hand and lit one torch along the far wall. Shadows and light played over his face, over his muscular body as she pulled him toward the make-shift bed. And when she turned to face him, she saw a thousand thoughts and emotions rush over his features.

She moved into him, until the heat and life of his body swirled around her and settled deep in her soul. "I want to be with you," she said softly as she rested her hands on his rock-hard abdomen.

His fingers landed gently on her shoulders, the brush of his skin against hers igniting a rush of hormones deep in her body. "*Kardia*—"

"Here, tonight. Like last night, only this time I want you." His eyes darkened at her words. "All of you, Demetrius."

"You can't. Your father—"

"It's my choice to make. I've waited a long time. And tonight I choose you."

"*Kardia*."

The emotion in that one word, *my heart*, stole her breath. Grasping the hem of her tank top, she tugged it over her head. The worn cotton landed against the dirt floor, but his eyes didn't follow. They were locked on her. Right where she wanted them.

"Touch me," she whispered.

His hand came up and she held her breath in anticipation as his fingertips grazed the swell of her breast. Her nipples puckered and a heavy ache settled between her legs. He stared at her breast, licked his lips, moved a fraction of an inch closer.

"*Yes*."

"I…" His eyes darted up to her face. "I think you should get some sleep."

He was gone before she could stop him. Before she even realized what had happened. "Demetrius?"

But he didn't answer. The only sound was his bare feet hitting the stone steps. Then the whoosh and slam of the great door at the top of the staircase.

Confused, she tried to figure out what she'd done to make him run. Every time something happened between them, he pulled back at the last minute. Almost as if he was afraid she wouldn't really want him if he got too close.

Her gaze swept over the room and landed on Jason's chest. *Every time, he pulls back.*

Her skin grew hot and damp as an idea took root.

A leader goes after what he wants. He doesn't take no for an answer. Her father had said that so many times it was ingrained in her mind. Wasn't it time she started acting like the leader she was destined to become?

Yes. Yes, it was. And what she wanted right now was Demetrius.

———

Demetrius stalled as long as he could. Until the chill night air sent gooseflesh all over his skin and he shivered in the great hall. The fire had gone out. He was too tired to light another and didn't think he had enough magick left inside to cloak the smoke this time anyway.

Okay, this was stupid. She had to be asleep by now. He'd just go in, grab a blanket, and slip right back out. She'd never even know he was there.

As he moved soundlessly down the steps to the Hall of Heroes again, he called himself ten kinds of stupid. He was an Argonaut. Hiding from a female. From the weak little princess, for crying out loud. If the guys ever caught wind of this…

He let that thought die as soon as it hit. The rest of the guardians were never gonna know any of this. Especially not anything that had happened between him and Isadora last night.

Dumb, dumb, really fucking dumb. That was him in a friggin' nutshell.

The chamber was quiet when he reached the floor. The torch across the room still flickered and burned, but it had died down and now cast only a dim glow over the heroes' trunks. Quietly, he moved toward the dark corner where Isadora—hopefully—was sacked out.

His night vision sharpened. He caught sight of her lying still on her side, one leg angled out in front of her, her hands tucked up near her face. She'd kicked the blanket off and the orange tank top rode up on her abdomen, giving him a nice view of her toned hip and creamy skin. The shorts, though baggy, were the perfect length to showcase her shapely legs and the winged omega marking on her inner thigh. Warmth gathered in his stomach as his eyes ran over her body.

Go. Now. Leave.

With a muffled grunt, she rolled to her other side. He tensed, afraid he'd awakened her, but when he looked closer he realized her eyes were still shut and her chest rose and fell in rhythmic succession. And that's when he noticed her breasts pushing against the strained cotton. That warmth turned to a white-hot burn that pooled in his groin. Hard.

Don't just go. Run.

He hesitated. What if her nightmares came back? If

he was all the way upstairs, he'd never hear her scream. She didn't have the nightmares when he was close, so maybe if he just slinked down in the corner…

It wasn't an excuse to get close to her, he told himself. He reached for an extra blanket from the floor, but as he drew near, her sweet feminine scent enveloped him and cut through what was left of his gray matter.

The corner would be uncomfortable. And the bed he'd made for her was easily big enough for two. He'd slept on it next to her last night and nothing had happened. And gods knew he was more tired tonight than he had been then. If he was going to leave her in the morning to hike around and find holy ground, he needed at least a few hours of rest.

Careful, so as not to wake her, he eased in beside her, tucked his arm behind his head, and lay down on his back. She lay facing him but—thankfully—was still asleep.

He released a breath. Closed his eyes. And fell instantly asleep.

~~~

The light rain hit Apophis's cheek with a sting he felt deep in the fleshy tissue of his skin.

Not *his* skin by birth, but his now by possession. He lifted the young Argonaut hand attached to this new body and ran it across his smooth, unwrinkled cheek. Power coursed through his veins. He was strong, not just mentally anymore but physically. And he was no longer confined to that bloody prison. He couldn't wait to test out this new body in every way possible.

The portal popped and sizzled as it closed. Crossing

the frozen ground, he tried to remember what those useless Argoleans had called him. Grant? Grim? No, Gryphon. Yes, that was it. The Argonaut Gryphon. Playing the character wouldn't be so important now, but shortly it would be. And this was the perfect time and place to experiment with his newfound persona.

Northern British Columbia. A frozen wasteland as far as he was concerned, but a means to an end. He narrowed his—Gryphon's—eyes and peered through the trees toward the main house some three hundred yards across the clearing. Night fell fast this far north, but the hour was late. Atalanta would already have dismissed her warriors to their barracks. The archdaemon resided with her in the house, but before turning in for the night he'd make a sweep through the outer buildings and check in with security.

Oh, Apophis wasn't a fool. He'd done his research, especially since siding with Atalanta. The archdaemon was the one he needed. It would know what she had planned.

He hovered in the shadows. Waited. Watched. Planned. Did Atalanta think she could outmaneuver him? Outthink him? She did not have a clue about what lingered deep inside him. From the edge of his vision he watched lights dim in the last bunkhouse, then the archdaemon close and lock the door behind him before turning for the field that led back to the main house.

Apophis's muscles vibrated. Magick gathered in the depths of his new hands. The power burst from his fingers and struck with deadly precision, taking the daemon down with one blow to the back of the neck that paralyzed his limbs within seconds. He was on the daemon before it could gasp, grasping its jacket and dragging the body into the trees so the security detail roaming these woods wouldn't be any the wiser.

He dropped the daemon at the base of a great pine tree, knelt down so he was face-to-face with the monster. "Your mistress took something that belongs to me. I want it back."

Recognition swept over the archdaemon's features and his eyes widened in horror. "You…you're not… a guardi—"

"No," he whispered, leaning even closer until the glow from his eyes turned the daemon's face, the ground, even the base of the tree just to his left, a blinding shade of blue. "I am your worst nightmare. And I can make you feel pain like you've never known. Tell me where the princess is and I will let you live."

The daemon trembled with such force, Apophis knew it realized death was but a breath away. "I…she…"

"Your fate will be a thousand times worse with me than your mistress, I guarantee it. The princess. Now. I grow tired of this conversation." He held up his hand for effect and watched the daemon's eyes grow even wider as it stared at the power pulsing inside his newfound skin, the blue glow backlighting the bones and veins and tendons within.

The daemon swallowed hard. "In the human realm. An island. She sent them to…Pandora."

"Who else is with her?"

"An Argonaut. At-Atalanta's son."

Apophis's brow lifted. Now this was an interesting bit of news. The conniving, vengeful goddess had a son who was an Argonaut. He wanted to know just how that had transpired, but a stronger curiosity left him wondering if the princess knew what evil lurked alone with her on that island.

The ramifications of what Atalanta might very well have done slammed into him. He needed the princess alive, with her virginity intact, if he had any hope of gathering the strength he needed to open the portal and draw his army of witches through with him.

"Pandora, you said?" He glared down at the shaking daemon. "How did she send them?"

"Th-through a portal."

Of course she had. One of the many benefits to being of the god class. You could poof people and things around the earth wherever and whenever you needed. Including yourself. But lucky him, even though he wasn't one of them—yet—he had the Orb of Krónos. And that was almost as good. Soon, it would be better.

"Thank you, daemon." He pushed to stand.

"Wait. My arms. My legs."

The left side of Apophis's—Gryphon's—mouth turned up. "You won't be needing them where you're going."

True horror erupted over the daemons features. "But you said—"

"Never trust a warlock." He blasted the daemon with one shot of energy, which severed its spinal cord. The daemon gasped; blood vessels burst in its eyes and skin. Its airway constricted until it choked to death on its own fear.

From across the barren field, a roar sounded in the main house, so strong it shook the forest where Apophis stood staring down at the lifeless daemon. Atalanta had just discovered her archdaemon was no more. He smiled as he reached inside his coat for the Orb resting against his chest from a chain around his neck.

"I'm coming for you, Princess," he whispered as he placed his index fingers over the sign of the Titans branded into the center of the disk. The portal opened before him. "And this time, you will be mine forever."

Chapter 16

HIS SKIN WAS ON FIRE.

Demetrius groaned at the flames rushing across his abdomen and hips. Something burned hot against his chest, but it didn't hurt. In fact, it felt good. Way too good. And that—oh, shit—that feathery sensation against his throat was pure heaven.

Electricity zinged along his nerve endings. Blood heated his groin, tightened his balls. The whispery-soft caress moved up to the base of his ear, then over his earlobe. Warm air blew across his neck to send shivers up and down his spine.

His whole body tensed, arched. Something silky brushed against his chest, his abs, the pressure point between his leg and torso. And his cock grew impossibly hard, just that fast.

"I've always wondered…"

Dimly he heard the sexy female voice, followed by what could have been a gasp or a sigh, he wasn't sure which. Either way, though, he knew that voice. It was the same one he'd been fantasizing about for years. The same one he'd been trying to keep his distance from the last few days.

Soft, sweet lips pressed against his belly button, his lower abs, the tendons in his groin, wiping away all thought. He groaned all over again, even as his hips lifted as if they had a mind of their own. But the dream, fantasy, *whatever* it was, didn't cooperate, because no matter which way he twisted he couldn't seem to get what he wanted.

"*Skata*." His cock absolutely throbbed. He wanted those lips *there*. Wanted her. Finally. Even if she was just a dream.

Quiet laughter rose up from his toes. Followed by pressure around the base of his cock as delicate fingers encircled his shaft. But what caught his attention wasn't the wicked touch. It was the fact the sound hadn't come from him. And it definitely wasn't in his mind. Where it was supposed to be.

He froze. His heart rate shot up. And very slowly he peeled his eyelids open to look down his body. His very *naked* body. Except—holy Hades—how the hell was he supposed to focus on anything when that small hand was stroking the length of his erection from base to tip, squeezing the head until he moaned, then repeating the caress all over again?

Ah, gods.

In the dim light he watched Isadora's mouth curl in a tempting smile. She leaned over his hips and pressed her lips against his groin again. Her hot little tongue snaked out just before she sucked the tender flesh. Heat erupted everywhere, spiraled in, and gathered beneath her hand, still squeezing, stroking, sliding up and down until he thought he'd die.

"I want to kiss you here, like you did to me. Is that okay?"

Okay? She wanted to know if that was *okay*? It was better than okay. It was exactly what he wanted. Everything he'd dreamed of. Paradise and Heaven and the Elysian fields all rolled into one.

He couldn't tear his eyes away from what she was doing. Had no idea what the hell had happened and why she was doing it, but he definitely didn't want her to stop. "*Kardia*…"

Carefully her lips found the base of his cock. His whole body tensed. Anticipation thrummed through his veins. She slid her hand higher, making room for her mouth. He groaned again as she kissed her way up his length, and arched his back.

"I'll take that as a yes," she whispered.

Her sweet little tongue flicked out to taste the tip. Pleasure arced through his pelvis, radiated outward from that one spot until it was all he could focus on. His whole body tightened as she ran her tongue along the flared underside. Then she lifted her desire-filled eyes to his and sank down until he filled her mouth.

"Ah…*fuck*." His head fell back as he gave in to the sensations. She explored slowly, with her tongue, her lips, licking him gently, then sucking, shallow at first then deeper as she grew more confident. He lifted his hips instinctively, lowered them, showing her what he liked. She caught on fast, her sucking picking up strength and speed until he thought he was going to black out. But it wasn't until she scraped her nails over his balls that he realized how gone he really was.

He needed to touch her. Wanted to drag her up his chest and dive into her hot, wet mouth. Wanted to feel her whole body tense in release as she came around him.

Frantic, he reached for her, only to realize his arms were pinned up near his ears and that he couldn't move them.

Hold on, wait. That wasn't right. That was—

She took him all the way back in her throat, cutting off his thoughts. He groaned as his climax steamed closer.

Yes, yes, *yes*. His cock grew impossibly hard in her mouth.

Just before he erupted, she let go. The pressure eased from his cock and balls. Her lips slid over his abdomen, his chest, then to his throat, where she nipped and kissed and drove him wild all over again with her warm breath and succulent lips.

"I want you, Demetrius." She kissed his ear, his cheek, worked her way across to his mouth, just like he wanted. Then her lips were on his, parting his, drawing him into her wet heat, blocking out everything but the need to feel her. Everywhere.

She eased back, smiled. Her eyes were a warm chocolate that glistened in the flickering light. He swallowed hard against a rush of emotions that pummeled his chest from every direction. "Wh-where did you learn to do that?"

"I read. A lot."

She *read*? Bloody hell, just what kind of books was she reading up in her castle suite?

Her hard little nipples brushed his chest. The downy hair between her thighs tickled his abdomen. As her hands came up to frame his face and she leaned down to kiss him again, he realized she was naked. Naked and straddling him right this second.

"*Kardia*...Let my arms go."

"I can't," she whispered between kisses.

"Why not?"

"Because every time you get me worked up like this, you pull back. I don't want you to pull back this time. I just want you."

He tried to clear the sex fuzz from his mind. Clenching his hands, he discovered they worked but his arms were definitely pinned back, and even though he was ten times stronger than her he couldn't free them. While she moved to kiss his jaw and neck, he glanced from side to side, then spotted the spell book from Jason's trunk on the floor beside their makeshift bed.

The little vixen had cast an immobility spell on him. His eyes shot back to her blond head, moving down his chest, back up to nip his ear. He should be pissed. He should be irate. But as her lips found his again and her hand slid down his torso to grip his shaft, he couldn't help but think that was the most erotic thing he'd ever known. His entire body trembled with renewed lust.

"Ah, gods," he whispered as he turned himself over to her touch. She stroked him, kissed him, drove him absolutely wild with her fingers and mouth and the heat of her compact little body. "I'm so going to hell."

"At least I won't be alone then."

He knew her words were meant as a joke, but they hit. Hard. Smack in the center of the chest. And when nothing else broke through his raging need, that did.

His conscience pushed in, dragged reality on its heels. Yeah, he wanted her to the infinite power, but this… this was wrong. This couldn't happen. This was exactly what he'd been trying to avoid for too damn long.

"Isadora. Wait."

"No more waiting. I've been doing that my whole life." She eased back. Her inner thighs brushed the outside of both of his. Her fingers found his cock again and she drew her hand up slowly, the sensation so intense it messed with his resolve. "I'm tired of waiting, Demetrius."

"You don't know what's at stake here. You don't know—"

"Yes, I do," she whispered. "I know exactly what's at stake. Everything."

He sucked in a breath as she settled over him, brought the tip of his erection so close it brushed her folds. "Let me…" *Oh, fuck*, she was so wet. Wet and hot and *his*. He swallowed hard. "Let me pleasure you."

"I intend to."

Panic rushed in as she ran his shaft over her clit, sighed in pleasure, and did it again. If she kept that up, he wasn't going to be able to stop himself. "Let me use my mouth."

She stilled over him, and her rich brown eyes lifted to rest on his face. In that one look he saw she wasn't quite as confident as she seemed. "Don't you want to make love with me?"

Something in his chest cracked open. The sound of her voice, the look in her eyes, the feel of her body ready to take him in…he wasn't sure what caused it. But it cracked open wide, right there for her. "Yes," he whispered. "Gods, yes."

"Okay, then," she said in a decisive voice as she moved back into place.

"Wait." She was rushing things. She wasn't ready. If she was bound and determined to do this, he wanted to make sure she enjoyed it. And he needed to cool himself down about ten thousand degrees before that happened so he'd stay in complete control. "Slow down. Let my arms go. Give me a minute to—" The head of his cock found her opening, and she sank down, just until he was buried inside her one reaching inch.

She gasped and froze. He groaned, closed his eyes, and clenched his jaw to the point of pain to keep from thrusting up into her scorching heat. She was so tight he was afraid he'd come right there and then if he did. "*Kardia…*"

She braced her hands against his chest. Her fingernails dug into his skin. And when she didn't move a single muscle, only breathed deeply above him as if she were in pain, he finally realized she wasn't nearly as close to going over the edge as he was.

His eyes popped open. He focused on her face, scrunched up tight. Then remembered that she was the heir to the throne. And female. And as such, by law, untouched. In every sense of the word. "Isadora—"

"You're bigger than I thought," she gasped. "Just… just give me a minute."

"Let my hands go."

"I…can't," she managed. "I'm…having a little trouble remembering the words of the spell right now."

He glanced at the book, just out of his reach. Knew he wouldn't be able to reach it without hurting her more. "Then give me your fingers."

"My—?"

"Your fingers. Put them in my mouth."

She looked at him as if he were insane, but listened and eased her weight onto her left hand. Slowly she brought her right hand to his mouth. He sucked her index and middle finger, got them good and wet, then pushed them from his mouth and said, "Touch yourself."

She hesitated; a flush rose up in her cheeks. And he couldn't help thinking how sexy she was right this minute. His command embarrassed her, but she wasn't embarrassed over the fact she'd tied him up, seduced the hell out of him, and now held him on the brink of sexual frustration. Nodding encouragement, he watched with rapt attention as she carefully lowered her hand, found her clit, and rubbed a slow, easy circle around the hard little nub.

"Oh…" Her body relaxed one muscle at a time. Her eyes slid closed. Her perfect face transformed from taut and scared to flushed with desire all over again. And as she worked her fingers over herself and he felt her growing wetter with each brush and stroke, he lifted his hips, a fraction at a time, deeper with every thrust, until finally he was seated fully inside her and her hips rested against his.

She opened her mesmerizing eyes, seemed startled at what he'd done. "That didn't hurt."

Not for her. But he had a feeling for him the pain was just beginning. "Let my hands go."

She glanced at his arms pinned back behind his head and bit her lip in indecision. "Let's wait on that."

Her mouth closed over his and her tongue slid out to tangle with his. She moved her hips slightly and gasped into his mouth and he realized, *bloody hell*, she wasn't gonna let him go.

The knowledge superheated his blood, juiced him to within degrees of boiling. His cock jerked inside her, teased by what was possibly the most erotic moment of his life. But he couldn't—wouldn't—give in. This was about her. He could grit his teeth and ride it out. And when she finally came around him, he'd pull out before it was too late.

Her hips picked up speed. He watched her ride

through heavy-lidded eyes, marveled at how beautiful she was, slicked with sweat and on the verge of orgasm.

He wanted this. He wanted her. He was inside her—finally—and every stroke and glide…it was the most incredible feeling in the world.

"Gods, yes. Ride me, *kardia*. Let me have your mouth." She answered with a kiss that stole his breath and pushed his hips higher, searching for that spot he knew she needed rubbed most. And when she tensed, when she pulled back and stared into his eyes and he saw she was close, he thrust harder, deeper, until she braced her hands against his chest, cried out her pleasure, and came all around him in a soul-deep tremble he felt everywhere.

"Demetrius…"

That was his name on her lips. That was his body deep inside hers. She was *his* soul mate and the only person in this world or the next that mattered.

The sound of her release, the feel of her tight channel gripping him, pushed him over the edge. His climax slammed into him, raced down his spine, and exploded before he could stop it. Brilliant white light erupted behind his eyes, pierced the center of his chest, until the blackness he lived with every day had nowhere to go but out. In that one moment, he knew what it felt like to be home.

She collapsed against his chest, drew deep, shattering breaths. He kissed her temple, her hair, whatever he could reach, and tried to keep reality at bay.

But the afterglow didn't last long. Now that his need was slaked, the truth rushed in on a tidal wave. Thanks to his never-ending weakness, nearly two hundred years of doing the right thing had just crashed and burned. And because of Hera's curse, he'd most likely just given Atalanta exactly what she wanted.

~~~

Isadora's heart raced so fast she thought it might sprout wings and fly right out of her chest. Sprawled over Demetrius, she breathed deeply and tried to steady her quaking pulse. "Wow…that was…I had no idea."

"Let my hands go."

She smiled, her entire body more relaxed than it had ever been, and pushed up to look down at him. Only when she saw the furrow in his brow and the way he was staring at the ceiling as if he couldn't wait to get away from her, wariness pushed out the euphoric feeling and replaced it with dread. "What's wrong?"

"I want my arms back. Now."

This suddenly wasn't the same guardian who'd rocked her world only moments before. No, this one looked a whole lot like the Argonaut who'd despised her for years.

You're letting your insecurities get the best of you. He hasn't changed. He still wants you.

She brushed aside the worry, gently disengaged, and reached for the spell book on the floor. "I didn't really think it would work. I've never cast a spell before. But Orpheus said my link to the Horae might give me extra abilities."

"Yeah, I'll just bet he did," he muttered.

"Here it is." She found the right page, flipped over onto her knees, and reached for his arms while she chanted the words. Even before she finished the last phrase his arms came down, he rolled away from her, and lurched to his feet.

Torchlight flickered over his toned body. Desire stirred deep in her core as she watched him grab his pants from the floor and wondered how long they had to wait until they could do that again. But then he straightened and the light hit his side just right. And she saw the fine white lines—the scars—all across his hips, his buttocks, and his upper thighs.

She gasped. And the conversation earlier by the fire flashed in her mind.

He pulled up his threadbare pants and buttoned them. "Books, my ass. Just what the hell else has Orpheus been teaching you?"

Her gaze lifted from his legs to his face. And she was startled at the disgust she saw in his features. Features that only moments ago had been flushed with passion and need. "I don't understand—"

"It's an easy-ass question, Princess. He's been teaching you fighting techniques and witchcraft, that much I already know. What have you been giving him in return?"

She gave her head a mental shake, struggled to keep up with him. Earlier he'd used her virginity as an excuse for why he didn't want her. Now he was insinuating she wasn't as pure as she was supposed to be? "What's going on here? I thought—"

"Fucking A." He raked his hand through his hair. "You really are clueless, aren't you? You play the virgin exceptionally well."

Her back came up, and the warm fuzzy feeling she'd been gliding on was yanked out from under her feet. A chill spread down her spine, and suddenly aware of her nakedness she reached for the blanket and pulled it over herself as she stood. "I *was* a virgin."

"But not untouched, like you're supposed to be."

The repulsion got through loud and clear. She swallowed hard, and images of the Underworld—of Hades—threatened to pull her down, but she pushed them away. "What changed all of a sudden? You seemed to enjoy—"

"You really are stupid sometimes, aren't you?"

Her head snapped back, as sharp as if he'd slapped her. Okay, yeah, he was having regrets now that all was said and done, but that was a low blow, even for him.

He bent down and whisked the spell book from the floor without looking at her. "Did you even bother to *ask* why I've been keeping my distance? No, because you're not that smart. If you had, I would have given you the skinny. That warlock you were shacked up with had his band of merry witches cast a fertility spell over you when you were at Thrace Castle."

His words didn't immediately register. But when they finally did, her eyes flew wide. "But I'm not…Argolean females are only fertile once every six months and my cycle ended not that long ago. I can't be—"

"It's called a spell, *Princess*. It kinda negates everything else, including biological cycles. And like you proved with your little bondage scene here, spells work pretty damn good."

No. It couldn't be. That's why he kept pulling away? Because he didn't want her to wind up—

She could barely even think the word. Her skin grew hot and perspiration dotted her forehead as she swallowed hard and turned a slow circle. She was the heir to the throne, single, and now…

Her mind spun with the ramifications of what they'd just done. But instead of being horrified, something warm burst in the center of her chest. If she did end up pregnant, it solved her father's problem. There would be a legitimate heir to the throne, one the Council couldn't overrule. And with Demetrius as the father—one of the strongest bloodlines of all the Argonauts—the Council wouldn't stand a chance at trying to overthrow her reign. Her father had originally picked Demetrius as her mate himself! Okay, yeah, they weren't bound yet and that created a problem in their patriarchal society, but only if someone found out about her pregnancy before the official ceremony. And so long as they kept quiet—

That warmth zipped along her nerve endings and the worry and stress of the last year began to dissipate. She turned to tell Demetrius exactly what she was thinking and faltered.

His jaw was a slice of steel beneath his skin, his eyes hard black slabs of coal. There wasn't a single thing friendly about his face, and the way he watched her with loathing, she knew there was no way he found the possibility she could be pregnant "okay."

"You don't want to have a child with me," she said softly, more to herself than to him.

"Why the hell would I?"

She winced. Okay, that stung.

"I thought I made it perfectly clear when your father tried to order me to bind myself to you that I wanted to have nothing to do with it."

Oh, he had. She remembered clearly the way he'd freaked out that day in her father's chamber, with all the Argonauts in attendance as witnesses. He'd said he'd rather choose death than be bound to her. And obviously he'd meant it.

A searing ache lit off in her sternum as if he'd taken his blade and stabbed her right through the heart. All the warmth and happiness she'd felt earlier leaked out through that one spot. Her throat grew so thick she wasn't sure her voice would work, but she had to know. "So this…here…us…It was—"

"One big fucking mistake. Just like I knew it would be."

The pain slowly dissipated until there was nothing left. No happiness, no excitement, no anger either. She'd given him something she'd considered sacred and he'd warped it into the cruelest moment of her life. And all she could think now was *What did you honestly expect?*

He grabbed his blade from the ground and brushed by her. But was careful, she noticed, not to touch her in the process. "I need some air."

He left her standing in the middle of the room, the blanket clutched to her chest, the torchlight flickering over her face and the remnants of the first heroes. It had to be close to morning but she didn't feel awake, energized, revived. She felt dead inside. As dead as she'd felt after she'd been with Hades. Except then she hadn't known what it was like to be happy. Or semi-happy. Or on the *verge* of happiness. Now she did.

Chapter 17

ISADORA SWIPED AT HER CHEEKS, TOSSED THE BLANKET to the ground, and found her clothes. Her hands shook, but she ignored the quiver and dressed in record time.

Forget fantasies of happily ever after. Forget trying to be what everyone wanted her to be. She'd been telling herself the last few weeks that she was the new Isadora, not the doormat she'd been for so long. Now was the time to prove it.

She moved to the ancient trunks and flipped the lids up one by one. Fatigue settled in and she paused to take a breath. It wasn't from lack of sleep and too much activity, she told herself. It was being away from Casey that was weighing on her, nothing more. And that was one more reason she was determined to find a way home, today.

Renewed determination rushed through her veins, gave her something solid to focus on. She found a small dagger with a black handle in Jason's trunk, stuck the tip into the belt loop of her shorts, and moved on to the next. After gathering what few items she thought might come in useful out there and slipping what she could into her pockets, she closed each lid, took another deep breath, and headed for the stairs.

She blocked the glare of the sun with her hand as she pushed the heavy door open and stepped into the great hall. No sound met her ears, so she figured that meant

Demetrius wasn't anywhere close. Which was a good thing. She most definitely didn't want to talk to him, now or ever, if she could avoid it.

Pebbles pushed into the soles of her bare feet, but after several days on this island walking around barefoot, she was getting used to the pain. Moving onto the front steps of the ruins, she scanned the horizon. *Any temples are going to be built on higher ground, farther inland.* That made sense. Early dwellers would have wanted their temples as close to Olympus as possible, just as Demetrius had said. A sliver of pain sliced through her heart at the thought of him but she pushed it away, pulled up her temper instead. It, if nothing else, was the fuel she needed to get through this day.

She stepped onto the grassy soil and pulled up short when she heard a voice. A vaguely familiar voice, calling from the bottom of the hill.

She squinted. Tried to see through the bright morning sunlight, then gasped when she caught sight of Gryphon climbing the slope steadily toward her.

Gryphon. No. It couldn't be. The last time she'd seen him, he'd been...

Bare feet forgotten, she took off running down the hillside. The dagger slapped at her hip. The small bag of rocks in her pocket jostled against her thigh as she jumped over stones and twigs sticking out of the ground. Excitement bubbled up in her chest because they weren't on this island alone after all. Gryphon was here. Gryphon was *alive!*

She pulled up short just before she reached him. Breathed deep and smiled wide. She wanted to throw herself into his arms, but she didn't want to knock him backward down the hill or shock the hell out of him. He was used to the shy, reserved, docile princess, not the take-charge female she'd become.

Her chest rose and fell as she worked to slow her breathing. She took in his white shirt, not the slightest bit dirty, his crisp pants, and shiny black boots. And her smile faltered when she focused on his face—his wind-swept blond hair, his clean skin and natural coloring, not tan like Demetrius or sunburned like her. He looked like he'd just stepped off a boat onto the island, wasn't the least bit worn and frazzled from days stranded here.

"Gryphon," she said when she found her voice. "What—? How did you—?"

"There you are, Princess. I've been looking for you."

Her eyes narrowed. He sounded the same, looked the same, but something was off. Something she couldn't quite pin down. A trickle of wariness coursed through her veins. "How did you get here? What happened to—?"

"I came through the portal."

"Portal? You came through a portal? Onto this island?"

"Yes." He held out his hand. "Come with me and I will take you there."

That wariness kicked up a notch. "Why can't you just open a portal home right here?"

He glanced to his right. "Something about this island…interferes with my abilities."

Okay, that made sense. Demetrius had said this place was as screwy as the Bermuda Triangle. And consid-ering Demetrius couldn't open a portal, it made sense Gryphon wouldn't be able to either. A little of her anxi-ety eased, but not completely. "How far is it?"

"Not far. Come with me."

He motioned, and her eyes cut to his hands. Big, strong, guardian hands. They were the same hands he'd used to unchain her from that bar in Thrace Castle where the witches had strung her up, and yet...something still felt off. Her gaze slid to his face. To his eyes. To his blue eyes that seemed brighter than before.

"What the hell...?"

She flinched at the sound of Demetrius's voice. Her heart rate kicked up and a flutter lit off deep in her chest. But instead of the rush of warmth his voice had elicited the past few days, today all the sound did was blast a hole the size of a crater in her stomach.

She clenched her jaw. Pushed down the humiliation and pulled up her anger. He'd made it more than clear how he felt about her: he didn't. And she wasn't about to play the blithering idiot, especially not in front of Gryphon.

She squared her shoulders. "I'm definitely ready to go home, Gryphon. Let's go."

But Gryphon was no longer focused on her. His gaze skipped past her to land on Demetrius. And something hard settled in his eyes as he focused on the Argonaut at her back.

"Gryphon," Demetrius said with what Isadora knew was also a hint of wariness. He stopped just to her right. And it was all she could do not to turn and glare at him. "How the hell did you get here?"

Gryphon's gaze shifted to her, then back to Demetrius. "I've been looking for the princess."

"You? Where are the others?"

Silence. Then, "Also looking. I came across a daemon who told me where to find her."

"A daemon?" Isadora asked. That wasn't right. How would a daemon know they were here? Demetrius had told her some kind of signal had crossed when he'd opened the portal from that field. Instead of taking them home, it had landed them here by mistake.

Gryphon's bright blue eyes shifted her way, but before he could answer, Demetrius said, "The Argonauts are here? On this island?"

"No," Gryphon answered, swinging his gaze back to Demetrius. "But I'm sure they will be quite pleased when I return with the princess."

Demetrius was silent beside Isadora. From the corner of her eye she saw his clenched jaw, his scrutinizing dark eyes. He wasn't happy Gryphon was here. Was it because he knew she was going to leave with the blond Argonaut and he was upset he wouldn't have another chance to belittle her? Or was there something else going on?

"Come, Princess," Gryphon said, holding out his hand to her again. Only this time his eyes never left Demetrius. "The portal is waiting."

"Isadora—"

Yeah. Like she was about to listen to Demetrius? Not a chance. She stepped toward Gryphon, but she didn't take his hand. "I'm ready."

"Isadora," Demetrius said again. "Wait—"

"No, thank you," she tossed over her shoulder as she brushed past Gryphon and headed down the hillside. "I'm done waiting. Really done waiting. Especially for you."

Demetrius didn't answer. And she didn't bother to look back to see his expression. But she was almost sure she heard a soft chuckle at her back. One that definitely hadn't come from Demetrius's mouth.

―∿―

Something wasn't right.

Forget the fact Gryphon had been near dead the last time Demetrius had seen him. Forget the fact there was no way Theron would ever have sent him off to search for Isadora alone. Forget even that there was something freakin' wrong with Gryphon's eyes and his speech pattern was off, like he was trying too hard to sound normal. What stuck like a burr in Demetrius's brain was the knowledge there was no way in Hades a daemon would know the location of Pandora, except maybe the archdaemon, Atalanta's right-hand monster. And he sure as shit wouldn't give it up unless he was on death's doorstep.

One Argonaut alone couldn't overpower the archdaemon. He was too big, too strong, and with enhanced abilities from Atalanta, not a simple grunt that could be easily taken down. Gryphon showed no signs of battle, not even a scratch. And he claimed a daemon had simply *told* him where they'd been sent? Demetrius wasn't buying it. Not for a minute.

He followed along behind Gryphon, curious and cautious about where they were heading. It was more than coincidence that Gryphon had put Isadora in the lead and placed himself between her and Demetrius, even though she didn't have a clue where they were heading. With every step they took, Demetrius's apprehension kicked up and his Argonaut senses went on high alert.

They walked on sunlit paths for at least an hour, deeper into the island's topography. He knew Isadora was tired, but she didn't slow her pace. And she didn't once look at him, didn't once acknowledge he was there. Then again, why the hell should she? After the way he'd treated her this morning, he was lucky she hadn't hauled off and stabbed him with that dagger hooked in the waistband of her shorts.

He slapped a tree branch out of his eyes, looked past Gryphon, and focused on her legs. Then her short shorts. Then the round curve of her ass, which flexed and moved under the baggy cotton. Heat rippled through his torso, slid down to his groin. This morning he'd wanted his hands there, right where he was focused now, urging her on and helping her ride. His mind flashed back to the image of her moving over him, the look of sheer pleasure on her face. And that heat went white-hot just that fast.

"*Skata*," he mumbled. Like he needed that vision now? She hated him again, just as he needed her to. It was stupid and useless to remember any of what had happened early this morning. Even more pathetic to wish things could be different.

Gryphon glanced over his shoulder, but there wasn't curiosity in the other guardian's too-bright eyes. There was malice. And very clear hatred.

Oh yeah, something was definitely off. Gryphon was the easygoing Argonaut. Everyone's pal, the non-shit-stirrer of the group. Though they'd never been best buds, they certainly hadn't been enemies. But right now? Right now it was crystal clear that's exactly what they'd become.

They moved out of the trees and headed for a small knoll covered in emerald green grass. As they drew close, Demetrius realized it wasn't simply the steadily increasing slope of a hillside. There was something underneath all that soil and grass, as if a structure of some kind had been buried long ago. Sure enough, as they moved closer and Gryphon called to Isadora to stop, Demetrius caught sight of an opening in the rocks near the base of the hill that looked like an entrance to some kind of tomb.

"What's down there?" Isadora asked, eyeing the stairs that disappeared into darkness.

"A temple," Gryphon answered. "To Demeter."

Isadora's gaze swept the landscape. This high there was nothing but hills and grasses as far as the eye could see. They'd moved out of the trees and were now surrounded by open sky. "Out here?"

"Are you implying this location isn't sufficient for the earth mother?"

"I didn't say that—"

"Good," Gryphon replied with zero humor. "Because Demeter knows a thing or two about purity. Unlike some people." He motioned her to follow him. "We go inside. The portal is below."

Gryphon moved down the steps, rounded a corner, and disappeared from view. A reddish yellow glow erupted in the tunnel, indicating he'd lit some kind of torch, which struck Demetrius as wrong once again. Had he brought matches with him? How would he have known he'd need them?

Isadora took a deep breath and moved toward the opening, but Demetrius caught her by the arm. "Wait."

She rounded on him so fast, he didn't expect it. But the sharp point of the dagger pressing into his side registered loud and clear. "Don't touch me."

He let go of her arm, held his hands up in surrender. Yeah, still seriously pissed. And could he blame her?

"I won't," he said calmly. The fire in her dark eyes was something he hadn't seen before. Even yesterday when she pulled the sword on him in the Hall of Heroes, there'd been a softness there, a vulnerability. Now, thanks to him, that was long gone. "Think carefully about this, though."

"About cutting you? I don't have to. If you ever touch me again there will be blood. And this time it won't be your choice, it'll be mine."

He didn't doubt that for a minute.

She lowered the dagger and moved one step down into the tunnel. The light was now gone and nothing but blackness beckoned, but Gryphon couldn't be far ahead.

"Isadora," he said quickly, panic pushing in before she disappeared. "I didn't mean about me. I meant about Gryphon. He isn't—" He stopped himself, unsure what the hell to say. Was he overreacting? Or was he simply jealous she so easily trusted Gryphon when she now hated him?

He didn't want to face that realization, so he went with his gut. "Things aren't always what they seem."

She glanced back over her shoulder. But her eyes were just as hard and cold as they'd been before, when she'd held the dagger to his side, not the soft chocolate brown he'd looked into as they'd made love. "And sometimes they are. I've learned that the hard way. You made sure of it."

She moved down into the darkness, turned the corner, and was gone.

Alone, his heart thumped hard. In his attempt to

protect her from himself, he'd done what he'd set out to do. He'd finally broken her. And as a result he'd turned her into someone who was as cold and unfeeling and hopeless as he was.

Regret and a need to make amends pushed him forward with a fierce determination. He stepped toward the opening, but instead of moving down into the darkness himself, his body hit an invisible shield with a crack that stole his breath and knocked him back to the ground.

What the…?

"Gryphon?" Isadora called from inside the tunnel.

Demetrius rushed to his feet, tried again, met nothing but a wall of air as strong as granite.

"Isadora!" He slammed his hands against the force.

"Gryphon?" Isadora called again. Realizing he could hear her as clearly as if she were beside him, Demetrius stopped fighting, placed his hands on the invisible wall, and listened. "Where are you?"

"I'm here, Princess."

"I can't see you," she called.

"Oh, you will," Gryphon replied with a chuckle. "Come closer and I will light the way."

A scraping sound echoed, like metal against rock, and Demetrius imagined the dagger on Isadora's hip hitting the narrow passageway. His chest grew tight. The scraping eventually died down, and he heard Isadora's voice again.

"Where…where are we?"

"In the main chamber. Where it will begin."

Begin? Oh, shit. Demetrius's anxiety pushed higher.

"Why can't I see you?" she asked. "I thought you had a torch."

"Oh, you'll see me, Princess. Very soon you will see all of me. In my true form, as you did before. Even though you are no longer a virgin, you are still of great use to me."

The dead voice, the too-blue eyes, and the hunch in Demetrius's gut all finally coalesced. And even before the blue glow erupted from the tunnel to spill out the archway and illuminate every stone and pebble, Demetrius knew he'd been right.

Isadora gasped. "Oh, gods."

"Not a god," Apophis said with that same menacing chuckle that belonged to Gryphon. "Not yet. But with your help, Hora, I will be soon."

Chapter 18

ISADORA SWALLOWED HARD AS SHE STARED AT THE blue glow coming from Gryphon's eyes. Her situation had just tanked. Big time.

No, not Gryphon's eyes. Whatever was *inside* Gryphon was definitely not Argonaut. Or Argolean. Or even human for that matter. It was…evil.

"I told you that you hadn't seen the last of me."

Apophis.

Panic jumped to heart-thumping fear. Isadora had no idea how the warlock had taken Gryphon's body, but she wasn't about to ask. She darted a look back down the darkened tunnel.

"Oh, your guardian won't be joining us," Apophis said in that same flat voice that sounded like Gryphon but wasn't. He took one menacing step closer, drawing her attention back his way. "Your escape from Thrace Castle was disappointing, but even I must admit…it brought other, more interesting opportunities to light."

He reached inside his crisp white shirt and drew out the medallion hanging on a chain around his neck.

The Orb of Krónos.

Oh, shit. The round medallion was as big as a man's palm, with four empty chambers and the sign of the Titans stamped into the center of the metal. She looked into Gryphon's—Apophis's—eyes. In that moment, every-thing made sense. And in that moment, mythological monsters, daemons, and even Atalanta were the least of Isadora's worries.

The Titans were the ruling gods before the Olympians. When Zeus and his brothers had risen up against them in their quest for power, Krónos had crafted the Orb and left it in Prometheus's care and told him to use it only if things became dire. Zeus and his brothers won the war and the Titans were imprisoned in Tartarus, where they still reside today. But Prometheus, a champion for humankind, had known the horror the Titans would unleash in their need for revenge if they were ever set free, so he scattered the four elements across the earth and hid the Orb from the temptation of both man and god alike. Peace had settled over the earth and for thousands of years the Orb had ceased to exist. Until, that is, it was rediscovered.

"The fact you are no longer a virgin is disappointing, Hora, but something I'm able to work around."

Isadora stepped back, slowly reached for the dagger at her hip. She knew Orpheus was the one who'd found the Orb, but she had no idea how Apophis had gotten it. The wearer of the Orb not only benefited from enhanced powers, but if he found the four elements and placed them in the empty chambers he would then possess the ability to release the Titans from their prison in Tartarus. And a power like that…Not only would it make him stronger than Zeus; if used, it would initiate the war to end all wars.

Apophis continued his advance. "There's nowhere to run, Princess. And this time, no one to save you."

No one but herself.

Her pulse beat like wildfire beneath her skin as she

waited for him to draw close. She'd seen him bleed. She knew he was mortal, even if he was blessed with an unnaturally long life. She had to hope that in Gryphon's body he was still as vulnerable as he'd been back at Thrace Castle. Hopefully more so.

The blinding blue glare coming from his eyes intensified as he stepped near. No, he wasn't Gryphon, not anymore. And he had absolutely no regret over what he planned to do to her.

She braced her feet against the floor. Clenched her teeth. When he was only a foot away, feeling confident and smug that she was the weak female he could easily overpower, she grasped the dagger at her hip and swung out with all her strength.

The blade caught him across the chest. He hollered and jumped back. Bright red blood seeped through the white cloth to stain his shirt. She didn't give him time to regroup. From her pocket she drew out the rocks she'd taken from Jason's trunk and threw them into his face, intent on distracting him while she attacked with the dagger again.

But the rocks never hit their target. Their momentum stopped midair to hover and swirl inches from his face. His eyes grew wide; the glow in the room increased. His gaze narrowed in on the stones circling in the air at eye level.

Magick rocks. Some kind of ancient Medean spell was keeping them from falling. Realizing this was her best chance for attack, Isadora charged.

Her dagger caught Apophis in the side. He roared, whirled her way, and swung out with his arm. The back of his hand caught the side of her face. She sailed through the air and the dagger flew from her grip. Her body smacked into a column near the temple's entrance.

Pain shot through her torso, exploded behind her eyes. She slid to the ground, gasped in a breath, rolled to her side, and tried to push up. When she looked up, though, Apophis wasn't coming after her as she expected. His roar shook the walls as he thrashed out with both hands at the rocks that shot out of the air to pummel him from all sides.

Her gaze swept over the floor, searching for her dagger, but she couldn't see it. She ground her teeth against the pain and pushed herself up, only to realize she was trapped. There was no way for her to get by Apophis and make it back through the same tunnel she'd come in.

That left hiding.

She wrapped an arm around her aching ribs, grabbed on to the column with her other hand, and righted herself. A quick look at the rock walls of the cavern told her that inside the temple was her best bet.

She stumbled through the enormous entrance, looked right and left. Ahead a raised stone altar was surrounded on all sides by marble benches and two large fire-burning torches that illuminated the space in an orange-red glow. A gigantic statue of Demeter graced the far wall. Along the periphery were small archways, no taller than a child, which looked like they led off into secret rooms or chambers.

Please, gods…for once be on my side.

She hobbled to her right, dropped to her knees near the first archway, and slithered through the space. The tunnel inside was dark, but one glance forward and she realized it went nowhere. Just ran the length of the wall and opened ten feet down to the next archway.

"Hora!"

Apophis's enraged voice brought her around. She scooted as deep into the tunnel as she could, past the last archway into a corner where no light shone. Drawing her legs in, she tried like hell to become invisible. Her heart pounded hard against her ribs and her labored breath was all she could hear in the dark. How long until he found her? How long until he made good on his promise to "work around" the fact she was no longer a virgin? And what—oh, gods—had happened to Demetrius outside these walls?

Wait. The portal. Excitement leaped in her chest. She was on holy ground. If she could pull herself together enough to focus, she should be able to open a doorway home. She closed her eyes, pictured Argolea, tried to concentrate. Nothing happened. Frustrated, she tried again. But her racing heart and what was happening outside this small tunnel were all she could focus on. That and the sharp stab directly in the middle of her back.

A scraping sound echoed in the tunnel as she shifted along the wall, and then she felt something drop to the ground behind her. Reaching back, she wrapped her hand around a small round shape.

She drew the rock in front of her, opened her hand, and looked down. There was just enough light coming through the closest archway to see what she held wasn't a simple rock. It was a diamond. As big as a coin and as clear as glass. And etched into the back wall of the stone, staring up through the shine as if it had been forged by magick, the mark of the Titans.

Her eyes grew as she stared at what she held, hardly believing it could be real. A loud crash echoed. Her gaze darted up just as the entire wall between her and discovery came tumbling down. Isadora yelped and covered her head with her hands. Debris crashed all around her. Before the dust settled, a hand latched on to her ankle and pulled hard.

A scream tore from her chest. She tried to grab rocks and stone, anything solid. But the hand was too strong, the force too great. She flipped over onto her stomach and grappled for something to stop her.

"I'm losing my patience with you, Hora!"

Apophis flipped her to her back. His irises glowed brighter than before, smothering the whites of his eyes until there was nothing but a blinding glare that illuminated the entire room.

"Trying to steal something that belongs to me, warlock?"

At the sickeningly familiar deep voice, Isadora's heart lurched in her throat. For the span of several seconds she didn't breathe, didn't move, couldn't think. When her muscles finally clicked back in gear, she turned her head toward the front of the temple where a man—*being*—dressed in worn denim jeans and a short-sleeved black T-shirt sat perched on the altar, his legs so long they reached all the way to the marble floor.

"Hades," Apophis growled.

"We've been through this before," Hades said in that jovial tone Isadora knew was anything but friendly. "Nice body, by the way. Step up from your last one." He winked, straightened. "What's mine is mine and what's yours is mine. And you know I don't take kindly to you trying to take my stuff."

Hades's piercing black gaze swung Isadora's way. Bile churned in her stomach as he stared at her as if he could see through every last stitch of clothing she wore. And in the silence each of his sick acts and wretched promises came back tenfold.

"You look shocked to see me, little queen. But we both know why I'm here, don't we?"

She swallowed hard. Didn't dare move. Had she thought Apophis was the worst of her worries? Oh, *skata*. She'd been so naïve.

"This does not concern you, Hades," Apophis growled again. "Go back to the Underworld and leave us be."

Hades's gaze snapped to Apophis. Their eyes locked, and some kind of other-being communication passed between them. Isadora flipped over, tried to scoot back, but met solid rock. The two held each others' stare so long, Apophis's mouth snapped closed and he visibly trembled. But it wasn't until sweat broke out on the warlock's brow that Hades finally broke the stare-down, hopped off the altar, and said, "No, I don't think I will."

He turned toward Isadora and held out his hand. Dressed as he was, with his jet-black hair tousled and his features relaxed, he almost looked handsome. If you ignored the fact he could grind you to dust with barely a flick of his pinky finger and enjoy it along the way. "Come, little queen. We have much to discuss."

Isadora didn't move. But behind Hades, Apophis couldn't contain his fury. His eyes grew so wide they nearly consumed his face, and that brilliant glow turned into a blinding spotlight that forced her to blink and duck her head. From the corner of her vision she watched as he lifted his hands, just as he had in the castle when he'd slammed Gryphon with some sort of energy force. But Hades whipped around before the blast left the warlock's fingers, and with one outstretched hand his powers hurled the warlock clear across the temple, out the main door, and blasted him into the far wall of the cavern.

Rocks crashed down, a loud roar erupted. Hades crossed the wide floor in three easy steps and was out the door before Isadora clued in to what had happened. A blood-curdling scream tore through the cavern, followed by a pop and sizzle, and then there was nothing but silence.

Fear rooted Isadora in place. She knew this was her chance to get up, to run, but she couldn't move. And when Hades stepped back into the temple, his expression set and jaw locked, she knew she was too late.

"Isadora!"

Demetrius's frantic voice from somewhere close brought her head up and around.

Hades glanced to the ceiling and frowned. "Damn heroes. Always trying to save the day." He crossed back to her, held out his hand. "He can't interrupt us, so don't worry. Now. The earth element, please."

His request shocked the voice out of her. "The…? I don't know what you're—"

"Talking about? Oh, I think you do. The diamond. In your hand. What was once coal and came from the earth and is now so much more."

Oh, shit. "How do you—?"

"Know about it?" he asked, finishing her sentence again. "You made a deal with my treacherous wife, little queen. Remember? She brought you to me so you could save your sister's soul. In exchange you gave her your power of foresight for one month. That one month has just begun."

The deal. Of course that's how he'd known. But still…

"She…she saw that I'd find it?"

"Mm-hmm. She sees everything now. Thanks to you."

The diamond dug into her palm as she tightened her fist around the jewel. So that's what Persephone was after. For one month she'd be able to see where each element was located. Now all she'd need was the Orb of Krónos and she'd have the power to release the Titans from Tartarus, bring about the war to end all wars, and have the strength to control what was left.

"Where…?" Her voice was nothing but a whisper. "Where is she?"

"Tied up at the moment. Literally." He knelt, rested his forearm against his knee. "You see, I know the bitch well. And wife or not, I'll not allow her to control something that should have been mine thousands of years ago."

His. He was talking about the human realm. His brother Zeus controlled the skies, his other brother, Poseidon, the seas. While he had free reign over the Underworld and all its levels of horror, he couldn't control the human realm. And that's what he obviously wanted.

"Why…why didn't you just come and take it before I got here?"

Disgust crossed his features. "Because I can't. Thanks to Prometheus, the ass."

When Prometheus scattered the elements, he must have put restrictions on how they could be found, Isadora realized. Or stolen.

"The only plus to the whole damn situation," Hades continued, "is that the wife will be spitting nails by the time I return to Tartarus. And I like her much better when she's hell on wheels, don't you?" His licentious grin churned her stomach. "Oh, don't look so horrified. I know you'll like her soon enough. Once you get used to her…tastes." His gaze traveled the length of Isadora's body. "And now that you're no longer a virgin, I can't wait to tell her she won't have to be so…careful with you." His soulless black eyes slid back to her face and held. "Just imagine what lies in wait for you when she returns to her mother for the summer and you're finally mine."

Bile rose in her stomach. She remembered clearly what she'd witnessed in the Underworld. The depraved acts he'd made her watch. Though he technically hadn't laid a hand on her, he'd wanted her to see and hear and remember what he had planned for her when she was his. And that memory still haunted her dreams and cast a shadow over what was left of her life.

"Of course," Hades said, leaning toward her, "I may be willing to make a trade. If you'd rather keep your soul instead, that is."

"A t-trade?"

His hollow eyes sparked. "Your soul for the diamond in your fist."

Her heart skipped a beat. "You…you'd give me my soul back? Just that easy?"

"Of course that easy. A deal is, after all, a deal."

Hope flared and a future, a real future, beckoned. But even before warmth spread up her torso, the flames of life grew cold and dark.

She couldn't give him the element. Apophis had the

Orb, but it was only a matter of time before Hades figured that out and took it back. Judging from the little power play he'd put on here minutes ago, taking the Orb back would be a snap. And if Persephone found the other three elements before the month was up…then the world as they knew it would be destroyed.

"It's a simple choice, little queen. Your soul. Yours once more to do with as you please. And I will be nothing but a memory."

"Isadora!" Demetrius's voice echoed from somewhere close again. A banging sound followed. Her eyes strayed to the dark ceiling of the temple, covered in gold-plated tiles.

Hades's gaze followed. "I'm getting really tired of his interference. If it weren't for that damn soul mate curse, I'd have lured you out days ago."

Soul mate curse? Her brows snapped together. "Lured me out? I don't—"

"Understand? Yeah," Hades said with growing impatience. "I remember that phrase well." He pushed to stand. "Now, little queen, I've had enough chitchat for one day. The element. And I'll be on my way."

Isadora's head felt like it might just explode. But one thing was clear. She was all that stood between Hades and the end of the world.

She pushed up to her feet, wobbled but caught herself. Her legs ached, her side was sore, and she was covered in dust. But she lifted her chin and squared her shoulders just the same. "No."

"What did you say to me?"

Her heart raced, her limbs trembled. He was at least seven feet tall and next to him she looked and felt like a child, but she held her ground. "I said no. I'll not give it to you. Not freely, at least."

His eyes went from coal black to bloodred, and before she could even gasp, his entire head exploded in a ball of flames. The face of a fire demon shot out from the blazing inferno. "Who are you to challenge me?"

The roar of his voice lifted the hair away from her face as if a great wind had swept through the temple. She gripped the diamond tighter and knew even if it meant losing her life and her soul for all eternity, this was worth taking a stand for.

From somewhere deep inside she pulled up every ounce of courage she had left. "I said go back to hell. You can't have it! Not now. Not ever!"

His roar was deafening. She slammed her hands over her ears to block the sound. Flames shot out from every part of his body, the heat so intense it singed the hair on her arms and legs. What was left of him swirled so fast, a giant vortex opened up in the middle of the room. Electricity crackled and popped, and then in an explosion that shook the temple, he vanished, leaving behind nothing but swirling dust and debris followed by bone-chilling silence.

No way that just happened…

Isadora's heart thundered against her ribs. He was gone. Just that fast. Her eyes darted right and left, searching, waiting for him to poof into reality again and backhand her into eternity.

"Very good, Princess."

She whipped toward the altar, but this time the voice was female, not male. And even before the face registered, somewhere inside she knew the being staring back at her was a Fate.

A Fate. Oh, gods. She tried to remember what each one was responsible for. Clotho spun the thread of life. Lachesis measured the thread with her rod. And...what was the name of the last one? Atropos, that was it. Atropos cut the thread when one's time was up.

Isadora's heart lurched into her throat. *Please, please don't let this be Atropos*. There was still so much she needed to do with this life. So much she'd been afraid to try before, but now...

The Fate, dressed in a thin white robe, floated across the ground and stopped a foot from Isadora. She was petite, smaller than Isadora, yet Isadora sensed she was stronger and wiser than any god.

The Fate smiled, the wrinkled skin around her eyes crinkling. "That was quite a show you put on."

Isadora stood rooted in place with the diamond clenched tightly in her hand, staring at the Fate, wondering how the hell this day could get any weirder.

From somewhere below, Hades roared, "Mine!"

The Fate glared down toward the floor. "Oh, go play with your three-headed dog, you bully."

He let out another ear-piercing roar, then silence descended once more.

The Fate winked at Isadora. "We don't have much time. I sense a temper tantrum coming on. He never learned to play well with others, you know." The humor faded from her voice when she said, "Fear not, dear one, I have not come to snip the thread of your life. If anything, I've come to—"

"You're not Atropos." A breath of relief swept through Isadora.

The Fate frowned. "I don't know why those from

your world keep mistaking me for that old hag. I'm clearly more attractive than the messenger of death."

Isadora stared wide-eyed as the Fate chuckled to herself over her own private joke. She wasn't sure what to say…what to do, for that matter. This meeting was beyond anything she could imagine.

"Oh, bah. Take my word for it. Atropos needs a face-lift or two." The Fate squared her shoulders. "Now, before our time is up, I'll get on with the purpose of my visit. You grow weaker by the day, as do your sisters. But fear not, for the strength you all seek is at hand."

"But the Orb of Krónos," Isadora cut in, remembering the medallion around Gryphon's—Apophis's—neck. "We lost it."

The Fate waved off her protest. "Where does your strength come from, dear one? Not from some magickal orb. It comes from that which is hidden deep inside each of you. Use that for the good of mankind and you won't be lost."

Isadora had no idea what that meant. "I don't understand. Why are you helping me? How—?"

"There are powers at work here no one expects you to understand. And I help you because you, unlike some others I know, are wise enough to listen. But ask yourself this: why *wouldn't* I help you, Hora? The Fates want balance in this world and the next as much as you do. I'm not telling you anything you don't already know. I'm simply encouraging you to remain steadfast. There are rules in this world, rules not even I can break. But know this, you were right in that you are all linked to the Titan Themis through your father's bloodline. Hold steady to that, and you and your sisters will find the answers you seek. The bonds the three of you share cannot be broken. Not by any god. Not by any spell. Not even by Hera's curse."

Hera's curse.

The ground trembled and Isadora's gaze shot to the floor again.

"I suggest you hurry." The Fate pointed toward the entrance. "Hades has a nasty temper. And you, clever girl, have succeeded in aggravating him greatly. Normally I would take much amusement in that, but not at the expense of your safety."

Isadora's head spun as she tried to make sense of everything the Fate had said. She took three steps toward the door then whipped back. "Wait. The witches in Thrace Castle…they cast some kind of spell over me. Is that…is that why I've been drawn to Demetrius?"

"I cannot answer your questions." The Fate tipped her head. "But ponder this: what does your heart tell you?"

Isadora searched her feelings. No. No, what she felt for Demetrius had come from the very center of her. No spell could make her feel the depth of emotion she'd felt the last few days.

"I knew you were wiser than most believed," the Fate said with a smile, drawing Isadora's attention again. "The attraction spell those witches cast was wrenched from your body when Apophis decided to punish you."

So her reaction to Demetrius really was her own. Isadora breathed a bit easier, though why she wasn't quite sure. But then another thought occurred. "Hades said something about the soul mate curse. He didn't mean…?"

The Fate lifted her salt-and-pepper eyebrows.

Isadora's throat grew thick. She couldn't believe

she was thinking this, let alone was about to say it. "He couldn't possibly have meant Demetrius is *my* soul mate, could he?"

"Argoleans, even those of the royal family, do not have soul mates. You know this."

No, they didn't. Only the Argonauts had soul mates. And thanks to Hera, they were intended to be a curse, not a blessing.

The disappointment was swift and consuming. As swift as a blade to the chest. And completely unexpected. Did she even want to be his soul mate? That was just—

"You choose whom you want to choose," the Fate went on. "But for Demetrius…there is only one he cannot deny."

Isadora's eyes slowly lifted. And she thought back to her night with Demetrius. To the struggle he waged between what he seemed to want but wasn't sure he deserved. To every time he'd rescued her and made sure she was safe. Even when she hadn't wanted him to.

Her. She was the one he couldn't deny.

She swallowed around the lump in her throat. "Then that means—"

"It means exactly what it is. And that causes Hades much grief because he can't infiltrate the subconscious of a hero's soul mate. Not when her hero guards over her."

Her hero. Her heart burst in her chest at the thought. That's exactly what he'd been doing this last week, wasn't it? Guarding her? She'd had dreams this week of Hades—horrible dreams, like always—but they hadn't lingered as they normally did. And in the mornings there'd been no residual effect. That was because of

Demetrius, she now realized. Because he'd kept her safe, slept next to her, made sure the Lord of the Underworld stayed away, even if he hadn't known he'd been doing it. Though she didn't understand why he kept trying to push her away with his cruel words, she knew now he would never be able to. Not completely.

Love blossomed in her soul. The kind she'd always hoped for but never expected. And as her mind swirled with the possibilities, she thought of her mother. And the cost of love.

She looked back to the Fate and knew this was her one chance to know the truth. Even though the Fate probably wouldn't answer, she had to ask. "Did she know? My mother? About my father's indiscretions? Is that why she left?"

Sympathy crossed the Fate's face and she glanced to the ground, pursing her lips as if choosing her words carefully. "Your mother loved your father deeply. And she was a good queen. A good wife to him. But your father…what does he love above all else, dear one?"

"His kingdom." The words left Isadora's mouth on a whisper, without a question in her mind.

The Fate's sad eyes lifted to Isadora's. "He still does."

He did. Isadora knew that better than anyone.

Sacrifice. Her father was always preaching about the responsibility of the monarchy and the level of sacrifice it took to rule. She'd never believed him before, but now…? Did it matter if she was Demetrius's soul mate? If he didn't want to bind himself to her because she was of the royal line, then she couldn't force him.

She looked down at her hand, opened her fist so the diamond sparkled up at her. She wasn't good at dealing with emotions. Her parents hadn't exactly taught her about never-ending love or what a good binding should be. She knew now that she did care about Demetrius, deeply, even with his dark moods and endless secrets and the way he kept himself closed off for reasons that didn't seem to make sense, but she couldn't walk away from her destiny either. She and her sisters…they were important. They were needed now more than ever. The face-off moments ago with Hades had reinforced just how important her position in this war really was.

The ground's trembling increased in intensity and the Fate began to fade. "Look within yourself for the balance you seek, dear one. I promise all your questions will be answered there."

Isadora didn't know what that meant, but the shaking walls jolted her out of her reverie. Rock and marble cracked, broke free to tumble down in a horrendous crash. Shielding her head with her hands, she ran out the entrance and down the three marble steps, sprinting across the dark cavern for the tunnel. From somewhere above she heard Demetrius's frantic voice calling to her, but the explosion of rock and granite at her back drowned out all other sound.

She reached the tunnel, darted through the long domed corridor, and spotted the stairs that led up to the surface. Rocks and debris tore into the flesh of her feet. She pumped her arms, gripped the diamond tight in her fist, and ignored the burn in her lungs, in her legs, as she ran harder. She wasn't going to die here. She had a purpose now, even if it wasn't the one she'd always wanted. Light shone down from the surface, a golden glow that urged her on.

Yes. I'm going to make it.

A thunderous clap echoed from above. She reached the first step and looked up just as the ceiling collapsed.

Chapter 19

"Isadora!" The force of the explosion shattered the invisible force field holding Demetrius back. He stumbled forward, caught his balance, and immediately began lifting pieces of debris out of the way.

Please, gods. He hurled rocks right and left. "Isadora!"

No sound met his ears. No answer. Great fissures had opened up in the earth, tearing through the grassy hillside, showcasing the mighty stones and pillars that had been hidden below. Jagged edges of rocks and marble ripped through the flesh of his hands as he dug deeper.

"Isadora!"

Sweat slid down his face, dripped onto his chest. The heat of the sun scorched his back as he kept moving massive pieces of stone, one at a time, searching. He'd heard her talking to Lachesis, damn it. Had heard every word they said. She'd been running for the exit when the ground collapsed. She couldn't be far from the steps that used to be right where he stood now.

Where is she?

Time seemed to drag on. Five minutes? Twenty? An hour? He wasn't sure how much time passed. All he knew was that she was here. Somewhere close, she was here.

Breathing heavily, his muscles sore from exertion, he stopped digging, wiped his forearm over his brow. A renewed sense of panic gnawed at his belly. Why couldn't he find her? Why couldn't he—

His spells. He could lift the rocks away with witch-craft. But which spell? His brain ran blank. He looked down at the amount of debris around him. A spell of this magnitude would drain him not only of physical strength but of mental strength as well. And if he was wrong, if he wasn't strong enough to cast it, he'd waste precious time he could use searching for Isadora with his bare hands.

Indecision warred as he raked his hands through his hair, grabbed on to the strands, and pulled until pain shot across his scalp.

You're not weak, Guardian, contrary to what you think. What you fear most may just have the power to save you. But only if you let it.

Lachesis's words from that night on the cliff—the night he'd taken that first step toward Isadora—ran back through his mind. Where they settled in. He took a deep breath. Then another.

Okay, focus. You can do this.

Closing his eyes, he held out his hands and regulated his breaths as words, phrases, chants tumbled through his mind. Spells he hadn't uttered in years but once had been as natural as drawing air. One grew stronger in his thoughts, like a beacon dragging him forward, casting shadows and darkness over all the rest.

His lips moved. Words spilled from his mouth. Rock scraped rock as he chanted in the warm, moist air and drew on the power of his ancestors.

His muscles bore the weight of the rocks. He gritted his teeth, lifted, and directed them away from the rubble with the sweep of his hands. One by one he moved broken pieces of marble and granite until his arms and

legs screamed in protest. Until he could see the first few
steps beneath the rubble.

Sweat poured down his temples. Fatigue settled in as
time slipped away. But he fought against both. He had
to find her. He wouldn't give up. He readied himself to
start again, only to stop short when his ears registered
the slightest sound.

A whisper. A squeak. Coming from somewhere in
the rubble. A rasp. A voice?

He dropped to the ground, placed his palms on
the warm rocks beneath him, and turned his head to
listen closer.

There. He heard it again. It sounded like…

"Isadora?"

The squeak echoed again. So faint he barely heard it.
His pulse picking up speed, he cleared away a handful
of rocks until his progress was stopped by a large slab of
marble that was as long as a car and too heavy to move
by sheer force. "Isadora?"

"Here," a small voice called. "I'm here. Down…here."

Relief flowed through his veins, as sweet as wine.
"Hold on, *kardia*. I'm going to get you out. Keep talking
to me so I know where to dig."

She did. Mumbling words he couldn't hear but which
vibrated all the way into his chest and gave him the extra
strength he needed. Closing his eyes, he focused again,
letting the chant flow from his lips at lightning speed
while he moved debris away from her voice.

"I'm here."

His eyes opened at the sound of her voice, clearer
now, and he realized enough material had been moved
to open a dark hole into the rubble. He rushed to the right

of the great marble slab and fell to his knees. Inside the hole, covered in a layer of thin white dust, she looked up at him, blinking into the bright light.

Holy gods. Thank you.

He pulled her out of the hole as carefully as he could, but with a frantic need to make sure she was in one piece. Once she cleared the lip, her weight shifted into his and he stumbled backward, wrapping his arms around her and drawing her close.

"I've got you," he whispered as he tucked her head under his chin and moved away from the debris.

"I'm okay," she said against his chest. Her body was warm. Her breath a soothing wind across his over-heated skin.

He eased down to sit on the hard earth. Seconds later, a massive crashing sound echoed from the rubble and they both jerked around to see the marble slab she'd been hiding under collapse into the hole.

"Gods." He pulled her back in tight and just held on.

Seconds passed in silence during which he worked on regulating his rapid-fire pulse. If he'd been any later… If his magick hadn't worked…If he hadn't moved those rocks first…

"I'm okay, Demetrius."

Yeah, but he wasn't. Not even close.

He pushed back so he could see her face. Dust covered every inch of her skin except where it had rubbed off one cheek that had been pressed against his chest. Her sun-kissed skin shone through to remind him she wasn't the ghost she appeared to be. She was real, alive, whole.

"I'm not hurt, Demetrius. I'm fine."

He wasn't entirely sure how that was possible. "What were you thinking?"

Her brow wrinkled to form deep lines in the powder. "What do you mean?"

He swiped at the dust on her forehead, her cheeks, her gently sloped, perfect nose. "Down there. With Hades. Don't you know what he can do to you?"

Fire flashed in her eyes. "Oh, I know. But I've finally wised up. He can't go against the natural order. When I'm dead, then he can do whatever he wants to me. But not while I'm alive. And he can't kill me to get me there faster."

Just the thought of her dead left a hitch in his gut. He motioned to the rubble behind her. "What the hell do you call that?"

She looked over her shoulder, then turned back to him. "A temper tantrum?"

He wasn't in the mood for jokes. His heart couldn't take it right now. "Isadora—"

"Okay, yeah," she said seriously. "He can cause natural disasters and send his minions after me if he wants, but he himself can't kill me. He can taunt me and show me what he plans to do to me when I cross over, but you know what? I'm not afraid of him, Demetrius. Not anymore."

"He offered you your soul back. And you said no."

"You heard that?" ·

"I heard everything."

A wary expression passed over her face, but she covered it quickly by glancing down at his chest. "Some souls aren't worth saving."

He tipped her chin up with his finger. "Yours is."

"No one's is. Not in spite of this." She lifted her hand, opened her palm. He sucked in a breath at the Titan symbol sparkling up at him.

The power of the earth element radiated from her hand and seeped into his skin even though he didn't touch it. As she turned the diamond in her palm, the confrontation he'd overheard between her and Hades rushed through his mind all over again. Even when she was trapped she fought. And not just for herself—she fought for her race. For people she didn't know and would never meet. For her sisters, for her warriors, for him. And sitting there on his lap, covered in a layer of grime from head to toe, she'd never looked more the queen she would one day become.

"*Kardia*—"

"I thought you didn't care, Demetrius. That's what you told me. What you've told me more times than I can count. And yet here you are. Whenever I need you, here you are." Her voice dropped to a husky whisper. "Tell me you don't care."

His heart picked up speed under her mesmerizing gaze and one by one, though he'd fought it for so long, he felt the last barriers of his restraint shatter and break.

"I do care," he whispered. "I care too much. That's the problem. That's always been the problem."

Her gaze roamed his face so long he tensed. "You hurt me."

Regret stabbed like a hot, sharp knife. But he deserved it. That and so much more. "I know."

"Don't ever do it again."

He swallowed hard. Didn't answer. Couldn't. Just as he couldn't tear his eyes from hers.

She braced a hand on his shoulder and pushed up to her feet. Warmth gathered beneath her fingers to trail a line of heat straight to his abdomen. He wanted to reach for her, pull her back into the circle of his arms, but stopped himself.

She took a wobbly step, caught herself from going down, and shot him a look before he could jump to her rescue. "I'm fine."

Not fine. She was weaker every day, and this situation with Hades and Apophis hadn't helped.

She took several steps down the dirt path, stopped, and looked back. "Dusk will be here soon. Aren't you coming?"

It took seconds to figure out what she meant. But when he realized she meant back to the ruins, instead of home to Argolea, he glanced at the rubble. At what was, technically, the holy ground they both knew they were looking for.

He had to take her home. It wasn't even a question. And yet…

And yet she obviously didn't want him to. And he wasn't nearly as ready as he thought he'd be. Now that they were faced with reality, he wanted more time. Just one more night to make up for all the shitty things he'd done and said to her over the years. She deserved that much, didn't she? If he took her home now, he'd never have the chance again.

He glanced back at her and knew the choice he made now would change his life. Once he gave himself to her freely, there was no way he could go back to pretending he didn't care. Knew also, because of who and what he was, if he made this choice, he was most likely sacrificing any kind of future he had with the Argonauts forever.

He pushed to his feet and stopped when he was inches from her. She craned her neck back to look up at him. "Ready?"

He scooped her into his arms and reveled at the gasp of delight that stole from her lips. "Yeah," he said as he moved down the path with her in his arms. "Yeah, I'm finally ready."

The warm sun, the heat of Demetrius's body, and the gentle rocking motion as he walked the path back to the ruins all coalesced and dragged Isadora toward sleep. She wasn't sure how long she'd been out, but when she awoke she was back in the Hall of Heroes, lying on the makeshift bed. Groggy, she sat up, rubbed her eyes, then gasped at the hundreds of flickering candles spread out around the room.

Her heart beat slowly at first, then picked up speed. The stone table in the center of the room was covered in a layer of blankets that were folded in half to lie across the middle, overhanging each side. Food was laid out over one end: a collection of fruits and berries of differing shapes and sizes, and more fish. Candles sat on the other end.

She heard footsteps to her right and Demetrius appeared at the bottom of the steps, holding two plastic buckets in each hand.

His face lit when he saw her, a reaction that warmed her deep inside. "You're awake."

She couldn't stop the smile on her lips, didn't

even try. "I must have heard you coming down." She motioned to the room. "What is all this?"

"Oh." He looked toward the middle of the room, and she wasn't sure, but she thought she saw his cheeks turn just the slightest shade of pink. "Trickery, really." He set the buckets on the end of the table and waved his hand through a nearby trio of candles. The image flickered and faded as his arm moved through, then solidified again when he was gone. He shrugged. "Optical illusion."

Amazed, she rose on limbs weaker than she wanted to admit and crossed to him, running her hand through the same space he just had. The candles flickered again and then the image reformed. "You can cast illusions? Wow." She looked up at him. "Can you teach me how to do that?"

He smirked, that easy grin he'd shown her yesterday at the beach, the same one that transformed his face from intimidating to gorgeous in the span of a second. "Party tricks are one of my many talents. I can't cast a protection spell worth shit, but if you need candles, I'm your guy."

He reached for the fruit, but her hand on his forearm stopped him. She waited until his eyes ran back to her before she said, "I think you have a lot of talents. And I know without them, I wouldn't be here right now."

Something soft flickered behind his eyes. Something she wanted to reach out and hold on to forever. But he didn't close the distance between them, and this time she wasn't going to make the first move. He'd brought her back here instead of insisting they go home to Argolea. For tonight, at least, she was going to be patient and see where this went.

He cleared his throat and reached for the food again. "You should eat."

He set a plastic plate of fruit and fish in front of her. She tried not to curl her lip in disgust but knew she wasn't successful when he chuckled at her side. "When you get home, you can have whatever you want. Here." His big hands slid around her waist and he lifted her to sit on the table with ease. Warmth gathered beneath his hands and inched its way up and down her rib cage. But his touch was gone way too soon, and he put the plate in her lap and stepped back before she could think of something to say to stop him. "What will you ask the cooks to make for you when you get back?"

She fingered an apple slice on the plate. "A steak. A nice big juicy one." As she sank her teeth into the apple and chewed, she imagined a rib eye instead. "With Cookie's good garlic mashed potatoes and a side of asparagus. And chocolate cake for dessert." She glanced his way. "What will you ask for?"

His lopsided grin faded as she ate. With one arm braced against the table, he looked down at his own food. "I don't know."

A strange foreboding trickled through her chest. What wasn't he telling her?

He ate a few bites, and when he noticed she wasn't eating much herself, took her plate and set it to the side. Neither of them, obviously, had much of an appetite. Her eyes followed as he moved around the table. "Lie back."

She glanced down at the blankets beneath her. "Why?"

He lifted the buckets he'd brought in with him when she awakened and said, "I thought you might want to wash your hair. It's too late to head down to the river, but I heated some water upstairs in case you wanted to clean up."

Her heart thumped in her chest. Candlelight flickered over his bare chest and the angles and planes of his muscular body. He was wearing the same low-slung black pants he'd worn for days, frayed at the edges and ripped in the knees, but he was no longer sweaty and dusty, as he'd been earlier. He'd obviously dunked himself in the river when she was asleep, and then he'd brought more water back here for her.

Tingles erupted in her breasts, in her abdomen, in her thighs as she nodded and swallowed back a rush of emotions. "I...I would. Thank you."

"Lie back then. And scoot toward the end of the table."

She did as he said, realizing the blankets were positioned to soften the hard surface. When her feet were hanging off one end and her head off the other, she looked up to see him peering down at her with an intense expression she couldn't name.

"Close your eyes."

Warm water flowed over her grimy hair, dripped down to the stone floor at his feet. She closed her eyes as he poured liquid over every strand, then relaxed into his touch as he began to massage suds into her scalp.

"Where did you get shampoo?"

"Same place I found the toothpaste."

She smiled. "Mm."

"Like that?"

Yeah, she liked it. So much. His hands were like heaven, rubbing, touching, massaging, and every one of her muscles relaxed as he worked. He poured more water over her hair to rinse away the lather, then carefully dried her short locks with an extra blanket.

"How did you heat the water?" she asked. "All we have are plastic buckets."

"Achilles's helmet is metal."

Her eyes grew wide. "You heated water in his helmet?"

"I don't think he's using it. Wish I hadn't?"

No, she wished that helmet was the size of a hot tub so she could climb into it with him and he could work his magic fingers over the rest of her body.

He set the damp blanket on the table at her side and used his fingers to comb the tangles from her wet hair. Then he slid his hands under her shoulders and pushed her up to sitting.

She brushed the wet hair back from her face and tried to think of something to say. His hands tugging at the hem of her filthy tank top stopped all thought. "Lift your arms."

Her heart picked up speed but she did as he asked. The tank slid up over her arms and dropped to the ground out of sight. Water sloshed behind her. Anticipation curled in her stomach. Then his hand landed gently on her bare shoulder, followed by a warm damp rag running across her back.

A sponge bath. He was giving her a sponge bath. The erotic implications of that puckered her nipples and arched her back.

"Too hot?"

"No, no. It's fine." More than fine. Better than fine. It was…paradise. She closed her eyes as he dragged the rag over her shoulders, down her spine, to the curve of her lower back and up again. Warmth gathered in her center, spread lower until she ached.

"I've been meaning to ask you something," he said softly.

"Hm?" He slid the rag down her neck, over her left arm. Water dribbled down to her fingers.

"What happened to your mother? We'd been told her party was ambushed."

Her eyes floated open to focus on a candle on the floor twenty feet away. He continued washing her arms, her back, her sides as her mind drifted. She knew what the Argonauts had been told, what everyone had been told. Thirty years ago, before the war with the daemons had picked up in intensity, her mother had taken a group of chaperones—soldiers from the Executive Guard and her own personal assistants—into the human realm for a "mini-vacation." A shopping trip, her father had called it. Andromeda had been as fascinated by human culture as the king, and every now and then he'd allowed her to cross over, so long as she was well protected. While there, they'd been overrun by a pack of daemons, and before the Argonauts had even been alerted, it was over. None had survived. But that wasn't what had really happened. That was simply the lie her father had told to cover up the truth.

"You know about my sisters, so I guess it's no big secret now. My father was never faithful to my mother. Three hundred years is a long time to be bound to one person, and when that person can't give you the one thing you want more than any other…" She shrugged, hating that she sounded so bitter but unable to keep it from her voice. "I guess he decided to move on."

Demetrius moved around to stand in front of her, and though she knew she was naked from the waist up and should be embarrassed, she wasn't. "A son. That's what he wanted."

She didn't meet his eyes, focusing instead on an inch-long scar under his left pec. "That's what he's always wanted. She was pregnant numerous times, but they all ended in either a miscarriage or stillbirth. Except me."

"What happened to her?"

Isadora sighed. "I think she finally had enough. She must have found out about his affair with Callia's mother. At the time, I didn't know who he was seeing, just that it was someone else. It was always someone else. Usually it was a female outside the castle, someone of lower status. But his own personal healer? That would have rocked my mother to her core. Especially since she and Anna were friends."

She couldn't help remembering how sad her mother had been the day she left. The way she'd hugged Isadora and said good-bye as if it was forever. "She didn't go into the human realm on a shopping trip. She didn't take any chaperones with her. She just disappeared. As if she'd never existed in the first place. And my father never searched for her. He made up that story about her being killed as an excuse to go on with his life, and he never looked back."

She glanced at her hands. Hands that were petite, just like her mother's had been. "I thought about looking for her. More than once. But my father…he forbade me from doing so." Her voice trailed off. Because, yeah, what was she ever going to be able to do? "I look like her. More than I do him. Aside from the fact I'm female and the only one of their children who survived, my nose is too small, my eyes the wrong color, and I'm timid, just like she was. That's never helped the situation with my father. In fact, I'm sure that's simply made it worse."

He didn't say anything, and she figured that meant her little sponge bath was over. She shifted and reached for the edge of the blanket beneath her legs to cover herself, disappointed she'd gone on in the first place instead of sidestepping his question. Even more disappointed she'd let the hurt get to her all over again.

Why did she let her father do that to her? Especially here?

He pushed the blanket from her hands. Surprised, she looked up into soft, warm eyes as the cloth fell against the table again. "I think your nose is perfect. And your eyes match your determined personality."

"Determined? No one's ever called me that."

A half smile curled his mouth. One that supercharged her blood and brought that ache back tenfold. "How many times have I tried to put distance between us? And how many times have you closed the gap? I'd call that determined."

Her heart stuttered. And in the silence she knew if she didn't ask the question, she'd spend the rest of her life wondering. "Is that what you want? Distance? Between us?"

"No."

She drew in a breath and held it as he twined one arm around her back and tugged her closer to the heat of his body. Her legs opened, sliding around his hips until his sweet male scent surrounded her and he was all she felt.

"And for the record," he said as he dipped the rag in the bucket at his side and trailed the warm, wet cloth across her collarbone so water dripped down her naked breasts, puckering the nipples to stiff peaks, "I don't think you're timid. Not anymore, at least."

His face was an inch from hers. His breath hot and minty and so intoxicating it left her light-headed. As he brought the rag around her right breast, she tensed, wanting his hand on her skin, his lips on her mouth, his length deep inside her as it had been last night. Except this time she wanted him controlling the pace, the mood, bending her body any way he wanted. "If I'm not, that's because of you."

"No, it's not. It's because of you."

She held her breath as his lips met hers. Once. Twice. As gently as if he were touching glass. She moaned as he kissed her again, as his soft and supple lips swept over hers. Bringing her hands up to his chest, she felt the corded muscles beneath his skin, the power, and tilted her head to give him more. He took the invitation and opened, sliding his tongue into her mouth to tangle with hers until she went a little mad at the taste of him again.

"Ah, *kardia*," he mouthed against her lips.

"I love it when you call me that."

He dropped the rag, wrapped both arms around her waist, and lifted her from the table. She responded by kissing him more deeply, sliding her legs around his hips and her fingers into his hair as she'd wanted to do from the first moment he stepped into the room. He carried her from the table, across the floor, and laid her out on the pile of blankets in the corner of the room, then peered down at her with eyes that weren't nearly as soft as she'd thought before.

No, these eyes were shimmering shards of onyx, filled with desire and yearning. And they were staring at her as if she were the only thing in the world he wanted.

She wasn't sure what had changed between this morning and now, but she wasn't about to ask.

"I want you to tell me what you like," he whispered. "What you want."

She ran her hands up his muscular arms and eased up to kiss him again. "I like you. I just want you."

He kissed her deeply and eased down into the vee of her body, and her heart filled when the hard length of his shaft pressed through the cloth separating them, right where she wanted it most.

He touched her, first with his fingers, then with his mouth, licking and kissing her most sensitive spots—the skin behind her ear, the base of her throat, the tips of her nipples—until she moaned in pleasure. And then he did it all again until she was panting for more.

His mouth made a slow trek down her stomach, paused at her belly button so he could trace the indentation with his tongue. Her muscles quivered; her body arched in anticipation. She watched with heavy-lidded eyes as he kissed her lower belly and expertly popped the snap on her shorts with his teeth.

The victorious grin he shot her curled her mouth, but it quickly faded into a moan of pleasure when he slid his hand into her shorts and moved lower to graze his fingers along her slit.

"Mm, Princess. You're wet for me."

She wasn't just wet, she was soaked, and she didn't want to wait. "Demetrius…"

He pulled his hand free, then tugged the shorts from

her hips. Cool air brushed her skin but was quickly replaced with his tantalizing mouth, blowing hot over her naked mound. She arched, groaned. He traced his fingers where he blew, careful only to graze the supercharged flesh. "I love the taste of you. Right here."

She pushed up on her hands, the erotic sight of him between her legs turning her blood to liquid fire in her veins. He lowered his head and she watched in awe as his talented tongue snaked out and made one long, lingering sweep of her cleft. *Oh, gods.* Her head fell back in pleasure. Her whole body clenched. She arched her hips to offer more and gave in to the ecstasy.

He flicked her clit, stroked and swirled, brought her close to the edge, then backed off. Sweat beaded her brow, slid down her back to pool at the base of her spine as she twisted and tried to show him just where she wanted more. But he knew how to tempt her. Knew just how to tease her into a maddening frenzy. And no matter what she did, the climax she needed hovered just beyond her grasp.

"Demetrius, oh, gods, I need you."

He lifted his head, wiped his mouth with the back of his hand, and flipped her onto her stomach so fast she gasped. Cloth rustled behind her, and then his hands slid under her torso, cupped her waist, and lifted. His warm, hard chest pressed into her spine, his strong bare thighs met the backs of her legs. One hand slid down her front and into her folds to tease her all over again. And his mouth, those sweet and tempting lips and that insanely erotic tongue, caught her earlobe and suckled.

"Should I bind your hands, like you did mine last night?"

Bind her? *Oh, yes*…His hot breath trailing her neck sent a shiver of delight through her whole body. His fingers teasing her flesh pushed her hips forward and back. His hard length pressing against her ass drew a moan from her lips. "Yes. Oh, yes, I don't care what you do. I just need…"

"What?" He nipped her earlobe with his teeth. But it didn't hurt. If anything, the bite felt…electric, amping her need higher still. His fingers slid lower, deeper, inside, and she moaned as he filled her. He teased her breast with his other hand until her nipples turned into stiff aching peaks. "Gods, you're so tight. Need what, *kardia*? Tell me."

"You," she managed. She found his strong thigh with her hand and squeezed. "I need you. Now. Right now."

His fingers left her sheath. He tilted her forward, and she gasped as her body shifted, but the arm of steel wrapped around her torso kept her from falling. And then his cock was sliding along her slippery folds and she didn't care about anything anymore. He could put her in any position he wanted, do whatever he needed to her body. As long as he found his way inside her, that was all that mattered.

He pressed against her opening. Pushed inside just an inch. Slid back out. "Is this what you need?"

"Oh, yes."

"Say it."

Her body quivered. "I need you, Demetrius. Fill me. I want to feel you."

He did, in one powerful thrust. Unlike last night, this time it didn't hurt. It was the most exquisite feeling in the world. As if her body was made just for his.

He was hard where she was soft, strong where she was fragile, and with every deep plunge, her climax barreled closer.

With one hand she gripped the arm wrapped tightly around her waist; with the other she clamped on to his thigh as he moved inside her. She moaned with every rock of his hips, with every drag and pull. Turning her head to his, she kissed him deeply, moving with him, against him, then nearly came apart when his fingers found her clit and he flicked in time with his thrusts.

"Yes, yes," she mouthed against his lips.

"Here?"

"Yes. Oh, yes."

"You like me fucking you here?"

"Yes." Oh, gods, his voice, telling her what he was doing to her in such a basic way, was so damn erotic. No one ever talked to her that way. No one ever dared. "Yes. Please…don't stop."

Her climax steamrolled its way toward her, but just as she reached the peak, he pulled out, twisted her around again so she fell against the blankets on her back. She groaned her frustration, but he captured it with his mouth, and then he filled her all over again in one mighty thrust. And she forgot everything but this, here with him, right now. She wrapped her arms around his shoulders, her legs around his back, and held on as he drove harder, deeper, as he kissed her as though he couldn't possibly get enough. Not ever.

"Now, *kardia*," he whispered. "Come for me now."

She was powerless to do anything else. Her climax slammed into her with a force that stole her breath. Her whole body arched as spirals of light and electricity rippled through every cell, dragging his name from her lips. He thrust again and again, faster, longer, and grew impossibly hard inside her. She heard his own cry of release and marveled at the way every muscle in his body turned to stone beneath her hands, against her skin, *inside* her body.

Seconds passed in silence as if they were frozen in time. Finally, he dropped his head against her shoulder and dragged air into his lungs. "I…oh, man…"

A smile twined its way across her lips as she ran her fingers through his hair and tried to regulate her own breathing. She pressed a kiss against his temple. "Me too."

He pushed up on one hand and looked down as if judging her words for honesty, and in that moment, with his hair mussed, his face relaxed, and his body sated, he didn't look a thing like the cruel, unfeeling guardian she'd known most of her life. Here, now, like this, he was simply the *ándras* she'd fallen in love with.

His gaze slid from her face to her breasts, and heat built in her veins all over again under the searing look. And then his gaze moved lower, to her abdomen, where it hovered. He pushed up. "Hold still."

The heat of his body was gone before she could stop him. He crossed the floor, his nakedness reflecting the flickering candlelight as if he were a statue carved from marble. He reached for the rag from the table.

Isadora looked down at her belly and saw the evidence of his release all over her skin.

"Here." He knelt by her side and used the rag to wipe away the remnants of his pleasure, then tossed it back across the room and eased down onto his side, tucking his arm under his head and pulling her into the curve of his body. "That's better."

Isadora wasn't so sure. Confused as to why he hadn't finished inside her, she ran through their lovemaking in her head, searching for something she'd done wrong. But she couldn't find a single moment that hinted of him not wanting her, not needing her as much as she'd needed him. Then she thought back to his infuriated reaction this morning. After she'd ridden them both to a blistering climax. *After* he'd finished inside her, then realized what he'd done.

You don't want to have a child with me.

Why would I?

She swallowed hard, and a shiver of doubt gnawed at her greatest fear. All this time she'd thought his coming back here tonight was a sign he was ready to take a step forward with her. Start anew. Make the greatest leap of faith there was. But she was wrong. This wasn't a beginning. It was an ending. The sweetest, most painful ending she'd probably ever experience.

Misreading her reaction, he reached for a blanket from the edge of the pallet and tossed it over their naked bodies. But he didn't pull away, and he never once let go of her, as if he couldn't bear the thought. He stroked her arm, her side, her stomach with his soft fingers and whispered the sweetest words in her ear, ones that, considering what she now knew, brought tears to her eyes.

"Sleep, *kardia*. You need your strength for the morning. We both do."

She closed her eyes tight. But she didn't sleep. She worked simply to keep from crying. Because her heart, which moments before had been so full, felt as if it were now leaking from a pinprick deep inside her chest.

Tomorrow she did need her strength. She was going home to Argolea. Finally. But somehow, instinctively, she knew he wasn't going with her.

Chapter 20

HE WAS IN HEAVEN. OR THE ELYSIAN FIELDS. OR wherever it was the blessed heroes went after they died. Glancing down at Isadora asleep in his arms, Demetrius figured, considering who and what he was, this was probably as close to paradise as he was ever going to get. And because of that he should be enjoying the moment rather than worrying about what came next.

Except…how in Hades couldn't he think about what came next?

That ache lit off in his chest again, the same damn one he'd been fighting the last few hours, lying here in the wee hours of morning with her. He didn't have another choice. He couldn't go back to pretending anymore, and he didn't trust himself to be with her. Not after what had happened earlier.

Who was he kidding? Even if there was a way to guarantee she'd never get pregnant, he still couldn't be with her. If she ever found out the truth about him… That ache intensified. He couldn't bear the thought of what that knowledge would do to her. What the Council would do to her. What would happen to their homeland if word got out the heir to the throne had shacked up with the enemy's son.

No. The only solution was to take her home, then get as far away as possible. This time for good. She needed to find a mate, to give the kingdom heirs, and cement the monarchy so the Council couldn't overthrow her reign and fuck things up, and he wasn't strong enough—not anymore—to sit back and watch her fall in love with someone else.

He closed his eyes, told himself this was for the best. The only thing he could do. The one thing he should have done long ago.

"You think loudly, Demetrius."

His eyes shot open and he looked down at Isadora. Her head rested on his shoulder and her sleek body was tucked tightly to his under the blanket, but her shimmering brown eyes registered the distance he'd already started drawing out between them.

"Was I talking out loud?" Shit. Had he voiced his thoughts?

"No, but I've been around you long enough now to know what you're thinking." She pushed up to sitting and drew the blanket around her torso, hiding her luscious breasts from view. "There's no way to change your mind, is there?"

Skata. She did know. "You're not well, Isadora. I have to take you home in the morning."

She nodded, looked down at her hands in her lap. "But you're not staying, are you? Once we go home, you're leaving Argolea."

His heart cracked. The heart he hadn't even known existed before her. He chose his words carefully because, as shitty as he'd been to her over the years, he didn't want to make this any harder on her than it already was. "I think, considering the circumstances, it would be best if I left."

"Best for whom?"

"Best for you."

Her eyes darted his way and the fire he saw flash there reminded him of the *gynaíka* who'd stood up to a god. And a warlock. And him, more times than he could count. "At least do me the courtesy of not lying. Not now."

She rose, taking the blanket with her, and crossed the floor to find her clothes. His illusions had faded, and what candles were left had burned down to almost nothing. Soft warm light spilled over her as she bent to pick up her shirt.

He sat up, reached for his pants. "Isadora—"

She tossed the blanket to the ground, tugged on her dirty shorts, and wriggled into her filthy tank top, the flash of skin in the low light hitting him on the most basic of levels. "I just want to know one thing. Why did you come back here with me if you were planning to take me home tomorrow and then split?" She waved her hand around the room. "What was the purpose of this?"

There wasn't one. Except for him being a selfish-ass bastard. He rose, pulled on his pants. "I don't know. I just wanted…"

"What?"

Frustrated, he raked a hand through his hair. "To be with you."

"Obviously not."

The bite to her voice brought his head up. Her short blond hair stuck out all over her head. Her cheeks were sun kissed, her skin brown, and staring at him from across the room with candlelight flickering behind her, she looked like a deity of the earth. Like one of the original Horae, the personifications of nature and the goddesses of balance and order.

The heart that had cracked earlier broke open wide. "Do you think I want this? I want you. But there's no way...*Skata*." He looked down at his forearms, covered with the markings of the Argonauts. "There's no way that will work."

"Why not?"

"Because it won't."

"Because of me."

His head darted up again. "No. This has nothing to do with you."

"Because I'm royal. Because of the monarchy."

"No. It's not about that. I don't care about—"

"Then what?"

He looked back at his hands. Gods, he was such a fake. He shouldn't have these markings. Shouldn't be allowed in Argolea. Sure as shit shouldn't be with her now. Her life would be so much better if he'd been thrown to the humans like his brother. If she'd never even met him.

His voice wavered even though he tried to keep it steady. "It's not about you, okay? It's me. I just can't..."

Yeah. Like he could finish that sentence? He swallowed hard.

"What aren't you telling me, Demetrius?"

"Nothing." *Everything*.

"Nothing," she repeated. Then louder, "No, I think it's definitely something." She crossed to the end of the bed and her voice, which had been steady before, dropped to a whisper. So soft and tempting, it called to the very center of him in a way nothing and no one ever had before. "Just tell me what's going on."

"I can't."

"Can't or won't?"

He shook his head even as that hole in his heart grew wider. "What's the difference? Either way it adds up to the same damn thing."

She stood still for several minutes, eerily silent. Finally, when he couldn't stand the quiet anymore, he looked at her, then wished he hadn't. Her face was drawn, her shoulders slumped, but it was the heartbreak in her eyes that would stay with him long after this conversation was over.

He reached for her. "Isadora—"

She moved out of his grasp. "No, don't. Don't say anything else." She turned toward the stairs.

Panic rushed in. "Where are you going?"

"I need some air."

"It's still dark outside. You can't leave—"

"I'm not suicidal, Demetrius. I won't leave the ruins. I'll stay within the walls. I just want some fresh air."

He shouldn't let her go up there alone, but he knew she was struggling to stay in control, just as he was. And after the way he'd just hurt her, he owed her a few minutes to collect herself.

She moved up three steps, then hesitated and turned back to face him. But she didn't meet his eyes. Instead she focused on his chest and bit her lip as if thinking through what she wanted to say. Firelight flickered over her features and he knew right then, soul mate curse or not, there was never going to be anyone else in his life that mattered as much as she did.

"You said I'd regret this." Her voice, usually strong and confident, was so soft he barely heard her. "Do you remember that? You said when I went home I'd look back on my time here with you and regret every moment of it."

He swallowed again, loathing the fact his warning had now come true. "Yeah," he managed. "I remember."

"And what did I say to you?"

When he didn't answer, she lifted her chocolate eyes to his. "Don't remember? Then I'll tell you. I said the most important things in this world are the ones we have to fight for. And I still believe you're worth fighting for, Demetrius. Even if you don't."

He stood where he was long after she disappeared up the spiral stairs. The door at the top opened with a hiss, then closed gently behind her as she left. And alone, his heart squeezed so tight, it hurt to draw a single breath.

He was doing the right thing. No matter how painful, no matter how upset she thought she was now…in the long run, ending it here, before she learned the truth about him, was the only thing he could do.

In the quiet, he turned a slow circle and glanced over the Hall of Heroes, stopping when his gaze landed on Jason's trunk. In the three thousand years after Jason's tragedy, Demetrius hadn't learned a thing, had he? He was still fucking things up, just like his forefather. History, obviously, loved to repeat itself.

Damn it.

He blew out a breath, ran his hands over his face then rested them on his hips. After ten minutes, he figured that was long enough for her to collect herself. It would be morning soon. She could start packing up whatever she wanted to take to Argolea. As soon as it was light, they'd set out for the temple again. And from there…

From there he didn't know where the hell he'd go.

The ache spread out from his chest like wriggling tentacles searching for pain receptors to latch on to and bleed dry. He made it to the top of the steps and pushed the heavy door open, pausing as chilled air slid around his hand and crept toward his body.

Had a cold front moved in? The temperature seemed to drop by the second. Isadora was wearing only a tank top and shorts. She had to be freezing up here. Before they headed for the temple, he'd make sure she grabbed a few blankets from down below. Shoving his shoulder against the door, he stepped out into the moonlight. And then froze.

The seven foot daemon holding Isadora against his body had one hand wrapped around her mouth to keep her quiet, the other over her abdomen to hold her still. Two other daemons stood behind the first, their grotesque faces awash in the moonlight trickling through the open ceiling above. But it was the figure draped in red, moving up on Demetrius's right, that nearly stopped his heart.

A vile grin spread across Atalanta's face. "Guardian, it's so good of you to join us. We've been waiting."

His gaze jumped to Isadora's wide, frightened eyes.

Atalanta stepped up to Isadora and bent to run one red-tipped nail down her cheek. The princess tensed. "You've done well," Atalanta said to him, continuing to study Isadora. "Very well, it seems."

Skata. How had she gotten here? And why now? When he was hours away from getting Isadora to safety?

Atalanta trailed her finger down the center of Isadora's chest, over the daemon's arm holding her still, then hovered her hand over Isadora's belly. A wicked smile turned her bright red lips higher at the corners. "Oh, yes. Extremely well, *yios*." She turned to face him. "But then I never expected anything less. I always knew my son would one day make me proud."

Isadora gasped beneath the gnarled hand clamped over her mouth before looking to Demetrius for some sign that what Atalanta said couldn't possibly be true. But there was nothing he could say or do to reassure her.

"And you, *yios*," Atalanta went on, obviously enjoying her torment, "have done that now. In nine months' time, the princess is going to bear me a child. The heir to the throne of Argolea. With my bloodline in its veins. And in doing so, she will gift me the link to the Horae that was stolen from me by the Argonauts."

His gaze shot to Isadora's face. Betrayal and revulsion raced across her perfect features, morphed to bitter hatred. And in the stillness that followed, Demetrius knew he'd been wrong. History hadn't repeated itself. Because in Jason's case, the only people who'd been affected by the hero's fuckups were the ones he was supposed to have loved. This time the whole world was at stake. And thanks to him, the enemy now had the weapon it desperately needed.

Chapter 21

THE BLACKNESS CIRCLED IN, SEEPING THROUGH Demetrius's ribs to condense in the space where his heart had been. A blackness he hadn't felt in days and hadn't once missed. Steeling himself against the familiar tightness in his chest, he shifted his gaze away from Isadora and focused on Atalanta.

He had to play it cool. He couldn't let her see his fear. Couldn't show he cared in any way.

The goddess turned to her minions. "Take her outside."

Panic pushed in. "You can't take her."

Atalanta's dark gaze swung his way. "I can do anything I want, *yios*."

Isadora grunted beneath the hand clamped over her mouth, struggled in the daemon's arms as he muscled her toward the doorway. Though he wanted nothing but blood, Demetrius didn't look. His mind spun with alternatives. If they took her off this island where he couldn't follow…

As if a light flicked on, he remembered the way Isadora had been sick once before at home. Before she and Casey had been joined as the Chosen. *That's* why she was weakening. Not because of the witches. Why the hell hadn't he figured that out before?

"She's sick," he said quickly.

"Halt." Atalanta's abrupt command stopped the daemon's forward momentum. Eyebrows drawn low,

the goddess crossed the stone floor to peer down at
Isadora, her bloodred robes fanning out behind her in
the moonlight as she moved. With one long finger she
tipped the princess's chin up and studied her pale face.

"She won't last nine months," Demetrius added. "Likely
not even nine days, given the rate she's weakening."

"What is this illness?" Atalanta asked, still examining
Isadora's face. "A spell?"

"Not mine."

"Then whose?" Atalanta's enraged face whipped
his way.

"It's part of the prophecy. You should know this. The
longer she's separated from her sister, the sicker they
each become. Blame Hades if you want, but not me." He
shoved his hands into the front pockets of his pants, hoping, praying he looked relaxed and not like he wanted
to rip her throat out with his bare hands. "And since you
sent us to this piece-of-shit island, what? A week ago?
That time's been running out."

Atalanta's eyes narrowed. Demetrius's pulse picked
up speed. They stood locked in a stare-down that
vibrated the blackness inside his chest and drew it to the
forefront. He knew she was looking inside him, delving
deep for the lie she sensed was hidden somewhere in
his words.

Just when he was sure she was going to strike him
down simply because she could, she turned to look back
at Isadora, then shifted her gaze to him once more.

She crossed the floor, lifted her hands in front of his
face, and muttered words he didn't catch. He tensed,
but before she even finished chanting, he felt something
shift in his hands and break open.

Her eyes grew to thin black points of darkness. "I was going to leave you here, where I could keep a close eye on you, but I've decided there are other, more useful plans for you now. I've unbound your ability to open the portal. On this island, however, you'll still need to get to holy ground, though I have no doubt about your abilities. You are, after all, my son. It's your loyalty now that concerns me. So I've decided to test it." She looked at Isadora, but her words were meant for him. "You'll return to Argolea, you'll find the Chosen half-breed, and you'll bring her to me. To your *soul mate*."

Isadora cried out under the grotesque hand still clamped over her mouth, but Demetrius still didn't look her way. He remained focused on his *materas*, on the female who, in a fucking twist of irony, had given him life and was now ripping it from his grasp.

Atalanta faced him again. "As you said, *yios*. Time is running out." Over her shoulder, she called, "Baal?"

"Yes, my queen."

"Take the princess outside."

The daemon dragged Isadora out of the hall. The other monsters followed. Every muscle in Demetrius's body clenched, ready to spring forward, but Atalanta, leaning in close, stopped his momentum. Her perfectly formed face, as beautiful as Aphrodite's, blocked his line of sight. "Your soul mate's life hangs in the balance, *yios*. Do not disappoint me."

She moved out the door, disappearing from sight. From outside he heard a pop, a sizzle, and then a scream—Isadora's scream. And then nothing at all.

He knew they were gone. He didn't even need to

look. Just as he knew he had one chance now, and time really was ticking.

He hit the doorway to the Hall of Heroes at a dead run, slithered through the widening gap as the door opened. Skipping stairs to get to the bottom fast, he ran through everything he might need. Candles and torches flared as he hit the ground, as if the dark magick inside him vibrated so strongly he didn't even need to harness it. He flipped up lids on the heroes' chests one by one and snagged the Pelican spear, a knife that looked like a circle of teeth—which he strapped to his thigh—and two daggers he hooked in the belt loops of his pants. Then he headed for the stairs.

Something flashed in the corner of his eye. Three steps up he paused and looked back toward the pallet he'd lain on with Isadora only minutes before. Quickly he crossed back to the makeshift bed and used the spear to flip up the top blanket. Lying near the far right corner lay the diamond with the Titans' marking. He bent and lifted it and immediately felt the heat and life of the earth radiate into his palm and up his arm.

You're the one who set the torches.

I am. It's sacred.

His gaze darted up and around the hall as he thought of his conversation with Lachesis. Bloody hell, *this* was the sacred ground they'd needed all along. She'd been trying to tell him, but he'd been too stubborn to listen. Isadora could have opened the portal at any fucking time. All she'd needed to do was calm herself and focus.

He dropped the weapons in his hands, shoved the earth element into his pocket, and brought his pinky fingers together. He focused his mind, thought of

Argolea. The Argonaut markings on his arms glowed as if backlit, growing strong in intensity. And then the portal opened in a pop and sizzle of light that shimmered all along the walls.

He stepped through the portal and into the Gatehouse in Argolea. Where a force slammed into his side and shoved him to the ground.

"What the hell?" he said.

"It's him. *Skata*. Get him!"

Four sets of hands grabbed on to him. He tried to push himself up but they shoved him back down to the ground. Blinding pain shot off behind his eyes as his head smashed into the stone floor.

"He's armed!" a voice yelled.

"Someone get to the Argonauts and tell them we've got him!"

"Get the fuck off me!" Demetrius hollered. A knee jabbed his back. His arms were wrenched behind him before he could break free and swing out. What were these morons doing? Didn't they know who he was?

He thrashed, knew if he got to his feet he could take all four of them down. Throwing his head back, he cracked his skull against the guard behind him. The guard cried out in pain, loosened his grip. Demetrius swung around. The blade at his throat brought him to a sudden halt.

"This little party's over," the guard muttered. He stripped Demetrius of his weapons while another guard searched his pockets.

"Look at this," the one to his right said.

The guard with the blade held the earth element out so Demetrius could see it. "Oh, Guardian, you *have* been a bad boy. Many have been looking for you, and I can't wait to see what they'll say when they get an eyeful of this."

"You don't seem pleased to be here," Atalanta said. "I'd think you'd be dying for real food after a week of nothing but berries and fish."

Isadora cut her gaze from the roaring fire in the enormous stone fireplace to Atalanta, seated at the other end of the long rectangular table in what she supposed was a dining room. Supposed, because she didn't care. All she could think about were the things the witch in front of her had said back at the ruins. And the fact Demetrius hadn't once denied them.

Atalanta lifted a large goblet and took a deep drink. Unable to watch, Isadora's gaze fell to the tall, grotesque metal candleholders in the middle of the table, dripping red wax like blood splatters onto the scarred wooden surface. The scents of spices and raw meat wafted on the air. Isadora's stomach rolled as she looked from the candles to the slab of oozing red meat on the plate in front of her. She didn't know where they were, only that it was colder than the top of the Aegis Mountains here and everything about this place was vile. The food, the temperature, the smell, the company. She wanted to go home. She wanted her sisters. She wanted…

Bile rose up her throat and she swallowed hard so she wouldn't think of Demetrius. She didn't want him. She couldn't. Not after what she now knew was true.

Dear gods. She couldn't be pregnant. Hours ago, that

had seemed like the perfect solution to all her problems. But now? Her eyes slid closed. She just couldn't be. The goddess was lying. No one could know so soon…

The soft chuckle at the other end of the table drew Isadora's eyes open. "I know much, Hora. And my son's seed now grows within you. Just as we planned it would."

What little food she'd eaten earlier rushed up and Isadora's stomach heaved. She covered her mouth with her hand, rolled out of the chair, and darted for the bathroom in the hallway Atalanta had let her use before ordering Isadora to join her for dinner.

Sardonic laughter followed as she slammed the door shut and reached for the toilet. Again and again her stomach heaved until there was nothing left. Until every muscle in her body ached from exhaustion. Until her soul was utterly and completely spent.

Tears rushed down her face as she dropped back on the floor and grabbed a towel from the bar to wipe her mouth. How could she have been so stupid? Why hadn't she seen the signs? Every cruel word and despicable thing Demetrius had ever done or said over the years came back tenfold in her mind to make perfect sense. She'd wanted to believe there was good in him. She'd built up a fantasy of who he was, when the truth had been staring her in the face the entire time.

He was Atalanta's son. The spawn of ultimate evil. And he'd tricked her to get what he—what Atalanta—wanted.

Her gaze strayed to her stomach. No, she couldn't possibly be…

She squeezed her eyes shut tight on a wave of misery,

unable to even think the word. And that's when she remembered the Fate's words.

Look within yourself for the balance you seek.

Chapter 22

CASEY'S EYES FLEW OPEN WIDE. ON A GASP SHE ROLLED out from under Theron's arm and lurched from the bed.

"*Meli?*" Groggy, Theron pushed up on his elbow and blinked Casey's way.

The first rays of dawn shone through the high-arching window of their suite in the castle, cascading over his rumpled hair, the dark whiskers on his jaw, his broad, bare, and muscular chest. His eyes were still sleepy, the lines on his face a harsh reminder that even in sleep he hadn't found peace. Exhaustion was wearing on him, and since he hadn't slept more than two hours since Isadora had gone missing, Casey had pulled out all the stops and lured him to bed with the promise she would ease at least a little of his anxiety first. Truth be told, she'd succeeded in easing them both, for a little while at least, and afterward Theron had finally fallen asleep in her arms, just as she'd wanted. But now...

"*Meli?*" he asked again, sitting upright on the white silk sheets. Confusion cleared from his eyes and the focused intensity she was used to seeing from the leader of the Argonauts returned to his features.

Her pulse slowed as she looked at him, as she took in the dimly lit room around her with its four-poster bed, lush rugs, and velvet curtains. Damn it. The hallucination, dream...whatever the hell she'd just experienced had killed their restful mood.

"I—"

"Casey!"

The sound of Callia's voice in the living room, at this hour of the morning, brought both their heads around.

Casey's heart rate shot up again. And one thought registered. The king. God, not now. Not with Isadora missing. Casey darted a look at Theron and saw the worry she felt reflected back at her. She reached for her robe from the end of the bed and headed for the door.

"Hold on, *meli*."

By the time she pulled the double doors open, Callia was already across the living room, her hand lifted to knock on the bedroom door. She wore baby blue silk pajamas, the cuffs of the pants brushing her bare feet, the sleeves falling to her knuckles. Behind her, Zander's face was pale and drawn, and from his twisted sweats and rumpled hair it was apparent his much-needed few hours of sleep were also long gone.

"The king?" Casey asked, her worry overriding everything else.

"What?" Callia's brows dropped low. "No. He's fine. I mean, I'm sure he's fine. That's not why I'm here. I—"

Relief was swift and consuming. And then Casey thought of the dream and dread spiraled in like a twister.

Casey reached for her sister's hands. "You felt it too."

"Yes," Callia breathed, gripping Casey's hands. "You did as well?"

Casey nodded.

"Can someone tell me what the hell is going on?" Theron asked.

"I vote for that," Zander muttered at Callia's back.

Casey'd almost forgotten about the males in the

room. She turned toward her husband. "I don't know. At first I thought it was a nightmare. It was so strong it pushed me right out of bed. But now I'm not so sure. I thought I felt—"

"A jolt," Callia finished. "And then a voice. It sounded like…"

As Callia's words trailed off, Casey looked back into her sister's wide frightened eyes, at the wild and tousled hair framing Callia's perfect face, at the stark reality mirrored back at her. One look and Casey knew the nightmare hadn't been a nightmare at all.

"Isadora's voice. You heard Isadora."

"Yes," Callia finished on a whisper. "Scared and alone and hurt. Casey, I'm starting to think I'm going crazy."

"Not crazy," Casey said. "I heard her too. She was calling out to us."

"Where?" Theron asked, excitement reverberating in his words as he stepped up next to Casey. "Where is she?"

They all knew this was the first real lead they'd had in over a week. Of course, Casey and Callia had tried repeatedly to use their link as the Horae to contact Isadora but nothing had happened, and the weaker they became the less likely they'd be any help. Now though, if there was a chance Isadora was reaching for them the way they were reaching for her…

"I don't know," Callia said. "Before, when Atalanta had Max and we tried to find them, we had the Orb to direct our energy. And we were all three together. This time—"

"This time we know more." Casey squeezed Callia's hands. "Touch and focus, remember? It's how we each use our gifts. We direct that, and then we focus on Isadora."

"And if it backfires?"

Callia was worried Atalanta would be able to see what they had planned again, like last time. The difference now was that they had nothing planned. They needed to find Isadora first. "Do we have another option?"

Callia's eyes held hers, darkened with understanding. "No."

"*Thea*," Zander started, but his worried voice faded to nothing as Casey closed her eyes and homed in on Isadora.

The Horae marking on her lower back began to pulse. The room spun and then she felt herself flying across space and time. Darkness pressed in, illuminated by tiny white lights all across the inky canvas like a thousand stars upon the heavens. She squeezed Callia's hands tighter, felt her sister's presence, and called out to Isadora with her mind. And was jolted by another sharp stab to the heart, this time stronger than the one that had propelled her out of bed.

I thought you'd never hear me.

Isadora. They'd reached her.

The Fate said balance, but I didn't really believe her. I'm just…I'm so happy I found you.

Casey had no idea what Isadora was rambling about. She was just thankful her sister was still alive. *We've been so worried, Isa.*

Are you all right? Callia asked. *Where are you? Tell us how to get to you.*

I…I'm fine. Tired and weak but not hurt. I…I don't know where I am. It's cold here. And dark. And there are daemons everywhere. But neither of you can come for me. That's what I needed most to tell you. Her voice hitched. *It's not about me anymore. Not even about us. It's bigger than that. We can't give Atalanta what she wants. Whatever you do, don't follow Demetrius. Don't let him bring you to me. He...*

The sob that caught in Isadora's throat was too much for Casey. *What did Demetrius do? Did he hurt you, Isa?*

Not physically, no. Isadora sniffled. *He...he's just not what everyone thinks.*

"Oh, gods, Gryphon was right," Callia whispered.

"Son of a bitch," Theron muttered from somewhere close.

Isa, think, Casey said. *Has anyone said anything, anything at all, about where they're holding you?*

No...nothing. I...I'm so sorry I'm not strong enough to get out of this on my own.

We'll find a way, Isa, Casey said, her own voice catching. *Do you hear me? Whatever you do, don't give up hope. We'll—*

I have to go. Fear filled Isadora's words. *She's looking for me. I don't want her to know we've been in contact. I love you both. I wish we'd had more time. Remember what I said. Please don't come for me.*

Isadora, wait. Callia's fingers tightened against Casey's. *Isa?*

Silence.

Casey's lashes lifted and she looked into Callia's worried eyes. But before she could turn and tell Theron what they'd discovered, the main door to their suite burst open and a member of the Executive Guard stumbled across the threshold.

"What in Hades is the meaning of this?" Theron asked.

"Sir." The guard's flustered eyes darted to Casey and Callia across the room. "My ladies, apologies." His gaze swung back to Theron and excitement filled his voice when he said, "We've got him. He came across the portal not more than thirty minutes ago. We've got the bastard. And he was carrying this."

He opened his palm to reveal the earth element, a shining diamond marked with the Titan symbol, the likes of which Casey had never seen before.

Callia gasped, and Zander moved in next to her for a better view. But what held Casey's undivided attention wasn't the gem or even the power she felt radiating from the guard's hand. It was the knowledge Demetrius was back. And he was the only person in the world who could lead them to Isadora.

—∿∿—

"Where in the bloody hell is he?"

Voices echoing down the dark staircase brought Demetrius's head up. Slowly, he pushed up from where he'd been sitting on the cold floor, leaning back against the stone wall, every muscle in his body aching as he waited for freedom.

The blackness inside rippled and rolled. When he got out of this blasted cell—after he found Isadora and brought her home—those fucking guards who'd tossed him in this hellhole were going to wish they'd never been born.

Heavy boots clomped on the stairs. Keys jangled and an argument with several participants broke out. He strained to listen, but his ears were still ringing and the pounding in his head made it hard to concentrate. More than a week on that miserable island, without anything substantial to eat and no decent sleep, had taken its toll. He was weaker than he'd realized. He couldn't call up a spell to spring the lock on these bars and he couldn't even hold his own against four measly guards.

Isadora. He had to get to Isadora. He had to keep it together long enough to find the others and...

The cell door swung open. He looked up just in time to see Theron lunge for him.

"You motherfucking son of a bitch!" Theron's fist plowed into Demetrius's jaw, slamming him against the wall.

"Theron!" someone screamed.

Stars fired off in Demetrius's vision but he didn't have time to defend himself. The leader of the Argonauts grabbed Demetrius by the arms as if he were nothing but a rag doll, pulled him forward, and slammed him back again. "Where is she?"

"Theron, stop this right now!" Casey's voice echoed in the room.

Darkness edged Demetrius's vision as Theron's fingers dug into the meat of his arms, sending blinding pain ricocheting to his head.

"Theron. *Skata.* He's not going to tell you where she is if you kill him."

Demetrius's gaze swung out and he saw Zander standing a good four feet back, looking as thin and weak as Demetrius felt. Then Casey, Theron's bride, next to him, worry and fear awash on her face. Demetrius's vision blurred but he shook his head to clear it, picked out Cerek and Phin behind her, and finally Titus standing outside the bars of the cell, watching the entire scene with a *Man, you're a dumbshit* look in his hazel eyes.

Two thoughts got through Demetrius's fuzzy brain. One, Theron was ready to tear him to pieces. And two, no one was about to stop him.

The guard's superior voice echoed back through Demetrius's mind and he realized in a rush they blamed him for Isadora's disappearance. Hadn't even once considered the fact there could be an alternate explanation.

The blackness erupted inside him, bubbled up from the depths of his soul where he'd always known true evil lurked. These weren't his friends, never really had been, and he'd been seriously mistaken if he thought they gave a rat's ass about him. They'd never believe him if he told the truth. He could see that now in the deeply carved lines of Theron's face, leaving Demetrius with an oh-so-fucking-clear picture of reality. His reality.

"Where is she?" Theron asked again from between clenched teeth.

Demetrius didn't answer. Only stared at the leader of the Argonauts and cleared his mind of everything. Everything they could use against him or twist into their own vile truths.

"If you don't tell me where she is right now—"

"He's not gonna tell you," Titus said from outside the cell. "You're wasting your time, Theron. He's put up a block."

Fury erupted in Theron's eyes. His fingers tightened around Demetrius's arms. But it was Casey's voice that stopped the guardian from ripping Demetrius's limbs off.

"Please, Demetrius," she said in a weak voice. "Please just tell us where Isadora is."

His gaze strayed to Casey, and he saw then that the king's half-breed daughter was pale and thin as well. As pale and thin as Isadora had been when he'd last seen her.

"We saw where you live," Theron said, dragging Demetrius's attention back to his face. "We saw your little lookout room, you sick fuck. We know you've had this planned for a long-ass time. And thanks to what Gryphon told us about your *materas*, we now know why. If you want to live to ever see the sun again, you'd better tell us where she is right this minute."

They'd been to his flat. They'd seen his pictures. And they knew Atalanta was his mother. Oh yeah, they'd already tried and convicted him. He wasn't getting out of this one.

"Shit," Titus muttered. "He knows where she is, but he's not going to tell us."

Menace erupted over Theron's face. "I ought to—"

"Not if you ever want to see her again," Demetrius finally said. Theron's eyes went wide with rage, but Demetrius didn't back down. "Now take your fucking hands off me."

The others must have read the fury on Theron's face, because they each moved forward, ready to pull Theron back. But the leader of the Argonauts easily shook off their arms. He released his hold but he didn't look away. "You sonofabitch no-good traitor. Do you have any idea what you've done?"

Demetrius swiped at his bloody lip. "Not everything's about you, Theron. The sooner you figure that out, the better off we'll all be." He looked at the others. "Titus is right. I do know where she is and I'm not going to tell you. I am, however, willing to make a deal."

"You're not taking Acacia or Callia anywhere. And we don't make deals with scumbag-sucking—"

Demetrius shot Theron a scathing look. "I don't need them. And you will deal if you want to save your soul mate's life. I'm willing to take you to where Atalanta's holding the princess, but once she's free you're going to do me a favor."

"You're higher than a kite if you think we're gonna release you after what you did."

"I don't expect you to. I want something else."

Theron's gaze jerked Titus's way, but the other guardian shook his head. "I can't read him. Your guess is as good as mine."

Theron's gaze swung back to Demetrius. "And just what do you want?"

"That, you'll find out later."

Theron scoffed. "Why should we trust you? Not only are you a witch but you're Atalanta's son. And thanks to you, Gryphon's gone. You could be leading us into a trap just like you did him."

Gone. Demetrius thought back to the way Gryphon had been on the island. Possessed. Which meant his soul was dead. Likely in Tartarus.

Not his biggest problem now. He couldn't do anything about it anyway. And considering everything else, the fact they knew he was part witch didn't even matter. The only thing that mattered was getting to Isadora before it was too late. "I could be," he answered with a shrug. "At this point, though, I'm the only option you've got. And contrary to what you think you know, things aren't always what they seem."

Theron turned away in disgust, looked toward Casey.

The half-breed's eyes reflected worry, fear, and indecision. "Theron."

He glanced to the other Argonauts, none of whom seemed to know what the hell to do. And in the silence, Demetrius prayed they would take him up on his offer. He knew exactly where Atalanta was holding Isadora, and thanks to the vileness that lingered inside him he was the only one who could get to her.

Theron turned to face him again and hatred brewed in his eyes when he said, "Fine. We'll agree to your terms. But that's where the hospitality ends. And you'd better pray we get to her in time, because if we don't I'm going to enjoy ripping you apart with my bare hands. Titus?"

"Yo."

"Get Orpheus over here. We're gonna need him. And tell the SOB we found the traitor who got his brother killed. That ought to light a fire under his ass."

--~~--

"It's as cold as the fucking Arctic up here," Phineus mumbled as he rubbed his hands together to ease the chill they all felt.

"It pretty much *is* the Arctic, dumbass," Titus said, shifting the toothpick in his mouth to the other side and stomping his boots in the thin layer of snow that covered the permafrost.

From his spot on the other side of the old-growth trees they were all huddled under in the frigid forests of northern British Columbia, Demetrius watched the banter with keen eyes. Next to him, Cerek shot Phin and Titus a glare. "Stop your bitching. It's better than Siberia any day of the damn week. Trust me, I know."

"Ladies," Theron said as he studied the rough sketch of Atalanta's compound that Max had put together for them. "If we're done gossiping, I could use some focus here."

The boy had detailed the main lodge, the training yard, and the barracks with chilling accuracy, but luckily he hadn't remembered just how to reach Atalanta's stronghold. That, thankfully, had kept Demetrius in the loop and had made his presence necessary.

They were half a mile away, hidden in the trees just outside the northern city of Fort Nelson. Moonlight cast looming shadows across the frozen forest floor. A slight breeze blew, rustling the evergreens in the dead of night. In addition to the Argonauts, Orpheus had agreed to join the raid, but he wasn't listening to Theron or studying the schematics of the compound. No, his icy eyes were pinned on Demetrius and murder brewed in their dark depths.

Get in line, shithead.

Beneath the thin dark jacket he wore, that blackness inside Demetrius shifted. The closer they'd gotten to Atalanta and her daemons, the stronger it had grown, giving him the power and strength he'd been lacking. Until now it was all Demetrius could do to keep it at bay. But soon enough he'd let it free. If his plan went as he hoped, soon enough it would consume him. And Orpheus just might get that murder he so desperately sought.

"Z?" Theron asked. "You ready?"

Next to Demetrius, Zander scowled. "No. I'd rather kick some daemon ass."

Theron folded the map and stuck it in his back pocket. "Too bad. I'm not risking you in your condition."

"I can't be—"

"You can be hurt. And none of us have time to haul your ass out of there if things get rough, which I fully expect to happen." His gaze swept each of the Argonauts and hovered on Orpheus. "Rescue mission only. We clear?"

The guys nodded in agreement, all except Orpheus, who still had a death stare dialed in on Demetrius.

Yeah, he deserved it, but a small space in Demetrius's chest pinched with the realization he was now the outcast. Though he'd never truly fit in with the others, he'd been a part of something greater than himself for a short amount of time. Now? Now they all regarded him as the enemy. Which, ironically, he was.

"O?" Theron asked.

Orpheus tore his gaze from Demetrius and looked toward Theron. But something shimmered over his face before he turned, and for a split second his eyes shifted to a glowing green before hardening once more. "Yeah, I'm ready. Let's do this."

The blackness inside Demetrius jumped to life, recognition sparking it into action. He hadn't been sure before, but now he knew for certain. Orpheus was—

"Zander," Theron said, "you know what you have to do."

"Yeah, yeah," Zander mumbled. "I've got it under control. He's not going anywhere. Just don't have too much fun without me."

Casting Demetrius a withering look, Theron turned and motioned the others to follow.

The Argonauts disappeared into the trees, their path a circular loop in different directions around the property, out of sight of Atalanta's sentries. Thanks to what Demetrius had told them and Max had confirmed, they were targeting the main house. But that wasn't where Isadora was being held. Demetrius stared out over the barren brown field. Far off in the distance, he sensed Isadora was close to Atalanta, in her stronghold, where her powers were greatest and where no one could get to her but him.

Zander shoved his hands into his pants pockets, jumped up and down a few times to ease the chill. "Fucking freezing out here."

The guardian was ticked he'd been relegated to baby-sitting detail, but Demetrius couldn't have picked better. And even though Demetrius was cuffed and Theron had brought Delia in to cast some sort of spell on the cuffs before they'd left so Demetrius couldn't use his magick to break free, he knew it was only a matter of time before opportunity presented itself. Now he just had to bide his time and wait.

Footsteps pounded in the trees no more than thirty yards away, followed by muffled voices and grunts that definitely weren't human. Or Argolean.

"*Skata.*" Zander tugged Demetrius back into the darkness of the trees. With his hands bound behind him, Demetrius watched from the shadows as three daemons, obviously running patrol, emerged from the woods and crossed the barren field.

Yes.

"Fuckers," Zander muttered when they were nearly across the field. "We're lucky they didn't see us."

Demetrius closed his eyes as a chant rose up in his mind. Calling on the magick that had been born into him, he reached out with an invisible limb, his power a dark mist curling along the ground until it reached the feet of the daemons, now more than a hundred yards away. Contact and pressure erupted in his hand. He imagined the mist wrapping around the ankle of the middle daemon and clamping down. Then he gathered his power and yanked.

A cry erupted across the field as the middle daemon was wrenched up and back to slam into the frozen ground. The other two jerked to a halt and looked back with perplexed expressions on their gnarled faces.

"What the hell—"

Demetrius shifted around to face his kinsman. "You've got about twenty seconds before they reach us."

"How did you—"

"The magick works like a beacon, Z. It's how they found me the first time. It's how they'll find us now. You can either stay here and be overrun, or you can unbind my arms and help me save Isadora."

"Save her? I thought—"

A roar erupted across the field and footsteps pounded the earth, signaling that the daemons had realized just where they were. Demetrius's pulse picked up speed. "Contrary to what Theron thinks, I didn't hand her over to Atalanta. And I'll do whatever it takes to get her back. Even sacrifice you if I have to."

Zander's eyes flashed from silver to gray, signaling he'd called up one of his legendary rages. "You sonofa—"

Another roar sounded, this one a hell of a lot closer.

"Five seconds, Z. You more than anyone know things aren't always what they seem. The others won't be able to get to her. I'm the only one who can. Help me."

Zander's eyes held Demetrius's, indecision warring within their gray depths. "Motherfucker."

Whether it was the plea or the truth that made up Z's mind, Demetrius didn't know. But Zander shoved Demetrius around without another word. Metal clicked against metal as the key slid into the lock, then the cuffs clanged together as they separated.

Zander thrust the ten-inch hunting knife from his thigh into Demetrius's hand and took a step away, reaching back for the parazonium at his back. "You'd better not make me regret this."

Demetrius didn't have time to answer. The first daemon plowed into his body, taking him down hard. His skull cracked against the frozen ground, but he arced out with the knife, catching the daemon at the jugular with the blade. Blood sprayed all over him and the ground. The daemon fell forward, his weight pinning Demetrius to the frozen earth. The beast wasn't dead, though, and Demetrius had seconds before it got its second wind.

He flipped the daemon to its back and scrambled out from under its weight. Grasping the sword from its clawed hand, he swung out and down, decapitating it before it had a chance to regenerate its strength.

"D!"

Zander's voice brought Demetrius's attention around. The guardian was battling two daemons, each coming at him from a different direction. Though Zander could probably handle them alone, Demetrius charged the one on the left and took the monster down with a few carefully placed swipes of his blade.

The fight was over within minutes, the carnage

around them a stark reminder of what they faced the closer they got to the compound. Breathing heavily, Zander braced his hands on his knees and leaned forward while he sucked air as if he'd just run a marathon.

"You okay?" Demetrius asked as he wiped his blade against his thigh.

"Peachy," Zander muttered. He leveled Demetrius with a steely look as he pushed up to his full height. "You'd better not be fucking with me."

Blood ran down Zander's right bicep to darken his thin black jacket. Sweat covered his brow. As Demetrius studied his kinsman, he remembered what Gryphon had told him. Callia was linked to the Chosen, and she was Zander's vulnerability, his Achilles heel. Theron's words and the thinness he'd noticed in Zander earlier finally registered. Isadora's separation from Casey was affecting more than just the two of them. Four lives hung in the balance if he couldn't get to Isadora in time.

"I'm not," Demetrius said. "Isadora's being held in an underground bunker near the back edge of the property."

"Why didn't you tell Theron?"

"Because I needed a diversion. If Atalanta suspects I'm not on her side, she'll have an army guarding the area. She knows I'll be coming for Isadora. I needed Theron and the others to draw them away."

Zander studied him, clenched his jaw. "Why are you the only one who can get to her?"

"Because I share more than just Atalanta's DNA."

"That magick trick you pulled with the daemons?"

"No." He thought about that black mist curling through him even now. "That's a gift from Medea. What I share with Atalanta is a helluva lot darker."

"How do I know you won't turn that on me when we get closer?"

"You don't. But I promise you this, my only goal is to get Isadora out of there and back to Argolea. I'll do whatever it takes to make that happen."

Zander's eyes held Demetrius's so long, Demetrius's pulse picked up speed. If Zander didn't help him now... If he called Theron or one of the others to come back...

"You've fallen for her."

Demetrius clenched his jaw, looked quickly away, and thanked Zeus that Zander couldn't read minds like Titus. "Yeah, that's it."

"Shit," Zander muttered. "You didn't just fall for her. She's your soul mate. Why didn't I figure that out sooner? Now it all makes sense. No wonder you didn't want to bind yourself to her."

Skata. He was obviously doing a bang-up job of hiding his emotions if Zander could see through him like tissue paper.

Demetrius handed Zander the hunting knife then looked over the field. "Can we just go already?"

Zander sheathed the knife and chuckled. "Oh, man. Hera cursed you but good."

No shit.

Demetrius turned for the tree line around the field. "I'm leaving."

Zander followed. "This just got a whole lot more interesting."

The guardian didn't know the half of it.

They stayed out of sight of any daemons in the area and thirty minutes later were crouched behind a small outbuilding on the far side of the property, waiting for the perfect moment to make their move. Ahead, an enormous warehouse-style building was illuminated by an eerie orange light.

"How many?" Zander whispered.

"Looks like four," Demetrius said softly. "Two just left. Theron and the others must be causing a commotion at the main house."

They were far enough away that they couldn't hear or see anything happening at the lodge a distance across the field. Though Demetrius had told Zander the truth and he did need the others to create a diversion, he hoped like Hades none of them got killed in the process.

Demetrius ducked back behind the shed. "Okay, we'll go around from behind. One sentry's walking each side. I'll take the right, you take the left. Try to make it soundless, then go for the guard on your side at the front door."

"Got it."

Hunched down, Zander disappeared into the darkness. Demetrius did the same. His heart pounded hard in his chest as he waited in the shadows for the daemon sentry to move past him. Then, when the beast wasn't expecting it, he struck.

He was the same height as the sonofabitch. Slipping up behind the daemon, he wrapped his hand around the fucker's mouth before it could shout out a warning and sliced its jugular in one clean sweep. The black mist inside him screeched to the forefront, but he ignored it, beheaded the monster, stepped over what was left, and tiptoed to the edge of the building.

Two daemons stood at the main doors, still as statues, their glowing green eyes scanning the landscape.

"Come on, Z," Demetrius whispered.

Twenty seconds later, Zander's head popped around the far side of the building. He gave Demetrius the thumbs-up, then disappeared again.

"Go time." Demetrius took a deep breath even as the blackness roared inside. Soon enough he'd let it out. He had to have faith Zander would be able to get Isadora out before he lost himself to it for good.

He waited for Zander to make his move. A swish echoed across the silence, then a grunt, and without even looking Demetrius knew Zander had thrown his hunting knife into the neck of the daemon closest to him. When the daemon on Demetrius's side turned to see what had happened, Demetrius charged.

His blade was a blur of metal as he struck from the back, decapitating the daemon in one strike. The other daemon cried out, his guttural howl like a blaring alarm. Demetrius jumped over the falling body of the first daemon and swiped out with his blade, catching the second across the back. Zander charged from the other direction, and seconds later all that was left between them were blood, body parts, and steam.

"Come on." Demetrius dropped to his knees and reached for the keys hanging from the first daemon's waistband.

He slid the key in the warehouse door, turned, and pushed it open just enough so they could pull the bodies into the darkness. They locked it from the inside, spun around and surveyed the vast space.

Demetrius moved like a wraith, one thought in mind as he headed for the door at the back of the building that led down into the tunnels. Zander didn't speak, but

Demetrius heard the guardian behind him as they eased down the stairs and into the corridor like silent black shadows, low and deadly in the eerie orange illumination.

It was just as he'd remembered—stone walls, lights in the ceiling, and an air of evil that seemed to coat every inch of space.

The acrid odor of brimstone was strong in the tunnel but this time it didn't bother Demetrius. The blackness inside burst forward, curling around every organ, tightening like a boa constrictor.

He stopped in front of the black door at the end of the tunnel surrounded by a pulsing halo of smoke and stared at the hideous warnings carved in daemonic text all over the burnt wood. He hadn't been able to read them the first time he'd been here, but now he could. Now, because the black mist inside was on the verge of consuming him, he knew exactly what they said.

"What the hell is this place?" Zander asked, covering his mouth and nose with his hand.

"What you think it is," Demetrius answered. "The doorway to hell. Hell on earth."

Give in. Come to me.

He reached out with his hand.

"Um, D? Maybe this isn't such a good idea."

"No matter what happens," Demetrius said without turning, "get Isadora out of there. Open the portal and take her home. Don't wait for me."

"Yeah, D, man. I know, but what if—"

"No matter what happens, Zander. No matter what I do or say in there. Just make sure she's safe."

He lowered his hand to the door before Zander could say anything else. Power sliced into his palm, raced up his arm, and exploded in his chest, invigorating him with phenomenal strength and the dark, vile energy of his lineage.

"*Skata*. D—"

The mist whipped into a whirlwind of evilness, whisking through Demetrius like a tornado. Until his vision turned dark, until his limbs grew light, until all he saw and heard and felt was the malicious wickedness that no longer existed only on the other side of that door.

Until, in one mighty pull, the blackness drew him home for good.

Chapter 23

ORPHEUS CAME TO A DEAD STANDSTILL. FRIGID AIR blew past his face. A tingle ran over his skin. Deep inside, the daemon he kept locked down roared to life.

He felt his eyes shift to green but couldn't stop it from happening. This time the pull of evil was too great, the mixture of witchcraft and darkness in the empty space that should hold his soul telling him one of his own had just turned.

Rustling to his right brought his attention around. In the darkness he watched Phineus and Theron slink from the shadows to take down the three guards on the north side of the building. A barren field surrounded them. They were using shadows and darkness to cloak their attack, but they weren't a surprise. The daemon inside him roared again, signaling the darkness was coming. It was coming, and it knew, and it was ready to destroy.

Urgency pushed at him, drew him, dominated every cell in his body. He moved in stealth mode to Theron's side, where the guardian was sheathing his blade. "She's not here. It's a trap. Get your guys the hell out of here."

"What?" Theron glared at him. "How do you—"

A roar sounded from the other side of the building. Theron's head jerked in that direction.

Orpheus's eyes glowed bright, illuminating the darkness in a surreal green light as he took a step away. "I'll get to Isadora. Just go!"

He closed his eyes, blocking out Theron and the others and what he hoped didn't happen, and instead focused not on the darkness that was so much a part of him but on the magick of his mother. On his link to Medea and what he'd sensed hidden in Demetrius from the very start. He let that guide him as he flashed from the frozen field, across empty space, through earth and solid walls. And hoped like Hades he wasn't too late.

A thick haze of darkness surrounded Isadora, pulling the breath from her lungs and settling deep in her bones.

Her heart beat was fast and erratic. An evil air hung heavy in the stillness, ratcheting her adrenaline and fear to epic levels. A sense of déjà vu washed through her, but she didn't know where she was, only that it was cold and dark and the stench of brimstone was strong enough to make her gag. And somewhere in the darkness, Atalanta lurked.

"I sense your fear, Hora."

Isadora's pulse picked up speed as she turned in a slow circle.

"You wonder why I have brought you here," Atalanta crooned from somewhere close. "I feel the energy vibrating within you."

Isadora felt it too, thrumming in her veins, battling the malevolence that surrounded her.

Light flared, cutting through the inky darkness in a burst of illumination. Isadora flinched, blocked the glare with her hand. As her eyes adjusted, she realized she was standing in the center of a vast room. Thousands of candles burned, but the maliciousness was still there, hovering over everything as if it could extinguish the flames with one heavy breath.

From the far end of the room, Atalanta moved into the light. "You feel it, don't you? The power of the darkness? Our gifts are not all that different, Hora. The key is how we choose to use them."

"Ours are different. You use yours for evil. And I…" Her voice trailed off. How the heck did she use hers? Aside from contacting her sisters, she hadn't yet. She didn't even know if she could.

A wicked smile spread across Atalanta's perfect face. "Your powers are young, but I can teach you. If you join me willingly, I can teach you a great many things. The world is at your fingertips."

The goddess was scheming. She never did anything without purpose. Was she worried that Demetrius wouldn't follow her instructions?

Her stomach rolled. "It's all for naught. Theron will never let Casey leave Argolea. He'll never allow Demetrius to bring her here. You're going to lose."

Atalanta's vile grin spread. "Do you think I cannot predict the Argonauts' next move? Even now as we speak, they are preparing to rescue you from the main house. And yet they will fail. They walk into a trap." She moved closer. "And I need not your sister, Hora. I never did."

Atalanta moved past her, and Isadora turned to follow the trail of her red robe. "I won't live long enough to…" She placed her hand over her stomach, barely able to think the words. "To give you what you want."

"Oh, you will," Atalanta said over her shoulder. She gestured to the room with a wide sweep of her hand. "My power gathers here, in this chamber, where it's fed by the darkness I harnessed from Tartarus. And with you here, the temptation will be too great for my son to deny." She turned to face Isadora again. "Knowing his soul mate is in mortal danger will bring him to this place. This time he'll come ready to wage war, consumed by hatred. And when that happens, he won't be able to resist the power of the darkness. When he finally joins me in his rightful place, he'll be strong enough to use his Medean gifts to keep you alive long enough to bear me the child that was stolen from me by your Argonauts."

Isadora's breath caught as the plan Atalanta so easily laid out before her took shape in her mind. She remembered the way Demetrius had healed her broken leg. "How?" she whispered. "How is it even possible…?"

"How is what possible?"

"That you, of all beings, are his mother?"

"I should have been one of the first Argonauts, Hora." The air stirred, whipping past Isadora's face with the force of the goddess's fury. "And you would be wise not to forget that."

The wind died down and Atalanta added, "You're honestly curious, aren't you?"

Isadora didn't know how to answer. She sensed she was walking a tightrope and that at any moment the string could break, thrusting her into the dark chasm of Atalanta's rage.

"The story of Demetrius's birth is actually linked to your existence, Hora."

Though fear lanced through Isadora's chest, she asked, "I don't…How?"

Atalanta moved to stare into the flame of a candle perched on a tall spire of twisted metal. "Three thousand years in Tartarus is not exactly my idea of paradise. But it was a condition of my deal for immortality. In fact, all gods are limited by their immortality. Did you know that?"

She turned to peer at Isadora. "Don't you think Hades would rather be here, among the humans he so loves to manipulate? Of course he would, as would all the gods, but their time in the human realm is finite. A day here or there, a few hours to meddle where they shouldn't be meddling. I was tired of Tartarus."

Isadora thought about the Fate, and how she'd left the temple so soon after arriving.

"Which is how you come in, Hora," Atalanta said. "You see, I couldn't allow the Chosen to be united, because it would render me mortal again, but the prospect...of being free of my bonds to Tartarus? Now that was tempting."

Isadora's mind twisted with conversations long past. She remembered Demetrius telling her he'd never known his mother. How he'd been abused by a father who should have loved him. She thought about what he'd said—that a female had seduced his father and he'd been the unwanted result. And that he had a brother who'd been raised in the human realm.

What would Demetrius have in common with a human brother?

And then she knew. His father hadn't just hated Demetrius's link to Medea. He'd despised Demetrius because he'd been duped by Atalanta in her quest for ultimate power. She'd wanted control of her immortality.

She'd been tempted to find a way around Hades's bargain. She'd thought conceiving her own Chosen—siblings that were the perfect balance of half god, half mortal—would do that. "You tried to get around the prophecy by creating your own Chosen."

Atalanta turned to face her. "I tried. But I failed. And lucky for me I did, because we wouldn't be together now." The goddess turned abruptly toward the dark end of the room before Isadora could answer. "Ah, there you are, *yios*. I was beginning to think you'd changed your mind."

A shadow loomed in the darkness, but it wasn't friendly. Malice spread from beyond the illuminated circle. Malice and a malevolent threat aimed directly at Isadora.

She swallowed hard. Took a step backward.

"Come into the light, *yios*."

Isadora's gaze shot to the shadows. The air stirred as Demetrius stepped from darkness into light. And one look told Isadora that if she'd held out any hope he was going to save her, she'd been a fool.

His eyes were hard, cold pools of obsidian. No spark, no light, no kindness anywhere in their fathomless depths. He didn't look at her. Didn't show even a hint of recognition. The darkness engulfed him fully, and though she knew it was useless she found herself wishing he'd turn into the stone-cold bastard he'd always been whenever she was around. Because this—this soulless being possessed by evil—was a thousand times worse than anything she could have imagined.

Isadora took another step back. Panic and fear settled deep in her throat. Her heart pounded hard against her ribs as she waited and watched and prayed…for what, she didn't know.

"You please me." Atalanta cupped his face and kissed each of his cheeks.

He didn't recoil. Instead he muttered something in a language Isadora didn't understand, which made Atalanta laugh. And then they both turned and stared at her.

Emptiness brewed in Demetrius's eyes. It was as if someone else was looking out at her. As if they were strangers. As if they'd never shared a single thing on that island together.

The Horae marking on her leg tingled. Two words swirled in her mind.

Remember me.

Somewhere deep inside she knew it was her only chance. No matter what he'd planned, no matter how he'd schemed with Atalanta, there had been a connection between them. She was his *soul mate*, damn it.

"We'll need a strong spell, *yios*. We need her alive for at least nine months. I don't care if she's unconscious all that time, but we need that child. Are your powers strong enough?"

"They're strong enough." His cold, soulless eyes didn't leave Isadora, and the tingle in her leg grew stronger as he took a step her way. "It won't be pleasant for her, but the child will not perish."

Oh, gods…

Remember me. Remember me remember me remember me…

She backed up until her spine hit something solid, blocking her path. Her pulse raced like wildfire as he stopped in front of her. His body was the same, his scent so familiar it surrounded her, consumed her, reminded her of every moment alone on that island with him. He lifted his hands and closed his eyes. A chant rose up in the air as his lips moved and that black mist swirled around him, mixing with the Medean powers he drew from somewhere deep in his soul.

Fear pushed her forward. She grasped his hands, threaded her fingers in his, and held on tight. That tingle turned to a full-on vibration that shook her entire body.

Remember me.

Energy—a power she hadn't known she could control—flowed from her hands into his, a host of memories flashing through her brain, traveling into her limbs and out again. Every cruel word he'd uttered to her in the castle in Tiyrns, the moment in her chamber when he'd accused her of abandoning Theron in the human realm, that wretched day he'd refused to bind himself to her in front of her father and all the Argonauts, the way he'd soothed her burns after rescuing her in Apophis's castle, the nights he'd slept next to her to keep Hades away, when they'd made love, and afterward when he'd held her like she was the most precious thing in the world.

Emotions stirred in her chest. They rushed out her hands along with the memories, flowed into him. And when his chant cut off mid-sentence, when his eyes flew open and he stared down at her with a confused expression, as if he felt the transfer too but didn't understand how, hope sprang in her soul.

Remember me, remember me, remember me…

"*Kardia…*"

Yes!

He shook his head as if to clear the haze, then stared down at her with the same blank, malicious expression.

No. Remember me, dammit!

She gripped his hands tighter, focused harder.

"*Yios?*"

This time he didn't take his eyes off her as his chant resumed. He squeezed her hands right back, until pain shot up her fingers and into her palms.

She was weak and no match for his strength. His chanting grew louder. She cried out as he squeezed tighter, pushing down so she was forced to the ground.

"*Yios?*"

Something moved in the shadows behind Demetrius, but Isadora was in so much pain she couldn't focus. Demetrius let go of her hands and swung around to face Atalanta. His chanting grew stronger; then he thrust out his hands forward. The goddess's eyes went wide with surprise, and seconds later her body flew backward past the circle of candles to slam into the ground somewhere in the darkness.

The shadow shifted, moved, streaked toward Isadora. "That's our cue, Princess."

Zander. Oh, gods, it was Zander.

He wrapped his arms up underneath hers and hauled her to her feet. "Let's get the hell out of here."

"*Yios!*" Atalanta's bellow from the darkness shook the entire room. The candles went out in one giant breath of air.

Demetrius answered by chanting again and disappearing into the darkness.

"Come on," Zander said, more frantic this time, hauling Isadora with him toward the other side of the room.

"We have to get to the surface. I'm too weak to open a portal down here."

She found her footing, held onto his arms with fingers that still burned, and tried to move with him. A dark doorway loomed ahead. They took five steps before a series of roars from that direction halted their progress.

"*Skata.*"

Atalanta screeched. An arc of electricity lit up the darkness. Demetrius's chanting cut off abruptly and a crash resounded.

The roars—closer this time—brought Isadora's attention back around. Terror raced down her spine.

Zander pushed her behind him and grasped his parazonium. "Get back!"

Isadora didn't have a weapon. She couldn't even see a foot in front of her face. The roars grew to explosive levels. She felt Zander's adrenaline thrumming in the air in front of her. At her back, Atalanta screeched again and another arc of electricity illuminated the room.

She turned to look back, and in the split second of light saw Demetrius sail through the air and crash into the wall fifteen yards away. She cried out for him, but the roars, the pounding in her ears, drowned out all sound. Her heart lurched in her chest. Instinctively she moved toward him.

She slammed into a massive body, fell back on her butt. Horrified, she looked up and froze when the eyes peering down at her began to glow, casting an eerie green light over the entire area.

Oh shit…

"It seems I'm always rescuing your ass, Princess. Is this three now?"

Orpheus? No way. Orpheus was here?

"Holy shit, O," Zander exclaimed from mere feet to her left. "We're about to be overrun."

"Then might I suggest alternate travel plans?" Orpheus winked down at Isadora. "I'll add it to your bill."

He brought his pinky fingers together and opened the portal with a snap and sizzle. The room burst with light. Zander turned and grasped her arm, dragging her to him, but in the chaos she saw the Argonaut markings down Orpheus's forearms—the markings that hadn't been there mere days before.

A battle cry erupted just beyond the door.

Zander pushed her forward. "Go, go, go already!"

Isadora took a step toward the open portal. Behind her, another arc of energy lit up the room, followed by another crash of body into stone, and again she watched as Demetrius sailed through the air as if he were a rag doll.

"Demetrius," she whispered, moving toward him and away from the portal.

"What the hell do you think you're doing?" Orpheus asked.

"We can't leave him."

"I think he's getting what he deserves."

"She's going to kill him."

"Who the hell cares? Get through the portal, Princess!"

The black door shook with a mighty force. Followed by roars that rocked the room.

"No." She wasn't abandoning him. Not here. Not with Atalanta. She turned to Zander. "We can't just leave him here."

"You will rue the day you were born!" Atalanta

bellowed in the darkness. A groan sounded somewhere across the room.

"Zander!" Isadora cried.

Zander looked to Orpheus. "She's right. We can't leave him."

"What the—?"

"I couldn't have gotten to her without him. He tried to save her, not kill her. It's the truth, O. I don't know what happened with Gryphon, but he didn't hand her over to Atalanta. Dammit, she's his soul mate."

"Motherfucker," Orpheus muttered. "Talk about screwing up a wet dream. Would you two get through the damn portal already?"

"But—"

"I'll get him," Orpheus said loudly, cutting off Isadora's words.

"Do you promise?"

The glow of his green eyes held hers. But even through the illumination, she saw the truth lurking in their depths. He thought he was such a badass, yet how many times now had he come through for her when she needed him? "Yeah, I'll get him. Now *go*!"

The door crashed in. Another series of roars resounded, these louder and closer and a thousand times more frightening. Zander grasped her arm. "Come on!"

From the darkness Atalanta screamed, "Hora!"

"Please," Isadora pleaded as Zander tugged her toward the portal. "Please bring him back."

"You so fucking owe me for this," Orpheus muttered.

She didn't get a chance to respond. Zander pulled her through the portal with one last yank. And then all sound dispersed as she went flying.

Chapter 24

ISADORA STOOD IN THE MASSIVE WALK-IN CLOSET OF
her suite in the castle of Tiyrns with a towel wrapped
around her body, staring at the clothes hanging from
the rack.

Not a single pair of pants. No blouses. None of the
modern items Casey had helped her gather weeks ago
when she'd decided she wasn't going to play the part
of the cloistered princess any longer. All she saw were
miles of crinoline, satin, chiffon, and silk. Dresses she'd
thought she was done with forever.

Water droplets fell from her wet hair to drip onto her
bare shoulders. Her stomach rolled all over again. She
hitched the towel tighter as one expensive fabric bled
into another.

She barely remembered the past two days. Callia
had told her she'd blacked out when Zander brought
her back. She'd slept straight through, her body so sick
and worn out that it had needed the time to heal. But
even after nearly twenty-four hours asleep, a platter full
of food that hadn't stayed down, and a fresh shower,
Isadora didn't feel healed. Or free. If anything, looking
at the clothes in this closet, she felt more confined than
she ever had before. Even on Pandora.

She grabbed the first dress her fingers touched,
dropped the towel, and wriggled into the claustrophobic
gown. She didn't notice the color or style or anything

about the garment. The only things she wanted were answers. And after everything she'd been through, she deserved them.

She zipped the back of the dress, finger-combed her short hair, then reached for the closest pair of shoes before turning out of the closet. And stopped when she came face-to-face with both of her sisters.

"I'd say she's feeling better," Callia said in that healer voice that set Isadora's nerves on edge.

"Much," Casey agreed with a smile that looked forced.

They were both dressed in slacks, Casey with a red fitted sweater and Callia with a blue button-down blouse. Both were close to the same height, with the same violet eyes and the same confident expressions. And both were studying her as if she were their latest laboratory experiment.

Isadora dropped the shoes and slid her feet into them. "Where is he?"

When neither sister answered, she looked up. Callia and Casey exchanged somber glances.

"What?" Isadora asked. "He is back, isn't he? You told me Orpheus brought him back. I need to talk to him."

"He's not…" Callia started, then closed her mouth. "You can't."

"Why not?" When neither answered again, panic settled in. "Is he…?" *Oh, gods.* "Is he hurt?"

"He's not hurt," Callia said quickly, taking Isadora's left hand. "He's fine. Orpheus found him in the dark and flashed him outside the bunker walls. He was a little banged up from the fight with Atalanta, but these guys—they heal quickly with their superhero Argonaut genes, you know." The healer tried to smile but it didn't reach her eyes. "He's lucky Orpheus was there, though. Anyone else...they wouldn't have been able to get away."

Isadora knew that. She owed Orpheus. In the hours since her rescue she'd learned that Theron and the others had defeated the daemons and that the ones who hadn't been killed had scattered, just as she'd learned Atalanta was now gone as well. Where, no one seemed to know, but whatever Orpheus and Demetrius had done to the goddess down there in that bunker had given the Argonauts the chance they needed to win the battle.

Her gaze strayed to Casey and she noticed her sister still looked worried. Something was wrong. If Demetrius wasn't hurt...

"What aren't you both telling me?"

Casey took Isadora's other hand. "Honey, I really think you should lie back down. You're not back to one hundred percent yet and I don't want—"

Isadora was so sick of everyone coddling her. It had to stop. Now.

She wrenched her hands free and took a step back. "No, you tell me what's going on right now. Where is he? Did he leave?"

Casey looked to Callia again, and the pitying expression on her face only sent Isadora's blood pressure higher. "He didn't leave, Isa."

"Then where is he?"

"He's..."

"He's in Erebus," Callia finished when it was clear Casey didn't want to go on.

Isadora looked from one sister to the next. "Erebus? The prison? But why?" She flexed her fingers, desperate for something to do. They still ached from where Demetrius had hurt her in Atalanta's chamber, but she knew now he'd done that to trick the goddess so she wouldn't suspect he'd turn on her. No matter what he'd done up until that point, no matter what his motives had been before, he'd saved her. "I don't—"

"Between Gryphon's testimony that Demetrius betrayed the Argonauts and what Theron found in his flat," Casey said, "the Council's charged him with treason."

"Wait." Isadora held up a hand. "Gryphon's gone."

"He was here. The guys found him after the daemons took you from the field. He told the others what happened outside the colony."

Her mind flashed back to that moment when she'd stepped through the portal from Thrace Castle and realized they were surrounded by daemons. Demetrius had been shocked. She knew in her heart he hadn't planned that any more than she had. "Gryphon was hurt. He wasn't thinking clearly. I was there. Demetrius tried to save us. I don't know what you're talking about with regard to his flat, but—"

"He's been planning your abduction for months, Isadora." At Callia's bombshell, Isadora swung her attention to her other sister. "He had pictures of you all over his flat. A telescope that looked over the rooftops into your suite. Drawings of you, maps of the castle. Isadora"—her voice softened—"he's Atalanta's son. You yourself told us he wasn't what we all thought."

Confusion welled in Isadora's chest. "I know what I told you, but…my gods, we're all related to someone we don't want to be related to. Do I need to remind you both about the hideous things our own father has done?"

Casey sighed. "It's more than that, Isa. His lineage and the evidence combined with his attitude are damning."

"What do you mean, 'his attitude'?"

"He's not talking," Callia answered. "When the king questioned him, when the Council questioned him. He won't explain where you two were, how you ended up with Atalanta, or what happened while you were gone."

Isadora glanced at her skirt. "Why wouldn't he just tell them the truth? Why would he…?"

Color swirled before her eyes, and she saw herself standing in her closet, staring at a sea of gowns, each one more stifling than the last. She wasn't *that* princess anymore. She wasn't meek and timid and easily pushed around any longer. If the last week had taught her anything, it was that she was strong and confident and that she mattered. The gowns were nothing more than a facade.

You can't save me.

Why not?

Because some things aren't worth the effort.

Her chest grew tight. And in a rush she understood why Demetrius had been so cruel to her. For so many years he'd been trying to protect her from himself— because of who and what he thought he was. But he wasn't like Atalanta. Yes, something dark lurked inside him, but it didn't rule him. Even when he'd been sur- rounded by temptation of the most evil kind, he hadn't given in to it to the point of no return. And now, to keep the Council and the king and the Argonauts from knowing what had truly happened between them on that island, he was reverting back to his old ways. Protecting her with the same I-don't-give-a-shit-about-anyone pre- tense he'd always used.

"*Ilithios*," she muttered, heat rising in her cheeks as she pushed past her sisters and headed toward the door. "It won't work, you big jerk. Not this time."

"Isadora?" Casey asked with worry in her normally confident voice. "Where are you going?"

"To Erebus."

"He won't see you," Callia said quickly. "He won't see anyone. We've already tried."

"Oh, he'll see me." She grasped the door handle and pulled.

"How can you be so sure?" Casey asked.

"Because I know a secret the rest of you don't. I'm his soul mate. And he can be an ass all he likes to everyone else, but not to me. Not anymore."

—⁂—

Voices dragged Demetrius's eyes open. He eased his head away from the cold stone wall where he'd been trying to sleep and peered toward the dark staircase that ran to the guard's station one level up.

His cellblock was isolated in the bowels of Erebus where he couldn't interact with any other prisoners. The bars were steel, the cot so damn uncomfortable he'd parked himself on the floor with his back against the wall and his knees drawn up while he tried to clear his mind.

It hadn't worked. Every time he closed his eyes he saw Isadora's face when she'd looked at him in Atalanta's chamber. The fear, the disgust. But mostly the pain.

The voices picked up—some kind of commotion was happening at the guard's station. Had the Council decided on his punishment already? It'd only been a few hours since he'd told them to fuck off. Since he fully expected to be executed at any moment, he'd have preferred that Orpheus hadn't hauled his ass back here, but the end result was going to be the same, now, wasn't it? At least Isadora would soon be free.

His heart clenched at the thought of her, but he ignored the feeling. Atalanta was gone—that was another plus—but she'd be back. He had no doubt the goddess would somehow find a way out of the Fields of Asphodel, where he and Orpheus had banished her by uniting their Medean powers. Ironic, really, that he'd fought his Medean heritage for so long and yet he'd needed it to defeat Atalanta. Ironic also that what he and Orpheus had done wasn't all that different from what those witches had done to keep Apophis locked in Thrace Castle for thousands of years. He was still more than a little surprised Orpheus was part witch, but he didn't have the strength or energy to care much about the *ándras*'s intentions now. The only question left burning his gray matter was whether Isadora was really pregnant or if that had been another of Atalanta's lies.

The voices died off and footsteps echoed down the stone steps. He pushed up, careful to keep his hands behind him, palms flat against the cold stones at his back while he waited for his fate.

The guard came down first, but there was no executioner in his wake. What followed was a swish of powder blue silk that lightened the entire room and looked like a breath of fresh air in this dark dungeon. His throat closed as Isadora moved down the last step.

She wasn't pale and dirty anymore. Dressed in the wide-collared light blue dress that showed off her dainty shoulders, she looked like the queen she would soon become. The bell sleeves made her hands appear that much more delicate. The nipped waist reminded him how he'd been able to span her rib cage with his hands. And the A-line skirt sent thoughts of the treasures hidden beneath rushing through his mind.

Her chocolate eyes fell on his, held. He didn't move forward, just tried like crazy to still his pounding heart.

"Leave us," she said to the guard.

"I…" The guard stiffened. "The king has ordered the prisoner not be left unattended in the presence of visitors."

Isadora glared at the guard. "My father will be dead in a matter of weeks and I'll be your new queen. If you don't leave us now, I guarantee I will remember your name. And the consequences will be severe."

"But the king made it clear—"

"Now," Isadora said louder.

Unease rushed over the guard's face, but he backed toward the stairs. "I…I'll be right upstairs. If you need something…"

His voice trailed off as he scrambled up the steps. And in the silence that followed, Demetrius couldn't help but be awed by Isadora's strength. Gone was the timid princess he'd mocked for nearly two hundred years. In her place stood a *gynaíka* who was calm and collected and the only female in this world or the next who he had ever truly wanted.

She was the first to break the silence. "Do you have anything to say to me?"

Yes. A thousand things. Not a single one of which makes a difference now.

Fixing an impassive look on his face, he crossed his arms over his chest and stared at the wall.

"Fine," she said. "Then I'll go first. I know you didn't plan to open the portal in that field outside the colony. But I want to know what happened there and how we got from that field to Pandora. I think you owe me that much at least."

He did. He owed her so much more. But why would she think he hadn't opened the portal to that field on purpose? His gaze shifted her way. Didn't she know about his flat? About the pictures of her Theron had found there? About all the other evidence the Council had trumped up to prove he was the traitor they wanted?

"I was in Atalanta's chamber before two days ago, wasn't I?" she asked. "Her daemons captured us in that field. You didn't turn me over to her. They took us to her stronghold, and when she saw us together she knew what you've known all along. That I'm your soul mate. And she saw an opportunity then to get what she really wanted. That's how we got to Pandora. She banished us there so you'd be forced to protect me and we'd grow closer, and then she came back to claim her prize when she figured enough time had passed."

Fury welled in his chest over the fact Isadora had been manipulated for the goddess's cruel plans. But it was followed quickly by surprise that Isadora so easily saw through his lies and was pulling out a truth he didn't want her to know. If she believed he was a bastard and that he'd used her for Atalanta's gain, she could forget him when he was executed and move on with her life. But if she believed the truth…

He moved forward to grasp the bars of his cell and added just enough contempt to his voice to get his point across. "You live in a fantasy world, *Princess*."

She stiffened but didn't recoil as she would have in the past. "The most logical answer is usually the right one."

"Not this time." His gaze traveled the length of her body, a condescending sweep he'd used numerous times before to put her on edge. "But if it makes you feel better to pretend something so you can sleep at night, by all means go for it, *Highness*."

He sneered the last word and knew it hit its mark when she narrowed her eyes. But she didn't turn and leave in anger as he expected. Instead she stepped closer to the bars. The sweet scent of her rose up to make him light-headed.

"You can be an ass all you want, Demetrius, but it doesn't work on me. Not anymore. And you can tell all the lies you want as well, but I know the truth. You never would have willingly turned me over to Atalanta."

He scoffed, turned, and was about to push away from the bars when her delicate hands closed over his, warm and tempting and so alive they froze him in place.

"I love you," she whispered.

His head jerked her way, and that heart she'd kick-started back on Pandora leaped to life in his chest. Even though…what was the point?

"I know exactly what you're doing," she said softly. "The same thing you've been doing my whole life. Trying to make me hate you so you can go on protecting me. Well, I'm not falling for it. And I don't need you to protect me anymore. Do you think I care what the Council thinks? What my father thinks? All I care about is what's right. Their condemning you for something you didn't do is wrong, just as your protecting me from the Council's archaic traditions is wrong. They'll all learn I'm pregnant soon enough. If you won't stand up and tell them the truth now, how am I supposed to do so later?"

No. Atalanta had been right. She really was pregnant with his…*Gods.* His stomach dropped.

"You…you have to get rid of it."

She leveled him with a yeah-right look. "Nothing's happening to this baby."

Baby. She'd already given it a title. Panic pushed in. "Isadora, what lives in me will live in it."

"Good."

Good? Had she gone mad? "You don't realize—"

"Do you honestly think I believe you're like her? Demetrius, who we are is not a result of where we come from. It's the combination of what we do and how we live that determines who we are. If I'm to condemn you simply because you're related to her, then I might as well damn myself in the process. Every Argolean can link his or her heritage back to the gods. And I don't care if it's Zeus or Poseidon or Hades, each one is as cruel and self-serving as Atalanta in one way or another."

His brow wrinkled as he looked down at her calm and perfect face. "You saw what lurks inside me. The black mist—"

"I saw it." Her fingers tightened around his. "But I also saw that you didn't give yourself over to it. Not completely. And as long as I'm here, I won't let you. Hera picked a pretty damn good soul mate for you, because I have the power of balance within me, thanks to my link to the Horae. And I gave it to you. Let me be your balance, Demetrius."

She had. In Atalanta's chamber, he'd felt the energy and power rushing from her hands into his, and it had been enough balance to keep the darkness in check.

Was it possible she could love him, even knowing who and what he really was?

He looked down at her stomach, hidden behind the powder blue silk of her gown. "That thing inside you—"

"Baby," she corrected. "Our baby. Conceived in love, even if you didn't like the fact I tied you up."

His gaze shot back to her face. And heat stirred in his groin at the memory. He'd loved what she'd done to him that night with her little spell. Loved every moment of it and only wanted more. "How can you be so confident when everyone else knows I'm the enemy?"

"Because I know you and those fools don't." When he frowned, she added, "Don't you see? The humanity you scoff at is what sets you apart from Atalanta. All I have to do is think about the things you've done for me—like not telling the Council the truth today because you don't want them to punish me—and I realize how heroic you are. I might not agree with your tactics, but I understand them. And knowing you're doing all this to protect me? It only makes me love you that much more."

He could barely breathe. She loved him. Really loved him. Even knowing the truth.

She moved closer to the bars, until her heat was all he felt. "I felt the connection we shared when we made love. I felt it every time you kissed me on that island. I feel it now, in the bars between us. You've been protecting me from yourself for years, but you don't have to anymore. I didn't come down here because I needed confirmation of your innocence, Demetrius. I already know that truth. I came down here because I need to know you didn't do all this just because some twisted sense of fate says I'm your soul mate. I need to know you really love me too."

He closed his eyes and rested his forehead against the bars even as her love wrapped around him like a warm caress. She was asking for the impossible. For something that didn't even matter anymore. The truth would only prolong her pain after he was gone.

"Promise me you'll get rid of that thing inside you."

"Not even close."

His eyes squeezed tighter. "Then at least give it away."

"It's not an it. And *he* stays. Tell me the truth, Demetrius."

"You could bind yourself to one of the other guardians." He glanced at her. The look in her eyes said, *Not in a million years*.

"The truth, Demetrius."

Gods, she was so stubborn. A major pain in his ass. She always had been, right from the start. "I can't."

She eased up on her toes until her sweet breath brushed the side of his face, until his heart squeezed so tight it was hard to get air. "You can. It's easy. All you have to say is 'I love you.' Listen," she said softly, her breath tickling his cheek, her words warming the cold space left in his chest. "I love you. I love you. I love…you."

"Isadora…"

Voices brought his head up. The ruckus grew louder
and footsteps pounded the stairs. Isadora turned just as
three guards appeared from the dark tunnel.

"What's the meaning of this?" she demanded. "I left
instructions we were not to be disturbed."

The tallest guard moved forward and grasped her by
the arm. "The prisoner's to be moved to the Argolion to
face sentencing."

Oh, shit.

"What?" Isadora refused to let go of Demetrius's
hands. "He's yet to stand trial."

"The Council, upon the king's request, voted unan-
imously moments ago to convict him of high treason.
We have orders, Princess. Let go of the bars."

Isadora's shocked face shifted back to Demetrius.
She knew, just as he did, what the charge of high treason
entailed. There was no such thing as a "sentencing" in
this case.

"No," Isadora whispered. Then louder, "No. I won't
let this happen. You tell the Council they—"

The tallest guard lifted her around the waist and
jerked back hard until she was forced to release the bars.
"I said let go, Princess!"

Things happened so fast, Demetrius barely tracked
them. All he knew was the guard had a death grip on
Isadora, she was struggling in his arms, screaming for
him to release her, and he was hurting her. The black
mist swirled in his chest and pushed forward, turning
his vision to a dark hazy red. When the closest guard
unlocked the cell door and the second moved to cuff
him, he charged, knocking them both to the ground
before going straight for the third. "Let go of her!"

He got in one good punch before the other two were on him. Isadora screamed. Voices rang in the air. A club nailed him in the small of his back, sending blinding pain to his skull. Another hit him behind both knees, forcing him to the ground.

"Get down, you son of a bitch!"

"Get her back!"

"Stop! You're hurting him!"

Blow after blow hit him from all sides, until his vision swam and stars exploded behind his eyes. Someone wrenched his arms at his back and slapped cuffs on his wrists. Another guard shoved his battered face into the cold, dirty stones. Behind him, he heard crying.

"Please stop!"

Isadora. *His* Isadora. This was the last time he was going to see her. He couldn't let this be her last memory of him. He'd already taken everything else from her.

The guards hauled him to his feet. "Get up, maggot."

The room spun. Warm sticky wetness slid down his cheek. He tasted the coppery tang of blood. He stumbled but the guards caught him. "*Kardia*," he rasped.

"I'm right here," Isadora answered.

He swung his gaze to the right and zeroed in on her broken voice, on the pale halo of blond around her head that made her look like an angel, on her perfect face that was, even now, fading in and out of focus. "You were right. You've always been right. About me, about everything. I only wanted to save you from this. I'm sorry. I'm sorry for all of it."

The guard shoved him hard in the back. He stumbled forward. "No one cares, maggot."

"Demetrius—"

"I love you, *kardia*," he said louder as the guard shoved him up the first step. He twisted around to look at her. "You have my heart. You always have. Just you. Just you, Isadora."

As they dragged him away, his last image was of her standing between both her sisters with tears streaming down her cheeks.

Chapter 25

ISADORA STARED AT THE EMPTY STAIRWELL THROUGH A sea of tears.

"Oh, Isadora," Callia said.

"Isa," Casey said softly on her other side. "I had no idea."

She wasn't going to let this happen, and she wasn't about to act like all was lost either. Isadora stepped away from both of her sisters and wiped her cheeks. Her mind raced as conversations and links swirled behind her eyes. He had a brother. In the human realm. Someone he might not get along with but who would undoubtedly hate Atalanta as much as he did. Someone who was closer than she realized. If only she knew where he was, so she could figure out a way to bring him back here and have him explain to her father—

"Oh, *skata*." Her eyes grew wide. "Nick."

"Nick?" Casey asked, eyebrows drawn together. "What does the leader of the Misos have to do with any of this?"

"Nick is Demetrius's brother." Isadora brought her hand up to her mouth. "Oh, gods. Why didn't I figure that out sooner?"

"Demetrius has a brother?" Callia asked.

"Holy crap," Casey muttered. "That's why Theron's always been confused by Nick. Because he's both Argonaut and human."

Isadora turned a slow circle. She had to get to him.

But he'd moved the half-breed colony to a new location somewhere in Montana, and she had no idea where that was.

"The Argonauts will never let you through the portal," Casey said, following her train of thought.

Isadora stopped. "Orpheus can get me there."

Callia looked at each of them. "You're seriously going back to the human realm after what just happened to you?"

"He'll want something in return," Casey said, ignoring Callia's question.

Yeah, Isadora didn't doubt that for a minute. Orpheus never did anything without something in return. "He can have whatever the hell he wants, so long as he helps me."

She headed for the stairs, frantic to get to Orpheus before it was too late.

Casey's hand on her arm stopped her. "Hold up." When Isadora turned, Casey and Callia exchanged glances. Callia nodded, then Casey said, "We're going with you. You'll need help convincing Nick."

"He likes us," Callia added with a half smile. "More than he likes you, at least."

Isadora breathed easier. But not by much. Because on this one, her sister was right. "We have to hurry."

"I have no idea what you're talking about." Orpheus grabbed his spell book from the shelf in the back room of his shop and shoved it into his bag. "All I did was bring the traitor back, like you asked."

Isadora stepped around the table so she was in his face again. "You're lying."

So what if he was? That was his prerogative and she could take a flying leap for all he cared. Being daemon was bad enough. Admitting you were part witch to the Council would surely get him blacklisted. While he didn't much care what people thought of him, he didn't have time to dick around. Helping the Argonauts with their little raid had already slowed him down. He had one goal now, and everyone else could go to hell. Especially Demetrius. So what if they'd united their powers to lock good ol' Atalanta away? Eventually the bitch would find her way out of that purgatory. But Gryphon would still be dead.

The daemon in him pushed forward, the need for retribution strong. Controlling the beast, he glanced around, mentally ticked off what else he'd need. Delia's witches had given him shit as to where he might find that rat bastard sonofabitch Apophis. In Gryphon's body, the warlock could be anywhere. His next step was to head back to Thrace Castle and see what leads he could pick up there. Maybe torture a witch or ten if he had to. From there…from there he didn't know where the fuck he'd go.

"I don't care about your heritage, Orpheus." Isadora stepped in his path, blocking him again. "And if you won't cop to the fact you had a hand in defeating Atalanta, fine. I don't care. My father thinks you're a questionable source anyway. What I need right now is for you to take me to Nick."

His jaw locked. "I'm not a fucking bus driver, Isa. And I'm on my way out, in case you haven't noticed. Besides, you already owe me way more than I'll ever be able to collect."

"You can have whatever you want. Whenever you want. As soon as we get back. I won't even argue with you." She moved closer. "Just please, *please* help me. You're my last hope."

Yeah, like he hadn't heard that one before. "Why should I?"

"You have no reason to. Except…" She bit her lip as if trying to decide which tactic to use next. "Except helping me will piss off the Council."

"I can do that any damn day of the week."

"This is different," Callia added behind her. "We're talking *seriously* piss them off."

"With a passion," Casey said in agreement.

He flicked looks at both sisters, then at Isadora again. The princess was clearly desperate, but he couldn't figure out why. Demetrius was Atalanta's fucking son. Why the hell was she so frantic to save his life after what the guardian had done?

He knew there was one surefire way to get her to back the hell off. He leaned in close. "I only want one thing, Isa, the same damn thing I've always wanted. You. But this time I don't just want you for a quick little affair. I want you whenever and however and for as long as I'm interested. Are you willing to relinquish your future in order to save his life?"

"Yes. Absolutely."

He drew back, shocked by her answer.

"I said yes, Orpheus." She blinked once, like it was no big deal. "Can we go now?"

"You…you don't even want to think about it?"

"I don't have to."

Holy shit. "You're in love with him."

"Yes." Honesty raced across her face. He looked to her sisters, who both nodded in support.

His gaze shifted back to Isadora. "How can you feel anything for him, knowing what he is?"

"The truth?" When he nodded, she said, "I love him more *because* of what he is. He could have given himself over to the darkness at any time, but he never did. The Council is wrong. He never tried to hurt me. He tried to save Gryphon in that field and he rescued me more times than I can count. And I will do whatever I have to in order to do the same for him. Including give myself to you. You can have my body. I don't even care anymore. Because my heart will always belong to him."

Orpheus looked to the sisters again and caught their disgusted expressions, but he barely cared. Was it possible someone could love pure evil?

"Please," Isadora said gently, stepping close and laying her hand on his lower arm. "Please help me."

He looked down at her fingers, resting on the Argonaut markings on his skin—the ones that should be on Gryphon's arms—and felt something stir in his chest. It wasn't his soul, because he didn't have one. It was some heroic fucking honor that had passed from Gryphon into him when his brother's soul had gone to Hades.

"Sonofabitch," he muttered. "I don't want this responsibility. I never wanted it. Do you get that?"

"No one will force you to serve with the Argonauts if you don't want to. On that you have my word." She squeezed his arm. "Please, Orpheus."

He ground his teeth and looked toward the door. He wasn't a hero. He wasn't ever going to *be* a hero. Helping her now didn't change that fact, and the Argonauts could kiss his ass for all he cared. "Fine. Whatever. But if you get kidnapped by witches again, just know I'm not saving your ass."

Relief rushed over Isadora's face. A relief that stirred whatever was in his chest again and made him wish like hell he just didn't give a damn.

But he did. Motherfucker, he did.

——〰——

"Well, if it isn't the Witches of Eastwick and the Grand Poobah himself." Standing in the middle of the empty hall in the colony's new digs, Nick Blades frowned at the newcomers he considered a major-ass interruption.

"You're just jealous 'cause I got the hotties and you've got a fucking migraine," Orpheus said.

Wasn't that the damn truth?

"How about this one?" Helene asked, holding up a box.

Nick pointed the pen in his hand toward the stairs to his right. "Third-floor kitchen, Helene."

As Helene disappeared around the corner, Nick caught the half grin on Casey's face from the corner of his eye. "It's nice to see you again too, Nick."

He leaned down so she could kiss his cheek, then straightened, refocusing on the task at hand. Activity flowed around him, the bustle of people moving to and fro as they worked to get the ancient castle, nestled in a fjord high in the mountains of Montana, fortified and stocked. It wasn't his first choice for a location, but since the Misos colony in Oregon had been destroyed, it was the only place he'd found big enough for his people. And built on an island in the middle of an ancient lake, it was as isolated and secure as they were going to get. For now, at least.

"Where's Hercules?" he asked Casey without looking up. "Does yesterday's hero know you're walking on the wild side today?"

Casey frowned at the mention of her husband. "He's fine. And no, he doesn't know I'm here." She glanced toward the cathedral windows that looked down over the crystal blue lake. "Nick, where on earth did you find this place? It's like Hogwarts, straight out of a Harry Potter movie."

Frustrated, Nick rubbed a hand over the long jagged scar on the left side of his face. The one that was a stark reminder of just how much those in Argolea cared about his people. The only reason he answered was that Casey was a Misos just like him. "You know there's a colony in northern Russia, right? Some Russian prince's servant's brother's cousin's aunt or some shit like that is a Misos. He had this castle built sometime back in the 1800s but never got here because he was killed. When I contacted the other colonies to see about moving our people around temporarily until we could find more permanent digs, the Russian leader told me about this place and offered it to us."

"Wow," Casey said. "Just like that?"

No, not just like that. There were conditions. And it didn't matter how much Nick liked Casey, he wasn't going to get into those conditions with her or the future queen of Argolea. Ever.

"What the hell are the four of you doing here, anyway?" he asked, nearing the end of his patience for the day.

The princess moved forward from the back of the group. "We came to talk to you about your brother."

Nick clenched his jaw and went back to his checklist. "Not interested."

"They're going to kill him," Isadora protested.

"Oh yeah?" He didn't look up or care who "they" were. "I'm sure he deserves it. Now if you don't mind, I've got work to—"

Isadora wrenched the clipboard from his hands before he could turn away. "The king knows Atalanta is his mother. And we know she's yours too."

The scars on Nick's back—more blasted reminders—tingled with awareness, reawakening the blackness deep inside. His fiery gaze shot to Orpheus, standing behind the women with his hands shoved into the front pockets of his pants. "Hear her out, Nico."

Fuck.

He pointed toward the closest door. "You," he said to the princess, "in there. The rest of you, stay put."

"But—"

Nick cut Casey's protest off with a look.

In silence he followed Isadora into the long rectangular room with its soaring ceiling and iron chandelier and windows that spanned an entire wall that faced the lake. He guessed this was some kind of dining room, but as he kicked the door closed with his boot, he really didn't give a rip.

Isadora glared from across the room. "The Council thinks Demetrius turned traitor. They're going to execute him unless you help me stop it."

"Why should I care?"

"Because he's no more evil than you are."

The blackness surged. "Be careful, Princess. You don't know what the hell I am."

She took a step forward and lifted her head, looking proud and regal and confident. "I know you didn't choose your fate any more than Demetrius did. You're both pawns in Atalanta's quest for vengeance. And I know you hate her as much as he does."

"Do you want to know what I hate? Not just her, but you and your world and everything it stands for. Do you know the story of me and my so-called brother?"

"Not all of it. Just that she conceived you in an attempt to complete the prophecy on her own."

"She didn't conceive us. She mixed together her own cesspool of vileness. Have you heard of superfecundation?" When the princess shook her head he said, "It's when a female does the nasty with two different guys on the same night and is impregnated by both. Twins with different fathers. Only Atalanta didn't just pick anyone. She chose Akrisios, an SOB guardian in his own right, and then to seal the deal with evilness, she found the most horrific human serial killer and did the hokeypokey with him too.

"Since it was clear right from the start that her little plan didn't work, she knew she had to get rid of us. Best option? Send us to Argolea so we could infiltrate the Argonauts. She had her daemons leave us in the human realm in a place she knew the Argonauts would find us. And they did. Took us both back to Argolea. From Demetrius's markings, they knew he was Akrisios's son. But me? Well, let's just say the Council didn't think I was Argolean material. They had me cast out to the human realm, where they left me to die.

"Of course, I didn't," he sneered. "I survived. No thanks to any of your Argonauts. Not even my so-called brother. So you tell me, Princess, why should I help you save him when you and your kind have never done shit for me?"

Isadora's gaze dropped to his hands. "You have the markings. That's why you wear long sleeves and those fingerless gloves all the time. You…" Her gaze lifted, her eyes wide with awe. "You're an original Argonaut, spawned from the union of a god and a human. That's why the Council banished you. They're afraid of you."

Nick clenched his jaw and looked out the windows to the calm blue water, wishing the serene image would dampen the firestorm brewing deep inside.

He didn't hear Isadora step closer, but he sensed her, just as he'd always been able to sense whenever she was near.

"Nick," she said softly. "I can't do anything about the past. I can only assure you of the future. My father's health is steadily failing. He'll be dead in a matter of weeks and the rule of Argolea and the Argonauts will fall to me. I guarantee I'll not let what happened before happen again to you or your people. But I need your help to set things in motion. And it starts with saving Demetrius's life and proving to the Council their reign ends here. Then we can focus on this war and finally defeat Atalanta for good."

He looked down into her chocolate eyes. "You know about the soul mate curse?"

"I don't think it's so much of a curse anymore."

"Think again, Princess. Demetrius and I, thanks to the whole super-fucking-twin thing, only get one. I've known you're ours since you first showed up at my colony with Casey, looking for Theron. I'm sure Demetrius has known for years."

Her eyes ran over his face and surprise flushed her cheeks a delicate shade of pink. "And that's why you were never nice to me either."

"Why should I be? No one should be subjected to either one of us. You don't have a clue what lurks inside us."

"Yes, I do," she said softly. "But your humanity is stronger. It's why you make a great leader for your people and why Demetrius is so valuable to our race as an Argonaut."

No, Demetrius wasn't just a valuable Argonaut. He read it in her eyes. His brother had come to mean something more to her. Reality chilled a space in his chest. "You're in love with him."

"I am," she whispered. "Deeply."

Her chocolate eyes softened with emotions, and looking deep, he knew she was telling the truth. Something pinched in his chest. "You could have been mine."

"Maybe," she said, not denying it. "In another lifetime, perhaps. But not now. I love him, Nick. I always will. Please help me save him."

He shouldn't. There were a thousand reasons he shouldn't get involved. But that damn humanity she mentioned wouldn't let him turn his back the way he wanted.

"Shit," he muttered. "Go get your Grand Poobah. I don't have all day for this, you know."

A bright smile spread across Isadora's face, making her look…like a goddess. A gorgeous, powerful, confident goddess. "Thank you. I won't forget this."

She rushed from the room, and as the blackness inside him settled he told himself he wasn't doing this for Demetrius. He was doing this for her. For the soul mate he was never going to have, thanks to the all-fucking-mighty gods.

Nick was just stripping the fingerless gloves from his hands when Orpheus came back in with all three women.

"I've got this," Orpheus said, bringing his hands together so his pinky fingers touched and the portal burst to life between them.

Brow drawn low, Nick glanced from Orpheus's newly marked hands up to the *ándras*'s face. "What the hell?"

"Long story. But I think we should avoid the Gatehouse and the Executive Guard. Since you can only open the portal there, I'm saving us some time. Isa? Daddy's chamber?"

"Yes, please," Isadora said.

With one last beaming smile, Isadora stepped through the portal, followed by each of her sisters. Scowling, Nick followed.

They appeared in some kind of sitting room in the castle in Tiyrns. A maidservant jumped to her feet with a horrified expression. "Dear gods…"

"It's all right, Althea," Isadora said quickly. She stepped past the others to calm the flustered servant. "We need to see my father."

"But the king is sleeping. He's—"

"This can't wait."

Isadora pushed open the massive double doors to the king's bedchamber. The curtains were drawn, casting the room in darkness. From the enormous bed on the far side of the room, a frail voice said, "Who's there?"

"It's me," Isadora answered, stepping into the room. The sisters followed, each moving to stand on one side of the king. Nick hung back near the door with Orpheus, not entirely sure what he was doing here and hating every minute of it.

"*Pateras,*" Isadora said. "I've come to ask you to spare Demetrius's life."

The old king pushed himself up in the pillows and narrowed his beady eyes. "He betrayed the Argonauts."

"No, he didn't." Isadora moved to the foot of his bed. "He saved my life. He tried to save Gryphon's. I was there. He never would have sided with Atalanta."

"He lied to us. He's Atalanta's son. The proof shows—"

"The proof is wrong." She moved around the side of the bed. "You told me once that a true leader knows when to listen to history and when to focus on reality. The history is irrelevant here. We've all made mistakes we wish we could change. You included. He can't change where he came from any more than you can change what happened to Mother. His mistake was simply that he kept his lineage secret from you and everyone else for fear of persecution. For fear of what's happening to him right now. He's not evil, Father. He's more heroic than you or I will ever be."

She softened her voice. "If it weren't for him, I wouldn't be standing in front of you now. He saved me from the warlock in Thrace Castle. He kept me safe over the last week and a half. He found me in Atalanta's stronghold and made sure I came home. He's not the enemy here. Please don't let the Council condemn him for something he hasn't done."

The king's eyes darted around the room, but they

didn't seem to focus. "You have no proof of what's in his heart. The Council convicted him based on the evidence at hand."

Nick saw the same thing happening to Demetrius that had happened to him. Isadora was right. He couldn't stand back and let it keep happening. If he did, he was no better than his brother.

"I'm your evidence," he said from the back of the room.

"Who's there?" the king asked, looking his way.

Nick caught Isadora's thankful expression and moved fully into the room. "Nico. But you, Your Highness, will probably only remember me as that child the Council wanted to get rid of."

The king winced. Nick told the same story he'd told Isadora, and when he was done silence settled over the room.

"I…knew not of your lineage," the king said. "Only that you were—"

"Yeah." Disgust rolled through Nick, but he tamped it down. "A threat. I got that loud and clear."

"*Pateras*," Isadora said, reaching for the king's hand. "Nick isn't any more evil than Demetrius. He's proof the humanity of the heroes overpowers anything Atalanta may have given them."

"My brother would never turn to Atalanta," Nick said. "No more than I would. And I can tell you flat out, my only goal in this lifetime is to defeat the bitch." He glanced at Isadora. "Considering what she put Demetrius's soul mate through during this last week, I can pretty much guarantee that's his goal too."

Isadora's eyes softened so much, Nick felt that cold space in his chest warm just a touch.

"Please," Isadora said, refocusing on her father. "Please spare him."

The king sighed. "I can't. The Council's already made its decision."

"You can stop it, though. All you have to do is pardon him."

"If I do that, I'll look weak in the eyes of the Council. And they're already looking for a reason to declare me unfit to rule."

"Fine, then abdicate the throne to me. I'll pardon him."

The king's brow wrinkled. "You?"

"Rule is going to fall to me soon, whether you like it or not. Pass it to me now."

"You're not ready."

"I've never been more ready."

"It's not that easy—"

"It is," she said, her voice rising. "I've faced down Hades twice. I saved the earth element from both him and the warlock. I'm not about to let the Council push me around. Our world is changing, but I won't be part of the problem. And as queen, I won't allow them to be part of the problem anymore either."

She moved closer to the bed, gripped the king's hand tighter. "*Pateras*. Dad. I've never asked you for anything before. I'm asking you now. I'm begging. I've already lost my soul. Please, *please*, if you ever loved me, if you ever trusted me to become the leader you taught me to be, don't take away my life as well."

The king's milky gaze held hers, and in the silence Nick saw indecision and pride in the old *ándras*'s face. And he couldn't help but feel the same pride in his own chest. She really was royal material, contrary to what everyone thought. And for reasons he'd never understand, she loved his brother. Eternally.

"Althea," the king barked, breaking the moment.

The maidservant rushed in. "Yes, Your Highness."

"Get me my wreath. Callia? Acacia? Help me from this blasted bed."

"Holy shit," Orpheus muttered at Nick's side. "I never thought I'd see the day."

Nick frowned. He didn't share Orpheus's awe. Even though he knew he'd done the right thing here, he'd also sacrificed something as well.

Althea scurried out of the room. The sisters helped the king stand. Isadora glanced toward the clock high on the wall. "We don't have much time. Hurry."

"Isadora," the king said. "Kneel. Here."

She did as he commanded, looking up with expectation and impatience.

Althea hustled back into the room with a golden box in her hands. Several other servants followed, curious as to what was happening.

The king handed the box to Casey. She held it steady while he opened the lid and extracted the gold laurel wreath each king and queen before had worn at their coronation. He held it high over Isadora's head. "The future lies not in the hands of the gods and goddesses nor in the kings and queens of old. It lies before us."

At his feet, Isadora circled her hand in a hurry-up-already move the old king couldn't see. And Nick chuckled. Oh yeah, she was going to be okay as a leader. In fact, knowing how persuasive she could be, he sorta dreaded dealing with her.

The king lowered the wreath to her head, but the

pomp and circumstance was lost on Isadora. She jumped to her feet and grasped her skirts before he could launch into another speech. "Orpheus, Nick, gather soldiers from the castle gate. We'll need some muscle when we storm the Argolion."

"Hot damn," Orpheus said, flicking Nick a look. "I do so love stirring the shit with the Council." He poofed into nothingness before Nick could answer.

The sisters helped the now-exhausted ex-king back into bed. Servants whispered in shock as Isadora stepped toward Nick, but her father's voice caused her to turn back. "Wait." To Casey, he said, "Bring me that box over there on the table."

Casey handed him the small rectangular purple box he'd asked for. He opened the lid and motioned Isadora back to his side.

"I suppose this is yours now," he said. "The guard's found it on Demetrius when he came through the portal. I hope you know what you're doing."

Isadora looked into the box and smiled. Reaching in, her hand returned with a fat diamond the size of a quarter, attached to a long golden chain. "Thank you," she whispered. "I won't let you down."

Her father only harrumphed as she slid the necklace over her head, offered his wrinkled cheek so she could kiss him, then eased back into the pillows. "I'm tired."

A servant moved in to help him. Isadora stopped in front of Nick. "I'll never forget what you did here."

Nick's chest pinched again, a feeling he didn't like and didn't want to get used to. "We'll see. You still have to save him, Prin—" He caught himself. "Queen. Just don't expect me to ever call him King if you do."

She smiled and squeezed his hand, and in the soft light coming through the windows he saw the Titan symbol sparkle in the diamond nestled in her cleavage. "I won't, Nick. I promise."

Chapter 26

IT COULD BE WORSE.

As Demetrius pulled in deep, painful breaths and wished for death, he figured it could be a helluva lot worse. At least Isadora wasn't here to witness this.

"Here, D." Zander held a glass to his lips. "Drink this."

The cool water was the best thing he'd ever tasted. He sipped slowly, felt the liquid dribble from his lips, land on his bare chest, and slide down to mix with the blood and sweat staining his pants.

"This is wrong," Cerek muttered on his other side. "This is so fucking wrong."

"No shit," Phineus said. "I'd like to string up the damn Council and give them each a taste of what they're doing to him."

Demetrius's vision came and went. He turned away from the glass when he was done, focused on simply breathing while his kinsmen's voices drifted around him. If he'd had any strength left, he'd have dug deep for his magick to get the hell out of this one, but he was too weak. His arms ached from the weight of his body pulling down on the metal hooks high above his head. Beneath his bare feet, a pool of blood had gathered, dripping from the wounds in his back where the *tria mastigio* had sliced deep into his skin during the cleansing portion of the execution rite.

He was strung up in the main Council chamber, on

the raised platform behind the great alpha seal stamped into the marble floor where Isadora usually sat when she observed Council proceedings. Twelve massive pillars rose around the room in a vast circle. Guards were stationed at the main doors, another two on each side of the platform. The twelve Council members weren't seated around the alpha seal as usual, but had taken up space on the far side of the room where they could watch the ritual in relative comfort. All except Lucian, their leader, who stood in the center of the vast room arguing with Theron and the cleanser, the hooded guard the Council had chosen to mete out the early portion of the ritual.

Footsteps echoed, and the Argonauts' voices died down as Theron stepped back onto the platform and moved close. "The cleansing's over. I got Lucian to agree he's had enough."

"Fuck," Titus breathed. "Theron, man, this is wrong. He's one of us. Doesn't matter where the hell he came from."

"I know," Theron answered.

"He saved Isadora," Zander said. "I was there."

"I know," Theron said again, running a hand over his brow as if he had the mother of all migraines. "I know all of that, but he wouldn't talk, and the Council's ruled. I can't stop this any more than you can."

"It's not right," Cerek added. "This ritual isn't ever supposed to happen. I don't want to have anything to do with it."

Footsteps echoed again, and Demetrius cleared his vision just enough to see the two guards stepping up on the platform. The guardians' voices died down as they all watched the first guard set out the seven jars, followed by the second, who placed a marble box in the center of the table.

"Hold it together," Theron said quietly to each of the Argonauts as the guard opened the box and lifted the roll of red satin. He set the roll on the table, moved the box to the floor, and slowly unrolled until all seven ancient daggers inside were lined up, the bloodred satin beneath an eerie promise of what the weapons were meant to do.

"Fuck," Titus muttered again, turning away from the table. "No way. I'm not doing this."

Demetrius's gaze landed on the symbols carved into each black handle of the twelve-inch daggers. The same symbols he'd seen on the trunks in the Hall of Heroes. Each blade had once belonged to one of the original seven heroes, and they were never used. Not unless an Argonaut was sentenced to death. Though he'd never witnessed such a ceremony—couldn't remember when or if there'd ever been one—Demetrius knew how this was going to play out. Each Argonaut would use the weapon of his forefather to inflict a punishing wound. Death would be prolonged until the last killing blow. Then his organs would be cut from his body and buried in the jars in the far corners of Argolea as a testament to the other Argonauts of the swift retribution for betraying the order.

"If we don't," Theron said as tension grew around them, "Lucian will let his guards do it, and they'll draw this out as long as they can." He turned to Demetrius, and though his vision was murky Demetrius saw regret, not contempt, in the guardian's eyes. "I'll go first. I'll make it quick, D. The rest of you"—he glanced over the other faces—"you'll have to go through with it, but I'll make sure he's already dead."

More swearing rose up. Demetrius didn't care who went first; he just wanted this shit over. He licked his lips, struggled to find his voice. "Theron."

"Yeah, D," Theron said. "I'm right here."

Demetrius lifted his head, pushed his weight on his feet so he wasn't hanging by his arms. His legs shook. "I told you...before I took you to Atalanta's stronghold to find Isadora...I wanted one thing."

"I remember," Theron said gently. "You name it and it's yours. Whatever I can do, I will."

Demetrius drew in a deep breath. "Isadora's pregnant. She won't get rid of the...baby. I already tried to talk her into it."

A host of whispered *holy shit*s and *skata*s rose up around him.

"She won't..." He rolled his shoulder to ease the pain. Didn't work. "She won't bind herself to one of the other guys either. I tried that as well. She won't listen to me."

"She's never listened to me either," Theron said with a sad smile.

No, she hadn't, had she? The *gynaíka* did things her way, for right or wrong, and he loved her more because of it. "The Council can't know about the pregnancy. They can't..."

Emotion closed off his words. He swallowed hard, tried not to sound like he was begging, but really, what did it matter anymore?

Theron laid his hand over the markings on Demetrius's

arm, high above his head. "I'll make sure they don't. And when the baby's born, Acacia and I will raise it as our own. You have my word on that, D. Isadora will be protected. And your son will serve with the Argonauts when he's old enough. Just like his father."

Demetrius closed his eyes. Drew in a deep breath. Let it out slowly.

Yeah. Yeah, okay. They could get on with this now. "Thank you," he said to Theron. To all of them.

Voices echoed around him. Words of regret and friendship from each of his kinsmen. They knew the truth about him now, and contrary to what he'd always thought, they didn't hate him. Funny that it had taken all of this to get to a place where he finally felt…like he was really and truly one of them.

"Theron," Lucian announced in a loud voice from the other end of the room. "It is time."

Demetrius opened his eyes, looked at each of his kinsmen, and nodded in reassurance. "Look on the bright side. No one has to…deal with my shitty attitude anymore." He swallowed hard. "No regrets here, guys."

No one laughed at his lame joke, but as they each moved away, he felt better. Lighter. Like at least his life hadn't totally been for shit.

Theron moved to the table and held his hand out over Heracles's dagger. He hesitated, then glanced up at Demetrius. "No regrets," he said softly.

Demetrius swallowed one more time. Steeling himself for what was about to happen, he nodded.

Some kind of commotion outside the council chamber brought Demetrius's head around. The guard's rushed to see what was happening.

Theron turned toward the others. "T, Zander, go see what the hell that is."

Lucian rose from his seat. "What's the meaning of this disturbance?"

"I don't know," Theron muttered as Titus and Zander jumped off the platform.

Voices echoed outside the doors, but only one cut through the chaos. Demetrius's chest squeezed tight. "Theron." *No. Gods, no.* "That's Isadora. Don't let her in. Please don't let her see me die."

"I won't," Theron said as he stepped off the platform and doled out instructions to Phineus and Cerek.

Hands bound above, powerless to move or even see what was happening, Demetrius held his breath as he stared toward the commotion and prayed with everything left in him that Isadora wouldn't walk through those doors.

Theron and the others disappeared into the hallway. Voices rose up in confusion in the chamber. Outside, the sound of a struggle echoed. His heart lurched into his throat as he waited; then the fight died down and the click of shoes against marble resounded.

His heart beat so hard it was all he could hear. Then a swish of powder blue rushed through the doors and his heart sped up until he was sure it would fly right out of his chest. Isadora, wearing a gold wreath in her hair, emerged, flanked by both her sisters and followed by Orpheus and—*no fucking way*—Nick?

Isadora's gaze immediately found him, and Demetrius's stomach dropped at the horror he saw in her eyes. She nodded at Orpheus. "Get him down from there."

Lucian lurched forward. "You have no right to interfere with these proceedings!"

Nick put himself between Isadora and the Council leader and held the sword blade out in his hand. "I suggest you rethink that move, old man. I've gotten rather good with a blade since we last met, and I have no qualms about slicing and dicing you."

Shock ran across Lucian's face, but he stopped mid-step.

As Orpheus, Callia, and Casey rushed over to unhook his arms from the bindings, Demetrius saw Theron and the other Argonauts haul Lucian's guards in and toss them to the ground along the wall.

Isadora stepped up next to Nick. "I'll take it from here." Nick moved back. She squared her shoulders, leveling her eyes on Lucian. "By the power of the monarchy, as is my right by birth, I pardon this guardian and clear him of all charges."

Fury erupted in Lucian's face. "You have no right!"

"I have every right!"

Voices and motion ceased in the room. Next to Demetrius, where he was unhooking his arm, Orpheus whispered, "Go, Isa."

"My father has abdicated the throne to me," Isadora went on in a strong and confident voice. "And know this now, Lord Lucian. Not you, not any member of this Council, can overrule my authority. If you thought I was simply going to roll over and let the Council use me as its pawn, you'd better think again. The charges brought against this guardian were the result of biased propaganda and I'll not let you use him in your political war against the monarchy or the Argonauts."

She moved closer to the leader of the Council, who

was now visibly vibrating with rage. "And when you address me from now on, you son of a bitch, you'll do so as Your Highness. Theron?" she called over her shoulder.

"Yes, my queen," the leader of the Argonauts said with a clear smile in his voice.

"Have the Argonauts escort the Council members out of the Argolion, please."

"With pleasure, Your Highness. Phin? Cerek? Care to help me?" he asked as he moved past her, stopping in front of the twelve lords, all dressed in their traditional robes, shock and awe across their faces. He held out his hand toward the door on the opposite side of the room. "This way, Your Lordships."

Demetrius could barely believe what was happening. His vision wavered as Orpheus and Callia supported his weight and helped him down the marble steps, but he knew the swirl of heavenly blue silk rushing his way was Isadora—his soul mate, his heart, his life—and somehow just her closeness gave him the strength he'd nearly lost.

"Oh, gods." Her arms slid around his waist and a trail of heat exploded wherever she touched. "Is he okay?"

"I think so," Callia said in a clearly shaken voice. "Some of these will need stitching, though."

He couldn't tear his gaze from her face. From her dewy skin, her dreamy eyes, that blond cap of gold that was like a halo around her head. "You..." His weight shifted from Orpheus to her. Her arms tightened, but she wasn't strong enough to support him when his legs went out beneath him.

She gasped as he went down. Voices echoed again, but all he could focus on was her.

"Demetrius," she said in a frantic voice. "Are you okay?"

"I'm…" He stared up at her face. "You fought for me."

She knelt in front of him and ran her fingers down his cheek. So warm, so soft…"Of course I did. I told you on Pandora you were worth saving. I meant it."

"No one's ever fought for me before."

A warm smile slid across her face. "Get used to it, Guardian. As long as blood flows in my veins, I'll be here fighting for you. Any and every time you need me."

The blackness that was so much a part of him settled in that moment. Just laid right down in the bottom of his soul as if she were the key to controlling it. And warmth filled the space left behind. "I love you," he whispered. "I love you so damn much."

Her smile grew even wider. "Oh, it's a good thing. Because I just made some serious enemies here today, and I'm pretty sure I'm going to need you now more than ever."

Her arms slid around his neck and she leaned down to kiss him. As he'd dreamed of for nearly two hundred years. As he'd been afraid of for too damn long. As he'd prayed for, this last lonely day. He wrapped his arms around her waist and pulled her close, reveling in the warmth of her body tight against his, just where she should be.

Home. She was his home. She always had been. No matter where he went or what happened from here, she always would be.

When she eased back, her eyes sparkled, but his brain was slowly coming back online and there was so much he still didn't understand. "How did you get your father to—?"

"Nick. He testified on your behalf."

His gaze shot past her face to where his brother was standing near the far door. Their eyes met, held, then Nick nodded once and disappeared out the door. Demetrius's brow wrinkled. "How—?"

"It turns out he doesn't hate you quite as much as you think," Isadora said, drawing his attention back to her. "And I promised him things were going to be different, now that I'm in charge. This isn't just our war. It's his too. He needs the Argonauts' help."

Pride swelled inside of him at what she'd done. At how she'd stood up to not only the Council but her father as well. At the lengths she'd gone to, to save him. "He's got mine."

She smiled, brushed her hand down his cheek, but before he could kiss her again the smile faded and she loosed her hold. "Just hold that thought. One minute." She must have seen the confusion on his face, because she eased back in to kiss him quickly. "I'll be right back. I promise."

She stood and looked around the room. Callia stepped up next to Demetrius to check his back. To the left, the Argonauts grinned like colossal fools.

Isadora grasped her skirts and disappeared out the door.

"Orpheus!" she called when she reached the hallway. The *ándras* stopped halfway down the long marble corridor and turned to look back. "Wait."

"I've got things to do, Isa. Places to be, people to torment. Make it quick. What do you want now?"

"Just to thank you. I—" She stopped in front of him, placed a hand over her still-quaking stomach. The image of Demetrius strung up in the Council chambers would live with her forever. If she'd been moments later…"I owe you more than I can ever repay."

"That's right. You do." A frown creased his forehead. "And how the hell am I supposed to collect on our little deal now? The whole freakin' kingdom knows you've got the hots for Hellboy in there. And what's the fun in seducing you when you're already damaged goods?"

Her lips curved up and relief—no, gratitude—rushed through her chest. He thought he was such a badass, but he wasn't. Underneath that devil-may-care attitude lay the heart of a hero. "I would have lived up to our agreement, you know."

"I know you would have," he said quietly. Their eyes held a moment, then he frowned again. "Which totally takes the freakin' fun out of the whole thing."

Her smile widened as she took a step forward. Oh, she did like him—always had. She'd just never trusted herself to see what lurked underneath his prickly exterior. Now she did. Her week with Demetrius had taught her that what you see isn't always what's real.

"Stay," she said, sobering. "Stay and help me. I need you. Our people need you. The Argonauts need you. You have the markings from the gods now. And though I don't quite know where Atalanta is at this moment or what she has planned next, I do know she's not gone for good. We won the battle, but the war isn't over."

"We both know I'm not hero material, Isa." His eyes flashed green before resettling to their normal gray, a reminder that what was hidden in him was a liability. But she didn't see it that way anymore. She saw it as an enormous asset. "You are, though. More than you realize."

"Not in this lifetime." His jaw clenched and he glanced away. "Look, I gotta go. Are we done here?"

"We're done. But before you go." She lifted the gold chain from around her neck and held the earth element out in front of him. In the lights from above, the diamond sparkled and shone. "Take this with you. It might come in handy."

He eyed the diamond as if he were afraid it would electrocute him. He knew what it was. And he knew its importance. "You're giving this to me? Why?"

"I'm loaning it to you. There's a big difference. I fully expect you to bring it back. And if you don't, I know six burly guys who'll be more than happy to hunt you down and haul you both back." He didn't smile at her joke, but that was okay. She knew she'd just shocked the hell out of him. She stepped close, gently laid the diamond in his hand, and closed his fingers over the stone. "It'll help you save Gryphon."

His eyes shot from the diamond in his fist to her face. "I'm not going after Gryphon. All I care about is the Orb."

"Sure, I know. Take it anyway."

He looked back down at his fist. Hesitated as if he was going to say something, then didn't. When he looked up again, his gaze strayed past her toward the end of the hall, where she sensed Demetrius standing.

Confusion cleared from his features, was replaced with his normal I-don't-give-a-rip attitude as he glanced back at her once more and pocketed the diamond. "Don't fuck up the kingdom while I'm gone, Isa."

She watched as he walked away. And in the silence that followed knew, even if he didn't, that he wasn't going after the Orb of Krónos as he claimed.

She heard Demetrius move close, felt the heat from his body wrap around and draw her in. Her heart picked up speed, and when she turned she found he was no more than a foot away, holding a blanket closed at his chest, his brow wrinkled in confusion at what he'd just overheard. His dark hair was a mess around his face, his cheeks hollowed out from the stress of the last week, his skin stained with blood and sweat. But to her he'd never been more handsome.

"Where's he going?" He nodded toward the end of the hall.

"To find Gryphon."

"How can you be sure?"

"I'm going on faith. And intuition. The same faith and intuition that told me to find Casey, to stand up to Hades, to trust in you. It hasn't let me down so far. I have to believe it won't this time either."

"*Kardia.*"

He opened the blanket. She moved into him without hesitation, sliding her hands around his waist, careful not to touch any of the wounds on his back. Lifting her face to his, she drew in a breath as his lips lowered to hers and she took a little of his weight, giving him back her strength tenfold.

His eyes were as soft as she'd ever seen them when he eased back to gaze down at her. And though she knew the horrors of this day were never going to leave her, neither would this moment.

"I've been floating in a black mist of death and

misery so long," he said, "I couldn't see that the one thing I was most afraid of had the power to save me. Lachesis was right. You didn't just rescue my body in there, *kardia*, you saved my soul. Just like you did on that island every time you trusted me, every time you touched me, every time you loved me. You're doing it now simply by looking at me like I'm everything you've ever wanted."

"You are," she whispered. "In more ways than you will ever know."

He brushed his fingers down her cheek. "I promise you, with everything that I am, that I will find a way to break Hades's contract on your soul. I'm not spending eternity without you. Not now, when I've finally realized you are my home."

Had she once been afraid of him? It seemed like a lifetime ago. "Some things can't be saved, Demetrius, but I'm okay with that. I'm not living my life for the future anymore. I have everything I want right here. I have you and"—she took his hand and placed it on her stomach—"the life you've given me. That's all I need."

He looked down where he touched her, and his eyes went so soft and dreamy her heart clenched. "Ah, *kardia*. Anything can be saved. I'm living proof of that. Believe in me like I believe in you. I won't let you down. I won't let either of you down ever again, I promise."

Emotion closed her throat. "I already do, Demetrius. I love you. I love you so much."

"You shouldn't," he whispered. "If I were stronger, you wouldn't. But I'll be damned if I'll keep fighting this." He lifted her around the waist and turned a slow circle with her in his arms. "I love you too, Hora, queen, soul mate, *mine*. Always."

His mouth captured hers again and he kissed her, just as she wanted. There were a thousand unknowns hanging in the balance—the fate of her kingdom, her rule, this pregnancy, the Argonauts, and a war she knew wasn't over—but this, how she felt about him, this was a truth that would never let her down. As long as she believed in that, nothing could ever tear them apart.

Not even Hades himself.

Eternal Guardians Lexicon

adelfos. Brother

ándras. Male Argolean

archdaemon. Head of the daemon order; has enhanced powers from Atalanta

Argolea. Realm established by Zeus for the blessed heroes and their descendants

Argonauts. Eternal guardian warriors who protect Argolea; in every generation, one from the original seven bloodlines (Heracles, Achilles, Jason, Odysseus, Perseus, Theseus, and Bellerophon) is chosen to continue the guardian tradition

Chosen. One Argolean, one human; two individuals who, when united, complete the Argolean Prophecy and break Atalanta's contract with Hades, thereby ejecting her from the Underworld and ending her immortality.

Council of Elders. Twelve lords of Argolea who advise the king

daemons. Beasts who were once human, recruited from the Fields of Asphodel (purgatory) by Atalanta to join her army

Fates. Three goddesses who control the thread of life for all mortals from birth until death

Fields of Asphodel. Purgatory

gynaíka. Female Argolean

Hora; pl. Horae. Three goddesses of balance controlling life and order

Isles of the Blessed. Heaven

ilithios. Idiot

kardia. Term of endearment; my heart

matéras. Mother

Medean witches. Followers of the teachings of the sorceress Medea who live in the Aegis Mountains

meli. Term of endearment; beloved

Misos. Half-human/half-Argolean race that lives hidden among humans

Olympians. Current ruling gods of the Greek pantheon, led by Zeus; meddle in human life

Orb of Krónos. Four-chambered disk that, when filled with the four classic elements—earth, wind, fire, and water—has the power to release the Titans from Tartarus

paidi. Medean word; child

patéras. Father

quai. Medean word; stop

skata. Swearword

Tartarus. Realm of the Underworld similar to hell

Titans. The ruling gods before the Olympians

thea. Term of endearment; goddess

yios. Son

Next in the Eternal Guardians series...

ENRAPTURED

For over two hundred years Orpheus has had an uneasy alliance with the Eternal Guardians. They've never quite trusted whose side he's on. Now he's been called to serve in the Guardian ranks. But that calling comes at a price—one that may eventually cost them all

An assassin has been sent by Zeus to seduce, entrap, and ultimately destroy him. A woman who will dredge up a past he doesn't remember, a love that once condemned him, and a dark and deadly secret as old as the Eternal Guardians themselves.

ORPHEUS FOLLOWED SKYLA UP THE THREE FLIGHTS OF stairs and paused in the hall of the old building near the waterfront with its water-stained ceiling and dirty carpet while she unlocked her apartment door.

As he stared at the back of her blond head, a waft of honeysuckle met his senses. The same fragrance he'd noticed in the bar where they'd met, in the alley when they fought of the daemons, and every second since. A scent that was oddly…familiar.

The key clicked, and she pushed the door open with her shoulder, stepped inside. As he followed, he reminded himself he wasn't here for fun. He hadn't followed her back here for anything more than information and a place to clean up after killing off a pack of daemons hot on her trail. He'd be damned if he was going to let her out of his sight without figuring out what the hell she was. Something told him she was linked to Olympus, and if she was…a thrill bubbled through his veins. If she was then he might have his first link to that vengeance he was so close to obtaining.

After he found the Orb, of course. The Orb of Krónos, the palm-sized medallion that held the four classic elements and had the power to release the Titans from Tartarus, was key to every one of his plans. He couldn't forget that, or be distracted away from it. Luckily, this female also knew the woman he'd been tracking for the last three months. The one who could locate the Orb for him in the first place.

Skyla closed the door once he stepped inside, flipped on the kitchen light. The place was a far cry from the Ritz. It didn't fit her, and he didn't doubt for a minute that this shithole was nothing more than a stopping ground. This place suited her as much as the Argonauts suited him.

She headed down the hall. He tipped his head as he watched the sexy sway of her backside in the short black skirt. He had to admit it was a nice view.

"The bathroom's here." She pushed open the door to the left, flipped on the light.

He followed, glanced into the small bathroom. An avocado green countertop and a mirror over the sink that reflected hollow cheeks streaked with blood, pale skin, and hair standing every which way.

He looked away from his reflection, moved into the doorway of the other room.

A full-sized bed with a disgustingly ugly burnt orange bedspread, a small dresser, a nightstand, and a lamp. He waited while she crouched in front of the dresser, pulled the bottom drawer open and extracted jeans and a T-shirt. "These should fit. While you get cleaned up I'll find bandages for your chest."

He didn't bother telling her he didn't need them. Instead he took the clothes she offered, then stiffened when she moved close. Pulling the garments against his chest so she could pass, he again smelled honeysuckle, and when her body grazed his, another burst of electricity rippled between them.

Only this was different. This wasn't just sexual, though there was certainly enough sexual heat ricocheting off both of them to power the whole building. No, this was something else. An awareness. A déjà vu feeling. A memory he couldn't quite bring into focus.

She hesitated, just long enough for him to know she felt it too. And his stomach tightened when her gemlike eyes found his and held.

Who was she? What was she to him? And why the hell couldn't he figure out how he knew her?

She cleared her throat and looked away. "Take your time."

He stood where he was while she disappeared back into the living room. Called himself ten kinds of stupid. *Mark—Orb—revenge*. Those were the only three things that mattered now.

He stepped into the bathroom and avoided the mirror. He didn't need to see his reflection to know he looked like shit. He felt like it too. And not just from the change of shifting into his daemon form. Months of searching only to be met with disappointment were taking their toll. Though his strength was slowly coming back and his wound was already healing, he needed more than a shower to recharge him. He needed food. A couple hours of shut-eye. And to find that damn dark-haired female before someone else did. He tossed the clean clothes on the counter, kicked off his boots and pulled off his shredded garments.

Steam filled the room as he let the water beat down on his battered body. He rubbed soap all over his skin, washed his hair with shampoo from a purple bottle that smelled way too girly, then flipped off the water and dried off with a towel from the rack. As he did he caught sight of the ancient Greek text on his forearms that ran down to entwine his fingers.

Man, if the Argonauts could see him now. No, nix that. He already knew exactly what they'd say or do if they'd seen the switcheroo he'd pulled in that alley. Daemons weren't just discriminated against in their world, they were the bitter enemy. If word got out he was half daemon, the Argonauts would be the first to crucify him, likely in Tiyrns Square for all Argoleans to see. Forget the fact he was the last living descendant of the famed hero Perseus. And never mind that he'd helped the queen and all the Argonauts more times than he could count. He tossed the towel away in disgust, jerked on the fresh jeans. To them he'd forever be nothing more than a daemon. A monster that was only useful one way: dead.

He tugged on the dark blue T-shirt that barely fit, shoved his feet back into his boots and finger-combed his hair. When he opened the bathroom door steam preceded him into the hall where the snap and crackle of food cooking and the scent of bacon filled the air.

His stomach growled, and he turned the corner to find Skyla, dressed in fresh clothes—the same short skirt, tight shirt, and kickass goth boots included—standing at the stove flipping bacon and scrambling eggs.

His vision blurred and the modern appliances faded into the background. Weathered stone, a baking hearth, and an old scarred table filled the space in front of him. And at the counter, the same female, stirring something in a ceramic bowl. Only this time she was barefoot, wearing a slip of a dress made of gauzy white and tied at her narrow waist with a woven gold braid.

The room spun. He reached out and gripped the hallway wall to steady himself.

She looked up. Her hand stopped moving. The bowl sat cradled in the nook of her other arm. A streak of flour ran across her right cheek.

A warm smile spread across her face. One filled with heat and mischief and knowledge. "Stop looking at me like that. Thou knows that is playing with fire."

She went back to stirring. Looked back down at her work with a victorious grin. Turned to reach for something behind her.

But Orpheus felt like he'd just been sucker punched in the gut.

The air left his lungs on a gasp. The room spun again, flipped his stomach end over end. He reached for the wall with his other hand, felt himself falling. Saw shadows barreling in from all sides. And was powerless to keep from fainting like a giant pussy.

"Daemon? Shit, can you hear me?" The voice was muffled. Distant. Something hard pressed down on his chest. "Come on, already. Wake up!"

A crack echoed around him. His eyes flew open.

"That's it. Criminy, you're worse off than I thought. Yeah, that's right, keep looking at me."

He couldn't do anything else. He stared up into amethyst eyes that sparkled like the Aegis Mountains in the early morning sunshine. And felt that rush of familiarity all over again.

"There you go. See? Not so bad after all." Her voice wasn't so muffled anymore. "Let's get you up."

He didn't fight her when she pulled on his shoulders, maneuvering him around to lean against the wall, his legs kicked out in front of him. While his head continued to spin like a top, she went back into the kitchen, flipped off the stove, reached for bandages and other supplies, came back and knelt next to him.

Honeysuckle wafted in the air around him as she grasped the hem of his shirt and lifted it, exposing his abs and chest. The hem of her skirt rode dangerously high on her thighs, but that vision of her in that old-time kitchen wouldn't leave his head. That and the know-ing smile she'd sent him that spoke of familiarity on a personal level. An intimate level.

Her brow wrinkled as she inspected his skin. "This is…already scabbed over. I know daemons heal quickly but…well, you are not at all what I expected."

Neither was she. Whatever the hell she was doing to him, though, he was about to put a stop to it.

He grasped her wrist, "I want…answers."

She looked down where he held her then focused on his eyes. She pulled her hand free with a quick snap of her wrist, a motion that told him she was stronger than she appeared, then rose to her feet. "You need food. We'll talk after you eat."

Screw that.

He'd never fainted in his life. Couldn't believe he'd done so now, especially in front of her. Whatever she was—witch, sorceress, immortal—she was playing some kind of mind fuck on him. Getting him to see and feel things that weren't real. His mother had been Medean. He'd studied her craft, knew how to cast spells himself when the time was right, and was well aware the power the dark arts could harness. He wasn't about to be manipulated by this female in any way.

He pushed to his feet. Before she reached the end of the hall he flashed in front of her, bringing her to a dead stop.

Surprise lit her eyes. Confusion followed quickly on its tail. Argonauts could only flash in Argolea. In the human realm they were limited to the same laws of nature as humans. Except him.

She dropped her supplies, took a step back. "What…? How did you do that?"

"I'm full of surprises." He took a menacing step toward her.

She moved back more. "What do you think you're doing?"

"I'm tired of playing games." He advanced until her back hit the wall. He knew his eyes were glowing green, illuminating the dark hallway around them. His daemon hovered right beneath his control, but he didn't force it back like he normally would. Right now he wanted its strength. And the fear it instilled. "I want answers, and I want them now."

He pressed a hand against the wall and leaned in close. Until the heat from her skin slid over his and the beat of her heart was all he could hear. "I want to know who the hell you really are."

Coming April 2012

About the Author

A former junior high science teacher, Elisabeth Naughton traded in her red pen and test-tube set for a laptop and research books. She now writes sexy romantic adventure and paranormal novels full time from her home in western Oregon, where she lives with her husband and three children. Her work has been nominated for numerous awards, including the prestigious RITA Awards of Romance Writers of America, the Australian Romance Reader Awards, the Golden Leaf, and the Golden Heart. When not writing, Elisabeth can be found running, hanging out at the ball park, or dreaming up new and exciting adventures. Visit her at www.elisabethnaughton.com to learn more about her and her books.